Dark Angel

DARK ANGEL

Geoffrey Archer

C
Century · London

Published by Century in 2004

1 3 5 7 9 10 8 6 4 2

Century Books
The Random House Group Limited
20 Vauxhall Bridge Road, London, SW1V 2SA

Random House Australia (Pty) Limited
20 Alfred Street, Milsons Point, Sydney,
New South Wales 2061, Australia

Random House New Zealand Limited
18 Poland Road, Glenfield
Auckland 10, New Zealand

Random House (Pty) Limited
Endulini, 5a Jubilee Road, Parktown 2193, South Africa

The Random House Group Limited Reg. No. 954009

www.randomhouse.co.uk

A CIP catalogue record for this book
is available from the British Library

Papers used by Random House
are natural, recyclable products made from wood grown in
sustainable forests. The manufacturing processes conform to
the environmental regulations of the country of origin

ISBN 1 8441 3803 8 (Hardback)
ISBN 1 8441 3804 6 (Trade Paperback)

Typeset by SX Composing DTP, Rayleigh, Essex
Printed and bound in Great Britain by
Mackays of Chatham plc, Chatham, Kent

To Eva, Alison and James

Acknowledgements

My research for the Korean War section of this story was greatly assisted by Don Barrett, who served there as a National Serviceman with the 1st Battalion the Middlesex Regiment in 1950-51. His remarkable historical record of that regiment's Korean campaign proved invaluable to me. For fictional purposes I have altered the sequence of events at times. Any misrepresentations are mine and not his. All members of the armed forces portrayed in this book are entirely imaginary.

My thanks too to Oliver Johnson for many years of support and good advice.

PROLOGUE

January 2004
London

IT HAD TAKEN courage for Tom Sedley to come up to London. Seeing his mother on the screen always stirred bad memories. But there she was now, the monochrome face smiling down at him in the cinema by the Thames, and it was all right.

And yet, seeing those hauntingly alluring eyes which his dead sister Sara had inherited, being here in the city where it had all happened, he couldn't help feeling uneasy. And guilty that so much remained unresolved after so many years.

It wasn't Maureen Stuart herself who was being celebrated in this retrospective at the National Film Theatre, but the whole genre of Second World War films produced in Britain in the 1940s and '50s. She'd starred in several of them. Somehow the NFT researchers had tracked Tom down and invited him to a viewing as bait for the media. He'd thought long and hard before accepting. London with its bitter associations was a place that he tried to avoid. But eventually he'd decided to attend. The showing had been preceded by a buffet lunch, where he'd been interviewed about his mother by a couple of young journalists whose reading of the cuttings had, to his relief, been surprisingly superficial.

The woman up there on the screen was considerably younger than Tom was now. She'd been beautiful then. It was later, after Sara was killed, that her famous smile had lost its seductive power.

Her old films came on TV from time to time, but Tom avoided them, because they took him straight back to that dreadful summer of

I

1948. He'd never been much of a movie fan anyway, preferring books to celluloid, and in recent years the simple pleasures of his garden in the Cotswold village he'd retired to from GCHQ more than a decade ago.

The film drew to an end. Polite applause rippled through the sparsely filled rows as the closing credits rolled. Then the house lights went up and Tom got to his feet. He'd been eager for the film to finish, because the longer it went on the less he could stem the tide of foreboding that was creeping up on him. At the age of seventy-two he felt he ought to be beyond the reach of these reminders of his past, but some events scar a person for life and his sister's murder was one of them.

'Enjoy it, Mr Sedley?' It was the young man who'd invited him here.

'Don't make them like that any more,' Tom purred non-committally, as they made their way up the aisle.

'Absolutely. Well, thanks so much for coming. It's been jolly nice meeting you.'

'Likewise.'

They shook hands, then Tom hurried through the foyer café, out into the crisp January air. He gulped it in, hoping the oxygen would blow away the feeling of unfinished business that clung to him like a cobweb. To his left, the sun was setting, bloodying the sky beyond the London Eye.

The showing of the film had finished earlier than he'd expected and the train he'd planned on taking back to Gloucestershire wasn't for another couple of hours. He walked over to the parapet and stared at the sinuous brown river, wondering how best to use the time.

He was on the point of deciding to head for Paddington and catch an earlier train when he suddenly became aware he had company. He didn't actually see the figure standing there looking at him, but sensed it. At his age and living in the country, Tom thought of London as a nest of muggers. Skin tingling with fear, he half-turned his head. It wasn't a thief standing there, however, but an elderly woman. Keeping a few feet away from him, as if plucking up the courage to speak.

Begging, he thought. He looked down at the river again, hoping she would go away.

'Tom.'

Her voice sliced through him. He'd not heard it for a very long time. Hoping his ears were playing tricks, he turned for a proper look. The white hair fooled him for a moment, then with a sickening jolt he realised it *was* her.

'Binnie . . .'

More than twenty years had passed since their last unhappy encounter. Her face had aged significantly. Deep lines where there'd been smooth skin. It was a face that he'd once known almost as well as his own. For years he'd seen it in his dreams.

'I guessed I might find you here,' she said, pointing back to the film theatre. 'I'm on their mailing list and saw the billing for your mother's picture.'

'I see.' So this was no chance meeting. She'd sought him out. The question in his head was *why*?

'I thought how nice it would be to see you again,' she said, answering it.

Tom didn't respond, knowing there'd be more to her stalking him than that. As he looked at her, still startled by her sudden appearance before him, he was affected by the same painfully conflicting feelings he'd felt long ago.

Binnie was the same age as him. The homes they'd been brought up in were next door to one another. Her hair was still short, he noticed. A lustrous brown once, instead of this snowy grey. Still with that straight teenager's fringe. She looked burdened, he noted, worn down by life.

'It's over twenty years . . .' she reminded him.

He tried to read her face. Was it desperation that he saw in her eyes? It dawned on him she might be here simply because she was lonely.

'Last time we met you were off to Australia to stay with your daughter,' he said, finally getting some words together.

'Well, I came back.'

'So I see.'

'I live alone now.'

'Ah.'

For a split second her obvious sadness caused the warmth he'd once felt for her to flicker back to life.

'Difficult, isn't it?' she said. 'To know where to begin.'

'Yes.' Or even whether it was sensible to begin at all.

'Shall we go back into the café?' she suggested, her face pinched with anxiety. 'My feet are freezing.'

'What do you want, Binnie? Why did you seek me out?'

She looked away. A water-bus hooted on the far side of the river, its mournful note echoing towards them like a tormented soul.

'Please, Tom,' she whispered. 'I need to talk with you.'

He steeled himself. There were unresolved issues between them. Questions that had bugged Tom for most of his life. If she was ready to answer them at last, then he owed it to himself to listen.

'Well, all right. But no coffees. You can walk with me if you like. I'm heading for a train.'

They started to move along the Embankment towards Hungerford Bridge.

The damnable thing was that, as Binnie matched his pace step for step, it felt the most natural thing in the world for Tom to have her by his side.

1948

I

September 1948
North London

THERE WAS NO shortage of greenery in the North London suburb of Wood Park. Sprawling trees and lush grass wherever you looked. Well-mown lawns in front of the houses. Playing fields for the children to run about in. Dappled woods nearby, reeking of leaf mould. The adults with enough wealth to buy homes here loved the fact that they were in London yet had so much space around them. Relished the social status that went with the mortgage.

For their older teenage offspring, however, the place bore a different image. Many felt stifled by the suburb. There was nothing to do. No pub or cinema for miles. No cosy gathering place where boy-girl relationships could fumble into life away from the inhibiting eyes of parents.

Two worlds. The adults coping with the aftermath of war, grateful to be living in peace, somewhere free of bomb damage. The young, aflame with hormones, longing for a new world filled with choice and excitement. A generation gap, which in some Wood Park homes was chasm-wide.

Then, on Tuesday, 14 September 1948, tragedy struck the community, uniting parents with their disaffected offspring in shared horror at what had been done to one of their own. At the epicentre of the crisis was the Sedley family, but the disaster gripped each resident, forcing them to confront the fact that an unspeakable evil had emerged within their idyll of a community.

The police had been called late the previous night, three hours after fourteen-year-old Sara Sedley had failed to reappear at her home for bedtime. Her mother was distraught, imagining the worst.

'Probably at a friend's and forgotten to phone,' the pinched-faced detective suggested, trying to calm the situation. He'd recognised the girl's mother as Maureen Stuart who'd played a Spitfire pilot's wife in a war film he'd seen at the Odeon a couple of weeks back. A flighty character. With her husband shot down and locked up in Stalag Luft something-or-other, both his legs severed in the crash, she'd gone off on a dirty weekend with his best mate. A woman not to be trusted. Which was what the detective felt about women in general and actresses in particular. Temperamental creatures. Burdened with overactive imaginations. And the missing daughter, he guessed, was probably a similar type.

The Sedley family – Stuart was the actress's stage name – had of course already rung everyone they could think of. Sara's friends from school, the woman who ran the tap dancing class. But nobody had seen the girl.

Tom Sedley, Sara's stocky, fair-haired, seventeen-year-old brother, had found himself taking charge of the crisis when his younger sister disappeared. Their father, Michael, was in Manchester on BBC business, producing a play to be broadcast live the following night, and couldn't get away. His absence had added to their mother's hysteria. Tom coped with his own growing sense of panic by organising things – ringing people and touring the neighbourhood on his bike in case Sara was wandering about in a daze. His mother imagined that she might have tripped on a paving stone and banged her head.

Now it was an hour before sunset on the day after Sara's disappearance. She'd been missing for nearly twenty-four hours. The police had decided to search the parkland and woods bordering the suburb, rounding up volunteers to help. There'd been no shortage of takers. Most of the fathers weren't back from work yet, but some twenty mothers and older teenagers home from school were now spread in a line at the edge of the long grass which bordered the open space of the park. Each volunteer ten paces from the next.

Tom, slight of build and shorter than most of his peers, stood in the middle of the line, close to the police Inspector. His sister's disappearance had wrung him dry. At first he'd been angry at her for causing such anxiety. Much as he loved her, she'd become an attention-seeking flirt in the last few months. Recently he'd taken to growling warnings about her behaviour, saying she'd get into trouble if she didn't become more ladylike.

When midnight came last night he'd begun to fear the worst. In the hours of darkness he'd sat with his mother, waiting for the phone to ring or a knock at the door. He was angry at his father for not being there. He was often angry at his father. It was as if a wall stood between them. Or as though they were different species. The man was artistically pretentious, whereas Tom was down-to-earth. Unreliable as a parent when Tom wanted someone to depend on. There was no point of contact. They had little in common except blood.

And now it had come to this. A search.

'For what, exactly?' he'd asked, hoping to be fobbed of with some lie. But the policemen's faces were deadly serious. 'For anything,' they'd replied. 'Anything relevant.'

Tom had been close to tears several times that day, visualising just what sort of 'trouble' his sister might have got herself into. He knew a little about prostitutes. Had seen them plying their trade in Soho where he and his friend Marcus sometimes went to look at foreign films, dirtying their chins to look old enough to get membership of the clubs where they were shown. Some of the girls in Wardour Street had been young. Almost as young as him and Marcus. Was this how they got there? Kidnapped from the suburbs, indoctrinated with the tricks of the trade, then put up for rent by some swarthy thug?

Tom glanced up and down the line. Marcus was there, trying without much success to smile reassuringly at him. Marcus Warwick who lived opposite the Sedley house in the Close. The same age as him, Marcus had been Tom's closest friend for as long as he could remember. And next to Marcus, Binnie. Binnie Rowbotham, the tall, slender girl who lived next door. Columbine, her parents had christened her, a name which made her cringe if it was ever used accidentally by her friends. For Tom, Binnie epitomised what a female should be like. Considerate. Gentle. Caring. And with that indefinable air of mystery that made girls different from boys. She looked very tense today. Pale. Paler than usual, even. Everyone's face showing the anxiety they all felt. Everyone knowing it was twenty-four hours since Sara had last been seen walking out of the garden, telling her mother she was off around the corner to see a friend whose cat had just had kittens. Back in half an hour . . . She'd never arrived at her destination.

Tom Sedley's heart thudded like a steam hammer. Until they'd begun lining up for the search, he'd been able to kid himself that things would turn out all right. That there could still be some simple explanation for

Sara vanishing. But the seriousness of what they were now doing filled him with dread. The blue-black uniforms. The grim faces as the Inspector quietly briefed his men. And an unspoken certainty in the minds of those around him that this could only end one way.

Tom gulped air, fighting to control his emotions. He'd been strong up to now because of the need to comfort his mother. But she wasn't with the search party, unable to cope with people staring at her tear-streaked face. Even at a time like this there was her image as a film star to consider. She was sitting at home being comforted by an actress friend with the help of a bottle of amontillado. Waiting for Tom to tell her that nothing untoward had been found.

Tom stared across the grass. In the middle of the park some two hundred yards away was a large clump of trees, known simply as 'the woods'. Neighbours walked dogs there. On the far side was a small amphitheatre where local amateurs performed Shakespeare in August. But above all, the woods were *their* territory, the playground for the boys of Wood Park. Rival gangs had formed when they were younger, each with their own camps amongst the trees and bushes, but with a common purpose. To keep out the girls. They'd spun their sisters stories about wild dogs, snakes, and old men in mackintoshes. When a few girls had dared venture in, they'd been hounded out with animal noises and wild charges from the bushes. In later years, when he and his contemporaries reached their mid-teens, the woods had become a place to smoke and to ogle pictures of bare-breasted women in the magazines left behind by the Americans who'd had a camp in the parkland at the end of the war.

And it was towards the woods that they would soon be heading. That male domain which Sara would never have entered on her own, but where Tom sensed this dreadful mystery would be resolved.

The police Inspector blew his whistle and raised an arm. Like a football referee, Tom thought. A hawk-faced ref. He caught Marcus's eye, saw his forced smile. Binnie's expression was a blank, her pale skin, round spectacles and small, thin-lipped mouth a mask of forced calm. The Inspector dropped his long, thin hand and they were off.

Tom noted how close Binnie was keeping to Marcus. He felt a little jealous of the attention she was giving him, despite being pretty sure his friend wouldn't respond to it. The two of them had often discussed Binnie behind her back, Marcus saying how unkissable she was, with her plain round face and owlish glasses. How with her flat chest and straight hips she looked more like a boy than a girl, a fact that didn't bother Tom particularly.

Binnie's crush on Marcus had emerged during the summer holidays. Tom worried that she would get hurt. There was a wild, almost dangerous side to Marcus which Binnie in her trusting way seemed unaware of. Tom feared she'd be damaged by Marcus. Robbed of the sweetness that he so prized in her.

Tom looked along the rest of the line, at all those other faces he'd grown up with but whose owners he hardly knew. For years he'd felt a misfit in the neighbourhood, and in the Sedley household. Mother a famous actress, father a drama producer, little sister a budding performer, dressing up and trying out greasepaint. The whole acting business bored him. Model aeroplanes, trains and crystal sets had been his own preferred playthings. He'd once overheard his mother describe him to a friend as dull. 'God knows where that one came from. Reads something called *Practical Wireless*, would you believe. I have the oddest of feelings he might've been switched at birth.'

In the last twenty-four hours, however, Tom knew he'd grown immeasurably in his mother's eyes. As they sat through the night in their living room, its walls hung with framed theatre posters, she'd told him he was 'mature beyond his years'. This, the reward for assuring her she wasn't to blame for Sara's disappearance. Telling her she was not a lousy parent. That, even if her work meant being away from them a lot, leaving them in the hands of au pairs, he and Sara had always liked the fact she had a glamorous career, because it set them apart from the crowd. Made them special, too.

Even to his own ears Tom had sounded grown-up last night. Coming out with the very words his father might have spoken if he'd been there.

'She's simply run away for a bit, Mum. Some silly girly reason. You know what Sara's like. She'll be back.'

But now, twenty-four hours later, he was ceasing to believe it.

During the morning, as news of Sara's disappearance spread, he'd seen it grip the neighbourhood. Passers-by slowed their pace and sneaked glances at the house, hoping to spot some famous face who'd come to give succour to the family. Despite what he'd told her, he hated his mother's fame for the rubbernecking it provoked.

The cul-de-sac where they all lived had been like a nest for him and his friends, a safe playground, which had made Sara's disappearance all the more shocking. A close community shattered. One of their young missing. Men in blue asking questions door-to-door, like in some 'B' movie. The stir caused had been the first real disturbance to the calm of the place since an errant V2 had destroyed the tennis club and a few nearby houses in 1944.

Half a dozen law officers were coordinating the search. They'd been allowed to remove their helmets. Most looked not much older than himself, Tom thought, as the line moved slowly forward. 'If you find anything, don't touch it,' the Inspector ordered. 'Call one of my officers. Let us decide what's interesting and what isn't.' The policeman's manner was brusque. Almost contemptuous. As if he had little time for civilians and was only using their help because he had to.

On either side of him people swished at the long grass with sticks. Tom watched Marcus Warwick beat at the cow-parsley and nettles with an old cricket stump. Then, to his alarm, Marcus dropped to his knees and called out to one of the officers.

'There's a cig packet here. Don't know if it's important. You said report anything.'

A police constable picked it up with a gloved hand and put it in a brown paper bag. Capstan Full Strength, Tom noticed. His and Marcus's choice, if ever they could afford it. Roll-ups were their usual fare.

Another shout went up. A child's sock fished from the grass on the end of a stick. Alarm flickered along the line until they saw how small it was.

Tom had heard Marcus lie to the police about his age when they'd asked an hour ago. 'Eighteen and above, please,' the Inspector had shouted as they'd gathered to help. Binnie Rowbotham was standing next to him and had lied as well. He knew that as his closest friends they couldn't not be involved in the search for Sara. They'd all grown up together. He and Marcus as two musketeers, with Binnie as a would-be third. They'd all watched Sara develop into a physically precocious teenager, Binnie trying not to be jealous of her shapely chest.

It was true that Binnie was beanpole-thin, and with her short, light brown hair and the dungarees and blue check shirt she was wearing today she could have been mistaken for a boy. Tom felt quite comfortable with her androgynous looks, however. He would never admit it and hoped soon to develop a taste for them, but he found women's breasts intimidating. He watched her now, wondering if her all too obvious infatuation with Marcus was the cause of the open space that had come between him and his friend in recent weeks. Marcus had begun avoiding him. Finding excuses why they couldn't spend time together. Stopped coming to the house. He didn't blame Binnie for that, but suspected that her desire to be with Marcus could have something to do with it.

He kept his eyes on them, looking for clues as to what there was between them. What secrets they shared. What they were excluding him from. Their faces revealed nothing, though, except the tension they were all under. They hardly spoke to one another, although at one point Tom heard Binnie say her stomach felt as if there was a brick in it.

Tom looked down at the ground, pushing aside the nettles with his feet. Soon they would be through the overgrown edge of the park and on to the trimmed grass of the recreation ground. He scanned the line again. He knew so many people here by sight but not by name. He knew Marcus better than anyone in the world. Next year they would both be leaving school and doing their National Service. Tom had discussed things, done things with Marcus he'd not done with anyone else. If it was all right to love someone of the same sex, then Tom would happily say he loved Marcus.

Which was more than Marcus would say about his own brother, Sebastian, whom Tom spotted further along the line, making his number with the dour police Inspector. Sebastian, two years older than them, an Oxford undergraduate already. Someone who considered himself a man of the world and who treated his younger brother like a child. Showing how adult he was by talking to the man in charge of this whole affair, Detective Inspector Wilkie. Even sharing a joke with him.

Binnie was trailing a little way behind Marcus now, as if he had her on a long lead. Tom understood why she'd fallen for him. Despite being nowhere near as good-looking as his older brother – gangly, with spots here and there – Marcus had a way of looking at girls, openly, carelessly, that made them melt. And there was another reason for her new-found infatuation. At the beginning of the summer Marcus had sketched a portrait of Binnie. Art was his main interest at school and he was constantly looking for sitters. She'd volunteered, remaining as still as a statue while he worked away with his pencil. Marcus had told Tom about it afterwards. Claimed to have cut through what he called her suburban smugness and seen for the first time Binnie the young woman. He'd got her to remove her spectacles. 'She was thinking about sex. I could see it in her eyes.' Tom had dismissed the idea, convinced that sex was not a preoccupation that filled the female mind. Marcus still considered Binnie to be a girl whose ambitions lay no further than the end of the street, but he'd flattered her with his drawing. Put in things that weren't there. Made her beautiful, he said. Even, as a joke, talked of signing the portrait 'Leonardo'.

The line of volunteers reached the mown grass and quickened its pace. Soon they were closing with the railings that fenced off the woods. In his mind Tom could smell the leaf mould in the rhododendron thickets beneath the oaks. Suddenly he heard a commotion and turned round. His mother was joining the search party, clinging to her actress friend whose face was even better known than her own.

'I had to be here, darling,' she whispered, touching Tom's cheek.

Maureen Stuart had thick auburn hair. This evening she had what Tom called her 'actress face' on, the look of the brave heroine waiting by the winding gear on a Welsh hillside for the rescuers to bring up news from the flooded mine. Tom wished desperately that she'd stayed at home. People were staring. All along the line heads turned to gawp at these two famous women.

Ignoring her, the Inspector gathered his volunteers together for the assault on the woods.

'The undergrowth's pretty thick in there. No point all of us going in.' He scanned the attentive faces, picking out those of the boys. 'Some of you lads probably know these woods quite well. I need a couple to point us to places we mightn't immediately think of.'

Tom saw Marcus flinch as the Inspector's eyes focused on him.

'How about it, you two lads?'

At first Tom didn't grasp that the other 'lad' was Binnie. Someone snorted with amusement as the realisation spread.

Tom disengaged himself from his mother's arm.

'Not her. Me. Marcus and I know these woods as well as anyone.'

The Inspector smothered his surprise at having mistaken Binnie's sex.

'All right. You two, follow me, please.' The policeman detailed four of his own men to accompany him and led the way into the wood, strutting ahead like a general.

The ground smelled mustily dry. There'd been no rain for weeks. Tom was filled with dread. Sara had always been scared of this place, yet he had an awful feeling this was where she'd come.

'Okay, lads,' said the Inspector softly. 'How many hiding places do you know of?'

Marcus and Tom glanced at one another. 'There's a good half-dozen,' said Tom.

'Any favourites?'

There was no avoiding it. No way of keeping secret the one place they'd always used whenever they wanted to be absolutely sure of not being seen by anyone walking through the woods.

Guessing the reason for their hesitation, the Inspector took out a packet of Players and offered them. They both shook their heads.

'Go on. I know you smoke. There's nicotine on your fingers.'

Marcus looked at his hands. To Tom's eye they were perfectly clean.

'I'd rather not,' he said.

'In case your mum sees you?'

'Something like that.'

Marcus's father had promised him fifty pounds if he didn't smoke until he was twenty-one.

'But you do come in here to smoke, don't you?'

'Sometimes,' Tom admitted.

'Show me. Where do you go?'

Tom felt utterly powerless. Like being poised at the top of a big dipper, awaiting the inevitable plunge.

'Well, it's over here.' Marcus led the way towards a particularly thick bank of rhododendrons.

'Looks impenetrable,' the Inspector commented.

'There's a bit in the middle where you can sit without being seen . . .'

The boys stood aside, expecting the constables to push their way through the branches.

'Show us. Lead the way. Slowly, mind, one step at a time so we can have a good look at the ground.'

Marcus was hanging back, so, with his heart in his mouth, Tom led the policemen to the other side where there was a small gap in the dark green leaves.

'In there.' He pointed.

'Lead on, lad.'

Above their heads a blackbird chipped away, alarmed at the disturbance. Pigeons clattered from their roosts higher up.

Tom pushed his way in, followed by the Inspector. Twigs cracked as they penetrated the thicket.

Then he saw her, not six feet away. He froze, sick with shock. Marcus came crashing in behind and yelped with anguish.

'No . . .!'

There, on the small piece of brown earth where the two of them had so often lain, looking at the sky through the branches, was Sara, her pretty face a ghastly yellow, her pink cotton blouse unbuttoned, exposing her breasts. The short blue skirt she'd worn most of the time that summer was bunched up at the waist and her white cotton pants were round one ankle.

'Don't touch anything,' the Inspector said.

'Check for a pulse, sir?' one of his men suggested.

The Inspector gave him a withering look.

'Been dead for hours,' he answered. 'Strangled. See the bruising?'

Tom stared disbelievingly at the purple-blue stripes on his sister's slender neck. It was make-up, he told himself. This was Sara's stupid game. Any minute she would leap to her feet and ask what they thought of her performance.

Then he looked at her breasts. He'd never really seen them before – she'd gone shy on him since puberty. They looked so firm. So perfect in their shape, as if fresh from a mould.

And the little dark smudge of pubic hair . . . Shocking for him to see. So coarse. So animal-like. So out of place on his angel of a little sister.

Her slim thighs were a little apart, streaked in places with a silvery sheen . . . At last it sank in what had happened.

'No . . .' Marcus backed away from the scene, shaking his head. 'No. It's not poss—' The words gagged in his throat.

Numbly, Tom turned and stared at him. Questioning. Wanting reassurance that this wasn't happening. Wanting Marcus to make things all right, as he'd so often done in the past. But his friend's face was white as milk. Marcus the problem-solver was at a total loss. So unable to cope that he turned and fought his way out of the thicket, lashing at the branches.

'Better take Tom back to his mother,' the Inspector said to one of the constables.

Tom felt hands guide him back into the open. He didn't resist. Everything was a blur, the branches swirling around him. All he wanted was for the spool to be rewound, to make all this a fiction. As they passed back through the gate in the railings Binnie was there, her face a block of stone. Then her composure broke. Her shoulders began to quiver. The two of them were little children again, both needing comforting but too young to do it for one another. They both began to cry, their faces contorting with the effort to control it. The shock of their emotions rippled through the cluster of volunteers surrounding them, triggering muted cries and stifled sobs.

Then Binnie ran from him, clutching her face, heading blindly away. A male arm caught her mid-flight and enveloped her. Instinctively Tom expected it to be Marcus's, but it was Sebastian who'd provided the shoulder to cry on.

Then his mother stood before him, all poise, all control gone. She clung to him, her face wet against his cheek.

'It's not true . . . It can't be. Tell me it's not true.'

But Tom couldn't. The image of his dead, violated sister was branded into his brain.

Suddenly he realised that they hadn't checked. Hadn't made absolutely sure. He pushed his mother away and rushed back towards the gate. A policeman barred his path.

'I'm sorry, son . . .'

'But she may be alive. Has anyone . . .? Her heart – maybe she's breathing?'

The policeman shook his head. Not just once but continually. The finality of that gesture brought it home.

Tom's chest felt gripped in a vice. He couldn't breathe.

'Who?' he croaked. 'Who did this?'

'We'll find out, son, you can be sure of that.'

Tom looked around wildly, as if the murderer might be amongst them. Some stranger lurking, watching. Gloating over their misery. Voices rang in his head. Cries, murmurs, angry exclamations. The crowd of helpers was incensed as well as shocked. He saw the Inspector questioning Marcus. Tom stumbled towards them, wanting to know what was being said.

'You knew the girl.'

'Of course. We . . . we all did.'

'When did you last see her?'

'I don't know . . . A few days ago.'

'And when did you last come into these woods?'

Marcus had a scared look in his eyes. He caught sight of Tom and appealed to him for help.

'When, Tom?'

Tom couldn't speak, unable to grasp what was being asked.

'Was Sara with you when you last went into the woods?' the Inspector asked.

'God, no,' Marcus protested.

Inspector Wilkie drew himself up to his full height.

'Now look here, lad, you ran away just now.'

'Did I?'

Yes, thought Tom. He did.

'Why was that, lad?'

'I dunno. I . . .' Marcus's voice dried. Then he began to snivel again.

'All right, lad. All right. We'll need statements from all of you later. When you've got over the shock.'

Suddenly Tom found his mother beside him again, icy calm. She glared at the Inspector.

'I want to see her.'

'I'm sorry, madam. The pathologist. Forensics. We can't let anyone near at the moment.'

'She's my daughter . . .'

'I'm sorry, ma'am.'

Tom glanced away, out across the grass. The volunteers were being dismissed by the police. It was over. He gripped his mother's arms. They both stared towards the woods, he knowing the precise horror of what had happened there, she tormented by what she could only imagine. Then Marcus loomed in front of him. Marcus whom the police had been talking to as if he were a suspect.

'Tom,' Marcus choked, 'Tom. Whoever did this, we're going to get him. Understand?'

'Yes,' said Tom, his head filling with wild suspicions. 'We'll get him. However long it takes.'

1950

2

28 August 1950
HMS *Unicorn*, off Pusan – South Korea

STANDING ON THE flight deck of the aircraft carrier, Second Lieutenant Marcus Warwick was as unprepared for the foul smell of Korea as he was for the whole extraordinary adventure he was embarking on. A reek of human excrement wafted from the shore as the giant warship made a slow turn for the entry into harbour.

'What a horrible pong. *Shit!*' His disgusted exclamation amused the man beside him.

'That's exactly what it is, old boy,' chuckled Lieutenant Richard Carter. 'Shit of the human kind. They fertilise the rice paddies with it. Foul practice. *Most* unhealthy.' He was from a landowning family in the Midlands and knew about such matters. 'Same in the New Territories. Surely you must've . . . '

'I wasn't in Hong Kong long enough, remember?'

'Ah. Yes, of course. Well, welcome to East Asia.'

'Thanks a million.'

The carrier HMS *Unicorn* had sailed from Hong Kong three days before, carrying Britain's makeshift response to the emergency in Korea. And now, after a passage dominated by PT and weapons testing, they were approaching the decaying port of Pusan. Their orders – to support the American-backed South Koreans against the Soviet-trained forces of the North who'd invaded across the 38th Parallel in June.

The mobilisation order had come just over a week ago. The Hong Kong detachment was the nearest British military force and the most prepared for action, but it had still been a scramble to get it ready in time.

With all the Hong Kong battalions undermanned, those assigned for Korea had had to draft in men from other regiments to make up the numbers. Lieutenant Richard Carter had been one of them.

27 Brigade's deployment was a stopgap measure, a rapid British response to the Americans' desperate plea for UN help. Their lack of equipment – no heavy guns or tanks – had caused some wags to dub it the 'For God's sake send us *something*' Brigade. A properly equipped unit was being mustered in England, but it would be months before it could get here and take over.

Marcus looked around him. Over a hundred officers stood on the aircraft carrier's deck, partly to impress the welcoming committee ashore, partly because they all wanted to see what they were getting into. Marcus knew few of the other officers by name yet and even fewer as friends, but he had struck up a bond with Richard Carter, despite their different backgrounds.

'Doesn't exactly fill one with confidence,' Marcus murmured as the decay of the port became more apparent.

'A dump,' said Carter. 'But one the communists can't be allowed to have, apparently.'

Marcus suspected that it might be better to give it to them and turn the ship around, but he kept the thought to himself.

National Service had come as a relief to him a year ago. Life in Wood Park had been unbearable since the murder of Sara Sedley the previous summer. Although her killer had been rapidly apprehended, the whole neighbourhood seemed to feel tainted by the crime. There was a collective sense of guilt at having let it happen, a guilt that Marcus had shut out to prevent it consuming him. He'd kept himself to himself for the rest of that academic year, locking away what he'd seen in those woods. School work had become his preoccupation. In particular, he'd painted and drawn for all he was worth.

In September last year he'd turned eighteen and been called up. After basic training he'd been selected for a commission, arriving in Hong Kong as a green subaltern to join the Middlesex Regiment, the 'Die-Hards', just days before the battalion was ordered to Korea. So far he'd hardly spoken to the men in the platoon he was to lead. When he'd arrived in the colony they'd been away on patrol, led by their sergeant. They were below him in the hangar, a lean, experienced bunch, their muscles toned from patrolling the hills bordering Mao's Red China. He knew he would have to win their confidence quickly, and suspected that it mightn't be easy.

The vile smell of human manure drifted down to that hangar through the huge lift openings in the carrier's deck. The soldiers of Marcus's platoon welcomed the stench because it meant their journey was nearly over. It was hot inside the ship. Despite their light tropical kit, the men sweated profusely. Beside them on the grey deck lay their packs and weapons.

''Ere, think they'd notice if I had a fag?' Private Jack Stokes hailed from the East End of London.

'Don't you fucking dare.' Sergeant Ron Bryant pointed at the fretwork of sprinkler pipes above their heads and tapped the side of his nose. The hangar had a permanent smell of oil and aviation fuel. At the far end, Seafire fighters stood with their wings folded like hands in prayer.

Bryant studied the faces of his men. A few, like him, were regulars, with battle honours from World War II. Others were National Service, almost as good as the professionals now, after the hoops he'd put them through in Hong Kong. And none was as green as the pale-faced young officer who was about to lead them to war. The sergeant was a fair man and would give Mr Warwick every chance, but there were others in the platoon, Stokes and Corporal Jagger in particular, who would make his life difficult unless he got the better of them.

The ship shuddered as it nudged the quay.

''Ere we go.' Private Stokes struggled to his feet and swung the bulging pack on to his back.

'Hold it, Stokesy,' said Bryant. 'It'll be a while yet. Enjoy the rest while you can. You won't get much of it from now on.'

Up on deck the officers stood to attention. Ahead of the *Unicorn*'s bows, the cruiser *Ceylon* was already tied up. It had brought the Argylls, the brigade's second infantry battalion. Marcus watched the Scotsmen preparing to disembark.

Pusan was a depressing sight close up, a flyblown shambles of rusting corrugated iron. Dusty and smelly. The wharf was lined with welcoming dignitaries and regimented schoolchildren waving Union Jacks.

Marcus Warwick's bony face had filled out in the past two years and his spots had gone. His thick dark hair was cut short at the sides and back. The muscles of his body had firmed up well and he felt fit. At the training camp on the south coast, he'd relished mixing with 'real people', the sort he'd seldom met during his middle-class suburban upbringing. But when the offer of a commission came he'd accepted it without question.

Down on the wharf a Korean band struck up a scrappy 'God Save the King'. Schoolgirls in navy skirts and white blouses struggled to trill the words, their wholesome cleanliness at odds with the filth all around. As the Argylls began to disembark from the *Ceylon*, two kilted soldiers climbed on to a gun turret and puffed up their bagpipes.

Buried in the midst of those Scottish soldiers as they descended the gangways to the quay was a small detachment from the Royal Signals Regiment. Amongst their ranks was Lance Corporal Tom Sedley, quite unaware that his one-time closest friend was less than a hundred yards away. He would have been discomforted to know it, because of the wedge that had come between them. Theirs was a friendship no more.

'Cor! If me mum could see me now!'

The words breathed in Tom Sedley's ear came from Private Pete Hewitt, a dark-haired lad from Durham who was following him down the gangway. Hewitt was a radio operator in Tom's section.

'Bloody band to welcome us, an' all.'

'She'd be right proud of you,' Tom confirmed.

'Your mum too, eh, corp?'

'I expect so.' Tom had avoided mentioning his relatives since signing up. None of his companions knew he had a film-star mother, nor that his family's troubles had been splashed all over the gutter press a couple of years back. He had no wish to talk about the death of his sister or the very public breakdown of his parents' marriage. No desire to be the focus of that sort of interest at all.

'Cor! Look at them Negroes!' Hewitt pointed down the quay where an immaculate US Army marching band was strutting along the wharf. 'That bloke with the stick – 'e must be seven foot tall!'

The giant of a drum-major twirled his baton as if it were a small twig. The tune being played was 'Colonel Bogey'.

'The Yanks are doing us proud,' Tom murmured, wondering if the clamour of their welcome reflected the desperation of the American and South Korean armies. He understood little of why they were here or what the war was about. But he did know that things were going badly.

'Wish I had a camera,' Hewitt said. 'I'd soon send a snap of this home.'

Home. Tom couldn't think of Wood Park without his stomach knotting. His sister's death had been just the start of it. A few days after the funeral and a man being charged with her murder, a Sunday newspaper had hammered a stake into the broken heart of his family with a dreadful revelation. On the night Sara was violated, their father, BBC producer Michael Sedley, had been having sexual intercourse in a Manchester hotel room with an unemployed actress in her early twenties. When the girl sold her story, it was as if a noxious substance had been spread round the perimeter of the Sedley home in Heathside Close. Neighbours looked away when they passed the garden gate. The milkman left his bottles there instead of at the back door. Even the neighbourhood children were affected, playing in their own gardens for a while instead of out in the Close.

The worst thing was that Marcus had turned his back on Tom completely. His mother had tried to smooth things over by saying: 'Friendships you have when you're young aren't always for ever. Boys grow out of relationships. They leave the nest and scatter.' The idea that Marcus had 'grown out' of their friendship only made things worse. Marooned inside his home in a whirlpool of recrimination, Tom had withdrawn into himself, listening to his parents fight over the remains of their marriage. Most of the time they'd argued in the privacy of their bedroom, but the muffled accusations and tearful outbursts had often penetrated the walls. His disgraced father had begged for another chance and his mother had eventually agreed. To get rid of the photographers, they'd put on their bravest faces and posed by the front gate, insisting that the past was the past and they were staying together.

But the damage was done.

Tom hated his father for betraying his mother. For betraying them all. At school his friends had all read the papers. He felt like a freak. An object of malign curiosity. He couldn't concentrate. And always in his thoughts was that dreadful sight in the woods of his adored sister's defiled body. His work had suffered and instead of the high grades expected of him, he'd barely passed his leaving certificate.

And so for Tom too the obligation to do National Service had come as a relief. In his call-up interview he'd mentioned his interest in wireless and been assigned to the Royal Signals. A stripe had soon come his way and he was shipped to Hong Kong, serving there for several months before the deployment to Korea.

For the first time in his life he was amongst people who knew nothing about him. Accepted him for what *he* was rather than for what his parents did. And he'd found contentment.

On board HMS *Unicorn,* the Middlesex Regiment was also preparing to disembark. Marcus itched to take the small sketching pad from the breast pocket of his tunic and capture the alien drabness of the quayside and the impressive ships towering above it. When first told that he was to be posted to Hong Kong he'd envisaged painting exotic oriental landscapes and wizened faces there. Even fantasised about senior officers commissioning him to do pictures of their daughters, over for the holidays from their Hampshire boarding schools. Dumpy girls with dull faces, whom he would transform into beauties as he had done with Binnie. And maybe go to bed with.

'So this is Korea,' said Richard Carter in a low murmur, as they lined up for the gangway. 'God help us.'

'May we get out of it alive,' Marcus replied.

'Amen to that.'

Marcus had written to his parents before embarking, his first letter to them for a long time. A hard one to write. By the time he left school, relations with his father had reached a low point. He knew he was second choice in the family. Sebastian was the star, launching into a fast-track career in the Civil Service. His own aspiration to be a painter was considered neither respectable nor financially sound. 'If the boy won't listen to my advice, he'll have to find his own way . . .' He'd been written off as a hopeless case.

Sara's murder had further soured his relationship at home. The police had interviewed him at length, as they had all the other young men in the neighbourhood. But the atmosphere of suspicion had infected his own parents. It had shocked him to see the doubt in their eyes. Then the tramp had been arrested and the air had cleared, but Marcus couldn't forgive them for suspecting him. He'd hardly contacted home since being called up, but faced with a campaign in which he might conceivably die, he'd felt a need to write. And, although he would hate to admit it, he did want their approval for what he was doing.

An airmail letter from his mother had crossed with his own, arriving a day before he sailed, asking if he was going to Korea. A letter from Binnie too, harping on about how close she felt to him. An earnest letter, which he knew was a probe to see how close, if at all, he felt to her. He hadn't replied. The past was the past. The present was an altogether different world.

And the future? Of one thing he was sure. Wood Park and all who lived there would not be featuring in it.

The journey north to the front line took a painfully long time. The men of 27 Brigade were crammed into a filthy train with as much equipment as they could carry, the rest being brought on by truck. It was dark before they set off. The seating in the cramped, evil-smelling carriages was hard. Ammunition had been issued in case of a guerrilla attack on the way. There seemed to be no air despite the open windows, only choking dust. Sleep was impossible except in positions of intimacy, which few of the men were prepared to adopt. The train moved in bone-shaking jerks, labouring up gradients and stopping with maddening frequency. At one interminable halt an officer got down to the track to see what was wrong. He found the driver sleeping on the ground and kicked him back into the cab.

Shortly before midnight the train arrived at its destination and the men transferred to American army lorries. Big open trucks driven by Negroes who smoked and chewed as they drove at breakneck speed along appalling roads. In the one carrying Lieutenant Marcus Warwick's platoon the driver sang spirituals in a delicately melodious voice. In the moonlight they could see distant hills and imagined the enemy dug in on their slopes, observing them from afar.

Eventually they arrived at the bank of a river, only a short distance from the front. The night air was cold. Here they made bivouacs with their ponchos, and bedded down to wait for the dawn and for their orders to go to war.

Tom Sedley didn't turn up at the assembly area until late the next day. The signallers had all travelled in their equipment-packed Bedford trucks and Land Rovers, on roads the like of which they'd never seen. When they arrived, the first thing they did was check that their radios hadn't been wrecked on the journey.

The brigade spent the next few days preparing to move to the line on one hour's notice. Plans were made, then unmade, an impression forming that their American commanders had little control over the situation. The US soldiers they had contact with expressed astonishment at 27 Brigade's lack of equipment. Soon they'd been dubbed 'the Cinderella Brigade'.

The men were showered with US army rations – grapefruit segments, pork slices and canned tomatoes for breakfast, tins of hashed meat, fruit juice by the gallon and coffee by the ton.

'If they're carting all this stuff round the battlefield, no wonder they're losing the war,' Richard Carter commented.

'Speak for yourself,' Marcus retorted. 'I love it. And don't forget what they say: an army marches on its stomach.'

'With this lot inside them they'll be crawling on their bellies.'

What nobody complained about was the free issue of cigarettes. Lucky Strikes, Chesterfields and Camels.

On the other side of the encampment from where Marcus had bivouacked with his platoon, Tom Sedley was integrating his section into the battalion headquarters.

Their task was to provide the Middlesex Regiment's communications link with Brigade. Being at the centre of things, Tom had a better idea of the state of the war. The fighting was close by and the sound of shelling frequently punctured the dusty air. It was a mystery to him why the Americans were doing so poorly, when they had such an abundance of supplies. The news was uniformly bad, with the communists still increasing their pressure on the 150-mile long defensive line which enclosed this last corner of non-communist Korea.

3 September 1950

Marcus sat on his bedding roll beneath the poncho he'd arranged as a bivouac, close to where his platoon was already sleeping. The British Brigade had moved further north. Tomorrow they would be facing the enemy for the first time.

During the last few days he'd worked hard to get to know his men and had established a rapport with Sergeant Bryant, making it clear that he'd be relying on Bryant's experience to see them through their first weeks of operations. He'd found the rest of the soldiers less communicative, the cynical looks of the older hands telling him he'd have his work cut out to convince them he wasn't useless.

'Look what I've managed to find.'

Richard Carter loomed out of the darkness, dropping to a crouch beside Marcus. A beer bottle in his outstretched fist was just visible in the moonlight. His other hand clutched a second one.

'Where'd you get those?'

'Don't ask.' The man had a permanent half-smile on his face, as if everything they were involved in was rather silly.

Marcus shivered. They'd been warned it got cold here in winter, but he had no inkling of the depth of the chill that lay ahead. He stood up and stamped his feet. Then they moved away from the others so they could talk and drink their beer unseen.

'My batman's an absolute idiot,' Carter complained, once they were out of earshot of the men. Marcus hadn't been allocated one and didn't mind at all. 'Asked him for a brew before we upped sticks this afternoon and he wandered off somewhere and didn't come back for a whole hour. Said he'd forgotten what I wanted him to do.'

'So you brewed up yourself?'

'Certainly not.' Carter sounded affronted. 'It's all right for you National Servicemen, but I'm going to make my life in the army. There are standards to maintain.'

They found a rock to sit on.

'Was your old man in the war?' Carter asked, raising the bottle to his lips.

'Went with the artillery on D-Day.'

'Talk about it?'

'Not to me. But then, he and I don't communicate much. He goes to reunions once a year. Tells friends he had a "good war". To be honest I think he misses it. Probably rather envious of me at this very moment.'

'What does he do?'

'Accountant. In the City. I've no idea what it involves, but from the look on his face when he goes off to work it must be incredibly boring. What about yours?'

'Father was evacuated from Dunkirk with a hole in his leg. Still walks with a limp. After that he managed the estate. There are four farms on it, all run by tenants.' Carter turned his head away as if preoccupied by something.

'What are you thinking?' asked Marcus after a while.

Richard shook his head.

'Go on.'

'Well, it's only that . . . I was wondering how I . . . how *we* will react when some of our men are killed and injured. I mean, have you actually seen someone you know dead?'

Marcus shivered. He'd never talked about Sara Sedley with anyone outside the boundaries of Wood Park. His instinct was to say no, to keep it all locked away, but he heard himself answer 'Yes'.

'. . . Once.'

By now he ought to be able to talk about it without getting into a state, Marcus decided. There had to be a safe way of tackling the subject. Filling in enough detail without revealing too much.

'It was two years ago.' He spoke in a soft, low voice that conveyed nothing of the unease fluttering in his chest. 'She . . . It was a girl we knew. All of us in the neighbourhood. She was fourteen. Sister of my best friend.'

'What happened to her?'

'She'd disappeared from home. Police were called and there was a search. We all helped look. In the end, she was found in the woods at the back of where I was brought up. She'd been strangled. And somebody had tried . . . you know.'

'What, rape?'

'Well, sex. Yes.'

'God. How dreadful . . .' Carter sounded outraged. 'My own sister's fourteen.'

'They caught the man who did it,' Marcus added quickly. 'The very next day. He was a tramp. We'd all seen him hanging around the area. Some people had even given him food. He denied murdering her, of course, but his blood group – you know. His sperm stuff on the girl – it matched. They can tell, apparently.' His heart was pounding by now.

'God. How sordid.'

'And they found fibres. From his jacket. On her knickers.'

Richard held up a hand.

'Spare me the details. You actually saw her . . . sort of as she was?'

'Yes. I mean I wasn't alone. The police were there. And her brother.'

Carter clicked his tongue.

Marcus felt sick suddenly. Talking about that dead child who hadn't been a child — a bad idea after all. He wished he'd kept the dreadful images of her in the part of his mind where he buried things that he would rather had never happened.

'What about you?' he asked quickly.

'A gun accident.' The countryman sounded dismissive. 'Fellow shot half his face away. Wasn't a pretty sight.'

'Someone you knew?'

'Knew *of*. Chap from the village. But he was a poacher. After our pheasants. Which sort of made it all right in a way. Different if it had been one of one's chums.'

'Yes.'

'Or like with you, a girl. From a family we knew . . .'

Marcus upended his beer bottle, then looked behind him. The camp was very still. Most were sleeping in preparation for what the morning would bring. It made him think of the production of *Henry V* that he'd acted in at school.

'Funny to think some of us here are going to die soon,' Richard whispered.

'Oh, thanks,' Marcus kept his own voice low too. 'That's really cheerful. Anyway, it may not come to that . . .'

'Of course it will.'

Marcus swallowed. 'Yes. I suppose it's bound to.' He sat up straight and tucked his chin in. 'Well, it's not going to be me.'

He was expecting his companion to come out with the same silly bravado, but he didn't. The moon had risen further and in its light he saw the young man's full mouth pucker as if tasting something sour.

'It'd be so unfair. I mean, to die. At our age,' Carter complained.

'Yes.'

'There are so many things we haven't done yet. And what would be the point? It's not like with our fathers. They were defending the homeland. Wives and children, hearth and home. But us? We're just here because some ruddy politicians think we ought to get involved.'

'We soldiers aren't meant to worry our little heads about such matters.'

'I can't help it. I mean, to be shot dead tomorrow. It'd be such a waste. With so many things still to do . . . I mean . . . well, there's *women*, for example.' He coughed out the word as if it had been catching in his throat.

'What about them?'

Carter shifted from one buttock to the other as if easing the pressure in his loins. 'You see, I've never . . . Have you? I mean done it? You know, the whole shooting match. In a bed?'

Marcus had no wish to discuss his paltry sexual experience. The one regret he'd had about coming to Korea was that he'd met a girl in Hong Kong at a regimental ball on the night the mobilisation order came through. Laura, the daughter of a senior official in the Governor's office, who'd just left school. At first he'd thought she was like Binnie, whose eagerness to settle into marriage and motherhood frightened the life out of him. But Laura had revealed a carefree, mischievous streak, convincing him that sex would have been on the cards, given time.

'I mean, I know what girls' bodies feel like on the outside,' Carter continued awkwardly, his leg jiggling, 'rubbing up against you in a smooch and so on. Perfume in the hair . . . But it's the inside I want to experience.'

'Won't be much of that here . . .' Marcus cautioned. 'Unless you're planning rape and pillage.'

Carter whinnied with embarrassment. 'Hardly. But you? I suppose you *have* done it. I'm probably the only virgin in the regiment. Hope to God my men never find out.'

'Nonsense.'

'Well? Have you or not?'

Marcus decided a little lie would do no harm. 'A couple of times.'

Carter looked disappointed.

'Actually, to be absolutely honest,' Marcus continued, trying to sound worldly, 'I think the whole sex business is overrated. And if we do end up in heaven, the angels will be much hotter stuff than anything down here.'

'Thanks a lot. You're a great comfort.'

'Tell you what. Changing the subject.'

'Go on.'

'How about taking bets on which of us bags our first North Korean?'

Carter grinned with relief. Wagering was something he *did* have experience of.

'A guinea says it's me,' he said.

3

**The following day
4 September 1950**

FOR TOM SEDLEY this war still didn't feel real, despite the frequent rumble of distant shelling. As he and his signals section followed the brigade's convoy towards the front line, he was lulled by the sight of pretty terraced hillsides, the scarlet flash of ripe pimentos and heavily laden apple trees. Then came paddy fields, wet, yellow-brown patches worked by women protected from the late afternoon sun by broad straw hats. Would they be there if danger was close at hand?

It was nearly two hours before they reached the place where the headquarters was to be set up. Tom had two Land Rovers for his section, each towing an equipment trailer. There were two signalmen under him and a technician to charge batteries and maintain the radios.

'The colonel wants the field telephones working as soon as possible,' the adjutant told him as they parked up next to the CO's tent. 'There are no tracks between us and Brigade, but we've recced the ground and the linesmen can do it in their jeeps. They should be on their way here already.'

'Right, sir. We'll be ready when they arrive.'

Tom set about organising his team. It would be dark before long.

The truck carrying Marcus's platoon broke down. By the time a replacement arrived the heavens had opened and drenched the men and their equipment.

In the gathering gloom the vehicle followed a mud road running parallel to the front. When they reached the Middlesex HQ it was night.

The CO scowled at their late arrival. He was a small man and a disciplinarian. A good commander but an unforgiving creature of whom Marcus had already learned to be wary.

The British were taking over ten miles of hills from an American unit needed elsewhere. The ground had been reconnoitred two days earlier and the prospects weren't promising. Lack of manpower would leave large gaps in the line which the enemy could easily penetrate.

Marcus felt utterly unprepared for what they were about to do. He sensed the fear and excitement of his men. Their skills learned on peacetime patrols in Hong Kong were to be tested against a real enemy. But his own ignorance frightened him.

They waited for an American guide to turn up, to lead them to where the rest of their company had set up its base.

'Time for a brew,' said Private Stokes.

'Excellent idea,' said Marcus. 'Get it going while I look at some maps.'

Marcus found the tent being used as an Ops Room. Inside was Richard Carter.

'Your transport break down too?' Marcus asked, surprised to see him here.

'No. My platoon's defending the HQ perimeter for the night. We'll be moving closer to the river in the morning when the colonel has a better idea of what's what.'

Carter spread out a map and showed him the company positions. Marcus's was on a bend in the river that separated them from the enemy, its HQ in a derelict house.

'The Yanks are in a hurry to get out,' Carter warned. 'Seem faintly amused as usual that we don't have any tanks.'

'Sounds like you've got the easy number, guarding HQ.'

'Actually I'm rather browned off. Prefer to be somewhere where I can bag a gook and win my bet.'

Marcus smiled. 'I'd better move. There's a brew on the go and I'm in bad need of a wet.'

Tom had completed the connection of the field telephone and was preparing to get his sleeping arrangements sorted when a startlingly familiar voice stopped him in his tracks. It came from the direction of the Ops tent. Disbelievingly, he peered into the darkness and saw

Marcus emerging, his face unmistakable in the light escaping from the lifted flap.

Instinctively, Tom backed away, shocked that the past should have caught up with him in such an unexpected way. Resentment rose up inside him. This was the friend who'd turned his back on him after Sara's death. Shunned him as if he were a leper. And now here he was on the same patch of earth on the other side of the world. And an officer, to boot.

Heart thudding wildly, Tom withdrew into the darkness.

Damn Marcus! If he saw him here, he might talk. Tell people who Tom was and what had happened in Wood Park two years ago. Destroy the privacy he'd carefully created for himself.

Suddenly he felt Sara with him again, her chin on his shoulder, whispering in his ear, just as he'd imagined many times in the months after her death. Always incomprehensible. A stream of burble, as if some fuse had blown in her brain, preventing proper words forming.

He clamped his hands to his head in an effort to shut out the noise. It was all coming back, the terrible feelings of loss. And of doubt. He could still hear Marcus's voice a few yards away, bright, vivacious and confident. What right did he have to be so chirpy? Why hadn't *he* been indelibly marked by Sara's murder as Tom had? The other officer spoke with the braying tones of the upper classes. The voice irritated him, but Marcus's hurt.

Then a soldier interrupted them, his accent from the East End of London.

'The Yank's here, sir. 'Im what's gonna show us the way . . .'

'Thanks, Stokes. I'll be right there.'

''E's in a fuck of an 'urry, sir.'

'All right.'

Tom heard muttered goodbyes, then Marcus disappeared with his soldier into the gloom. Tom stayed where he was for a few minutes, letting his anger subside. Then he returned to the signals Land Rovers where his section had their bivouacs.

One day soon he and Marcus would come face to face, he realised, as he buried himself in his bedroll. It was inevitable. And when they did, the chances were that he wouldn't have any darkness to hide in.

★

35

By the time Marcus rejoined his platoon, they'd abandoned their brew-up and the men were hoisting packs on to their backs. They set off on foot, led by the American sergeant, their progress helped by light from the moon and stars. After twenty minutes the dark outline of a squat building loomed in front of them. This was the derelict farm where the company had its HQ. Their American guide left them there and hurried away to rejoin his unit.

'Lieutenant Warwick. At last.'

Major Whittle, Marcus's company commander, took him to a corner of the headquarters and with a shielded torch showed him a map of the ground.

'The American position you're to relieve is about a mile down a track to the west.'

He took him to the door, pointing to a vague smudge of worn ground just visible in the moonlight, which led off through the trees.

'Take your platoon there right away. The Americans are on a bluff near the Naktong river bank. They badly need a break. Had a bad time. There are bodies about. Rather smelly.'

'Yes, sir,' said Marcus, swallowing his disquiet.

'And don't rely on your maps. They're based on a Japanese survey done in 1932. I'm told that half the hills are in the wrong place and others are missing altogether.'

'I'll watch out for that, sir.'

'Good luck.'

'Thank you, sir.'

Marcus assembled his men and told them they were moving on straight away.

'What, still no brew, sir?' Corporal Jagger complained. 'Been on the go for hours.'

'The men we're relieving have been on the go for weeks, corporal. You'll have to wait a little longer. Come on. Let's get moving. And keep your ears open. The gooks are not far away. Sar'nt Bryant?'

With his platoon sergeant leading, they set off. Although the rain had stopped some time ago the ground underfoot was soft and often slippery. They moved slowly, stopping frequently to listen.

Eventually the path, such as it was, began to traverse the southern face of the ridge they were to take control of. The stony earth was sparsely covered with bushes, which brushed against their legs.

Marcus followed a few yards behind his sergeant, learning from his field craft. This all still felt like a game, an extraordinary yet serious adventure. He kept wondering what his parents would say if they knew what he was doing at this moment. Would they admire him? Fret about his safety? Or merely pray that he wouldn't let down the family name?

Ten minutes later they were challenged by the American sentries, then warmly welcomed.

'How many guys do you have?' asked the lieutenant in command.

'Thirty-four.'

'Jeez.' The American platoon was twice the size. 'And no heavy weapons?'

'One two-inch mortar and a three-point-five rocket launcher.'

The American sucked his teeth. 'Then you won't be here for long.'

Marcus was led into the tent used by the three officers. They showed him on a map where their men were dug in on the forward slope of the hill overlooking the river. Then they briefed him on the last known positions of the enemy on the other side of the Naktong.

'Last few days it's been quiet, but a week ago they tried to take this position and shredded us. A couple of ours killed and twenty wounded. We got about thirty of theirs. You'll smell them when you're in the foxholes.'

'What are your plans?'

'We don't have any order to withdraw yet. Guess it'll come in the morning. Your men had better share our positions for the night. You're welcome to squeeze in here with us if you want, lieutenant.'

'Thanks. But I'll stick with my men. It's been a long day. We'll have a brew-up and get some rest.' His voice sounded archetypally British amongst the American accents.

'A final word of advice, lieutenant.' The US officer stuffed a fresh tablet of gum into his mouth. 'Don't get too clever out there. Those communists are subhumans. When you've once seen what they do to prisoners, you'll understand what I mean.'

Sleep didn't come easily for Marcus, worrying about the day ahead when he would be in sole command of this position. Responsible for the lives of more than thirty men and for preventing a communist breakthrough on this stretch of the line.

He did sleep eventually, then awoke with a start, dislodging the blanket and the greatcoat he'd draped over himself. There was a noise. Much noise. Engines firing up. Voices. Feet crunching on dead sticks. And torch beams, shaded pinpricks of light moving behind him like fireflies.

The Americans were on the move.

Marcus checked his watch with his shielded flashlight. Two in the morning. Surely they'd wait until dawn, unless there was some very, very pressing need to leave.

The wind had changed direction. Blowing from the north now, from the side of the ridge where the dead lay. He could smell them – a sour, sickening stench.

He got up. Sergeant Bryant was also awake.

'They're fucking off out of it,' the older man growled. 'Did they say they would do this, sir?' There was an edge to the word 'sir', as if he suspected his officer had been cutting him out of the loop.

'Not a word. Not a bloody word.'

Marcus went in search of the American officers' tent but found it gone. He walked on in the direction of the engine noise in time to see the outlines of the tanks as they disappeared down the hill.

'Christ . . .'

He returned to where his men were, the cloud-shrouded moon giving just enough light to see their outlines.

'Nice. Really nice. Polite, like,' Corporal Jagger complained.

'Makes you feel all warm inside, don't it?' The broad cockney of Private Stokes.

'Agreed,' said Marcus, needing to re-establish control. 'But it makes no difference. We're here to do a job.'

The sudden departure meant that no watch was being kept over the river now. And they needed one. But crawling around in the dark trying to find the Americans' abandoned trenches was hardly wise.

'I want sentries out. Two men from each section. Up on the crest of the ridge. We'll dig in properly at first light. Until then, the rest of you get your heads down again. Sar'nt Bryant . . .'

'I'll fix it, sir.'

The sergeant took over before more grumbles could be voiced. Marcus left him to it and returned to his bedroll. He knew sleep wouldn't return easily, but getting the blanket over him would help until the first glimmer of dawn.

It couldn't come soon enough. To be defending a piece of ground with no idea of the lie of the land was not the way he'd hoped to start his war.

4

MARCUS AWOKE WITH a start. He'd been dreaming about Binnie. It was her he'd been dancing with at that ball in Hong Kong, not Laura. Trying in vain to get away from her. He should have answered her letter, he realised. Made it clear that he didn't share whatever it was she felt for him. To him she would always be that bony ten-year-old from across the road who wanted to play with boys rather than girls, an alien creature whose pale nakedness he and Tom had explored when playing doctors in Tom's attic.

As the dream vaporised, he listened to the sounds of the night, but could only hear his own breathing. It was perfectly still, with the sky lightening to the east. Checking his watch – it was shortly before four a.m. – he shed his blanket and pushed his fingers through his thick dark hair. Close by, he saw the glow of stoves, the men heating water to shave and make tea.

'Count me in on the brew,' he told one of them as he stood up.

He walked up to the ridge and dropped down beside one of the sentries on the crest. The man's Lee Enfield rifle lay on the ground beside him.

'Anything moving?'

The ground fell away in front of them and at the bottom of the slope a shawl of grey mist marked the course of the river as it wound through the dark valley. The terrain beyond it, enemy territory, was a dark, formless mass, with only the hilltops catching the pre-dawn glimmer.

''Aven't seen nothing, sir.'

Marcus peered down at the forward slope of the hill, looking for the Americans' foxholes, but it was not yet light enough to see.

'Remind me, I've forgotten your name.'

'Walker, sir.'

'*Walker*, yes. And what do you feel about being here?'

'Don't know yet, sir. Bloody cold, that's all.'

'Quite right.' It was a stupid thing to ask.

Marcus scanned the far bank through binoculars, but it was too dark to see much.

'Another half-hour . . . What's your first name, Walker?'

'Danny, sir.'

'Where are you from?'

'Can't rightly say, sir.'

'Why's that?'

Walker made a throat-clearing noise as if he didn't really want to talk about it.

'Well, there's just me mum and me, sir. And we keeps moving, see?'

'Really? Why's that?'

'Because the blokes me mum owes money to keeps finding us.'

Marcus wanted to laugh but the boy sounded deadly serious. He was glad that his own mother couldn't see him now. She'd be tight-lipped with anxiety, not daring to reveal how afraid for him she was. Never once in his entire life had he seen her let an emotion fracture her composure.

He heard a footfall and Sergeant Bryant crouched beside him.

'Need to get the lads in position before it gets much lighter, sir. Two sections here on the ridge, with the third down on the river bank.'

'Fine.'

'I suggest we take over the Americans' slits for today, work out what needs doing to them, and dig in again tonight if we need to.'

'Good plan,' said Marcus. 'Let's take a quick look around.'

Crouching, they moved sideways along the contour, taking note of what the Americans had left them. The position they were defending was a small circular hill with a long, sloping ridge running westwards which ended down on the river bank.

As they dropped towards the water the sickly smell of rotting flesh became stronger. It wasn't long before they saw the cause of it. In an exposed area impossible to reach without risking fire from the enemy's guns, several bodies lay on the stony ground, bloated by the sun and the rain. The uniforms looked Korean.

'They tell you what happened here, sir?' asked Bryant.

'A week ago, a North Korean patrol crossed the river on a raft. Probing to see if this section of the bank was defended.'

'And it was.'

'The Yanks lost a couple of their own men in the action.'

'But nailed plenty of theirs.'

Death. The first Marcus had seen of it here. He wondered if it would become so familiar that it wouldn't bother him any more. And if it would ever stop reminding him of Sara.

'Be even more revolting when the sun gets up.' Marcus sniffed. 'Shouldn't we bury them or something?'

'Not unless we want to be buried with them, sir,' Bryant retorted.

Marcus lifted his gaze towards the far side of the river. A range of high hills swept round to their left, their flanks turning purple in the morning light. Somewhere in there was the enemy, in numbers that could only be guessed at. Directly in front of them on the other side of the water, running east, a ridge followed the line of the bank. Where it ended, a large wedge of flat ground extended back inland for some distance before becoming mountainous again.

They moved on, crawling through scrub to reach the river bank. As they approached it they saw a series of low mounds which the Americans had dug positions into.

'Looks like a local burial ground,' said Sergeant Bryant. 'Those mounds are useless for protection. Wouldn't stop a machine-gun bullet, let alone a tank round.'

They crawled forward to the largest of the excavations and found an American field telephone beside it in a smart leather case.

'They certainly left in a hurry,' Marcus commented, 'not to have taken this with them.'

'There's plenty more where that came from,' Bryant remarked. 'Always is, if you're a Yank. There's a load of 'em back where they had their platoon HQ. Enough for each section.' Bryant looked down into the shallow trench, screwing up his face at the gum wrappings and other detritus left there. His distaste for the American way of doing things was intensifying by the minute. 'The lads'll have to live with this today, but tonight they can dig proper slits.'

Across the water all looked still and beautiful in the strengthening light.

'You'd never think there were thousands of soldiers over there,' Marcus remarked, searching the terrain with his binoculars.

'A good place for a Bren, this,' Bryant growled.

'And a perimeter of barbed wire, perhaps?' Marcus suggested.

'I'll fix that, sir.'

They made their way back up the hill, using the reverse side of the ridge for cover. It was getting lighter by the minute. The sergeant was eager to get his men in place. Bryant's calm efficiency was making Marcus feel distinctly inadequate, so he decided to do something about it.

'I'm going to take out a patrol, Sar'nt Bryant. See what we can spot.'

'Yes, sir.' The sergeant didn't demur. 'I'd suggest Corporal Jagger and a couple of riflemen. Stokes and Walker should see you right.'

'Right, then.'

'I'll tell them, sir.'

Half an hour later, when Marcus had shaved and eaten, he had a brief talk with his company commander on the No. 88 VHF radio, telling him what he planned. Then he gathered his patrol group and spread out a map.

'I've had a look at the ground. There seems to be plenty of cover down this way.' He indicated where he meant. 'The gooks may also have patrols out, so keep alert.'

Marcus spotted a sidelong glance between Corporal Jagger and Private Stokes. A look that said: 'Are we *really* wise to be following this green lad into the unknown?'

'They 'ave snakes in this part of the world?' Stokes asked.

'I don't know,' Marcus answered, feeling it was something he should have found out. 'But if there *are* any, they should be more frightened of you than you are of them.'

'Yeah, but do *they* know that, sir?'

'If you find one you can ask it. Now listen, my plan is to follow the river bank to the east. The company commander has asked us to keep an eye out for the enemy laying sandbags across the river as an underwater bridge. Sounds fanciful, but we've been asked to look, so we will.'

There was a snort of derision from Jagger.

'Won't need that, sir. From what I heard the commies can walk on water.'

'Don't you believe it.' He looked from face to face. Rifleman Walker, the only one younger than himself, chewed his lip. 'The main aim of this patrol is simply to see if there's any sign of the enemy. Of course, if we can kill some that'll be a bonus.' There was mockery in the eyes of the old hands, which he knew he would have to defuse. 'Corporal Jagger . . .'

'Yes, sir?'

'If you see me doing something stupid, feel free to tell me.'

'Oh, I will, sir. You can be sure of that.'

They sorted their kit, checking ammunition and grenades and the bolt action on their weapons. Marcus carried a Sten as well as a revolver. He told himself it would be a piece of cake. Like his forays into the woods with Tom when they were young. All a bit of a lark.

Marcus led the way down the slope, Corporal Jagger following a few feet behind. Then came Walker, with Stokes bringing up the rear. Where the cover made it possible, they walked, otherwise they moved at a crawl. Marcus tingled with fear as they neared enemy territory. They'd all heard what the North Koreans did to prisoners. Wrists bound with barbed wire, then a bullet in the back of the head.

Every few yards they stopped to listen and look. A hawk circled above, watching them as if they were mice. The sky was clear blue by now, with a sun that was showing its heat. On a flatter piece of ground close to the river bank they hid amongst the scrub, aided by dappled shade from the pines. The water was less than fifty yards away. Beyond it, on the far side, the wedge of flat land he'd seen earlier led away from the river towards distant hills. Marcus put the binoculars to his eyes. There, about a quarter of a mile from the river, was a village. Mud-brown walls and thatched roofs. But no sign of people. They'd have fled, he guessed. Or been killed. He let the lenses linger on the small cluster of buildings, watching for the slightest movement that would reveal the presence of the enemy. It was eerily peaceful. So much so that he had an urge to stand up and stretch.

Marcus decided they would stay put for a while, watching and listening. He used the binoculars to check the ground further along their side of the river bank. There was an open patch to cross when they moved on.

After a few minutes Jagger began whispering to him.

'Movement in the village. Two men running between the houses, sir.'

'Armed?' Marcus asked.

'Couldn't see, sir.'

'They may have spotted us. Better get going.' Marcus pointed along the river bank. 'I'll go first. When I'm across the open ground, wait for my signal, then send Stokes. Walker next. One at a time. You follow after that.'

Marcus calculated the distance. It was only about thirty feet before a low sand dune would provide cover again. He psyched himself up and went for it, pulse thumping as he threw himself to the ground on the far side of the gap. He looked back and saw Corporal Jagger watching, his small, ratlike eyes just visible beneath his knitted cap-comforter. Marcus beckoned on the next man.

A few seconds later Private Stokes dropped to the ground beside him.

'Move on,' Marcus ordered hoarsely. 'Get amongst those trees.' He pointed to a clump at the far end of the dune. Stokes crawled away.

Marcus watched Private Walker raise himself to a crouch, then start his sprint across the gap. The boy was halfway over when a massive explosion heaved the ground beneath him. Earth spattered Marcus's face and something heavier zinged into the dune beside him. His ears rang.

'Christ . . .'

His first thought was a mine, then he heard the shout from Corporal Jagger.

'Mortar! Get clear, sir.'

Jagger began to wriggle backwards, distancing himself from the clearing where Walker lay motionless. Marcus felt paralysed. Terrified. Cringing in expectation of the next shock.

A second explosion lifted him from the ground and showered him with sand. The dune had been hit. His ears rang. It felt as if blood was pouring down his face, but when he touched the skin his hand came away dry. He looked across at the trees where Stokes had gone and saw him heading for the hill, keeping low.

Out on the open ground Walker lay still. My fault, thought Marcus. *My* stupid, bloody fault. He got to his feet and ran towards the soldier. There was a gash in Walker's leg and a lot of blood. The boy's lips quivered.

A third bomb detonated, further away this time, but the blast still knocked Marcus down. When the dirt stopped flying he got to his feet, slipped his hands under Walker's armpits and, half-lifting, half-pulling, dragged him back towards the place where they'd first lain in watch.

Suddenly Jagger was by his side. Together they carried the wounded private to safety and hobbled back up the slope. Deep in the shade of some trees they lowered Walker to the ground. The boy was moaning. Trembling uncontrollably.

'Be all right, Danny,' Jagger hissed. 'Just a scratch.' He ripped open Walker's trousers and pressed a field dressing to the narrow but deep wound in the thigh.

Marcus felt vomit rise in his throat and looked away. He was trembling too.

'You done good, sir,' Jagger assured him. 'Done good.'

A few minutes later Stokes caught up with them. Unharmed, to Marcus's relief.

'Need to get this laddie back up the ridge, sir,' Jagger stated.

'Yes. I'll take an arm.'

'The two of us can do that. You just lead on and get us there.'

When they reached the platoon base Sergeant Bryant took charge, calling Company HQ for a stretcher party and morphine. Then he sat down beside Marcus and forced a billycan of tea on him.

'Drink it,' he ordered.

'Was that wrong, Sar'nt?' Marcus needed to know. 'Wrong to take out a patrol?'

'No, sir. Look, the boy got hit, but he'll live. It does no harm. The lads'll be doubly alert now they know the enemy's really there. And the gooks know we're here, too. Know we're not going to sit on our backsides waiting for them.'

Marcus nodded. 'Thanks, Sar'nt Bryant.'

The sergeant got up again. 'You'll be needing to make a report to the major,' he reminded him. 'Pretty damned quick.'

'Yes. Okay, I'll be fine in a minute, sergeant. Thank you.'

Marcus finished off the tea. So he'd done all right. Not a disaster after all and he seemed to have earned the respect of his men.

5

14 September 1950

TODAY WAS THE second anniversary of Sara's death. Tom had remembered it the moment he awoke. During the morning he tried to think of some way to mark the day, without doing anything that would draw attention to himself.

More than a week had passed since Tom had learned about Marcus's narrow escape when on patrol. He'd been handed a casualty report on Private Walker for onward transmission to Brigade. The realisation that Marcus could have been killed – might still be killed any day now – had made him rethink his feelings towards his former best friend. Bitter at Marcus's withdrawal from him after Sara's murder, he nevertheless still felt a bond. A longing for things to be as they used to be. Marcus and Tom. Blood brothers. He'd been trying to think of ways to bring about a reunion before it was too late, but had reached no conclusion.

The war seemed static, the enemy having made no attempt to break through their defences, even though intelligence suggested that they were massing. The brigade's only fatality had been a young private who'd crashed a jeep into a shell crater.

Despite the boredom they all felt at battalion headquarters, Tom was perfectly content. Sometimes when off watch he would scan the airwaves with a small radio he'd built in Hong Kong, picking up snatches of Korean that he assumed came from the enemy lines. He'd also started teaching Signaller Pete Hewitt to play chess. The lad was an apprentice electrician by trade, a Geordie National Serviceman from a background very different to his own.

In the late afternoon Tom sat on a rock a few yards from the signals Land Rover, watching the sun sink towards the rice paddies in the valley behind their lines. From his tunic pocket he pulled a photograph of Sara. She was wearing a tutu, a snap taken at her ballet class when she was twelve. Not a particularly good picture, but it showed her smile, her already shapely body, and above all the bright sparkle in her eyes. He'd missed her dreadfully in the months after her death. Still did. And today he felt decidedly emotional, even though it was two years since he'd lost her.

As Tom sat there on his rock, brooding about what Sara might be doing now if she'd lived, he didn't notice Pete Hewitt come up beside him.

'Gi' us a look, corp.' The Geordie reached for the print. He had a cigarette in his mouth. 'Girlfriend? Or is it your mum?'

Tom tried to stuff the photo into his tunic. This was private. But Hewitt snatched it from him.

'Aw, she's sweet. Bit young for you, though.'

'My sister, actually.' Tom swallowed the lump in his throat. 'And give it back.'

'Nice-looking wee kid.' Hewitt twisted his body away, holding on firmly to the photo.

Tom thought of ordering the Geordie to hand it back, but knew how inappropriate that would be. And as the seconds passed he realised that he didn't actually mind the lad looking at her. One day he was going to have to open up to someone about what had happened, and Pete Hewitt was as good a person as any.

'She's dead, unfortunately.' Blurting it out like that brought a salty taste to the back of his mouth.

'You're joking.'

'Unfortunately not.'

'What happened, mon?'

Tom swallowed and wiped his nose on the back of his hand.

'It was two years ago today. She was murdered.'

'Flippin' heck, mon!'

Hewitt plonked himself down beside Tom who looked into his soft, brown eyes and wallowed in their goodwill.

'They catch the bastard?'

Tom nodded. 'Yes. He was sentenced to hang, only the execution's been delayed because of appeals.'

'But they'll not let him off?' Hewitt handed Sara's picture back.

'I don't know. It's a question of his sanity, apparently. They say he wasn't all there.'

'All the more reason to top the bloke. People like that need locking up.'

Hewitt frowned, partly at the foolishness of what he'd just said, partly at something else that had just come into his head.

'Can I 'ave another dekko?'

Tom passed him the picture again.

'Was this . . . was this in the papers?'

Tom grimaced. He'd hoped to avoid having to go into the rest of his story.

'Well, yes. Actually it was. That very picture.'

Hewitt stared at him, mouth gaping, the Woodbine stuck to his lower lip. He peeled it off and squeezed out the ember, saving the rest for later.

'It's all coming back. Me dad was always talking about it. This kid's mother – she's some famous blooming actress, isn't she?'

'Yes, but . . .'

'Hee! I've just realised – she must be *your* ma too! That's amazing, mon. I'll tell all me friends. My oppo, Lance Corporal Tommy Sedley – he's bleedin' famous!'

'No . . .' Tom snatched back the photo. 'Please. I don't want people to know about all this. They'll never stop.'

'Sorry. Sorry.' Hewitt patted Tom's knee and puffed out his cheeks. 'Sorry, corp. Got carried away, like. Of course. Mum's the word.'

'That's all right.' Without thinking what he was doing, Tom touched the place on his leg where Hewitt's hand had just been, wanting to extract the most he could from that brief contact. 'It's just that I haven't told anyone here about my mother. Or Sara.'

'You can trust me, corp. Won't say a word. Promise.' Hewitt squinted at the sun dropping behind the distant hills. 'You never know when it's going to happen, do you? Like with your sis. I mean, there's us sat here. You an' me. Just one mortar bomb on our heads and we'd be history.' His wide mouth spread into a smile. His teeth were unusually white. 'Hey . . . D'you think if we went in a flash, all sudden like, together, that you and me would be oppos for the rest of time? Sort of welded together for all eternity?'

49

'God, you do talk bollocks.' As Tom put Sara's photo back into his tunic pocket, however, the idea of being welded to Hewitt had a certain disturbing appeal.

'Wouldn't be so bad up there, eh?' the young man continued. 'You could still have the stripe and tell me what to do. And then you could introduce me to your sis . . .'

Tom flinched at the lad's insensitivity.

'Sorry. Sorry, sorry.' Hewitt stared down at the ground. 'Never did know when to button me lip. My dad used to clip me round the ear to shut me up.'

'Perhaps I should do the same.'

But Tom felt good talking with Hewitt. Since they'd been here on the line he'd developed a strong liking for the lad with his puppyish ways. *Lad.* They were the same age, yet Pete seemed a lot younger than him. Younger and more carefree.

'Sara would be sixteen by now, if she'd lived,' Tom said, wistfully. 'I have a feeling you'd have liked each other if you'd met.'

Hewitt was silent for a moment, then made a confession. 'Truth is I wouldn't have the ruddy nerve to talk to her if we met up beyond the pearly gates. Here's me, a bloke who babbles away all the time, but introduce me to a girl and the cat gets me tongue.'

'I know what you mean.'

Women were a largely unexplored pasture for Tom too. A combination of shyness and a lack of self-confidence meant he'd never had a girlfriend. That and the fact he couldn't envisage ever doing anything intimate with them. He was also rather self-conscious about his fair hair and soft-skinned face, suspecting that women would think him unmanly. But Hewitt, with his thick dark brush, handsome, chiselled chin and well-formed limbs, would, he imagined, have no problems with the fairer sex.

'Where was it you live?' Hewitt asked.

'In North London.'

'Somewhere posh, I'll bet.'

'The houses are quite big.'

'Yeah, but you speak posh too. I mean, you'd have to, wouldn't you, with your ma being an actress and all.'

The setting sun was leaching red from beneath a band of cloud. 'Posh' was not how Tom wanted others to see him.

'I mean, you should've got a commission, with all your education.'

'They offered it. But I didn't want one.'

'Shit! Why not? You'd have your own batman to wash your undies for you . . .'

'Maybe, but I don't feel comfortable with the sort of people who inhabit officers' messes,' Tom said tartly.

Hewitt murmured his approval. 'I know what you mean.'

'You see,' Tom went on, straightening his back, 'I happen to believe all people are equal.' He knew he was sounding pretentious but couldn't stop himself. 'You, me, the others. We're all as good as each other, whatever sort of school we went to. As people, I mean. There shouldn't have to be bosses and workers. Officers and other ranks. With special treatment for one lot and not for the others.'

'You sound like a communist.'

'Maybe I am.'

'So you're on the side of our enemy?' Hewitt sounded shocked.

'No, of course I'm not. This is a war about one lot of Koreans trying to force another lot to live like they do rather than the way they want to live. Just because one half are communist doesn't make me support what they're doing here.'

'But Joe Stalin's an all-right bloke as far as you're concerned?' Hewitt pressed. 'Bumping people off left, right and centre.'

'I'm not saying that either. What I mean is, I like the idea behind communism, not the way it's being implemented.'

'Yeah, well, anyway, I'm quite happy with the way things are. Back home and here in the army, thank you very much. Quite happy to have other people decide what's good for me.'

'You'd make a good wife for someone.' Tom smiled, the words slipping out.

Hewitt gave him a sideways glance to check that he'd meant it as a joke. 'Aw, bugger off, corp. And don't get any funny ideas.'

Wives. Whenever Tom visualised himself married, it was always to Binnie. It wasn't that he really loved her, or even desired her. It was simply that she was the only person of the opposite sex and of a similar age who'd always been there in his life. After the dreadful events of two years ago she'd made a point of coming to see him. Asking how he was and if there was anything she could do. Almost as if she'd been compensating for Marcus's abandonment of him. Then in the following year she'd changed. Grown up a lot, giving up trousers and wearing dresses. More and more she'd come to epitomise for him what a wife should be. Warm and motherly. Honest and fair. Affectionate without being overly so. Poised, and with the bearing of a lady.

Tom thought again of what Hewitt had just said about letting others take the decisions. That's how he would want it in a marriage. Him in charge. Would Binnie be happy with that, if it ever got to that point? As he lay in his bedroll at night, he sometimes visualised her making a sudden unexpected visit here. Just to see how he was. He would give her a tour of the HQ and introduce her to everybody. Sometimes he visualised a home with the two of them in it. Her at one end of the kitchen table and him at the other. All quiet in the house. Children asleep. And yet the physical act of creating those children with her was something he could never envisage.

'So, corp, what's the plan for tonight?' Hewitt rubbed his hands together. Small hands with short, straight fingers, Tom noticed.

'Am I doing the watch on my own, or does your belief that all of us is equal mean you'll be keeping me company some of the time?'

Tom thought that keeping him company would be just fine.

6

21 September 1950

A WEEK LATER, WHEN General MacArthur's Marines landed at Inchon 150 miles to their north, cutting the enemy's supply lines, there was a hurried spate of letter-writing in Marcus's platoon. The UN forces were going on the offensive. With one death in the battalion already, their intelligence officer missing and a handful of men injured, the risk of not surviving the days ahead had become rather more real.

Marcus scribbled a note to his parents, beginning it with a pencil sketch of a soldier heating a billycan, substituting his own face for that of the man he'd been drawing. 'Me enjoying lunch!' he'd scrawled as a caption. On the reverse side he explained how bored they'd all become, waiting for action, and how keen they were to be moving forward – words chosen to slip by the censor and to warn his parents of what was to come.

In the two weeks since his first alarming experience of enemy fire, Marcus had relived his brush with death by sketching it. In pencil at first, then in ink to make it more permanent. He'd been pleased with the result – two soldiers bearing away their wounded comrade as a mortar exploded behind them. Jagger and Stokes had pronounced it a 'Rembrandt' and suggested giving it to Walker as a memento. Marcus had other intentions. Assuming that he got out of here alive, he planned an exhibition of his work when he returned to London. An exhibition to launch a career.

As the battalion boarded trucks for the move to the Naktong River crossing point, Marcus spotted Richard Carter looking anxiously in his direction.

'Seen any more action?' Carter asked.

'Nothing, although one of my men bayoneted a pig. Made a nice change from C rations.'

'I'm dreadfully jealous. Don't let the colonel hear about it. He's forever banging on about having respect for civilian property. Oh, by the way, I take it our bet's still on?'

'Absolutely.'

'Excellent. Did we decide on the prize?'

'You mentioned a guinea. How about something more useful?'

'Bottle of whisky?'

'Perfect.'

'Do we need independent verification, or is the word of an officer good enough for you?'

Marcus smiled. He liked Carter, but with a bottle of Scotch at stake he was going to want proof.

'Independent verification, I think. Since the rewards are so high.'

Carter grinned. 'This time tomorrow I'll be demanding my prize. With witnesses. You'll see.'

The truck convoy reached the stony river bank in the late afternoon. A small, deserted village sprawled along the water's edge, its jumble of tiled roofs and twisted corrugated iron set in a swirl of filth. A dilapidated steam ferry had been requisitioned to carry the vehicles across, barely a square foot of its painted superstructure having survived the onset of rust. The vessel had broken down, causing a hiatus.

Because of it, the trucks would have to make a long detour upriver to find another crossing point. The men, however, used a pontoon bridge built by US Army engineers, carrying enough stores on their backs to last them the first twenty-four hours.

It took a couple of hours for the whole brigade to cross, under sporadic enemy shelling. Dusk had fallen by the time they reached the hills where the enemy had been. The next phase of the assault would wait until dawn. As the British soldiers made themselves as safe and comfortable as they could, they listened to the eerie *chip-chip* of the North Koreans digging new defensive positions further back.

22 September

Just before first light while the men were shaving, Marcus received his orders. The hill to their left was to be taken by the Middlesex, the one to the right by the Argylls. The North Koreans were expected to resist strongly because the positions controlled the road north.

In the grey dawn light the British soldiers hoisted their packs and, with bayonets fixed, made their way up the lower slopes, sprinting from one sparse piece of cover to the next. Bullets ricocheted off rocks and stripped bark from the stubby pines, but they carried on unscathed and began to scale the hill's steep flank. Sergeant Bryant led the way, with Marcus a few feet behind. On the road to their right a pair of American tanks rolled slowly forward, ordered in to support the battalion's attack.

To their joyful surprise, they reached the top unharmed, sweating profusely. Then, as they peered along a ridge to the next hill where the enemy had withdrawn, a machine gun opened up on them.

'Take cover,' Marcus yelled, somewhat superfluously. His mortar and Bren sections were already hacking at the thin topsoil with spades.

The ridge that stretched away from them dipped like a saddle before reaching the next high point. Grey-uniformed North Korean soldiers were retreating along its more distant flanks. Hundreds of men, but out of range. A perfect target for artillery, but the guns whose support they needed were American and their spotters had yet to join them.

'Sar'nt Bryant – we need to get that sodding machine-gunner. Where the hell is he?'

Bryant wriggled closer and pointed.

'Ten o'clock. 'Bout five hundred yards. Pile of stones just to the left of the saddle. See the smoke?'

Marcus saw the puffs as another burst was unleashed. One of their own Brens opened up on it.

'Too well protected,' Bryant complained. 'Mortar's the only way. But it's on the edge of the range.'

'Try it. We'll be worse than useless here unless we can silence him.'

Marcus watched their first shell explode short. They would have to get closer.

'Let's send them back down the hill, then round to the right of the ridge. They might be able to get along the flank out of sight of the machine gun and end up in range.'

'Worth a try, sir.'

Under covering fire from the Bren, the mortar team set off. Marcus watched them edge along the ridge. Behind him another platoon was waiting for the enemy outpost to be silenced before moving along the saddle and taking the far hill. The battalion's progress depended on them.

Eventually their mortar was in place. The first shot was long, but the second and third found their target. A cheer went up.

'Ruddy brilliant,' Marcus purred. He'd prosecuted his first significant act of war and it had worked.

In the hours that followed, they watched the other platoon attempt to take the ground ahead of them. Towards midday came the shocking news that its commander had been killed. Marcus knew the lieutenant only slightly, but it was a sobering moment.

Soon after noon they were joined by an American gunnery officer who began directing artillery on to the North Korean positions. The shells punched holes into the far hill, silencing the enemy's weapons. It thrilled Marcus to see the components of battle slotting into place. He did a rapid sketch of the scene in his notebook.

All morning Tom Sedley kept an eye on the casualty reports, fearing to see Marcus's name. Fate having placed them both in this war, it would be a cruel twist if one of them died before there was a chance of winding back the clock and becoming friends again.

Tom hadn't slept for nearly thirty hours and was feeling it. The battalion's vehicles had driven twenty miles to the east before finding a way across the river. It was the small hours of the morning before they'd caught up with the infantry and established the radio link to Brigade.

At midday they received a press visit. The reporter from the *Daily Echo*, driving his own jeep and accompanied by a sickly-looking captain from public relations, was given a rapid briefing, then directed forward to where he could proceed on foot to the scene of the battle.

After he'd gone Tom got up from the radio and handed over to Private Hewitt, feeling in need of a rations break. Out in the open he stretched and looked up at the sky. Silhouetted against the high cloud he saw the outlines of fighter-bombers heading for the front.

He selected a can of frankfurters and beans from the small brown cardboard ration box and proceeded to heat the contents.

Private Hewitt – Pete, as Tom usually called him now – had shown a continuing interest in the details of Sara's death. On the drive yesterday they'd talked at length about the case and Hewitt had asked the question that had most troubled Tom ever since the arrest of the tramp John Hagger. How had his sister ended up in the bushes with such a man? She wouldn't have gone of her own free will. And if he'd abducted her, why had no one heard screams for help? The question had remained unanswered at the trial and had lurked at the back of Tom's mind ever since. He badly wanted to talk to Marcus about it. To bounce off him his nagging concern that an injustice might have been done.

Marcus received orders to take a section forward to where Lieutenant Black lay dead. His platoon had got itself into trouble and had lost the will to fight. Marcus left Sergeant Bryant in charge and set off with Corporal Jagger's section, heading back down the hill and taking the same route round the side that the mortar team had used.

They found the beleaguered men sheltering in shallow trenches, pinned down by heavy small-arms fire. The platoon sergeant was seriously wounded, together with a section commander and a couple of the riflemen. With all their ammunition gone, they were demoralised and in shock. Marcus told Jagger to set up the Bren and return the enemy fire while he checked the condition of the casualties.

He was debating whether to try and carry some of them to safety or to wait for a stretcher party, when he spotted a figure sitting a few yards down the slope. A man in his forties wearing much of the paraphernalia of war but who clearly wasn't a soldier. There was a camera round his neck and a notebook in his hand whose pages curled at the corners. The reporter was smoking a cigarette and his escort officer was nowhere to be seen.

'How did you get here?' Marcus asked.

'On my knees, same as you. My escort's sick. Dysentery, I think. The dead lieutenant's over there.' He pointed further down the slope.

'I know.'

'Not a pretty sight. Friend of yours?'

'Hardly knew him. What's your name?'

'Terry Franks, *Daily Echo*.' He stretched out a hand.

'How d'you do?'

It seemed daft to be shaking hands in the midst of a battle. There was a burst of firing from the top of the ridge as Corporal Jagger let loose with the Bren.

'How's it going? Are we winning?'

Beneath the rim of his US-issue helmet, Franks had a lined, lived-in face, with pale, bloodshot eyes. He looked as if he hadn't slept properly for several weeks.

'That's something you'll have to ask headquarters.' Marcus had never met a reporter before and felt constrained as to what he could say.

'Deadline,' Franks said, as if that justified his need for an answer. He stabbed a finger at his notebook. 'Need every scrap of info I can get. Any casualties in your platoon?'

'No.'

'Can I have your name?'

'Look, I've got things to do.'

'Course. Sorry. You carry on. I've got enough anyway. I'd better get back and see if my jeep's still there.' Franks jotted down another couple of phrases, then started down the slope at a crouch. He had an M1 carbine with a folding stock slung round his neck and a pistol in a holster on a webbing belt.

Marcus got a couple of his men to help him recover the body of Lieutenant Black, moving it out of the line of fire. The officer had been shot in the head and was unrecognisable as the rather reserved young man whom Marcus remembered. He felt unaffected by the death. The man had been nothing to him when alive. Even less as a corpse.

Later that day, the 1st Middlesex seized control of their objective. From the top of the hill they watched the retreating North Koreans being cut to shreds by American shrapnel. As darkness fell the British troops dug in, two men to a slit, and prepared to take turns at sleeping, two hours at a time. Marcus was exhausted and found an old Korean trench for himself, carefully scattering earth in the bottom in case it had been used as a latrine. After eating some of his rations he wedged himself into it to sleep.

The reports about the day's fighting affected Tom Sedley strongly. Five members of the regiment killed, the young officer and four private soldiers. His job was to treat them as mere names on a signal sheet, but he knew that when dawn broke on the other side of the world five mothers would be weeping.

23 September

The next day, Tom learned from the radio that the Argylls had got into trouble overnight. The objective they'd captured, Hill 282, was being heavily shelled by the North Koreans. A call for divisional artillery support had met with a negative response. The American guns were needed elsewhere. Casualty figures were rising steeply and urgent calls were coming in for more ammunition to be brought. Tom logged the radio traffic for his own battalion's use, the desperate scene described in the cursory messages ratcheting up his fears that a major disaster was unfolding.

Towards midday came the welcome news that American fighter-bombers were at last flying to the Argylls' aid. When Tom heard the Mustangs growling overhead, he handed over to Hewitt and stepped outside the Land Rover to watch. He saw the planes rise up and circle the Argylls' hill, searching, he assumed, for the enemy guns. They climbed until they were dots in the sky, then rolled into a dive, small, black darts tumbling towards the ground. Cannon fire echoed from the hills as they strafed, then they pulled up and banked away.

Suddenly Hill 282 erupted, great balls of flame spreading over its crest, the thick black smoke identifying the cause as napalm. Tom's breath caught in his throat. He wanted to cry out, to protest. The planes had mistaken the Argylls' positions for those of the enemy.

Mesmerised by the trajectories of the diving planes, Marcus gazed in horror at the unfolding catastrophe. With Sergeant Bryant beside him, he watched dumbstruck as fire ballooned across the hilltop, turning its stunted pines into torches.

'I don't bloody believe it . . .' Bryant hissed. 'Wass the matter with them? Are they *blind*?'

'Poor blighters,' murmured Marcus. 'There won't be many left alive up there.' Through binoculars he could see men running to escape the inferno, then collapsing when it engulfed them.

'Sir . . .'

Marcus knew what was coming.

'They're going to need all the help they can get, sir.'

'Yes.'

'There's more'n enough of us Die-Hards to hold this position, even if the gooks counter-attack.'

'You think I should ask company HQ if we can go and help?'

'Or *not* ask, sir. They might say no.'

Marcus thought about it but not for long, because if they were going to move, it needed to be soon.

'You're right. I'll take eight men. You stay here.' Marcus had thought of sending Sergeant Bryant but felt compelled to see the disaster for himself.

'I'd be more use coming with you, sir.'

'I need you to command the rest of the platoon,' Marcus told him. 'One of us abandoning our post without authority is bad enough. If we both go, it could end up in a court martial.'

Thick, acrid smoke blew down on them as they crossed the valley. The first of the casualties were being stretchered to waiting trucks by the time they reached the base of the steep crag. Bodies that stank of burnt meat, with skin hanging off like paper. Scorched visages with obliterated features, only recognisable as faces because of eyes that stared fixedly from them, staring into nothing.

Mortars exploded higher up the hill, the North Koreans taking advantage of the disaster to intensify their attack. Marcus heard the hammering of outgoing machine-gun fire as he and his men began to climb, levering themselves from one rock to the next. They reached a point halfway up, where the ground levelled. Several of the walking wounded had come down this far, but with their strength failing they needed help to descend the steepest part. A few medics had arrived moments before them, carrying stretchers.

'Oi, you!' one of them said, pointing at Marcus and ignoring his rank. 'That bloke over there.' He gestured to a man lying on the ground beside an azalea bush whose torso was a mass of burns. Uniform and hair all gone. Skin a livid red or purplish brown, some of it an oozing mess – yet the man was alive. Alive, and singing the idiotic words of a popular song.

The almost comic banality of the lyrics somehow made what they had to do bearable. Marcus and three of his men grabbed a stretcher and laid it beside the soldier.

'W-we'll have you out of here in no time,' Marcus stammered, choking back his revulsion at the man's injuries. 'No time at all.'

The soldier's voice deteriorated into a tuneless ululation, but it confirmed that he was still alive.

Then the sound stopped.

'Got a fag, mate?'

Private Stokes stuck a cigarette between the remains of the man's lips and lit it. The casualty sucked the smoke into his lungs. When Stokes removed it for him, part of the man's lip came away.

They secured his peeling body as best they could, then the four of them lifted the stretcher and began to descend the hill. It took fifteen minutes to negotiate the slope to the valley floor. By the time they reached the field station the man they'd been carrying was dead.

7

October 1950

THE TRAGEDY OF the Argylls left a deep impression on Marcus's mind, which stayed with him even as the war moved quickly onwards. Autumn set in and the retreat of the North Koreans turned into a rout as the American-led UN forces charged northwards.

As the days passed, the nights grew ever more bitter. The under-equipped British Brigade, still dressed in their thin jungle-greens brought from Hong Kong, came close to losing men through the cold. Their thicker winter clothing arrived in the nick of time.

Then, to speed up the northwards advance, Marcus's regiment was embarked on a fleet of Dakotas, bound for a field near Seoul. The men were issued with parachutes and instructed in their use. None had jumped before. As the twin-engined transports took off in the middle of the night, an insane rumour spread that the British soldiers were to be dropped on to Kimpo airfield to clear the enemy from it. In the event the rumour was false. The planes landed uneventfully and the men found themselves in an already well-established American camp. Mess halls and canteens ringed the aerodrome perimeter, serving meals and hot coffee around the clock. After months of combat rations, for Marcus and his platoon it was like arriving in heaven. Particularly when they were told they would have to spend a few days there, waiting for their transport and supply vehicles to catch up with them.

For Tom, the journey north was far less agreeable – a thirty-hour trek by Land Rover on Korea's winding roads. The destruction and dilapidation of the communities they passed through appalled him. Villages burned to the ground, farm carts wrecked, and miserable refugees crouching forlornly by the side of what passed for a highway. He kept asking himself who this war was being fought for, because the ordinary Korean people certainly weren't benefiting from it. He and his section arrived at Kimpo bruised and exhausted.

After checking that their equipment had survived the journey, the priority for the signals team was to eat, have their first proper wash for weeks, and get their heads down.

Three-quarters of an hour after arriving, Tom and Private Hewitt were in the queue for the showers. Watching the entrance to the ablutions tent, the moment he'd half longed for, half dreaded suddenly came about. Emerging with his shirt off and a towel over his shoulder was Marcus.

Despite knowing that such a meeting was bound to happen soon, Tom felt hopelessly unprepared for it. The first thing he noticed was how thickset Marcus had become, after being so gangly as a teenager. He felt a little intimidated by this new-found maturity and for a moment considered turning away so as not to be seen, postponing the reunion until he felt readier for it. But, realising he would never be readier than now, he stepped out of the line into Marcus's path.

'Hello.' Forcing a smile, Tom watched nervously for his friend's reaction.

'Tom! Good Grief!' The blood drained from Marcus's face. 'Crikey! What on earth are you doing here?'

'Same as you. Serving King and country.'

Marcus blinked in confusion. Tom thought he saw fear in those eyes that he'd once known so well.

'Amazing. What unit are you with?'

'At Battalion HQ – the rear link.'

'A signaller?'

'That's right. With a stripe. And this is Private Hewitt, one of my section.'

'How d'you do, sir,' said Hewitt.

Marcus glanced briefly at the soldier, then grasped Tom's hand and shook it vigorously, rapidly recovering from his initial alarm. 'But this is quite extraordinary. We live next door to one another for eighteen years, then end up in this stinking hole together.'

'I hope to be stinking a lot less after I've been where you've just come from.' Tom grinned. 'The first wash below the chin since God knows when.'

'Not half! It's ruddy brilliant in there.'

'Some things the Yanks are good at, eh?'

'A few. And have you seen the scoff? I've stuffed myself since arriving, and drunk about sixteen cups of coffee!'

'Nice change from C rations, eh? You're certainly looking well on it.' Far *too* well, thought Tom, unable to stifle his resentment at Marcus's self-assurance.

'You, on the other hand, look pretty dreadful, if I may say so,' Marcus countered, smiling superciliously.

'So would you, if you'd been bounced around in a jeep for the past thirty hours.'

'Oh dear. You had to drive. What rotten luck.' Suppressing a smirk, Marcus took a step backwards. 'Well, I'd better let you chaps get at the hot water. See you around, no doubt.'

Startled by Marcus's readiness to end the conversation so quickly, Tom grabbed his arm. 'Hang on a minute. You and I need to talk.'

Flustered, Marcus shook his arm free. 'Of course we'll talk, Tom. I wasn't saying—'

'There are things I need to discuss with you.'

'Of course.' Marcus's watery smile failed to disguise his unease. 'Lots to catch up on.'

'Indeed. When's a good time?'

'I'll have to see. Not sure what's in store for us. The battalion, I mean.'

'Let's make it today, while we have the chance.'

Marcus stared into the middle distance, trying to stem his panic. 'Well, it'd have to be this evening, I suppose. I've got briefings this afternoon.'

'This evening's fine. Where?'

Marcus scanned the airfield, trying to think where would be safest.

Tom felt his anger rising. He knew damn well Marcus was going to pick somewhere as public as possible, to make a private conversation hard to engage in.

'Let's meet at the canteen they call Hank's Diner. Have supper together. There's no segregation between officers and men here. The Yanks like it that way.'

'Fine.' It would do as a starting point. They could go somewhere quieter later on. 'About six-ish?'

'Perfect.' Marcus reached out his hand again. 'Bloody good to see a friendly face. Till later, then.'

Tom watched him stride away towards a bivouac encampment on the far side of the airfield, distressed to find that beneath Marcus's bonhomie there was still a clear hint of hostility. What had he done to deserve it?

'Looks a nice bloke.' Hewitt's voice cut into his thoughts. 'Bet your sister liked him.'

Tom turned and stared at his signaller. It had never occurred to him that Sara's roving eye might have settled on Marcus any more than on the other boys in the neighbourhood. He frowned, trying to remember if it had been so.

'I really don't recall. Perhaps she did.'

By the time he reached his bivouac Marcus was still trembling. Seeing Tom again had caused dark memories to tear themselves from their graves. He batted them back into their holes, determined not to let himself be engulfed.

He needed a plan. Needed to think of safe things to discuss later. The war, yes, and their roles in it. Plenty to talk about there. Their parents – hard, considering what had happened to Tom's. But possible. In fact, they could cover almost any topic – except Sara's death.

Marcus pulled himself together. Tom didn't seem to have changed much. Still the wistful manner. The limpid eyes. That soldier he'd been with – a pretty-faced boy. It all fitted with what he'd suspected Tom would become.

He got a grip on himself. Never mind Tom's inclinations, the point was, damn it, that he had nothing to fear from a conversation with him. Sara's case was closed. The police had caught the killer. The man had confessed. Been found guilty by twelve good men and true. Society had deemed that John Hagger and John Hagger alone had been responsible for Sara Sedley's untimely death.

Marcus had washed his kit earlier and had laid it out in the sun. Testing it with his hand he found it to be still slightly damp. One shirt and a pair of underpants were dry enough, so he put them on. In this late-morning heat the rest of the moisture would soon evaporate.

Tom felt rather light-headed when he emerged from the ablutions. Despite Marcus's clear reluctance to talk about the past, he'd made up his mind to have it out with him that evening. One way or another he would discover the reason for that puzzling off-handedness and would try to set their friendship back on solid ground. He still craved the closeness they'd once had, even if Marcus didn't appear to. Needed his friend's common sense and insight to help rid him of his doubts about the conviction of John Hagger for his sister's murder.

That wasn't the only reason why Tom felt a warm glow as he walked back to his section's encampment, however. Inside the shower cubicle, standing next to a naked Pete Hewitt, their gazes had met and lingered. Brief as such moments of unspoken communication always were, it had been enough to cause him to cut short his washing and cover himself with a towel before his arousal became apparent.

Tom was rather uncomfortable with the fact that naked male flesh still stirred him. He told himself that it was something he *would* grow out of one day, but he was beginning to wonder when. He did worry about being thought queer. Despite being used to effeminate men in his parents' circle of friends, homosexuality bore a stigma as far as he was concerned, and in the army it was severely punished. On the eve of the deployment to Korea he'd overheard speculative comments about his own sexuality from some of the older men in his regiment and had made up his mind to establish his hetero credentials once and for all as soon as the battalion returned to Hong Kong. A night out in the red-light district of Wan Chai should guarantee that he broke his duck.

'I'm dead,' said Hewitt, as they reached the bivouac. He began unrolling his sleeping bag. The other two members of their section were already asleep.

'Me too,' said Tom, carefully avoiding looking at him. 'I could sleep round the clock.'

'Don't forget your chum, corp. Six o'clock, he said.'

Tom had no intention of forgetting Marcus. He looked at his watch. It was just after midday. If he could quieten his febrile mind he might have a reasonable rest.

At the appointed hour Tom joined the queue outside Hank's Diner, craning his neck for a sighting of Marcus. His heart was thumping so loudly that he feared others would notice.

The canteen was already busy. Dozens of US soldiers queued with an assortment of Britons and Australians for the free and unlimited issue of food and soft drinks that betokened this respite from the war.

Tom could see no sign of Marcus at any of the tables in the canteen. As he scanned them he was struck by the sizes of the platefuls being consumed. Gluttony was rampant.

Suddenly he felt a tap on his shoulder and spun round. Marcus stood an arm's length away, eyeing him cagily.

'I still can't believe this, you know.'

He was dressed in a battledress tunic with a lieutenant's pips on the shoulders. A cigarette hung languidly from the side of his mouth.

'Meeting here, I mean. It really is the most extraordinary coincidence.'

'Blood brothers, remember?' said Tom meaningfully. 'We always said nothing could keep us apart.'

Marcus lifted his eyes and looked past him. 'Yes, well . . . We were rather young in those days.'

'What's in the book?' Tom pointed at the volume clutched somewhat obviously in Marcus's hand.

'This?' Marcus held up his sketch pad. 'My art. My future – assuming I survive Korea. I'll show you what I've done when we've found somewhere to sit.'

'You're painting pictures of the war?' Tom had almost forgotten Marcus's artistic pretensions.

'Just drawings at this stage. To be turned into paintings when I get home. For my first exhibition.'

The queue moved forward at a steady pace.

'You don't expect to make a living at that game?'

'Going to give it a damn good try. The parents think I'm mad, of course.'

'You've heard from them recently?'

'Got a letter a week ago. Didn't say much. Mother meets her friends for lunch at Lyons Corner House and father does the garden at the weekends. Nothing's changed. Same dreary routine.'

'I suppose they're worried about you.'

'Mother didn't say. But then she wouldn't. She thinks it's infra dig for a grown-up person to express feelings.'

'I wish my mum was like that. Her letters arrive wringing wet. A sob on every line. In the last one she urged me to pretend to be ill so I could go home. "You're not the son of an actress for nothing."'

67

They laughed at the foolishness of parents.

'What about you?' Marcus inquired. 'Any thoughts on what you'll do after this little caper's over?'

'Nothing decided yet. I may end up working with radio.'

'Producing programmes like your father?'

'No. I meant radio as in playing around with the equipment.'

'Ah, I see.'

They reached the serving counter.

'Any recommendations?' Tom stared down at the steaming vats of food.

'Compared with the ration packs it's all bloody brilliant.'

They filled plates and took their heavily laden trays to a long trestle table with two free spaces at one end.

'Good Lord! They even have ice cream here!' Tom exclaimed, nodding towards a couple of soldiers tucking in further along.

'War? What war? Makes you almost believe the Yanks when they say it'll be over by Christmas.'

'Just when 29 Brigade arrives from Blighty to replace us. There'll be nothing left for the bastards to do.'

'Lucky sods.'

They sat down next to two Americans and began to eat.

Tom was not at ease. He sensed that Marcus was playing with him. An officer condescending to converse socially with a man of lower rank. There was no feeling of this being a long-overdue reunion. He was tempted to be reckless, to plunge straight in, confronting Marcus with his unhappiness at having been abandoned two years ago. But he held back, afraid of cracking the veneer of rapport they'd managed to establish so far.

'So, how's it been for you?' Marcus asked. 'Bit of a quiet life back at Battalion HQ, I imagine?'

'Don't you believe it. We've had shells landing pretty close and we're on the go the whole time.'

'How come you didn't get a commission?'

Again the tone of condescension. Tom explained about not wanting to spend time with people who thought they'd been born to rule. When Marcus bristled at this Tom realised it was a subject to avoid. They needed to talk as equals, not with Marcus pulling rank on him. Which meant talking about the past instead of the present. He decided to waste no more time.

68

'We never really talked about Sara's murder, did we?'

Marcus's left eyelid began to flicker, then his face lit up as if he hadn't heard what Tom had said.

'You know, there's something I've been itching to tell you, Tom. Happened to me on my first day at the front. I got bloody ambushed!'

'Marcus . . .'

'Don't you want to hear about it?'

'I know already. I saw the official report when it went to Brigade.'

'You did?' Marcus looked faintly alarmed. 'Oh, but that would have given you no idea what it was really like. Listen . . .'

Before Tom could stop him, Marcus launched into a graphic description of that first patrol when Private Walker had been wounded, spinning the account out for all he was worth. Tom listened with growing irritation at being so deliberately sidelined. Then his annoyance became tinged with disquiet. Marcus was relishing his story in a rather conceited way. Portraying himself as a hero, the man who'd saved the day, rather than a platoon commander who'd nearly got a soldier killed.

'Look. Here it is.' Marcus flipped through the pages of his sketchbook until he found his picture of the ambush. 'What d'you think?'

To Tom's eye the image had an almost comic-book quality, full of bloodthirsty naivety. The two US airmen sitting next to them glanced briefly at the drawing, then looked at one another and shook their heads at the weird habits of their English co-combatants. With a shrug they got up and left.

'Well, you've certainly captured the drama of it,' Tom commented, unable to shake off the habit of playing second fiddle to Marcus's exploits – a hangover from their childhood.

'I think so too. When I get back, I'm going to turn all my sketches into proper paintings.'

'Well, your regiment might like this for the officer's mess. There's a real *Boy's Own* quality to it.'

Marcus looked offended. 'You don't understand, Tom. I'm trying to show the horrors of war, not the heroics of it. Look . . .' He turned the pages until he found his drawing of wounded Argylls being carried off by stretcher from Hill 282.

Again, Tom found the picture disturbing, as if Marcus had extracted a vicarious pleasure from the Argylls' suffering.

'People back home have got to be made to understand what it's really like out here.'

'Well, you won't be sparing their feelings with that one,' Tom responded, not intending it as a compliment.

'Thanks.'

Tom sensed that Marcus's diversionary tactic had run out of steam. He seized his chance again.

'Look, there's something *I* want to talk about. Something that's been troubling me for a long time. About Sara's murder.' Tom saw his friend's eyelids flicker again.

'Oh?'

'I'm not convinced John Hagger killed her.'

Marcus pursed his lips as if coping with a sour taste in his mouth.

'Really? Why's that? Something happened with his appeal?'

'Sentence commuted to life imprisonment. Diminished responsibility. It was in the last letter from home. But that's not the point.'

'Still guilty, then.'

'Depends.'

'On what?'

'How certain we can be of that.'

'Can't think why on earth you're questioning it, Tom. Looked pretty cut and dried to me.' Marcus shifted uncomfortably on the bench.

'It's the question of how she got there. In the woods, I mean. With a man like that. It came up at the trial, you'll remember, but was never really answered.'

'That was two years ago,' Marcus grunted. 'Why rake over the past?'

'Because it's important. Don't you see? I mean, to my mind there's no way Sara would've—'

'Look . . .' Marcus's eyes blazed suddenly. 'It's no good you obsessing about her, Tom. Particularly with me. As far as I'm concerned Hagger's guilty and that's all there is to it.'

Tom was shaken by Marcus's vehemence. Discussing Sara was plainly as unacceptable now as it had been two years ago.

'Why would you never talk to me about it?'

'What d'you mean?'

'You turned your back afterwards. Wouldn't bloody well speak to me.'

'That's ridiculous.' Marcus tried to laugh it off.

'No, it isn't. You stopped coming round. It was as if our friendship had never existed.'

Marcus rubbed his temples, trying to hide his embarrassment at Tom's outburst.

'Look, it was a bad time for all of us. Not just for your family. Every one of us was completely devastated.' Marcus spread his arms, as if that was all he needed to say.

'All the more reason for talking about it,' Tom countered bitterly. 'A bloke needs his friends at a time like that.'

Marcus screwed his face up. 'Oh, Tom . . .' An apologetic look came into his eyes. 'Come on. Let's face it, us not seeing each other wasn't because of Sara. Was it?'

Tom frowned, not understanding. 'What do you mean?'

Marcus looked away, shaking his head. '*You* know . . .' His face began to redden. Then he lurched forward suddenly as a hand thumped into the middle of his back.

'*There* you are! Been searching everywhere for you.'

Tom recognised the braying tones of the officer he'd seen Marcus with that first night at the front. He looked up at the bucolic face that the voice belonged to, seething at the untimely intrusion.

'Richard!' Marcus beamed with relief. 'Can I introduce my oldest friend, Tom Sedley? Tom, Richard Carter. Tom's a signaller. With the battalion rear link.'

Tom nodded, trying to make it clear to the man that he was interrupting a private conversation.

'Ah yes, I've seen you in the HQ.' Carter sat down beside them, a grin spreading from ear to ear. He clapped Marcus on the back again. 'You owe me a bottle of whisky, old chum.'

'Do I indeed?'

'My platoon sergeant will vouch for it. I got two of them. One with the Sten and one with the bayonet.' Carter's big face glowed with pride.

'Killed his first gooks,' Marcus explained, shooting a conspiratorial glance across the table.

'Congratulations, sir,' Tom muttered.

'We took a bet on who would be first to do it,' Marcus explained. 'The bastard's beaten me.'

'Must be very disappointing for you.'

'It is. And now I'm going to have to find a bottle of whisky for him.' Marcus got to his feet.

'You're going?'

'Have to, yes. We'll have another chat, Tom. Loads of time for that. But when a gentleman has a debt to pay he has to get on with it.'

Tom hated Marcus at that moment. Hated him for having adopted the self-indulgent exclusivity of the officer class. Hated him too for evading the issue of Sara's death, and for leaving the reason for his ending their friendship unexplained.

Marcus glanced back briefly, his lips twisting with something that might have been guilt. 'Take care of yourself, old friend.'

Tom didn't reply. He watched the two officers walk towards the big open tent flap, Marcus clutching his damned sketchbook. He loathed their chumminess and their aura of invincibility.

Then, as his anger subsided, Tom began to analyse what had just happened. He'd learned something about Marcus in the last few minutes. Learned that he'd got him badly wrong when they were younger. Not a paragon as he'd always imagined, but a flawed character who'd manipulated Tom then as he had just now. His one-time best friend was a twister. With words or pencil Marcus bent life's facts to suit his own ends. Enhanced details when he wanted, or rubbed them out. It had always been that way; Marcus's ability to deny the existence of problems had been awe-inspiring when they'd been boys. But at this time, in this place, it was wrong. And downright unacceptable.

But what exactly was Marcus shying away from in the matter of Sara's death? Did he really think it was a closed book, or was there something else? Could his evasiveness be because he knew rather more about the case than he was willing to admit?

8

IN THE DAYS that followed, the chance for Tom and Marcus to meet again was prevented by the momentum of war. The advance was continuous, the sweep north against crumbling opposition making the British servicemen believe that 'Home by Christmas' was ever more likely.

'Home' would be a return to Hong Kong for most of them. Marcus had many months of National Service still to serve. He wondered if Laura would still be there when he got back. And whether the spark that had attracted him two months ago would seem as bright. He wished he could have written to her from Korea, but in the rush to leave for war he'd omitted to get her address.

The brigade advanced rapidly towards the 38th Parallel, the original dividing line between north and south. The plan had been to halt there, but it soon changed. General MacArthur wanted communism expunged from the entire Korean peninsula.

On they went and by mid-October Pyongyang was in their sights, UN units vying to reach the North Korean capital first. The primitive roads were jammed with tanks, trucks and towed artillery. At times dust was so thick that it was impossible to see more than a few feet. Sergeant Bryant and the other old hands muttered about the recklessness of the Americans' headlong advance, no attempt being made to secure the territory they'd overrun. They began to fear North Korean hangers-on might attack them from the rear.

Pyongyang fell on 19 October. The following day the 1st Middlesex led the newly expanded Commonwealth Brigade into the western outskirts, their arrival greeted by crowds waving South Korean flags. Allegiances changed quickly in Korea, Marcus noted. The Northern leadership had fled in good time, but truckloads of less fortunate communists were being driven from the town by their South Korean captors for summary execution.

'They're massacring the buggers,' hissed Sergeant Bryant as the platoon sat beside their vehicles, eating their rations. 'All as bad as each other in this stinking place. North, south – Koreans are all the same. Murdering bastards, the lot of them.'

There was a murmur of agreement. Marcus knew that every man in his platoon despised the people whose dispute had caused them to be brought to this godforsaken country.

He stood up, slung his Sten gun over his shoulder and stretched, then lit a cigarette. They were all weary. The drive from Kimpo had been long and gruelling. Soon they'd be pushing north again, towards the border with China. Throughout their time on the road Marcus had been keeping a wary eye out for the Land Rovers of the signals detachment, having no wish for another conversation with Tom.

A horn tooted beside him. A jeep had pulled up. Beside the driver was Richard Carter.

'Jump in. We're going on a tour of the town.'

Marcus glanced back to where his company was settled, thinking he should ask permission of his major.

'Come on. I've just been made Battalion Intelligence Officer. The other chap's gone sick. We're not going to be long.'

Exhilarated at the thought of doing something different, Marcus swung his leg over the side of the jeep and settled on to the back seat.

'Dacre's my batman,' Carter explained, slapping the ginger-haired driver on the shoulder. 'An ace behind the wheel. Useless at everything else. Foot down, Stirling Moss. Let's find out what the North Koreans do when they're having fun.' He turned to Marcus and winked. 'Never know. Tonight could be the night!' He made a lewd gesture with his fist.

Carter had obtained a map of the town, which he held out for Marcus to see. They passed through the outskirts of the heavily shelled city. US tanks and APCs stood watchfully at main road junctions but there were few signs of local people.

'They're all cowering in their houses,' Carter suggested.

'More likely run away, sir,' said Dacre.

Soon they were heading down a broad avenue lined by substantial stone buildings. Outside one of them a couple of wild-looking men were loading boxes into the back of a jeep.

'Stop the car!' Carter ordered, banging his hand on the top of the door. The vehicle slowed sharply and turned to pull up beside the other jeep.

Marcus and Carter got out. One of the men wore a Stetson, the other an American-style helmet. They were dressed in military fatigues, with rifles slung across their backs and sheathed daggers on their belts.

'What's going on here?' Carter asked.

Marcus thought he recognised the lined face beneath the helmet.

'You're the reporter from the *Echo*, aren't you?'

The journalist peered at him. 'Oh, it's you. We met on some blasted hill or other, the day Lieutenant Black got killed.' He came forward with his hand outstretched. 'Terry Franks. And the chap with the hat is from *The Times*. Just got here?'

'A few hours ago. What are you up to?'

'Just had ourselves some breakfast, courtesy of Joe Stalin. Caviar and champagne.'

Marcus looked up at the building behind them. There was a flagpole but no flag.

'What is this place?'

'The Russian Embassy. They left in one hell of a hurry, leaving it wide open. There were half-full glasses of bubbly in the bar. French stuff, not the Georgian rubbish.'

'What's in those boxes?' Carter demanded.

'Booze. We're liberating their cellar.'

'Some amazing vintages,' the *Times* man added. 'Plenty for everyone here. And vodka galore, of course. You should take a look. Help yourselves.'

'I don't think so,' Marcus said, wondering if they should be arresting this pair.

'Looting's not in our remit,' Richard Carter added. 'Unfortunately.'

The *Times* man took out a couple of bottles of clear liquid and gave them one each.

'Warm you up on a cold night. It's a present,' he added when they protested. 'Don't have to say where it came from.'

'Well, thanks,' said Carter, taking his. Marcus followed suit.

'Having a look round, are you?' Franks asked.

'Yes. The battalion's moving on again in the morning, so we're told.'

'No respite for the wicked, eh? Well, watch the junction at the end of this road. We took some incoming there. Small arms. Not very accurate, but it shows there are still communists about. Syngman Rhee's moved in a squad of South Korean police to control this place. Perhaps you've seen them. Trained by the Japs during the last war, so they're a bunch of thugs. You know they've started execution squads?'

'We saw the trucks driving out of the city.'

'Full on the way out and empty coming back.'

'Exactly. Will you be writing about it?' Marcus asked.

'We've filed it but I doubt it'll get past the censors,' Franks replied. 'The South Koreans are supposed to be the good guys, remember?'

His colleague from *The Times* was already back behind the wheel, so the *Echo* man jumped into the passenger seat with his rifle at the ready.

'We're off to take a peek at the boss man's palace. See if we can find some of his silk undies as a souvenir. Want to come?'

Marcus glanced at Richard.

'Why not? In for a penny . . .'

The journalists shot off down the road with Private Dacre glued to their tail. Kim Il-Sung's palace was grotesquely Stalinist. A few South Korean soldiers hung round the entrance but made no attempt to stop them entering. On the first floor, quilted double doors led from an antechamber to the impressive inner room, which had been the domain of the premier himself. They trod a long mulberry carpet towards the massive carved, polished desk, flanked by busts of Stalin and Kim Il-Sung himself. Heavy black silk curtains, crimson-lined, hung from the tall windows. Someone had vandalised a second figure of the North Korean leader, removing his head.

'*Nouveau riche*, I'd call it,' said the *Times* man, sniffing in distaste. 'Wouldn't you, Terry?'

'Absolutely, old boy.'

They heard footsteps behind them, a South Korean officer checking that they didn't steal anything. The reporters took a few pictures, then they all left.

'Keep your heads down,' Terry Franks shouted as they parted company outside.

Marcus watched them go.

'What a pair!' Carter commented. 'The gentlemen of the fourth estate. Wonder where they got that jeep from.'

'Some of the Yank supply sergeants sell anything for a price,' Private Dacre explained. 'Their quartermasters have so many jeeps to spare they don't notice when one goes missing.'

'Then it's high time you got one, Marcus,' Carter told him. 'Must be somebody in your platoon you could rope in as a driver.'

They climbed into the car and headed back to the battalion. As they passed through the centre of town it felt eerily deserted.

'Looks like the ROK police have murdered the entire population,' Carter postulated. 'What bastards they all are.'

Back at Battalion Headquarters, Tom Sedley was summoned by the adjutant, who'd written an angry report about the executions. He ordered him to encode the text and send it to Brigade for forwarding to the US Division that commanded them.

'The only people with a chance of stopping those disgraceful murder squads are the Americans,' he said. 'Though I don't think there's a hope in hell they will.'

Tom had been making strenuous efforts in recent days to grasp what this war was all about. He'd listened to BBC short-wave radio broadcasts whenever he could and studied the teletyped briefing papers on Syngman Rhee, before passing them on to the colonel. The American-appointed South Korean leader had returned from US exile in 1948, he'd learned, soon becoming a tyrant as ruthless as Kim Il-Sung. What he still didn't understand was why they were fighting to save such a regime.

Tom had had quite enough of this war by now. He was tired of the constant upheaval. Fed up with sleeping on hard ground in temperatures that seemed to have no limit to the depths to which they could sink. Sickened by the waste of their own young lives and the stench of the land they were fighting over. He felt like making a stand, declaring he was here against his will. More and more he worried about people close to him being killed. Pete Hewitt. Marcus, even.

The night was still. They were all in their bedrolls. Tom pulled the blankets up to his chin. The air froze his ears and the tip of his nose. He prayed that 29 Brigade got here from England before the bitterest of the winter set in, allowing them to return to the warmth of Hong Kong.

He pricked up his ears. There was a sound he hadn't heard before here in Korea. An owl hooting.

There'd been owls in the woods near their house. Tom had heard them on the night Sara died.

The next day, as the battalion moved north again, Marcus observed the world from the front seat of a Bedford truck. When the jolting of the vehicle allowed it, he took notes for later drawings. Most of the villages here were intact, their houses raised on stones with fires underneath to heat them. The wealthier homes had tiled roofs, upturned at the corners like the toes of oriental slippers. The poorer cottages wallowed under heavy grey thatches.

At each new village they stopped to check for enemy soldiers. Inside the houses, old men squatted on polished wooden floors, stroking thin wisps of beards. The women were swathed in bright colours – crimson, pink, vivid emerald green. Mothers suckled their young, breasts swinging free beneath nursing aprons.

On the roads between the villages, families walking with bundles on their heads and children on their backs were forced into the paddies by the passing war machines. Here and there a child waved a flag or shouted a welcome. As the light faded the convoys would stop, the men bivouacking in fields for the night. Soon the pace of their advance began outstripping their supply columns. Rations ran short and the fear of what MacArthur was leading them into intensified.

At last they were allowed a day of rest. It was a Sunday.

At 10.30 a.m. Marcus lined up with his platoon for a church parade. All attended, whether religious or not, because avoiding it might be tempting fate. The colonel praised their courage and fortitude, then told them to take it easy for the next twenty-four hours.

'All very well for you,' Richard Carter complained when he sidled up to Marcus afterwards. 'I suppose you'll be dashing off a sketch or two this afternoon. But an IO's job is never done.'

'What's up?'

'Got a recce tonight to see if the gooks are still around. There's a village a mile up the road, which we have to pass through. Reports of the enemy dug in there.'

'I'd come with you, given the chance.'

'I'm better at this sort of thing on my own. Or at least just with Dacre. I learned to stalk when I was twelve. You don't want other people crashing about when you've got your prey in sight.'

'*Crashing about?*'

'You know what I mean. No offence.'

'Well, don't do anything rash. There's a bottle of whisky coming your way, remember. When I can find one.' The American camp at Kimpo had proved dry and the NAAFI still hadn't caught up with them.

Marcus did sit down with his sketchbook that afternoon, trying to capture what he'd seen during the last few days. He had trouble with the women's faces, however. Flat and featureless, most of them, and he found it impossible to tell what character, if any, lay beneath. It annoyed him, because faces were what he most liked to draw. Female faces in particular.

That night the battalion command considered the enemy sufficiently distant for it to be safe to light fires. The British soldiers sat around them after finishing their inadequate rations, singing 'Nellie Dean'. The moon was up and the light was silvery. It was a night of sombre beauty with the war feeling far away. Then, in the distance, they heard other voices raised in song. The recently arrived Australians, countering with 'Waltzing Matilda'.

Later, as they were preparing to sleep, the mood changed. A patrol brought two prisoners in, men who'd been spying on their encampment. One was Chinese. Fears intensified that the rush north had been a mistake. That a new, much more powerful Red Menace was about to flood the country and drive them back.

Few slept easily that night. Shortly before dawn their foreboding deepened, when news spread that shots had been heard and the battalion's intelligence officer had not returned from his recce.

9

WHEN THE SUN came up, it was Lieutenant Carter's batman they found first. Wounded in the shoulder and one leg, Private Dacre had dragged himself well beyond the perimeter of the village which the pair of them had been investigating. Hidden under a pile of rice straw, he saw Marcus's platoon advancing and yelled so they wouldn't think he was Korean.

Marcus knelt beside the man while a first-aider attended to his wounds.

'Mister Carter's a goner, sir.'

The blunt fact of Richard's death didn't register at first.

'Burp gun got him in the head and chest,' Dacre explained. 'I was fifteen yards behind 'im, covering our rear. He was peering into a court-yard. We thought the place was deserted. No sign of life. Then bang!'

'How many were there?' Marcus asked.

'Couldn't rightly see. But must've been at least six. After Lieutenant Carter went down, they came looking for the rest of us. But there was only me and I ran. They got me in the shoulder and leg. I bunged a grenade at them. Saw a couple of 'em fall. In the dark they must've thought there was a whole lot of us, so they ran back.'

Marcus felt numb. 'You're quite sure Lieutenant Carter was killed?'

'They was right in front of him, sir. Like I said, burst of SMG straight in the chest. Knocked backwards, he was.'

Marcus flinched at the description of it. Then he told himself it was better to die quickly than be taken prisoner.

'I owed him a bottle of whisky,' he murmured.

'I'll 'ave it, sir,' said Dacre, quick as a flash.

Marcus stood up and turned away. Had death become something to make light of?

A stretcher party carried Dacre to the rear. The Americans were to be asked to send a helicopter to fly him to a M.A.S.H. The red-haired soldier looked happy to be getting out.

The village where the shooting had happened lay less than half a mile away. Through binoculars it appeared devoid of life. To reach it they had to cross flat ground with little cover. Three American Sherman tanks assigned to the battalion went first, followed by the foot soldiers of Marcus's company.

The tanks took no chances, firing shells into a couple of the houses, but when they entered the village and the infantry searched they found the place deserted. Richard Carter's body lay where he'd fallen, outside the doorway of a small thatched house, thrown back by the force of the shots, just as Private Dacre had described. The blood caked on his face and tunic made him barely recognisable. At the sight of the corpse Marcus felt a ripple of shock, but it only lasted a moment.

As the company commander said a quick prayer over the body, Marcus and a couple of his platoon stood with heads bowed. A blanket was found and they placed Carter's body in the back of a truck while they waited for the chaplain to be brought over from Brigade.

Marcus thought about Richard's family in Leicestershire. He pictured them dressed in tweeds in a rambling country mansion surrounded by tall trees that dripped with autumn dampness. A house reeking of Labradors. How would they learn of their son's death? By telegram, like in the last war? Or would someone from the regiment drive round to see them in a black official car?

Marcus handed command of his platoon to Sergeant Bryant. Then, while the soldiers secured the village, he organised a party to dig a grave beside the road on the outskirts. The dark soil and the stench from the nearby paddy made him think it was a terrible end to a life. To fight a shitty war and end up buried in the stuff.

It was midday before the chaplain arrived. Marcus was touched by the way he made the funeral personal. The man had hardly known Richard Carter, yet sounded as if he were saying goodbye to a friend. As the grave party shovelled earth into the hole and stuck a makeshift cross at its head, Marcus remembered their first real conversation together – Carter's dread of dying before he'd proved himself with a woman. It had come to pass. Marcus resolved not to let the same thing happen to him.

When Tom Sedley learned about the death, the news saddened him. After their brief and unpromising introduction at Kimpo, Carter had made a point of saying hello whenever he was in Battalion HQ. And when his father had sent him copies of the *Daily Telegraph* to read, he'd given the crosswords to Tom.

1 November 1950

The brigade's advance halted twelve miles short of the Chinese border on the Yalu River. The men were told to rest. For the first time in weeks they removed their cracked boots and cut away stinking socks. There were hot baths in 44-gallon drums. Unit barbers had an orgy of clipping. Then it all turned sour when an American unit encountered a concentrated enemy force a few miles up the road. The Chinese had entered the war.

The battalion fell back in the next few days and waited for orders, but the divisional net stayed almost silent. The US command structure seemed to have fallen apart. The 1st Middlesex had no idea where the other units were and felt uncomfortably isolated.

In an effort to glean something, Tom scanned other frequencies on the home-made set he'd brought from Hong Kong. He met with little success, until a torrent of Chinese suddenly filled his ears. The sound chilled him. The signal strength was high so they were damned close. He alerted the battalion second-in-command, but with no interpreter in the headquarters there was little to be done with the intercepts.

'Let's hope the Yanks' intelligence people are tuning in,' the major commented. Knowing the poor intelligence briefs that came their way, neither of them thought it likely.

Soon the transmissions ceased. If anything, the ensuing silence was worse. Tom sensed that they were being watched, thousands of slit eyes all around, waiting for the moment to strike.

He took off his headphones. For four hours he'd been sitting there concentrating and he reckoned he deserved a break.

'Going for a leg stretch,' he told Hewitt, who nodded without looking at him.

Outside the bivouac Tom lit a cigarette and looked up at the sky. A grey, overcast day. With luck the clouds would make the coming night less cold. He crouched beside a sentry lying on a groundsheet.

'Anything happening?'

'People walking down the road.' Tom looked where he was pointing. 'Hundreds of 'em.'

'Refugees.'

'Probably from that town we went through on our way north. Where they welcomed us with big smiles, remember? Anybody left behind will pay a price for that when the communists come back.'

Amongst those refugees was a bewildered 21-year-old youth called Lee Ho Shin. He had broad-set eyes and fine black hair, which lay in a slick across his forehead, and he was one of the few in that group to have a good pair of shoes.

Lee Ho Shin looked about him in distaste. He'd never expected to end up in such company. They were strangers, the others. People from the countryside whom he'd been forced to fall in with.

Lee Ho Shin was the younger son of parents who'd died in a traffic accident in Pyongyang during the Second World War. His brother was nine years older than him with a young wife already, so an uncle had assumed responsibility for Lee's upbringing and education. His guardian was a committed communist, who'd used his Party contacts to secure his nephew a place at the Department of Engineering in Pyongyang University – and to get him excused military service when the invasion of the south was planned. Lee had no interest in politics, but was grateful for the advantages that had flowed from his uncle's connections.

Two weeks ago his life in Pyongyang had fallen apart. There'd been rumours that the war was going badly, but news that the enemy was close to the capital had come as a terrible shock. His brother, whom he'd idolised as a child, had already fled to Moscow with his wife and baby daughter. His uncle's family had stuck it out until the last minute, then had taken him north in a panic-stricken stampede. They'd had a car for the first part of the journey to cousins living near the Manchurian border, but it had broken down. The last leg had been by pony cart.

Then news had come that the Americans were closing in again. His uncle had begun drinking and announced that they could flee no further. He'd taken Lee Ho Shin aside and told him he must make his own way from now. To complete his education in whatever sort of country Korea became, communist or capitalist. He should try to return to Pyongyang, or even to Seoul, wherever there seemed an opportunity for life to resume.

Lee Ho Shin had felt cast adrift, but as he set off he'd understood the sacrifice his uncle was making. As a well-known member of the Communist Party he would be a dead man when the South took over.

Lee Ho Shin had begun his trek two days ago. He had money for food, but was unused to caring for himself. His first sighting of American soldiers had been frightening. They'd stopped and searched him, before waving him on. Then, seeing these other refugees on the road, he'd hoped for safety in numbers and joined them.

But where they were all heading he no longer knew. A tide of human misery had swept him up. All he could do was let it bear him along.

IO

November 1950

IN THE WEEKS that followed, Marcus and Tom both began to fear a military catastrophe. The UN forces had fallen back steadily, the smell of defeat sapping the men's spirits. The British blamed General MacArthur for driving the UN spearhead too far north, and felt let down by their American commanders for not ordering their troops to stand up to the resurgent enemy.

'Bug out' became the catch phrase amongst the American soldiery – as in 'Let's bug the hell outta here'.

To compound their difficulties, the Korean winter arrived with a vengeance. One night, a bitter wind from Siberia howled through their bivouacs bringing twenty-two degrees of frost. Suddenly their stoves couldn't cope. Water took one and a half hours to boil. Mugs of tea turned to brown slush if you put them on the ground. The men's clothing proved hopelessly inadequate and urgent orders for extra supplies were sent. The cold snap passed in a few days but it was a bitter foretaste of what was to come.

Eventually the UN forces had fallen back far enough and were ordered to hold their ground. A counter-attack was planned for Thanksgiving Day, in the belief the communists wouldn't expect Americans to fight on a sacred national holiday. But the US Army had long prepared for the celebrations, so brought them forward a day. On 23 November every UN soldier was fed on turkey, mince pies, shrimps and stuffed olives.

'There's something obscene about all this,' Marcus complained as his platoon sat round their campfire, eating their fill. 'Gobbling turkey while the peasants around us are fleeing for their lives.'

'I heard the Yanks offered us ice cream, but the brigadier turned it down,' Corporal Jagger whined, ignoring this point of principle.

'Ice cream?' Marcus spluttered. 'It's five bloody degrees below freezing. Who the hell wants ice cream?'

'Wouldn't have said no, sir,' said Sergeant Bryant. 'If that's what everybody else is having.'

The next day, when the new offensive kicked off, the Commonwealth Brigade was held in reserve, which was fortunate because that was when their longed-for extra clothing arrived. Thick, pile-lined parkas, woollen underwear and socks.

Three days later the new offensive turned sour. The Chinese forces ranged against the UN were so vast that they were being described as 'hordes'. From the buzzing on the net Tom knew that the battalion would be heading south again. He couldn't wait to get moving. Anything to distract him from the difficult situation he'd created for himself.

It was during the unreal atmosphere of the Thanksgiving feast that Tom had made his blunder. There'd been a deal of smut bandied about – men bragging about sexual conquests and the size of their genitals – which had left him uncomfortably aroused. Buoyed up by tots of rum, he'd persuaded Private Hewitt to take a stroll with him away from the others. Then, in a moment of madness while hidden amongst the trees, he'd grabbed hold of the other lad's hand and pressed it against the bulge in his trousers.

The response was not what he'd expected. Hewitt had punched him in the chest, saying, 'Don't bloody get queer with me, corp.'

For Tom it was one of those landmark moments when a person looks back at something he's done and thinks how incredibly young he must have been at that instant of time. And how much older and wiser he is as a result. Afterwards, when he'd sobered up, Tom had taken an important decision. To put his juvenile habits behind him, once and for all.

On the night of the incident he'd hardly slept afterwards, terrified of being reported to the colonel. The next day he'd apologised to Hewitt, saying he'd just been 'mucking about'. Hewitt suggested that they should never refer to the matter again.

As they loaded their Land Rovers for the next move, trucks laden with stretchers passed by – an American field hospital moving back to safer ground. The sight of it made Tom shiver. He had a vision of Marcus being one of those casualties before long. Marcus dead, and the reason he didn't want to talk about Sara's death dying with him.

When Lee Ho Shin reached Pyongyang with the column of refugees, he was shocked to see the city he'd been brought up in. Everywhere he looked, open spaces were piled with military supplies. Fuel tankers churned through the streets, drenching the pavements with mud. Tracked vehicles had reduced the poorly metalled roads to rubble. And his uncle's comfortable home had been taken over as officers' accommodation. Seeking some thread of continuity with his past, he made his way to the university, only to find its classrooms now a barracks.

Lee Ho Shin was exhausted from his journey. He eventually found friends who hadn't fled the city. They fed him, despite not having enough for themselves, but warned that they themselves were about to go south. The only hope of normality lay far, far away from the battlefront, they said.

And so the next morning he began walking again, his sights set on Seoul. He had cousins there whom he'd never met, but his uncle had said that as blood relatives they would have to take him in.

The UN collapse continued, with forces falling back towards Pyongyang. North of the city the 27th Commonwealth Brigade received orders to dig in south of a seven-mile mountain pass through which the retreating US 2nd Division would be forced to withdraw.

Many of the British contingent's own trucks had broken down and been abandoned, so they were relying on the Americans again. The transport didn't arrive, however, so the soldiers set off on foot.

The icy wind cut like honed steel through their woollen caps and fleece-lined US-issue jackets as Marcus led his platoon into the canyon on which the US retreat depended, a long line of pack-bearing soldiers. From beyond the ridges to their left and right they heard the distant roar of machine guns. The enemy was preparing to choke off the UN retreat.

When darkness fell they rested but, with no sign of the promised transport and continuing unease about where the Chinese were, they soon resolved to trudge on. Snow had begun to fall. Eventually they saw the lights of a truck column coming up the pass towards them. The vehicles turned in a circle on an open patch of ground and waited for the soldiers to reach them.

'Climb aboard, you cock-sucking Limeys,' yelled one of the drivers.

Footsore and weary, they flopped into the back and were taken the last few miles to a flat area of paddy beyond the mouth of the pass.

It was three in the morning and the north wind continued to mock their new clothing. They scoured the frozen fields for rice straw to pad out ponchos and blankets. Then, as they lay exhausted in their bedrolls, the company commander walked round with a ration tin, pouring rum down each eager throat.

30 November 1950

Morning dawned with a clear sky, but still the icy wind blew.

Radio communications were bad, with no word from Brigade since last night. Eventually the battalion's orders arrived by jeep. They were to head north again to the southern end of the pass. A small Chinese contingent had blocked the road where it went through a village. The Middlesex Regiment was to drive them out and keep the way clear for the US 2nd Division to withdraw along, later in the day.

The hamlet where the Chinese had been sighted was deserted when the British troops reached it, but there was an ominous sign that they'd been there not long before. A US jeep stood in the centre of the village, facing south, its windscreen riddled with bullets. An American full colonel and his driver were slumped in the front seats, caked with blood.

There was a sinister stillness about the place. The sky threatened snow again. Marcus shivered. Further down the street other platoons were clearing the small wooden houses. No sign of life anywhere. It felt like the most desolate place on earth.

Suddenly they heard shooting. Another Middlesex company, advancing across open ground, had found the enemy, the Chinese rising from the corn stooks and opening fire on them. The battle raged for several minutes before the Chinese fled, leaving many dead. That the enemy had been routed so easily gave the British soldiers heart.

At Battalion HQ a couple of miles back from the village, Tom Sedley was struggling to establish radio links, his colonel desperate to speak to Brigade.

'It's the distances, sir,' Tom protested. 'Must be too far away for the 62 set. We need to relocate.'

'Don't tell me what I need to do with my headquarters, corporal,' the colonel snapped. 'Brigade is on the move, that's the problem. And we don't know where.' He made it sound as if that were Tom's fault too.

After sucking ferociously on his pipe for a few minutes the colonel ordered Tom to take one of the signals vehicles and find a place where the radios worked. He detailed a subaltern with three soldiers in a jeep as escort.

Tom felt very scared. Little was known about the enemy's dispositions. But an order was an order and while Private Hewitt packed the equipment Tom studied a map with the second lieutenant, trying to work out where to go.

Marcus's company was ordered north from the deserted village. To the left of the road was an isolated low hill, a mound shaped like a pudding. They suspected that the Chinese held it, but it was a position they needed to take if they were to control the exit from the pass.

Marcus's platoon was to mount the assault. Flexing his fingers to maintain their function in the bitter cold, he led his men forward, crawling through undergrowth until they were at the base of the mound. Then, his throat bone dry, they charged up the slope, reaching the top without meeting any opposition.

'Don't like this,' muttered Sergeant Bryant as they lay amongst the bushes covering the knoll's crown. 'Feels like a trap.'

Beyond their hill were several more ridges, many with a commanding view of the road.

Suddenly an explosion showered them with earth and stones.

'Told you,' breathed Bryant. 'Mortar.'

A second detonation hurled shrapnel through the branches above their heads.

'Withdraw!' Marcus yelled. With no protection it would be madness to stay.

'Bastards,' he hissed, as they regrouped halfway down. His hands were shaking. He checked that none of his men were hurt, then looked back up at the hill.

'Where the hell are they firing from, Sar'nt Bryant?'

'Didn't see. But I've a nasty feeling they're ruddy everywhere, sir.'

'Except on this hill. Which we need to take again. I think we should try one of the flanks.'

Further away they heard the thunder of enemy artillery. It was some distance off, but close enough for the ground to shake.

'Sounds like somebody's getting it halfway up the pass,' said Corporal Jagger.

'Ruddy lunacy, this is,' said Bryant. '2 Div should've cleared the hills first. If the Yanks drive down that pass with the Chinese on their flanks they'll be sitting ducks.'

'Well, we'd better make sure we've got *our* end of it under control, at least,' Marcus snapped. 'Let's get the men back up the hill, Sar'nt Bryant.'

They kept to the right-hand side of the mound this time, with a view of the road but out of sight of the hills where they assumed the Chinese were. Before long they'd established a vantage point without attracting further enemy fire. The men dug deep scrapes, having no way of knowing how long they would be there.

It was two hours before they saw any movement.

'What the hell's that?' Bryant hissed, pointing to where the canyon road emerged from behind a bluff.

Marcus adjusted his binoculars.

'Refugees.'

A bullock cart piled with possessions. As it came closer they made out a man walking beside it, with two women and three children behind him. Perched on top of their belongings was a straight-backed patriarch in white, a tall black hat balanced on his head.

As they drew nearer, Marcus saw flashes of colour beneath the women's outer garments and guessed that this had been a well-to-do family once. The younger of the two women had a bundle on her back. As she grew larger in the binocular eyepiece he realised the bundle was a child.

A few minutes later they heard the grinding growl of tanks. A glance behind revealed two Shermans rumbling towards the pass, their turrets swinging as they sought the enemy.

Suddenly, from the hills flanking the mouth of the pass, heavy machine-gun fire streaked towards the road, tracer shells kicking sparks off the ground a hundred yards short of the tanks.

'Got it, sir!' Corporal Jagger shouted. 'My ten o'clock.'

Marcus followed where he was pointing. Tiny puffs of smoke from the top of a rocky outcrop.

'In range of the Bren?' Marcus asked.

'Worth a try, sir.'

They opened fire with tracer, but the rounds fell short. The tanks had seen the Chinese position too, their guns settling on the target, although not yet close enough to engage it.

Caught in the crossfire, the refugees' animal had taken fright and dragged the cart off the road, tipping it on its side and propelling the old man from the top. The family's precious packages scattered across the ground as machine-gun bullets raked the road.

The tanks rolled forward, trying to bring the enemy within range. As the lead Sherman thundered past the cowering family, it crushed their possessions beneath its tracks.

Suddenly a mortar round exploded beside the second tank, halting it. Marcus swung the glasses round. The vehicle's track was damaged and smoke came from the engine. The first tank opened fire, its first shell exploding behind the enemy machine gun. It fired again, silencing the gun, but mortars continued to bracket the roadway. Cowering in the dirt, the refugee family huddled together in terror. Then a fountain of filth erupted in their midst.

'Oh God,' Marcus croaked.

'Poor fuckers,' said Bryant. 'There was kids down there.'

The lead Sherman turned and headed back, its gun still swinging. The fire threatening to engulf the second tank had worsened. Smoke billowed from the engine as the crew clambered out. They jumped down, then scrambled aboard the other tank when it stopped to pick them up.

After the surviving Sherman clattered back to safety, a shocked stillness descended on the scene. All movement had ceased on the road below their hill. The refugees were dead.

★

Tom's mission to find a transmitting base did not start well. The driver of their escort jeep misjudged a turn and the vehicle slid off the road into a frozen paddy. It took the best part of an hour to haul it back on to the carriageway.

Eventually, he did manage to establish communications with Brigade, whose HQ had moved further west than anticipated. Tom and Hewitt had set up the equipment in hilly ground about half a mile from the road leading to the pass. The subaltern doubted whether the colonel would want to relocate his own HQ so far from the main route south, but called up on the short-range radio-telephone to propose it.

Tom climbed on to a bluff, carrying his binoculars. The clouds had cleared again and there was a sparkling clarity to the air. Looking north towards the mountain pass through which the US 2nd Division was to withdraw, he saw columns of black smoke. Explosions echoed round the hills, shattering the stillness.

He looked down at their small cluster of vehicles, thinking how vulnerable they would be if the Chinese were nearby. He caught sight of Private Hewitt eyeing him from the back of the Land Rover. Since the embarrassing incident a few days ago their relationship had been strained, despite the agreement to ignore what had happened.

The subaltern put down the radio and walked over to talk to him.

'As I thought, the colonel won't come here because it'll put him out of contact with C Company. But we're to stay in this position for the time being. Monitor the Brigade net and report to the colonel on the 88 set.'

'Very good, sir.' Tom returned to the vehicle and took his place beside Hewitt.

One thing he'd learned during his contact with Brigade HQ a few minutes ago was that they hadn't heard anything from the retreating US 2nd Division. No indication of where they were, or of what state they were in.

Half an hour after the mortaring of the Shermans, Marcus's platoon saw the first elements of the US force emerge from the pass. They'd been expecting tanks to lead the column through as it wound down the road towards them, but it seemed to be jeeps and trucks. Tracer streaked from the hills on each side of the road, ripping into the leading vehicles. Mortar bombs bracketed them.

'Get out of the trucks, for God's sake,' Marcus whispered. Infantry were useless sitting in vehicles. 'They're not even firing back.'

One truck caught fire, blocking half the road. When the vehicles behind struggled to pass it, another misjudged the edge of the road and tipped on its side.

'Jesus, what a mess!'

Several minutes later the first of the jeeps rattled past a hundred yards to their right, the driver's arms rigid on the wheel, his stare locked on the road ahead. As the vehicle swerved round the still-burning Sherman tank, they saw that its seats were piled with wounded and dead.

For the next hour the British soldiers watched in the bitter cold as a terrible scene unfolded. The road kept getting blocked with burning vehicles, which had to be pushed aside. The convoy was nose-to-tail, hardly moving. It took some time before Marcus realised why the soldiers in the trucks were doing nothing to save themselves. Most were already dead.

Mustang fighters pounded the hills on either side of the pass, in a desperate attempt to silence the Chinese guns. Eventually tanks appeared and pushed aside the burning trucks.

Marcus stared in disbelief. The mighty US Army, which had fought so valiantly in the Pacific just five years earlier, had been reduced to a rabble.

By four p.m. the last trickle of southbound traffic had ceased. The road from the pass was strewn with abandoned vehicles. In the far distance Marcus saw Chinese infantry move in to finish what their machine guns and mortars had started. They heard the pathetic crack of small arms as the surviving Americans fought for their lives amidst the shambles on the road. Men were still coming out of the pass on foot, limping, dragging injured friends, some of them sobbing with shock.

Marcus began to be concerned for his men's and his own safety. The light was fading and the Chinese would be following through, driving south again. He was on the point of calling his company commander for instructions when they got the order to withdraw.

The battalion regrouped at the village where the day had begun. Several houses were ablaze now, set on fire by US troops bent on revenge for what they'd been through. Any sort of revenge, on any sort of gooks.

The platoon commanders gathered to be briefed.

'There's no transport, surprisingly enough,' the major told them, his voice heavy with sarcasm. 'If you can find space on something with wheels, then grab it, otherwise start walking. With a bit of luck they'll send something back for us before we've worn through the soles of our boots.'

Tom also had been ordered to withdraw. And not a moment too soon. The subaltern had spotted soldiers in grey battledress scurrying down the hillside above them. The British men covered up the equipment and bounced down the frozen cart track to the road.

Hewitt was driving as they hugged the back of the escort jeep, its occupants tensely scanning the terrain. The soldiers signalled them to keep their distance so they could get a clearer field of view.

None of them saw the mortar shell arcing silently through the sky. It detonated between the two vehicles, blowing Tom's Land Rover on to its side.

Tom banged his head on the door frame as Hewitt crashed on top of him. He felt a sharp pain in his chest.

'Fuckin' hell!' Hewitt croaked, his mouth next to Tom's ear.

'Get off,' Tom hissed. 'You're breaking my ribs.'

Hewitt pushed out the remains of the shattered windscreen and climbed through the gap. What he saw when he stood up terrified the life out of him.

'Quick, corp. They're coming!' He dropped to his haunches.

The pain in Tom's side was excruciating but he levered himself through the hole in the screen. Gunfire crackled all around. He crouched down, trying to take it all in. It hurt him to breathe.

'Where?'

Hewitt pointed towards the hills they'd just left. A line of enemy soldiers was advancing, firing as they came. Their own escort had jumped down from the jeep and were firing back, but it was an unequal contest. Wild-eyed, Tom looked around. They were in the open here and needed cover.

'Get the guns,' he ordered.

Hewitt reached in for the rifles, but could only find one.

'Never mind,' said Tom. Staying put meant certain death. The escort would give them cover if they ran. Too far to the road with its comforting line of dark green vehicles, but a hundred yards towards it he spotted a small hillock with a copse.

'Come on.' Clutching his side, Tom began to run.

Each thump of his feet sent a blade of pain into his chest, but the fear of death overcame any inclination to stop. His own breath thundered in his ears and he could hear Hewitt panting behind him. They swerved to confuse the enemy's aim.

He heard an engine rev and saw the escort jeep career down the track towards the road. His heart sank, knowing they should have thrown themselves on to it when they had the chance.

Now it was just him and Hewitt, against God knew how many enemy. With a single rifle between them.

They reached the tiny copse and pressed on into the centre of it, dropping behind some boulders. Hewitt was whimpering, his eyes wide with terror, his left upper arm a mass of blood.

'I've been shot, corp. I'm dying.'

'Don't be bloody daft.' Tom sounded calm, but inside he was panicking.

'Do something, corp, for God's sake.'

Tom opened the pouch where he was supposed to carry field dressings, then remembered that he'd emptied it to make more room for rations.

'Dressings,' he said, as if it were Hewitt's responsibility.

'Top left.'

Tom felt in the pouch and pulled out a small packet. He'd never applied one before but knew how. He tore open the tunic above Hewitt's wound, exposing the flesh. Wincing at the sight of the shredded tissue and protruding bone splinters, he pressed the inadequate dressing in place and bound it tightly round Hewitt's upper arm.

'You'll be right as rain,' Tom said, far from confident.

As soon as the final knot was tied he looked away, about to be sick. But the nausea died the moment he saw the line of Chinese soldiers closing on the copse. He snatched up the rifle lying by Hewitt's side.

It was Sergeant Bryant who noticed what was happening off to their right. Marcus had been preoccupied questioning an American lieutenant about the disaster in the mountain pass.

'Sir, there's some of our lads in trouble.' Bryant pointed to the copse about three hundred yards away.

'Can't see anything.'

'There was two of them. See their Land Rover?' He pointed further to the right where a vehicle was burning. 'They're in those trees. And there's enemy soldiers moving in fast.'

'Can't see them, either.'

'The gooks have taken cover. But it looked like a platoon's worth.'

'Right. Let's go.'

They fanned out across the scrub and ran, stopping every few seconds to fire in an effort to keep the enemy down.

Tom surprised himself. He brought down two of the Chinese, causing the rest to hit the ground. But it couldn't last. He was nearly out of bullets.

Hewitt lay behind him, shielded by a rock, slipping in and out of consciousness. Tom had no idea how much blood he'd lost. How much blood a man *could* lose before he died.

Then came a sound that chilled him to the marrow. The piercing shrill of a tin whistle. The Chinese rose from cover in a single line, the fire from their submachine-guns sounding like ripping canvas. As bullets zinged off the rocks Tom took careful aim and fired. One man fell. He picked another target and squeezed the trigger, but this time there was a click. His last round was gone.

Out in the open, Jagger let loose with the Bren, felling the Chinese soldiers like corn. But some were already amongst the trees. When he saw that, Marcus didn't hesitate. He rose from the ground and propelled himself towards the hill, snapping the spike bayonet on to the muzzle of his Sten. The icy air surging in and out of his lungs froze his nostrils.

Tom cowered behind the rock where Hewitt lay, trying to reconcile himself to the idea of dying. He heard the subhuman screams of the men scrambling to kill him. It wouldn't be long.

Feet crunched on fallen twigs, then an alien face appeared, pale and thin, topped by a helmet. Eyes no more than slits. A boy no older than himself and just as scared. Tom experienced a weird sense of detachment as the burp gun seemed to float upwards and the soldier prepared to fire. He imagined the bullets that were about to pour from its muzzle would be like bluebottles which he could swat aside with his hands. He reached

96

out towards the Chinese soldier – whether in a plea for mercy or to block the stream of lead, he wouldn't have been able to say.

In the half-light beneath the trees, Marcus saw the outline of a tensed-up enemy soldier jerking from the recoil of his gun. He fired a burst and the man fell back, his bullets spraying the branches as he went down.

Hearing a yell of pain, Marcus began to run forward, spotting two British soldiers, one prone and motionless, the other a crouching NCO with his back to him, staring in horror at his mangled hands.

Then, before he could reach them, a new Chinese soldier appeared. Marcus levelled the Sten and squeezed the trigger. Nothing. He worked the bolt but the gun had a jammed. He dropped to a crouch, amazed that the enemy soldier hadn't seen him.

The Chinese youth seemed mesmerised by the two injured soldiers in front of him, yet he didn't shoot them. Out of ammo? His gun jammed too? Marcus's mind raced. If they were both in the same boat, it would be bayonets. Stomach clenching, he rose to his feet to press his attack. At that moment, the crouching British corporal turned his head and Marcus saw that it was Tom.

Blinking with astonishment, Marcus took another pace forward, then stopped, his mind running wild.

Tom couldn't believe his eyes. It was a miracle. Marcus had come to save him. His blood brother after all.

And yet . . . He wasn't moving. Just standing there, staring at Tom as if he were already dead.

Tom sensed the world around him slowing down. The Chinese soldier bringing down his blade to strike. Marcus immobile, watching. The enemy bayonet starting the journey that would finish Tom's life. Marcus still not budging.

Do something! Tom screamed the words in his head, but Marcus seemed detached from reality, uninvolved, like someone watching a cinema screen.

Tom's life began to unravel. Fragments of his past flashed through his mind. The eyes of his mother, weeping. A school classroom. Sara – whispering in his ear again. Hissing, burbling frenziedly. Struggling to find the words, as always.

As the blade pierced the air, plunging towards his throat, Tom locked his stare on Marcus's in a last desperate appeal.

Suddenly the mouth twisted. Marcus lunged.

His bayonet met a momentary resistance, then slid between the Chinese soldier's ribs.

II

Marcus watched the Chinaman die, transfixed by the sight of the blood pumping through his tunic. The man had fallen sideways over the rock, the bayonet still deep in his chest. Marcus jerked it out, then peered in astonishment at his victim's feet. He was wearing mud-caked canvas shoes.

Marcus became conscious of men from his platoon running past him, pursuing the remains of the enemy. Then the gunfire stopped, quite suddenly, as if a switch had been thrown.

Marcus turned to where Tom lay. He'd fallen backwards, gibbering from shock and from the pain of his mangled hands, which he still held outstretched, as if not believing they were his.

'Tom . . . Are you hit anywhere else?'

Tom looked as if he hadn't understood.

'Apart from the hands?' Marcus was already pulling bandages from the pouch on his webbing. He looked closely at Tom's wounds. Two of the fingers were at odd angles but the source of the bleeding seemed to be the palms. He pressed dressings to each of them and tied them in place.

'Thank you,' croaked Tom, calmer now.

'D'you think you can walk?'

'I meant thank you for saving my life.'

Marcus winced, knowing that he nearly hadn't.

'On your feet Tom. We've got to get away from here. What about your mate?'

Hewitt had regained consciousness, his face twisted with pain.

'Hit in the shoulder,' Tom explained. 'I put a dressing on it.'

'Sir!' Sergeant Bryant burst into the copse. 'We need to fucking move it. There's more of 'em.'

While the rest of the platoon gave covering fire, Marcus and Bryant helped the casualties back to the road. When they reached it they found a column of US trucks being held at gunpoint by a British company sergeant major. Theirs.

'Get in quick,' he yelled. 'These Yank bastards are ready to murder me for holding them up. Get the casualties in, too. We'll offload them when we find some medics.'

Tom sat wedged in one corner of the truck, with Hewitt slumped beside him, his head against Tom's shoulder. The truck was crammed with bodies, many wounded, others just plain exhausted. Tears trickled down Tom's cheeks and he didn't care who noticed. He kept seeing the eyes of the Chinese soldier who'd tried to bayonet him. Like himself, a child-man, living by one simple rule. Kill or be killed.

Tom's ribs hurt at the slightest movement and his bandaged hands throbbed. He wished he could see them, fearing irrationally that they might be damaged beyond repair. And Pete beside him with a smashed arm – he felt it was all his fault.

Tom wiped his tears with the sleeve of his parka. The incident was going round in his head like an endless loop of film. Marcus appearing suddenly. The hesitation. The waiting for him to act that had felt like a lifetime. Had Marcus *really* nearly let him die, or was it only a split second's hesitation spun into an eternity by the imminence of death?

Whatever the truth, Tom felt a new upsurge of warmth towards his old friend. The point was, Marcus *had* saved his life.

Marcus rode in the jam-packed truck behind the one carrying Tom Sedley. He sat in a daze. They'd passed hundreds of US troops, wounded, shocked and exhausted. Walking south, oblivious to what was going on around them. There'd been huddles of bodies by the roadside from time to time, the wounded waiting forlornly for attention, or just exhausted men who would soon freeze to death if left out there in the plummeting temperatures.

Marcus began to blank out what had happened in the copse. The thoughts that had passed through his head were not ones he wanted to remember. It had been an appalling day.

When they reached the grim, blacked-out town that was to be their next holding point, it began to snow. Fine icy crystals.

It was a while before Tom Sedley and Private Pete Hewitt got their wounds properly treated. The British Brigade had no field hospital of its own and the American facilities were overwhelmed by the disaster that had befallen the 2nd Division. Tom and Hewitt received first aid, then the day after the shooting both men were helicoptered south to a M.A.S.H. and onwards by air to Japan for further treatment and convalescence. The doctors told Tom that his ribs were cracked but not broken. It hurt him to breathe but the pain was tolerable. And his hands were less damaged than he'd at first thought. Flesh wounds rather than broken bones. After they'd been seen to, the surgeon asked if he played the piano.

'Yes. Jazz, mostly.'

'Then you might experience a slight loss of dexterity. If you work on it, it could come back, but I can't promise anything. Playing pool, now, that should be no problem at all.'

Hewitt's wound was more serious. A bullet had shattered his left upper humerus. His convalescence would take longer. He'd got it into his head that he owed his life to Tom, the actual details of their escape being a blur. Tom didn't entirely disabuse him of the idea, happy to be thought a hero by him. The embarrassing incident on Thanksgiving Day appeared to have been firmly forgotten. A bit of horseplay rendered insignificant by the frighteningly grown-up experience they'd both just gone through.

Tom learned that he would be sent back to Korea in three weeks if his wounds healed well. Back in the ice and the filth in time for Christmas. Finding himself warm and comfortable now, sleeping in a proper bed, being well fed and attended by pretty nurses, he didn't look forward to it at all.

In the December days that followed, the UN forces continued their flight south, trucks, tanks and transporters nudging along the roads like ice floes in a river. Plans for new defensive lines were conceived, then quickly abandoned. Intelligence reports said that the Chinese had fielded sixteen divisions in Korea. And word soon spread about the size of the disaster the American 2nd Division had suffered. 3,000 men dead or missing in their flight through the mountain pass.

On the outskirts of Pyongyang, the Middlesex Regiment came across the long-awaited 29th Brigade, sent from England to take over from them. Fully equipped with the latest Centurion tanks, they'd been positioned to defend the city, but were ordered to join the rush south. 27 Brigade's hopes of a rapid return to Hong Kong were quickly dashed. The collapse of the UN offensive meant that every man available would be needed to hold the line – whenever their American commanders decided a line should be held. As they left Pyongyang, thick, acrid smoke obscured the sky, the Americans burning vast dumps of fuel, clothing and ammunition, abandoned in the rush to get out.

The bitter weather set in. Whenever the convoys halted, men jumped down and lit fires from anything that would burn, scorching their uniforms in an effort to get warm. Water trucks froze solid. When shaving, the metal of the razors stuck to men's skin.

When he could, Marcus sketched what he saw by the roadside. Refugees in white trouser suits. Old men with tall black hats. Others bearing their worldly goods strapped to huge wooden shoulder-frames. In the villages were crippled children. Children with festering sores, dirty eyes and noses. Revolting scraps of humanity, yet Marcus admired them. Because they were surviving. Surviving against terrible odds.

Mid-December

Eventually the UN retreat halted with the Chinese left far behind. Marcus's company took up positions in the hills a little way north of Seoul. Shovelling through thick snow, they hacked shelters out of the sides of slopes, covering them with materials salvaged from nearby ruined villages. The positions they built were made to last. This shanty town was intended to be their home for some while, part of a defensive line designed to hold back the Chinese advance once and for all.

Two days after their arrival, Marcus received a summons to his Battalion Headquarters, which had been set up in an old shoe factory. The colonel had taken over the manager's office with its wide mahogany desk and ancient leather chair. He sat stiff-backed, his round spectacles and toothbrush moustache giving him the appearance of an officious sparrow. Marcus remained standing.

'Just been listening to the BBC,' the colonel began, trying unsuccessfully to make this interview feel informal. 'D'you know what that idiot prime minister of ours has been saying? That Britain has no quarrel with the Chinese. That's what he said. Can you believe that? Man ought to be dragged out here by the scruff of the neck and stuck in a trench for a few days.'

'Yes, sir.' Marcus shifted from one foot to the other, wondering why he'd been summoned.

'That's not why I got you here, of course.'

'No, sir.'

'Two reasons. Firstly, it is my duty to inform you that your action to save the lives of two of my rear-link signallers has been brought to my attention.'

'Sir.' Marcus flushed with embarrassment.

'Sergeant Bryant considered it an act of extraordinary valour. He has written a report confirming that without your action the men faced certain death.'

'Well, I . . .'

The colonel's scowl silenced him.

'You will be mentioned in dispatches.'

'Sir . . . well, thank you.'

'I'm simply doing my duty.'

'Yes, sir.'

'That's all I have to say about that, except . . . well done!'

'Thank you, sir.'

'Now . . . the main reason I called you to see me is that I'm posting you.'

'Sir?' Marcus blanched. Having been praised one minute it sounded as if he was now being punished.

'The Public Relations Service has asked Brigade to supply someone to escort journalists and cameramen around the battlefield. They've had one of their chaps go sick. I told them I thought I had just the man. You've a bit of an eye for a picture, so I'm told. Thought it might suit you. Plus you've had experience of battle, so you won't get any of those press fellows killed. They behave like children half the time.'

'But sir, I'm very happy with my platoon.'

'Your replacement arrived this morning. He's a line officer straight from training. Sergeant Bryant is just the person to break him in. The PR Service are sending a jeep for you at two this afternoon. So you'd better say goodbye to your men, get your kit together and bring it here. I'm sure the men will be sorry to see you go, but you deserve a break after what you've been through.'

The colonel stood up and held out his hand.

'Good luck.'

The interview was over. And Marcus's destiny had been sealed.

12

Japan
15 December 1950

THE WAR IN Korea could well have been taking place on another planet, as far as Tom was concerned. The hospital was on a US airbase near Tokyo and from the ward windows he could watch the sun go down behind snow-covered mountains.

Pete Hewitt had the bed next to his. The hospital was short of places to sit, so despite both of them being perfectly able to walk about they spent most of their time in the ward. Tom's hands were still bandaged and he needed assistance with eating and dressing. Hewitt helped a little when the nurses were busy but with only his right arm usable there was a limit to what he could do.

Since his decision that by one means or another he urgently needed to find a woman to go to bed with, Tom had tried to visualise himself actually doing it. Here in the hospital there was no shortage of titillating magazines to look at and he'd studied them, trying to psych himself up for his planned night out in the red-light district of Wan Chai when he got back to Hong Kong.

There were several attractive nurses in the hospital, one in particular to whom he'd been giving the eye. Nurse Michiko spoke convoluted English with an American accent and was a good ten years older than himself. She had a shapely figure and sometimes left the top buttons of her tunic undone. Tom was far from alone in being interested in her. Michiko had been nominated the hospital's number one pin-up by the Americans who made up the majority of the casualties.

It was mid-afternoon and an orderly came round with a bag of post, stirring the hopes of all the men in the ward. To Tom's surprise three letters were for him. He'd only been there a week and the mail had found him already. He wedged the envelopes between his bandaged hands and tore them open with his teeth. The first was a short and unwelcome letter from his father saying that despite the divorce's finalisation and his decision to move to Manchester, he hoped they would see something of each other when Tom's National Service was over. The one from his mother he put aside to read later, knowing that it would be another emotional helter-skelter. The third was an airmail envelope containing two pages of closely typed script. Tom didn't recognise the address at the top and turned to the end to read the signature.

It was from Binnie. His heart beat a little faster as he began to read.

My dear Tom,

You are no doubt puzzled by the Earls Court address at the top of this letter. To be honest I myself am a little surprised to be living here and at the things that have happened to me in the last few months.

I am now Mrs Warwick. Sebastian and I were married at the end of November.

Tom felt a leaden blanket descending on him. Binnie and Sebastian. Inconceivable. This was a bad dream. And, if true, a terrible, terrible mistake. He felt deeply upset, cursing the fact that National Service had dumped him on the wrong side of the world. Binnie, sweet, trusting Binnie, was to have been his, once she'd got over her schoolgirl crush on Marcus.

The wedding was a rather rushed affair. For the usual sordid reason, I'm afraid. I've been very stupid, Tom. And Sebastian was downright careless. But there's no point crying over spilt milk and we decided to get on with it and do the right thing.

He closed his eyes in dismay. Binnie pregnant. A shotgun wedding between two of his friends, people he'd grown up with. If it had been Marcus, he might have understood it, but she'd got herself impregnated by the other Warwick brother. He could imagine no one in the world less suitable for Binnie than Sebastian. And the thought of that obnoxious creature sticking his revolting tool into her upset Tom dreadfully.

Our first home is this rather small flat off the Earls Court Road. A living room with kitchenette and a bedroom. The bathroom is very small and rather revolting, but it will do for now. My father offered me an allowance so we could find somewhere nice, but Seb insisted that he was going to be the provider. He's quite the little caveman! So we live in genteel poverty on his not very generous salary from the Ministry of Defence. I miss Wood Park dreadfully. And you and Marcus, of course.

'Genteel poverty'. Tom could hear the soft sarcasm in her voice through the printed words.

Please forgive me for typing this letter. I finished my course in the summer and badly need the practice. How are you? I often think of you both out there in the bitter cold, facing all that danger. Have you met up yet? I suppose that would be too much of a coincidence. The photographs in the newspapers make it all look utterly miserable. Sebastian works in the Defence Minister's outer office so he hears all sorts of things about the war. Apparently the Americans are talking about using the atom bomb in Korea, which I find quite terrifying. If they do explode it, please, please, please make sure you're miles and miles away.

I've been trying to understand what this war is all about, but the more Sebastian explains it to me, the more confused I get. It seems as if the Americans helped create the mess by putting that horrid dictator Syngman Rhee into power in South Korea. And in that case I really think the Americans should sort the thing out by themselves without dragging us into it. Sebastian says I don't understand and insists that if we don't support America in the UN against the communists in Korea, then America will stop supporting Europe against the communists in Russia. It all seems rather far-fetched to me. I'd love to know what you feel about it. Being there, you must know so much more than we do.

Tom glanced up and noticed Hewitt perched on the edge of the next bed watching him, his large, puppy eyes pinched with envy. To hide his own longing for news from home, Hewitt quickly began adjusting the sling that supported his plaster-encased left arm.

'Tha's a big letter, Tommy. From your girlfriend, is it?'

Tom had told Hewitt he had one, as a way of reassuring him he wasn't queer.

'Well, from a friend, yes. A girl I've known for years. Just got married, actually.'

'That's nice. Big wedding, was it? Pretty grand? Film stars and the like?'

Hewitt had been unable to shake off his distorted vision of life in Wood Park.

'I don't think so. It was kind of hurried. But she hasn't actually described it yet.'

'Okay. Well, tell me when you get to it, will ya?'

Turning the pages was difficult for Tom. His hands were like two mittens. But he didn't want Hewitt offering to help and peering over his shoulder, so he managed it.

'No letters for you today, Pete?'

His friend shook his head and looked away. The Hewitt family weren't great writers.

Let me tell you a little about the wedding, since it's meant to be the highlight of a girl's life. In the circumstances it wasn't, of course. Mother pushed me into a corset to disguise my tummy but it didn't stop the priest being awfully suspicious. We were married in the Catholic Church in the Finchley Road where we've always gone as a family. Just a handful of guests. My parents didn't want their friends to know, you see. And neither did the Warwicks. I'm afraid it wasn't exactly a joyous affair. Mother has been pretty sympathetic, but father was furious when I broke the news and quite ready to kill Sebastian until he agreed to marry me and become baptised into the Catholic Church.

This is so not the way I intended it to be. Dear Tom, I wish, wish, wish you were here so I could tell you all about it. I shall have just turned twenty when the baby is born and I dread being a mother. I'm so unready for it. My friends think I'm a complete idiot or worse for getting into this state. It really is very lonely here. I suppose I will come to love Sebastian one day, but to be truthful I don't really know him at all. He can be quite cruel at times. And to be absolutely totally honest, I'm a little afraid of him.

If you can bear to, please write to me. And do be careful.

Your loving friend, Binnie.

Tom gulped. Binnie afraid. He desperately wanted to comfort her, but what could he do from so far away? It should never have been this way.

What was her God thinking of to allow this to happen?

'Well?' asked Hewitt, eager for more details.

Tom shook his head, not trusting himself to speak. It was all so awful. He put the letter back in the envelope, wishing he'd never received it.

'Not so good, eh?'

'Yup.'

Hewitt let out a long sigh. 'Sometimes I think it's for the best that I hardly ever get any post.'

Tom stared out of the window, trying to pull himself together. There was nothing he could do. No point in crying over spilt milk, as Binnie had put it.

Before long Nurse Michiko entered the ward. He gave her the best smile he could muster in the circumstances and she stopped by his bed.

'How you today, Tommy? You looking vewy han-som.'

Tom felt himself blushing. 'Very well, thanks.'

'You get letters?'

'Yes.'

'Fom girlflend?'

He hesitated, then said, 'Yes.'

'She vewy lucky girl.' Nurse Michiko giggled and walked on into the ward.

'Never has chats like that wi' me,' Hewitt complained. 'Knows me tongue would stick to the roof of me mouth, I suppose. Bet she doesn't even know my name.'

'Nonsense.'

'It's true. Some fellers have the touch and some of us doesn't. And you've got it. *Tommy*, she called you. You'll be all right there. Get her to put the screens round your bed and show her what you've got, mon!'

Tom felt uplifted by Hewitt's admiration and even found himself becoming mildly aroused by what he was suggesting. He watched Michiko's progress down the ward, noting with pleasure that none of the other patients was meriting the same warm intimacy he'd received from her.

The chair he was sitting on became uncomfortable after a while, so he decided to climb back into bed. When he'd done so, he opened the letter from his mother.

'Fancy a game of chess?' Hewitt asked.

Tom saw the letter was full of the usual trivia. He skipped through it, looking for some mention of Binnie's marriage. When he didn't find any, he began to suspect that his mother might not even know about it. Her contact with the neighbours, never strong, had diminished even further since the marriage break-up.

'Okay. But let me finish this first.'

'I'll set the board up.'

Tom would actually have preferred to have read a book. He'd found a copy of *Brave New World* buried amongst the cowboy fiction in the hospital library. But having instigated his friend's interest in chess he felt obliged to help satisfy it. Pete was improving fast, though he hadn't beaten Tom yet.

The 'board' was a small travelling set, with the pieces slotting into holes. Hewitt flattened the blankets beside Tom's legs and took the lid off the box.

'You know that bloke in the next ward? The Argyll with the burns?' Hewitt whispered.

'Yes,' said Tom.

'He borrowed me this.' Hewitt produced a dog-eared copy of a *Health and Efficiency* magazine from beneath his mattress. 'Naturists, they call themselves. A right laugh. Want to see it?'

Tom kept it flat on the bed and let Pete turn the pages for him.

'What's the difference between a naturist and a nudist?' he asked, trying to sound indifferent to the pictures.

'No idea. The same thing, I think. Look at that bloke's muscles! Mister bloody Universe. Not much of a willy, though, eh? Could you ever do that? You know, wander around without a stitch of clothing on? In front of loads of other naked bods? Women and all?'

'Never.'

'I mean, suppose you saw someone you liked and got all hard? It'd be so embarrassing.'

'Quite.' Tom knew he would be embarrassed himself if the bedding was suddenly snatched away. The pictures of unclothed men and women weren't particularly alluringly posed, but with Hewitt talking about it and Nurse Michiko striding up and down the ward his hormones were pumping.

'See that? She bloody smiled at you again,' Hewitt complained.

'She smiles at every chap in the ward.'

'No, she bloody doesn't.'

'Here. Put this thing away before she sees it.'

Hewitt sneaked the magazine under his mattress again, then edged closer to Tom's pillows.

'Have you ever thought what you would do if you found yourself alone with her in a darkened room? Like, say, on your last night here before being sent back to Korea?' Hewitt looked up at Tom as if certain that he would have an answer. ''Cos I've heard on the old grapevine that she's done that wi' some of the blokes.'

'Really?' Tom felt both alarmed and excited at the prospect. 'First thing would be to kiss her passionately, I suppose.'

'Then what? Rip her clothes off quick before someone came in?'

'I'd have to be sure it was what she wanted,' Tom answered cautiously. If such a thing ever happened, he suspected he would be banking on *her* taking the initiative.

Hewitt shivered. 'Makes me go all hot thinking about it.'

Tom looked away, desperately hoping for another sighting of Nurse Michiko so that he could concentrate his thoughts on her. Because what he *really* desired was to be in a darkened room with Pete Hewitt.

13

Korea
21 December 1950

THE POST CAUGHT up with Marcus in the week before Christmas, a letter and a parcel delivered to the house in Seoul where the UK Public Relations Service was billeted. He opened the package first. As he did so, the corporal who was the unit's driver placed a record on the wind-up gramophone, which to their great delight had been in the house when they commandeered it. Marcus knew the tune well. 'Mona Lisa' by Nat King Cole. He hummed along with the melody.

The parcel was from his grandmother and contained tea and thick socks. An early Christmas present. He felt unexpectedly emotional at this seasonal contact with home. The handwriting on the letter was his mother's, sparking an unaccustomed wave of homesickness. Fearing he might disgrace himself by shedding a tear, Marcus took it into the privacy of the bedroom to read.

He was expecting the usual carefully controlled content, so the first line took his breath away.

Dear Marcus,
    You will be interested to hear that Sebastian got married yesterday.

How on earth could something so significant have been allowed to happen without his knowledge? They hadn't even told him Seb had a girlfriend.

Binnie Rowbotham is now Mrs Columbine Warwick.

'Binnie . . .' He gulped. This was insane.

Marcus stared at the name, thinking he was seeing things. Any minute now, the Binnie word would transform itself into something else.

It was a quiet wedding which took place in her church, that rather ugly Catholic one on the Finchley Road. It was all rather sudden, a matter of necessity really, but Sebastian said he knew what he was doing.

Marcus was appalled. A matter of necessity, indeed . . . Seb had clearly forced himself on Binnie and made her pregnant. She would never have submitted willingly to him. And marriage – it couldn't have been love. Binnie was far too sensitive a soul to go for his arrogant older brother. And she'd been keen on *him*, for heaven's sake! Even though he hadn't wanted her for himself, he was experiencing a degree of hurt pride.

And to have married in a Catholic church, Sebastian must've converted, Marcus realised. What on earth was going on? This shocked him more than anything. He searched for some reference to this but found none. It didn't surprise him. With his mother's abhorrence of papists, writing about it would have made the pen fall from her hand.

They looked lovely standing there together, even if terribly young. The handful of people who came said Binnie's dress was simply gorgeous and your brother looked terrifically smart.

Marcus clicked his tongue. He had an awful feeling this was his fault. If he'd responded to Binnie's letter in Hong Kong, acknowledged her feelings for him in some small way, this mightn't have happened. He looked up, listening to the words of the song *Mona Lisa* being played in the next room. Something about hiding a broken heart.

Was that what he'd done? Broken Binnie's heart? Had she married Sebastian in revenge, knowing how sick it would make him feel? He felt deeply depressed.

In contrast to that piece of cataclysmic news, the rest of the letter was of little consequence. His mother wrote about electricity cuts and the smog. And how she was looking forward to Christmas, even if Marcus couldn't be with them. The newly married couple would be at Binnie's parents for the twenty-fifth, she reported, but coming to them on Boxing Day.

'Oh God . . .'

The cycle of dreary suburban existence was perpetuating itself. Binnie had her own man, her own home and soon her own family. What she'd always wanted.

Marcus felt sorry for his mother. He could imagine her disappointment at the circumstances of her first-born's marriage. Knew how she would have suppressed her reservations, keeping them bottled up inside her like acid. And how detached his father would have been, performing his duty at the altar like a sidesman.

He read on to the end. Buried in the last paragraph was another bombshell.

I thought you ought to know that John Hagger is dead. He was stabbed by another prisoner. The newspapers made a big thing about how he'd always maintained he was innocent of Sara's murder. Now, I suppose we'll never know the truth of that.

Marcus shivered. The truth was far more complicated than any of them would ever know.

Nat King Cole fell silent in the next room. Marcus needed noise. Needed company. He folded the letter, put it back in its envelope and rejoined the others to ask for the song to be played again.

It was two weeks earlier that Marcus had transferred to the Public Relations Service, his reluctance at the posting tempered by being given the temporary rank of captain and an increase in pay.

The unit in Seoul was run by a reservist major called David Adams, a Home Counties local newspaper editor in civilian life, who grumbled continually about the financial hardship his family was enduring as a result of his call-up. Before Marcus joined them, the PR unit had commandeered a pleasant, solidly built house in a residential district of Seoul, which had been left unclaimed by its owner when the city was recaptured from the communists. The floors were covered with matting made from rice straw. There were elegant chests of drawers in black lacquer with mother-of-pearl inlay, and some of the previous occupant's silken clothing hung on wooden pegs. The kitchen was equipped with heavy iron pots and cluttered with huge earthenware storage jars. A Korean 'boy', one of the many jobless in the city, cooked, washed their clothes and kept the place clean.

A second Korean had been recruited as translator, a refugee who spoke passable English. Lee Ho Shin had told the major that he was an engineering student in Seoul, who had lost his home and family when the communists first invaded.

Marcus had grown to like the major, who was far less overbearing than many of the senior officers he was used to. They slept in the same room and on his first night in a real bed for many months Marcus had slumbered so deeply and so sensuously he'd woken with a powerful erection, which he'd found hard to conceal. The major had joked about it, suggesting various addresses in Seoul where he could 'get it seen to'.

'But for God's sake use a johnny,' the major had warned. 'Some of the local women have diseases the medics haven't even heard of.'

Marcus had embraced his role as press liaison officer with enthusiasm, enjoying the blunt charm of the press men who passed through their office. Some were old hands who'd seen as much action as any soldier. Others preferred to get their news second-hand, hanging around the press office for scraps of information, or at the bars of the Chosan Hotel where UN officers went to unwind.

There was a lull in the fighting, the UN retreat having been so rapid and so deep that it had far outpaced its communist pursuers. Marcus's first escorting duty was to take a BBC man to visit the recently arrived 29 Brigade. He was mightily impressed by their equipment. Vehicles, tents, weaponry and clothing, no expense spared in preparing them for this war, contrasting strongly with what had befallen his own regiment.

The weather became more bitter than ever, with regular temperatures of minus twenty degrees Fahrenheit. The battle to keep warm was the only one that mattered for now. Fires blazed night and day on the rear flanks of the hills that the British troops were defending. Bunkers had been expanded into two- and three-bedroom apartments with wooden roofs and sides, the men as proud as Boy Scouts of their shanty towns and apparently happy to stay there for as long as they had to.

There was little to do in the press office for much of the time, so Marcus used the hours to make full-size drawings from the pencil sketches in his notebook, sometimes imitating the styles of artists he admired.

'This one's like that Nash bloke,' Major Adams remarked one day. 'What was his first name?'

'Paul. Nobody better at making war look bleak.'

'What's the matter? Haven't you got a style of your own?'

Marcus wasn't sure if he was being insulted or having the mickey taken.

'It's only by trying different styles, sir, that I can find out what I do best. But I'm impressed that you recognised it as Nash.'

The major sniffed disdainfully.

'You know what Sigmund Freud said about artists?'

'No, sir.'

'That by definition they are inadequate people, who turn to art because they can't manage life.'

'Thanks very much, sir.'

'Don't worry. He said it about writers too, so we're both in the same boat.'

On the day after his mother's letter arrived, Marcus felt restless. He told Major Adams he wanted to get to know Seoul better. The older man pursed his lips.

'Still got a stiffy, lad?'

'No, sir.'

The major laughed at him.

'Go on. Take a good look at what war does to a capital city. Might give you some more ideas.' Then the twinkle went from his eyes. 'It's pitiful, actually. There's tremendous hardships being endured. Get Lee Ho Shin to go with you. He should know the place inside out.' Then, with a stage wink, he added, 'And if you do fancy a lucky dip, he might negotiate a good price for you. It *is* the week before Christmas, after all.'

'Sir, really, that's not . . .'

'I know, I know. Just pulling your leg. Take the jeep. Corporal Ivory's a little hung-over this morning. He was drinking with the Reuters boys last night.'

Lee Ho Shin was an enigma to Marcus. Much of the time he sat in the corner of the press office, staring blankly in front of him. Whether he took in any of their banter, Marcus had no idea. What was quite clear was that Lee, as they all called him, relied totally on the small amount of money they paid him every week.

'Where do you live, Lee?' Marcus asked as they set off in the jeep.

'At my uncle house,' Lee Ho Shin replied.

'What happened to your own place?'

'They burn it. After my parents killed.'

'I'm sorry.'

'It happen to many people.'

'Yes.'

The silence that followed seemed heavy with reproach. Marcus didn't dare ask which side had been responsible for the loss of Lee's home.

The Public Relations house was on a hill, and as they drove down into the city, terrace upon terrace of small roofs spread out below them, their rough tiles tilted up at the corners. Some houses were like small fortresses, raised above street level on stone embankments. On a hilltop half a mile away Marcus saw office blocks of concrete and stone which could have been any modern town.

As they neared the centre, the destruction inflicted on the place when the Americans retook the city was more widespread. Whole blocks had been demolished. Rubble towered on street corners. They saw increasing numbers of refugees, gawping silently as they passed, the children's red faces polished by the wind. Tears streamed from eyes. Noses ran.

'Many poor people here,' Lee Ho Shin repeated, over and over again.

The Capitol, the seat of government, lay well back from the dual carriageway that led to it. It was a massive building in grey granite with a dome on top, covered in scaffolding and boarded over. A sagging banner hung from it, bidding welcome to the UN. Around it there were fine brick and concrete buildings.

'Government offices?'

'Yes,' said Lee after a moment's hesitation.

Near the Capitol was a small bazaar. Few of the open-fronted shops were staffed, but those that were displayed dried fish and brightly coloured food that Marcus couldn't identify.

'Where's the University, Lee?'

'Excuse me?'

'The place where you studied. Engineering, wasn't it?'

'Yes.'

'How do we get there?'

For a few moments Lee didn't reply. Marcus had a curious feeling that he didn't know the way.

'Not want to go there, Mister Wowick. Maybe someone know me.'

Marcus glanced sideways at him, but the face was as inscrutable as ever. He tried to think what Lee meant and concluded that he didn't want anyone he knew seeing him sitting in a UN jeep.

'You want eat Korean food?' Lee Ho Shin asked, out of the blue.

Marcus hesitated. From what he'd seen of the stuff and smelled on people's breath, it didn't appeal.

'You like eat kimch'i?' Lee Ho Shin persisted.

'What's that?'

'All Koreans eat it. Very good. You try.'

'You cook it yourself?'

'No, but my aunt.'

'The one you live with?'

Lee Ho Shin nodded. 'They have restaurant.'

'Oh really?'

'All family work in it.'

'It's big?'

Lee Ho Shin wavered, not having enough experience of such places to judge. 'Quite small. You like we go there?'

Marcus wasn't sure what military regulations said about soldiers mixing with civilians but decided it would probably be all right. And there might even be a drawing in it for him. Something to add some domestic colour to the battle scenes in his portfolio.

'All right. Where do we go?'

Lee Ho Shin seemed uncertain. He looked about him as if trying to find landmarks he was familiar with. Eventually he did.

'I show you.'

He directed Marcus to retrace their route back up towards the Public Relations house, then guided him down narrow streets with low doorways through which the red glint of cooking fires could be seen. They emerged eventually in a commercial district, almost untouched by the war, where cafés abounded. American servicemen were sitting in several of them.

'You stop here, please,' Lee Ho Shin directed.

Marcus looked at the house where they'd halted. On two floors and made of wood with a tiled roof, it had shuttered windows that prevented him seeing inside. Above the door was a board painted with Korean lettering.

'Please to wait. I go talk to my uncle.'

When Lee Ho Shin opened the door of the restaurant and went inside, Marcus caught a glimpse of low tables and several people sitting at them. He began to feel this was a bad idea, likely to leave him hospitalised with dysentery.

'Hey, lieutenant!'

Marcus looked to his right. An American military policeman was approaching, swinging a stick.

'You wouldn't be thinking of leaving that jeep unattended, sir?'

'I . . . I hadn't thought about it. We're going inside to eat.'

'Round here it'll be gone before you've had time to wipe your mouth, lieutenant. This town's about to take to the road and jeeps are kinda popular.'

'Thanks. Thanks for the warning.'

'My pleasure, sir.'

Was that the reason Lee had got him here? So the jeep could be stolen by an accomplice? Before he could digest this uncharitable thought, his translator emerged from the restaurant with a burly young man in an American infantryman's thick winter cap and parka.

'My cousin – he will look after jeep,' Lee Ho Shin explained. He gestured towards the door. 'My uncle say you very welcome.'

The cousin bowed to him, but the young man's Eskimo-like face was a blank. Marcus still had a lingering suspicion he was being set up.

'You come?'

'All right. If you're sure the vehicle's safe.'

'Yes, yes. Safe, safe.'

The door to the restaurant was low and Marcus had to bend to get in. The smell of garlic and other spices was overpowering, but the idea of eating food that tasted of something, after months of bland army rations, was beginning to attract him. A large collection of footwear stood by the door. Lee Ho Shin indicated that they should remove their boots.

A middle-aged man blocked their way, then bowed low three times. Unsure of the etiquette, Marcus bowed back.

'My uncle,' Lee explained. 'He say you most welcome.'

'Thank you. Please tell him how honoured I am to be in his restaurant.'

Marcus looked around him. There were perhaps twenty people sitting at low tables, all men and none of them westerners. One table well away from the door was conspicuously free of customers. He suspected that some benighted locals had been forced to squeeze up with strangers to make room for him.

As they were led over to the vacant table Marcus was conscious of every face in the room staring at him. The table was set with bowls and chopsticks. He and Lee Ho Shin sat cross-legged on the floor, which was warm from the heating beneath it. Marcus looked around him. When he met another person's eye, there was a courteous bow of the head, but for the most part he felt under suspicion.

'Is it true that everyone in Seoul is planning to leave?' Marcus asked, still a little surprised at what the MP had said outside.

'I don't know, Mister Wowick.'

Lee sat straight-backed, looking awkward and uneasy at the situation he'd created.

'But do people think the UN can stop the Chinese, or not?'

'Chinese have many, many soldiers. People are afraid.'

A steaming bowl was placed on the table, served by a girl of about Marcus's age. She wore a long, high-waisted skirt, with a short embroidered jacket in green silk over a white blouse. Marcus glanced at her face, expecting to see the flat, expressionless visage he'd become used to amongst the refugee women. Instead, her cheeks were pricked with colour and her eyes had the startled look of a forest animal.

'Thank you,' he whispered, staring fixedly at her.

She bowed twice and backed away, her gaze locked on his, as if still trying to make him out. He watched her turn and glide effortlessly towards the doorway that he assumed led to the kitchen.

Lee Ho Shin encouraged Marcus to help himself to the soup.

'What's in it?'

'I don't know how you say in English.'

Marcus peered into the tureen.

'Beans,' he said.

The girl returned, bearing rice and a bowl of pungent-smelling vegetables.

'This kimch'i,' Lee Ho Shin explained.

'Kimch'i,' the girl repeated. Her voice was birdlike and frail.

'You speak English?' Marcus asked, hopefully.

'She my cousin,' said Lee, defensively. 'No speak English.'

'She's very beautiful,' said Marcus, the words out before he could assess whether it was an acceptable thing to say. Her face wasn't square like those of most Koreans, but tapered towards the chin. Her skin made him think of peaches.

'Tell her what I said.'

Lee Ho Shin didn't. Instead he shooed the girl away. Marcus kept his gaze on her as she backed off, still bowing. When he saw Lee's disquiet at the blatancy of his interest, he felt a little ashamed.

'She has a very interesting face,' he explained. 'I'd quite like to draw it.'

Lee Ho Shin frowned uncomprehendingly.

'Make a picture of her,' Marcus explained. 'I'm an artist. You've seen the sketches I've done back at the house.'

Lee Ho Shin gestured for him to try the kimch'i.

'I suppose she's married,' Marcus went on, trying to sound as if it was of little interest to him. 'And her husband would object.'

'You know how use chopsticks?'

'I've never tried.'

'Very easy.'

Lee Ho Shin demonstrated and Marcus struggled to imitate. It took him a few minutes to get the hang of it.

'Kimch'i good, yes?'

Marcus was unused to fiery food and screwed up his face at the peppery taste. It seemed to be mostly cabbage.

'Interesting,' he croaked, taking some rice into his mouth to absorb the heat.

They ate without speaking for a while, Lee Ho Shin slurping noisily. Marcus had the odd feeling that his translator was almost as much of a stranger in this house as he was.

'Are you a close family?'

Lee Ho Shin looked confused by the question.

'You and your cousins. Did you see them all the time when you were growing up?'

'No.' Lee Ho Shin glanced away to avert further questions.

Marcus saw the girl emerge from the back again, carrying dishes for another table. She caught his glance and smiled at him, causing his heart to miss a beat.

'What's her name?'

'Who name?'

'The girl. Your cousin.'

'Lee Cho-Mi.'

'That's almost the same as your name.'

'Lee is family name.'

'I see. So we've got it wrong up at the house. We should really be calling you Ho Shin instead of Lee. And she's Cho-Mi . . .' He looked at her again, entranced by the graceful way she moved.

'Call me Lee is all right,' Lee Ho Shin insisted.

Marcus decided not to pursue the matter. 'Does Cho-Mi mean anything in particular?'

'It mean beautiful.'

'Of course.' Marcus watched her bowing to the table she'd just served. He felt a sharp pang of jealousy, wanting her exclusive attention.

'Lee, tell her to come over here.'

'Have you finish? No like kimch'i?'

'Yes, I like, but I don't want any more. Just get her over here.' Marcus pulled the notebook and pencil from his pocket and began to draw, glancing up at Lee Ho Shin. 'Go on. I want to talk to her.'

Reluctantly the translator caught his cousin's eye and beckoned her over.

Marcus sketched furiously. In the time available he could only do a caricature of Lee, but the picture was soon recognisable. After a couple of minutes he was conscious of the girl standing a few feet to his right, watching him draw.

He smiled up at her. 'What d'you think? Looks a bit like him?'

She frowned, not understanding.

'Translate for me, Lee. What does she think of the picture?'

There was a burst of awkward conversation between them. Short, staccato sounds. Marcus itched with frustration, not entirely trusting Lee Ho Shin to do what he asked.

'What does she think?'

'She say you very clever.'

'Tell her I want to do a drawing of her. But bigger and better. A proper portrait.'

'She not want that,' Lee insisted, his eyes smouldering.

'Ask her.'

Again the burst of tones that Marcus couldn't understand. His gaze flicked between the girl's face and Lee's, trying to see if Lee was directing how she should respond.

'She say she not worthy,' he translated. 'But I can tell she no want you to make her picture.'

'Worthy?' Marcus exclaimed, looking into her bottomless dark-brown eyes. 'Of course you're worthy, Cho-Mi. It is *I* who am unworthy . . .' He knew he was sounding ludicrously theatrical. If any of his old platoon had been in earshot, they'd have fallen about laughing. 'I could come back later this afternoon with my bigger sketch pad. An hour of your time, that's all it would take.'

The girl looked towards her cousin for guidance and he waved her away again. Marcus noticed the other customers were staring more intently than ever. It suddenly struck him how it must have looked. The old cliché. Conquering foreign soldier sees pretty local girl and propositions her. Except that there'd been no conquest and his intentions were innocent.

'It's only to draw her face,' he said forlornly.

'I think maybe we go now.'

'I'd better pay. Call the girl back for the bill.'

'No pay. You are guest of my uncle.'

Marcus felt even worse. He'd abused the old man's hospitality. As they made their way to the door, however, the uncle bowed again and showed no sign of displeasure. Marcus thanked him profusely.

Outside, the jeep was still there, with the burly youth asleep behind the wheel. Lee Ho Shin shook him awake and the boy went back inside.

Marcus sat in the car, stunned by the experience he'd undergone. It wasn't just the girl's beauty that had gripped him: she'd had an aura about her, some indefinable presence. He was no believer in fate, yet something had clicked between them in that restaurant. She'd felt it, too. He'd seen it on her face.

'Lee . . .'

'We go now?'

'Lee Ho Shin. I want you to go back in and persuade Cho-Mi to sit for me.'

'I think we go now, Mister Wowick.'

'Not until you've got her agreement.'

There was a long silence before Lee Ho Shin said he didn't understand.

'You like your job as translator for us?' Marcus asked.

'Yes.'

'You want to keep it?'

'Yes.'

'Then go back in there and persuade Cho-Mi to sit for me. Either here – I can come back with my sketch pad – or else up at the house.'

'But Mister Wowick . . .'

'If you want to keep your job, you will do this for me.'

Marcus had surprised himself with his own ruthlessness. But it worked. Lee Ho Shin stepped down from the jeep and went back inside the restaurant.

The Korean seethed with bad feelings. It was humiliating to be ordered around by foreigners in his own country. And the task he'd been given was the last thing in the world he wanted to carry out. He feared the outcome of letting Cho-Mi have her picture drawn by this Englishman. She was a girl whose head was full of dreams. Easily tempted by anything that promised an escape from the hardships of family life.

And Lee Ho Shin cared about her. Since coming to live with his cousins, he'd become fond of her. He might even say that he was strongly attracted, even though he hadn't dared to reveal his feelings. It would hurt him deeply if she were to show interest in this pretentious young Englishman.

As he walked through the dining room to seek out his cousin, he thought of his older brother. *He* wouldn't have stood for this. Was he still in Moscow, he wondered, or would the resurgence of the northern armies have brought him hurrying back to his homeland to help rub out capitalism from the Korean peninsula? Lee was certain of one thing. Wherever he was, his brother would be working his fingers to the bone to drive these foreigners out.

For a good ten minutes Marcus waited impatiently in the jeep. He watched hawkers squatting in the gutters and selling American cigarettes. A couple of shops next to the restaurant displayed odds and ends of clothing, cheap stationery and toilet goods. There was a café with plates of tiny cakes and doughnuts in the windows, with American servicemen going in and out, their faces half buried in the fur of their parkas.

Marcus shivered. The wind had got up and the clouds overhead were thickening. He imagined being in a warm bed with Cho-Mi.

When Lee Ho Shin emerged, his face was pinched and drawn.

'Well?'

'Tomorrow morning. I bring her to army house when I come.'

'Brilliant! Well done, Lee. You won't regret this.'

'Now we go, Mister Wowick.'

'Yes.'

Marcus started the engine and followed Lee Ho Shin's directions back to their billet, feeling undeservedly happy.

14

The next day, 23 December

A T FIRST LIGHT Marcus was up, fretting over what he was doing. He'd hardly slept, racked by self-doubt. Was he making a fool of himself? Letting himself be seduced by a pair of eyes? He'd thought about Cho-Mi most of the night. Imagining conversations they could have if there were no language barrier. Imagining the smooth skin of her naked body pressed against his own.

The previous evening he'd had a strip torn off him after telling Major Adams about Cho-Mi's arrival in the morning.

'Who the hell do you think you are, bringing your totty here?'

'Sorry, sir.'

'Your job is to assist the media in their work, not indulge your private fantasies. And, anyway, we can't have Korean nationals in our office left, right and centre. Seoul is thick with spies and saboteurs.'

'It won't take long, sir.'

'It had better not.'

Eventually the major had agreed to the portrait sitting going ahead. 'But I shall have strong words with Lee when he gets here. He's paid as a translator, not as a pimp for his sister.'

'She's his cousin, sir. And I'd be most extremely obliged if you didn't say anything to him. I appreciate I shouldn't have done what I did, but if you take it out on Lee it could undermine my authority with him.'

'Should have thought of that before.'

'If I'm to work with him, it's important he respects my orders, sir.'

Again, Marcus surprised himself with his forthrightness. But he knew Major Adams would back down. The older man was weary of this war, wanting nothing more than to get back to his newspaper desk.

'All right. But this is positively the last time. Any repetition of this sort of indiscretion and I'll have you sent back to the line.'

There was only one place in the house where he could do his drawing, a room used for visiting pressmen to doss down in if they had nowhere else to go. No furniture except for a couple of chairs. Plenty of light. And away from the main press office with its radio transceiver and occasionally working landline.

Lee Ho Shin arrived soon after nine, his gaze downcast. Marcus suspected that he was furious with him, but he didn't care. A frightened-looking Cho-Mi followed meekly behind him. Major Adams and Corporal Ivory made a point of ignoring her.

Marcus drank in her appearance, relieved that she was as beautiful as he'd remembered.

'It's wonderful to see you again, Cho-Mi.' He was struggling to sound calm and detached, wanting it to appear as if painting portraits was something he did every day. 'Please. Come into my studio.'

He heard Ivory snort with derision. Lee Ho Shin followed the girl into the room.

'I don't have a third chair,' said Marcus, hoping that Lee would take the hint and leave them alone together.

'I sit on floor.'

Marcus shrugged, suspecting that Lee was under instruction from the family not to let Cho-Mi out of his sight.

He took the girl's arm and guided her towards the chair. She wore a heavy woollen coat, which he helped her remove. Underneath she was dressed in a long cream-coloured robe, which looked like silk. A high waistband flattened her breasts.

'Perfect,' Marcus said. Nothing to distract from her face. 'If you sit here . . . and turn this way so the light from the window . . . that's it. Perfect.' He caught a light whiff of garlic on her breath, an imperfection that sharpened his desire.

Cho-Mi glanced at Lee Ho Shin, hoping for some explanation of what Marcus was saying, but none was forthcoming. Her cousin was staring at his feet, trying to disconnect himself as much as he could from the proceedings.

Marcus sat opposite her, with the sketchbook on his knee and his pencil poised, heart thumping. His hands would need to stop shaking if he was to proceed. He began to look, his eyes following the shiny river of black hair flowing down from her crown into a bunch at the back of her head. A wisp of it had broken free and lay across her forehead. He noted the broad spread of her cheekbones and the indentations below them. The full lips and slender neck. He studied the shading of her skin, more vellum than peach. Then he looked at her eyes, almonds of anthracite darting from side to side in wonderment and fear.

'You must relax, Cho-Mi.'

She had no idea what he was saying.

'Can you please tell her, Lee. Tell her to keep her eyes still. She needs to look at me, not all over the room.'

Lee Ho Shin spoke to her so harshly that she made herself as stiff as a statue, her eyes locked ahead like a soldier's at attention.

'But relaxed, Lee. She must relax. Tell her to just be herself.'

Eventually Cho-Mi understood and Marcus began to draw. From time to time he smiled or pulled faces in order to get some animation in hers. Slowly she began to loosen and he could see her curiosity grow. She leaned forward a little to see what he was doing. Gradually Marcus felt her opening up to him. Sensed himself getting beneath the foreignness of her face, reaching out for her character. She was as insecure as any young girl, he realised. Like Binnie had been when he sketched her: wondering if he thought her beautiful, fearing his intense stares might see into her mind. Would he think less of her for posing for him? Was she debasing herself by doing this?

Marcus held the pad away from him, unhappy with the way he'd started. The shape of the eyes was wrong. And the forehead. It was a while since he'd done a formal portrait and he began to fear he'd lost his touch. He rubbed out a section and drew it again. She could see his uncertainty and was disturbed by it. And her unease unsettled him. A telepathic communication that threatened to destabilise the sitting.

'Always happens,' Marcus sighed. 'The first few pencil strokes are the hardest. Can you explain that to her, Lee? Tell her it's all perfectly normal.'

Lee Ho Shin did what was required of him, but it took several more reassuring smiles from Marcus before Cho-Mi relaxed again.

Slowly the portrait took shape. Marcus was pleased with the hair and her chin and neck. But the eyes were still eluding him. The eyes which were the mirror to the soul. And he couldn't get them. Something about the upper lid's tightness, relieving it of expression.

He thought back to the picture he'd done of Binnie. He'd been able to play with her character, bringing out an unseen free-spiritedness, glimpsed only because of something she'd said. Because he could talk to her. And he couldn't with Cho-Mi.

Marcus put down the pad. This was impossible. Yes, he had a likeness, but he wanted more than that. Somehow they had to communicate. He wished Lee Ho Shin wasn't there. Left on his own with her Marcus was sure they could converse, by sign, by smile, by touch. Particularly by touch.

Suddenly there was the sound of heavy boots in the hall outside. A visitor. A pressman, judging by the greetings Marcus heard being exchanged.

He quickly shaded and refined what he'd done, fearing that time was running out. The sound of voices had made Cho-Mi's eyes flicker. She too sensed that the session would soon be over.

She said something to him.

'She want to see what you done,' Lee explained.

'It's nowhere near finished. But all right.'

Marcus turned the pad to face Cho-Mi. She gave a little laugh and covered her mouth with her hand. Then she laughed again and reached out for a closer look.

'You like it?'

Lee Ho Shin stood beside his cousin.

'She ask is that really her?'

'Of course it's her.'

Cho-Mi's words sounded scornful, but she was still smiling.

'She say it not her because this girl beautiful.'

'Cho-Mi *is* beautiful. Tell her.'

The girl giggled as her cousin reluctantly translated.

Then the door opened and Corporal Ivory poked his head inside.

'The major says he has need of your services, sir. You and Lee. There's an escort needs doing.'

'Bugger.'

'Right away is what he said, sir.'

'Thank you, corporal.'

Ivory left them again.

Lee Ho Shin was already explaining the problem to his cousin, embellishing the fact that she was going to be cast aside, now there was work to do, with the odd 'I told you so'. The girl looked alarmed.

'I need another sitting, Lee,' Marcus insisted, determined to see her again. 'Fix a time with her.'

'We drive Cho-Mi back home?'

'Well, yes. If we can. Let me find out what this is all about.' He touched Cho-Mi on the arm and gave her a reassuring smile. 'I'll be back in a minute. Don't worry.'

In the major's office he discovered that their visitor had a familiar face.

'Well, well. Look who it is!' Terry Franks's tin helmet lay upturned on the major's desk and his M1 carbine leaned against it.

'You two have met?' Major Adams asked, surprised.

'We were pinned down together on a hill next to the one where the Argylls got blitzed,' Franks explained. 'Then met again in Kim Il-Sung's boudoir.'

'Did you indeed?' Adams looked rather annoyed. 'Well, Captain Warwick will take you wherever you want to go.'

'*Captain*, eh?'

'Acting captain,' Marcus explained. 'Goes with the job. Nice to see you again, Mr Franks.'

'It's Terry, lad. Terry.'

'The *Echo* are doing a build-up-to-Christmas story,' Major Adams told him. 'I've called up your old battalion – they're expecting you. Then you can go on to 29 Brigade to get pictures of the Hussars' Centurions. You'll be cutting across country somewhat, so I suggest you take Lee with you in case of problems on the road.'

'Yes, sir. I was wondering if we could first take Miss Lee—'

'No time for that,' Major Adams glared over his half-moon reading glasses. 'You'll need to get a move on if you're to cover the ground before dusk.'

'Have to file a piece this evening, you see,' said Terry Franks. 'Bit of a rush. Sorry, old boy.'

'Then I'll get my things together.' Marcus turned to leave the room.

'I've got the maps ready for you,' the major told him.

'Thank you, sir.'

Back in his makeshift studio, Cho-Mi was on her feet, looking agitated.

'Sorry, Lee, but she'll have to make her own way home. You and I have work to do.'

'But I promise to my uncle that I bring her back.'

'Then it's a promise you're going to have to break.'

Marcus helped Cho-Mi on with her coat. She felt frail as a bird as he guided an arm into a sleeve.

'Have you discussed another sitting with her, Lee?'

'She say she want to take picture now.'

As if on cue, Cho-Mi picked up his sketch pad and clutched it to her chest.

'You give her the picture?' Lee asked.

'But it's not finished,' Marcus insisted, desperate not to part with it. 'And a picture always belongs to the artist until it's complete.' Gently, but firmly, he took the pad back from her. 'One more sitting. That's all. Tell her, Lee. Tell her that when I see her again and finish it, she'll think it the most beautiful thing she's ever seen.'

'Then you give it to her?'

It hurt, but Marcus agreed, knowing that without that promise he would probably never see Cho-Mi again.

Grudgingly, Lee Ho Shin translated all that he'd said.

Tears welled in the girl's dark eyes. Marcus's throat dried. Could it be that she'd fallen in love with him? Like Binnie had? A startling new sign that his art could seduce the female mind? If so, this time he was more than ready to respond.

'Good bye, Cho-Mi,' he breathed. 'We'll see each other again, very soon, I promise you.'

Lee Ho Shin took his cousin to the door and saw her off down the road. Marcus watched from the threshold. He hoped she would glance back, but she didn't.

When he re-entered the house, Major Adams was scowling at him.

'Why you can't just take a photo of the damned trollop, like any normal man, instead of this arty malarkey, God alone knows.'

Marcus seethed at the major's description of the girl. In his own eye she was a saint. But he kicked himself for not photographing her too. The truth was that he was still so unused to using a camera, it had never occurred to him.

★

The 1st Battalion of the Middlesex Regiment was still stationed on high ground to the north of Seoul. There'd been several changes of personnel since Marcus had left them. While Corporal Ivory and Lee Ho Shin brewed up with some of the riflemen guarding the headquarters perimeter, Marcus and the *Daily Echo* man were treated to a briefing by the new second-in-command.

'Where's the enemy got to, major?' Terry Franks asked, drawing deeply on a Camel cigarette.

'Vanished into thin air. Been no sign for weeks. Oh, by the way, your visit here's pretty timely. We're expecting a visit from the US Eighth Army commander, General Walker. 27 Brigade's being given a presidential citation for being such a bloody brilliant bunch of men. Maybe you'd like to interview him about it.'

'That'd be handy,' said Franks. 'And congrats on the award.' He drew in on his cigarette. 'Pity Walker's such a useless bastard. He's the main reason the Yanks haven't stood and held their ground.'

'Have to say no comment to that one, old boy.' The major winked to show he agreed. 'We're under orders to show him all due respect and deference.'

'Of course. When's he arriving?'

'Should be here by now. Don't know what's kept him.'

The major took them to a company position further up the ridge, so that the reporter could interview soldiers about the prospect of spending Christmas here.

'Heard any football results?' several of them asked.

It had snowed a lot recently, creating a deceptively seasonal landscape. The mountainside shelters were warm and dry and decorated with Christmas cards and pin-ups. Parcels and letters had been pouring in. Terry Franks scribbled furiously as the men showered him with messages for home.

Marcus had hoped to see his former platoon, but they were at a different part of the front. Being amongst fighting men again gave him mixed feelings. He missed the comradeship, but he knew that if he'd stayed with them he would never have met Cho-Mi.

Within half an hour Terry Franks was ready to move on. Back at Battalion HQ, they found Lee Ho Shin taking a keen interest in the rear-link radio sets.

Marcus asked the signallers if they'd had news of Tom.

'Heard they fixed him up in Japan and sent him back. But he's with 29 Brigade, sir. If you're going there next, you might see him. Knew him in Civvy Street, did you?'

'Yes. And I was there when he got shot.' In truth Marcus was more interested in avoiding Tom than in meeting him.

Five minutes later they were driving back towards Seoul where 29 Brigade's Centurion tanks were guarding the Han River bridges. Marcus sat in the back of the jeep with Terry Franks.

'Where'd you get your translator from?' Franks asked in an aside designed to be inaudible to Lee Ho Shin and Corporal Ivory who were in the front.

'Apparently he just turned up one day, looking for work. Finding a gook that speaks English is as rare as hens' teeth, so the major snapped him up.'

'Know anything about him? They're all potential spies as far as I'm concerned.'

'Lee's all right. Says he was studying engineering in Seoul.'

'And that Korean girl you were entertaining?'

'His cousin. And I wasn't "entertaining" her. I was sketching her.'

'That's what they all say. Fancy yourself as an artist, do you?'

'I'm planning an exhibition when I get back home.'

'Really? You *are* serious. Better show me some of your stuff. Might be able to give you a plug.'

Marcus bowed his head appreciatively. 'That's very good of you.'

'Tell you what, bring 'em to the Chosan Hotel on Christmas Eve. I'll be dining with some of the others. You and the major are coming as our guests – did he tell you?'

'No, he didn't. But thanks, I will.'

As the jeep bounded from one rut to another, Marcus was aware that the journalist was still observing him. Then he felt a hand on his arm.

'A word of advice, lad.'

'Yes?'

'I'm quite a lot older than you . . . Tell me if I'm speaking out of turn.'

'Go on.'

'Well, being absolutely blunt, if you're thinking of doing it with that girl, be careful. When the brown stuff hits the proverbial here in a few days' time and everyone tries to get out of the city, you may find her tying herself to your legs. And if you've had it off with her and don't take responsibility for her, the family will be round with knives. Trust me. If you want to get your leg over, pay for it. There's no comeback then. So long as you use something. Some of the diseases . . .'

'. . . The doctors can't even identify. I know.' Marcus felt intense irritation at being told what was best for him. 'I've heard all about them.'

'Good.'

Franks continued to eye him. Marcus couldn't tell if he was being envied for his youth or pitied for his inexperience. Either way, the journalist had sullied Marcus's feelings for Cho-Mi by assuming that his interest in her was only sexual. The truth was that for the first time in his life he knew what it was to yearn for someone with every fibre of his being. To feel an ache in his stomach at the very thought of her. She'd taken possession of him.

As they neared the outskirts of Seoul, the road became blocked by refugees. Cold and bedraggled, they stumbled doggedly towards the river. Many wore the long white pyjama suits of North Korean peasants.

Franks sucked his teeth. 'Bad sign. Means the Chinese are on the move again.'

Lee Ho Shin began remonstrating with them to clear a path for the jeep. Slowly Corporal Ivory eased the vehicle through. Few seemed to notice their passing, each stooped figure concentrating on the backs of those in front.

'What d'you think will happen?' Marcus asked.

'When the Chinese get here? You're the soldier. You should know.'

'The Americans don't seem to have any fight left.'

'Because they're badly led. God knows they *can* do it. I was in the Philippines in forty-four. They need to dump Walker and put in a general with bigger balls.'

'So it'll be a bug-out again, then.'

'I imagine so.'

The river suburbs were a maze of winding streets, lined with wooden shanties, roofed in corrugated iron or thatch. People stood in small, anxious groups, some of the women carrying babies tucked into nests of cloth perched high on their backs. After a few seconds Marcus realised he'd been unconsciously scanning the faces for Cho-Mi's.

'Final tip,' Franks murmured, leaning closer to him. 'If you *are* looking for a tart, go for the refugee girls. Fresh ones, new to the game.

They're grateful for whatever you pay them and less likely to have the pox.'

'Thanks, Terry.' Marcus was beginning to dislike the journalist quite strongly.

'You know about An Kiu's Victory Dance Hall, I suppose?' Franks asked.

'No.'

'Gawd, where've you been? It's a popular pick-up joint with the lads. Quite an orderly place 'cos the cops cream off half the takings.'

'Really.' Marcus pointedly turned his head away.

Before long, the road opened out on to the broad spread of the Han River. The sandbanks by the shore were pock-marked with snow. Ice covered the river itself, except where the frozen surface had been broken by the floats of a pontoon bridge.

'Which side are the tanks on?' asked Franks.

'The other side,' said Marcus. 'We have to cross.'

'Damn. It'll take an age and then we have to get back again. Still, a picture of the lads in front of their amazingly clever Centurions will make my story.'

Marcus knew what Franks was referring to. The Centurion was more advanced than any other tank in Korea, with a unique gun-stabilising system enabling it to fire accurately while on the move.

'The MoD hopes to sell it to the Americans,' Franks told him in a loud whisper. 'Did you know that?'

'What, the Centurion?'

'No, its gun mechanism. Way ahead of them, we are. Which is why we're so shit-scared of letting a tank fall into the enemy's hands. I heard the lads lost one during the withdrawal from Pyongyang. Broke down and got left behind in the rush. Had to send special forces back to blow it up.'

'You seem to know an awful lot about it.'

'It's my job to hear about such things.' Frank tapped the side of his nose.

Corporal Ivory tucked the jeep in behind a South Korean truck convoy which was heading across the bridge. The sand flats seemed to go on for ever, then the iced-over river itself proved to be at least two hundred yards wide. In the middle was an island of sand, beyond which lay more frozen water before a final short climb back up to the road.

Using the map provided by Major Adams, it wasn't hard to locate the Hussars' base.

'And there they are,' said Terry Franks, pulling his camera out of the webbing bag slung round his neck. 'The big metal beasties.'

Marcus looked at the sleek, heavy tanks, dug into emplacements on the river bank. Lee Ho Shin was craning his neck to see them too.

Tom Sedley emerged from the 29 Brigade signals truck, straightened his back and stretched. He'd been awarded a second stripe on his return to Korea and had eight men under him this time, managing the brigade's communications with the US division that commanded them. He didn't particularly mind being back in the war, although he wished Pete Hewitt was still with him.

He lit a cigarette and sucked in a lungful of smoke while idly watching a jeep pull up. A Korean was sitting beside the driver. One of the men in the back was wearing an American helmet with the straps flapping. From the far side, a British officer climbed out. Realising suddenly who it was, Tom felt a rush of panic.

Marcus. What was he to say to someone who'd hurt him deeply by rejecting his friendship, but who'd then saved his life?

Tom remembered the moment in the copse when he'd thought Marcus would let him die. But then he hadn't. Whatever the explanation of that terrifying hesitation, Tom was alive today and wouldn't have been but for Marcus. He needed to thank him, that was for sure. Yet the other questions – the ones about Sara – were still begging for answers. No opportunity to get them could be allowed to pass.

Tom watched the two men approach, steeling himself. The one with the US helmet had a camera round his neck. Tom thought he recognised him as the reporter who'd passed through the Middlesex battalion HQ the day before the Argylls were bombed. He and Marcus were heading for the cluster of vehicles and tents that made up the Brigade Headquarters. Marcus had acquired a captain's pips, Tom noted.

When less than six feet of the snow-covered ground separated them, Tom stepped forward and made a half-hearted attempt at a salute.

'Tom!' Marcus looked rattled. 'They told me I might find you here. How the devil are you?'

Tom showed him his hands. 'Scars healing nicely, thanks. Ribs still giving me gyp, though.'

'When did you get back?'

'A few days ago. Just in time to join the bug-out by the look of it. I see you've got promotion. Congrats.'

'You too. Mine's only temporary. I'm with the Public Relations Service now.' He looked a little shamefaced when he said it. 'This is Terry Franks from the *Daily Echo*.'

Tom nodded a greeting. 'A chance to talk later?'

'Don't know. Mr Franks is on a tight timetable.'

'You can manage a few minutes, surely. So I can thank you properly for saving my life.'

'Oh, that . . . Lucky timing, that's all.' Marcus pointed to the cluster of tents they were heading for. 'Which of those is Brigade HQ?'

Tom pointed it out, realising that he would have to bide his time. Then, as the two visitors began walking again, he called after them. 'Have you heard about General Walker?'

'Is he here?' asked Franks, spinning round. 'I want to talk to him.'

'No, sir. He's dead.'

'*What?*'

'Killed in a car crash. It came over on the divisional net ten minutes ago. He'd been on his way to see 27 Brigade.'

'Bloody hell.' Terry Franks looked unnerved. 'Bang goes my interview. Any details?'

'Only that he was killed, sir. No more info than that.'

'Then we'd better be quick here, Marcus. I'll have to file a news piece tonight as well as the feature.'

Tom watched them go into the Ops tent. He finished his cigarette and settled down to wait. Whether Marcus wanted it or not, they were going to talk.

Inside the tent Marcus hovered near the entrance while Franks got briefed by the brigade's intelligence officer. General Walker's death had given him the perfect excuse to keep any chat with Tom to the minimum. Franks needed to be back in Seoul as soon as possible – as did he, so that he could lay plans for seeing Cho-Mi again. He nodded to himself. Yes. He would tell Tom about the girl. That should fill what little time they had for talking. It'd be like in the old days when he'd never tired of finding things to impress Tom with.

★

Outside, Lee Ho Shin sat in the jeep with his arms folded. He was deeply troubled. Not only would he be in bad odour with his uncle for failing to bring Cho-Mi safely back home that morning, he'd been considerably alarmed by the Englishman's obsessive interest in her and her childishly trusting response. One way or another he was going to have to ensure they didn't meet again.

He looked across at the foreign soldiers and their tanks. From the men's alien faces, most of which he found hard to tell apart, he could see that none of them cared a jot about his country or his people. He realised they didn't want to be here, most of them. Like himself they were victims of the power games played out by people far higher up the tree. But it didn't excuse the way they'd turned his country into a landscape of dereliction under the tracks of their war machines.

The tanks themselves, however, standing about twenty metres away, fascinated him with their menacing bulk. He'd never seen inside one and had a strong urge to do so. He swung his legs out of the jeep.

Terry Franks cut the briefing short, in a hurry to get pictures of the Centurions and obtain quotes from their crews. He and Marcus were led outside by the Hussars' adjutant, an Ulsterman who sounded as if he'd rather be on a horse than on anything made of steel. He'd already lined up a tank crew for Franks to meet.

While Franks got on with his work, Marcus and the adjutant stood to one side, admiring the machines.

'It's a great piece of kit,' the Ulsterman told him. 'Only disadvantage is it's as slow as a cart horse and runs on petrol instead of diesel. Which means if you get hit, you burn like a candle.'

Marcus shivered at the thought of being incinerated inside one of these monsters.

'I say . . .' the adjutant murmured. 'That translator of yours. All right, is he?'

'How d'you mean?' Then he followed the Hussar's gaze. Lee Ho Shin was climbing aboard one of the Centurions.

'Reliable?'

'Oh, I think so. He's studying engineering, apparently. So I should say he's a bit of a techno wizard.'

'Is he indeed . . .' The adjutant stepped briskly forward, waving his arms. '*Not in the turret, Corporal Leahy.*' Then he stepped back again. 'Can't be too careful, you know.'

'Of course.'

'Actually, I think I'll just go over and listen in.'

Tom had held back from approaching Marcus again, knowing he'd get short shrift while the adjutant was with him. But seeing him on his own now, he hurried across.

'Getting what you wanted?' he began, trying to sound casual.

'Yes, I think so. The reporter looks happy, which is a good sign. So tell me, what are you up to?'

'Brigade communications. Down to the battalions and up to division. And we're listening out for the enemy as well.'

'How d'you mean?'

'Monitoring their radio frequencies. It's unofficial, because all that sort of thing is down to the Americans. But whatever they're getting, they're not passing much of it on. It was my idea to try it ourselves. We've adapted one of our radios. It's not perfect but it's better than nothing.'

'And you have someone to translate it?'

'Of course.' Tom cleared his throat. This wasn't what he wanted to talk about. Marcus was doing it again. Sidelining him. 'By the way, I got a letter from Binnie the other day.'

'Ah, yes. The new Mrs Warwick. I learned about that from my mother. Never heard anything so ridiculous. She must be mad, marrying my brother.'

'She's expecting.'

'I know. But she could have got rid of the thing.'

'Hardly. She's RC.'

'Then she shouldn't have gone to bed with him in the first place, should she? Silly little sinner.'

'I always thought it was you she was keen on, anyway.' Tom bristled.

'Yes, but the point is *I* wasn't keen on *her*.' 'I suppose she decided getting her claws into Seb was better than not having a Warwick at all.'

Tom winced at his arrogance. 'Marcus, you remember what we started talking about when we met in Kimpo?'

Marcus froze. 'I've forgotten.' He looked towards the tanks, hoping to see Franks finishing his interviews.

'Then I'll remind you,' said Tom coolly. 'I was telling you how I didn't think Hagger killed Sara.'

'Oh yes.' Marcus snorted with derision. 'Well, you're on your own with that. Even his fellow prisoners seemed sure he was guilty.'

'What d'you mean?'

'Haven't you heard? They did him in. Stabbed him to death when they learned he wasn't going to hang.'

For a moment Tom was speechless. He felt a terrible loss. That solitary voice, which had never ceased to maintain its innocence of Sara's murder, silenced.

'I can't believe it.'

'Heard it from my mother. In her letter.'

'But that's terrible.'

'Not really. There's a pecking order in prison. Hagger's type – child-killers – they're at the very bottom.'

'But he claimed he didn't do it.' Tom felt derailed.

'So do most criminals.' Marcus took a step towards Franks, as if to hurry him along.

'Hang on a second.' Tom was determined not to be deflected again. 'Just explain what could possibly have persuaded my sister to go into the woods with a man like that?'

'Ah!' Marcus ignored the question. The reporter was closing his notebook into a pocket. 'We'll have to be going.'

'No. Wait. Explain it, for God's sake. It just makes no sense, Marcus.'

'Explain what?'

'Christ! Can't you stop pretending? You know bloody well what I'm talking about.'

Marcus folded his arms and pulled himself up straight, using his height advantage to look down on Tom. 'For God's sake – get it into your head, old boy. The right man was convicted and now he's dead. It's over. End of story.'

'Not for me it isn't.'

They glared at one another, but Tom knew he wasn't going to get his answer. He could go on asking until the cows came home. Marcus would never concede that his doubts about Hagger might be justified.

Seeing the beaten expression on Tom's face, Marcus began to relax. Franks had started a new conversation with the adjutant however, so he decided he'd better distract Tom a little more. 'Come on. We ought to be talking about today, not the past. Tell me about Japan.'

For a few moments Tom didn't respond. He'd understood there was no way back into Marcus's heart. It hadn't merely been a rift two years ago: the friendship had actually died then.

'Well? How was it?' Marcus demanded.

'Okay.'

'What about the nurses?'

'Why does everybody ask that?' Tom felt himself begin to blush.

'Because *most* blokes are interested in bits of skirt.'

The sneer in his voice brought Tom up short. Did Marcus, he suddenly wondered, think he was queer? Was *that* what he'd been hinting at Kimpo – the real reason for the frost that had descended on them two years ago?

'Well, since you ask,' said Tom, determined to demonstrate he wasn't homosexual, 'they weren't bad, some of them.'

This, however, was not a subject he wanted to pursue. On his last night in the hospital, Nurse Michiko had conformed to her reputation and enticed him into a linen room. But when faced with achieving the very thing he most wanted, his nerve had failed him. With trembling fingers he'd undone her blouse, but when she unbuttoned his trousers she'd found him as limp as a ball of wool.

'*Captain Warwick!*' The Hussars adjutant called over to them. 'Just taking Mr Franks to see the brigadier.'

'After that I'll want to be off,' Franks added brusquely. 'Pretty damn smartish.'

'Ready when you are,' Marcus assured him.

Marcus and Tom watched the two of them march towards the tents, Tom's mind a whirlpool of fresh insecurity.

'Looks like we'll be on the move again in a few days,' he said, desperate to fill the silence that had descended on them.

'Not too soon, I hope,' Marcus replied, delighted at being handed a way in to talking about Cho-Mi.

'It was on the divisional net this morning. They're starting the civilian evacuation of Seoul tomorrow.'

'Damn! That *is* too soon.'

'Why? What difference does it make?'

Marcus gripped him by the shoulders. 'My dear old friend. You'll never believe what's happened to me.'

'What?'

'I've met a girl.'

Tom found it hard not to laugh at Marcus's thespian earnestness. 'What, in this God-awful place? Who?'

'A creature called Cho-Mi. She's beautiful, Tom. Absolutely ravishing.'

'A *Korean* girl? You're pulling my leg.'

'No. I'm deadly serious. She and I met yesterday . . .'

'*Yesterday?*' Tom almost choked.

'And we clicked. Just like that.'

'For heaven's sake . . . What did she say to hook you so quickly? "*Do what you like to me so long as you get me out of this stinking country?*"'

Marcus shook his head. 'Absolutely not. Anyway, it wasn't words that passed between us.'

Tom laughed out loud. 'You mean . . . she doesn't speak any English? Marcus, you've gone mad.'

'You wouldn't say that if you'd ever been in love, Tom. It hits you just like that. Out of the blue. There's nothing you can do. But the terrible thing is, if Seoul empties in the next few days I might lose her for ever.'

Tom stared, trying to work out if the concern on Marcus's face was in any way genuine.

'Have you . . . you know, *done* it with her yet?'

Marcus donned an affronted look. 'That's not what it's about.'

'No?' Tom wondered for a moment if it was about Binnie. A reaction to her marrying his brother. Marcus desperate to have a girl for himself. Or maybe, like himself, he was still a virgin, urgently looking for a chance to alter that state of affairs.

There was a shout from the direction of the headquarters vehicles. Tom saw that he was being summoned.

'I've got to go. Don't do anything daft, Marcus. And don't lose any sleep over that girl. There'll be more where she came from.'

'You simply don't understand, Tom . . .'

Tom grimaced. 'Maybe I understand rather better than you think.' With that he turned and headed back to the communications truck.

As he walked, a ghastly sense of failure descended on him. Hagger's death at the hands of another prisoner had increased his conviction that an injustice had been done. Yet any hope he'd had of discovering what Marcus knew or thought about the matter had been well and truly dashed.

With a heavy heart Tom climbed back into the radio truck and put on his headphones. Suddenly he had that weird feeling again, stronger than ever, that Sara was with him in that small confined space, whispering her unintelligible nonsense through the background hiss in his ears.

Relieved to be free of Tom, Marcus kept his gaze on the brigadier's tent, urging the reporter to finish quickly so that they could head back across the river.

Suddenly Lee Ho Shin was by his side, his face alive with excitement.

'This very good tank, I think.'

'One of the best,' Marcus replied.

'I very much like to see inside, but they don't let me.'

'They're a little sensitive. Some of the equipment . . .'

'But Mister Wowick, I not interest in secrets. I only want to see how much room for soldiers.' He laughed disingenuously.

'Even so . . .'

'You help me, please? Tell them it all right for me to see inside.' His expression became grimly determined. 'You help me, Mister Wowick.'

'I'm not sure I can, Lee. It ain't my tank.'

'Yes. You must help me.' The eyes had become pebble hard. 'Because you want see my cousin again . . .'

Marcus stared at him in astonishment. The tables had suddenly been turned. No tank turret, no Cho-Mi.

'All right, you little bastard, I'll see what I can do.'

He strode to the nearest Centurion and spoke with the crew. They stuck to the rules at first, but Marcus pulled rank. Taking good care to ensure that their adjutant was still out of sight, they let the young Korean climb into the turret.

'Be quick, Lee,' Marcus snapped. Then, beneath his breath, he added, 'And don't you dare renege on your side of the bargain, you little shit.'

15

But lee ho shin did renege on it. When they returned to the PR house at the end of that afternoon he took himself off to the centre of Seoul, promising to arrange another meeting with Cho-Mi. He didn't return.

Corporal Ivory kept playing the *Mona Lisa* song, the words reaching into the room where Marcus sat disconsolately tinkering with his sketch of Cho-Mi. The lyrics seemed to reflect his own uncertainties. Was she real, this girl, or just a lovely, lonely work of art?

He still couldn't get the damned eyes right. Apart from his personal longings, that was why he needed Cho-Mi there in front of him. Needed the light and shade of her. The feel of her presence.

24 December 1950

It snowed overnight and now it was Christmas Eve. The kitchen boy didn't show up, so they breakfasted on ration packs. Marcus kept looking at his watch, wondering where Lee had got to.

'I've just heard on the radio that the Americans have a new commander,' Major Adams announced as they sat down to eat. 'General Matthew Ridgway. Has a tough reputation.'

'Yeah, but how long before he can turn his men back into fighters, sir?' asked Corporal Ivory.

'Too long. We'll lose Seoul, I fear. The retreat will continue for now.'

'Where will they all go, the South Koreans?' Marcus hoped his reason for asking was not too obvious.

'Into the sea if we don't hold the line somewhere.'

'But how will they get out of Seoul?'

'By train, a lot of them. And there are some cars around. The rest will walk.'

'They'll die in this cold weather,' said Marcus. 'In their thousands.'

'Yes, they will.'

With an aching heart Marcus pictured Cho-Mi, spreadeagled in some frozen paddy like the wretches he'd seen on the road from Pyongyang.

'Sir, would it be all right if I had a little drive around the city to see what's happening?'

The major gave him a knowing look.

'Sorry. Can't allow that. We may have escorts to do. And just remember, Captain Warwick, the Korean populace are not our problem, however sympathetic we may be towards their plight. We're here to fight a war, not go trolling around on some humanitarian mission.' He narrowed his eyes. 'Even if the life you're concerned about belongs to a reasonably attractive young female.'

As the day passed with no sign of Lee Ho Shin, it began to dawn on Marcus that the family might already have fled, Lee included. He felt a terrible emptiness, as though a once-in-a-lifetime opportunity had slipped from his hands.

Then, in the middle of the afternoon, the translator turned up, sullen-faced.

'Well?' Marcus asked, when he'd got him on his own. 'Where's Cho-Mi?'

'I don't know.'

'What d'you mean, you little rat? We had a deal.'

Lee claimed not to have seen her. And when asked about the situation in town and his relatives' plans for leaving the city, he was non-committal. Marcus's frustration was absolute.

It transpired that they didn't have any press visitors that day. Christmas had started early for the media. The major told him about the invitation to join the scribes for dinner at the Chosan Hotel and said that tomorrow they would return there to eat turkey and Christmas pudding. War permitting. It all seemed so unreal.

The snow had kept away during the day, but as evening drew in it began to fall again and the temperature plummeted.

The Chosan Hotel had survived the war intact, serving as a billet for senior UN officials and American staff officers. An island of civilisation in a sea of devastation and misery. Inside its dining room, four-course dinners were consumed, accompanied by fine wines, while outside, refugees trudged past in forty degrees of frost.

Marcus had never been in the hotel before. A fuggy warmth hit him. The lobby was crowded with uniformed westerners, many of them drunk already. It felt like the Last Chance Saloon and by night's end, he guessed, the bars would be dry.

They'd brought Lee Ho Shin with them to the city centre, with the intention that he should walk home from the hotel, after a Christmas drink. The Korean recoiled at what he saw. This was not a place for the natives of the country. The extravagant revelry of these foreign armies disgusted him. As Major Adams tried to lead him to the bar he backed away.

'I go now.'

'Come on. Don't mind them. Have a drink. You lot love alcohol, I know that for a fact.'

'My family. They wait for me.'

'Just a quick one.'

'No . . .' Lee Ho Shin pushed through the throng towards the door, shouting 'Happy Christmas' over his shoulder, but his eyes bore no sign of goodwill.

'Day after tomorrow,' Adams shouted back. 'In the office as usual. Right? Don't let me down.'

But Lee Ho Shin had been swallowed by the crowd.

'Probably the last we'll see of that little bugger,' Adams muttered.

'Why'd you say that, sir?' Marcus asked, devastated that his link to Cho-Mi might have been lost for ever.

'I paid him until the end of next week. Christmas goodwill and all that. Little eyes big as plums when I handed over the cash.'

Marcus's heart sank. There would be no happy Christmas for him.

The bar was raucous with drunken soldiers of all ranks, clutching heavily made-up Korean girls. The major decided they should head straight for the dining room, in the hope that the journalists had commandeered a table. In the jam-packed entrance to the restaurant they came across Terry Franks, trying to attract the attention of a waiter.

'The sods have overbooked,' he growled in Marcus's ear. His breath reeked of spirits. 'Still, nice to see you, old boy. And happy Christmas. Did you bring your pictures?'

'Sorry. I forgot.'

'Maybe just as well in this madhouse.'

A table was eventually secured and Marcus made a determined effort to get in the party mood. He drank two large glasses of beer in quick succession, then switched to wine when the food came, but the journalists were far ahead of him. And he lacked their stamina.

The food was remarkable. Marcus had never eaten foie gras before and felt like an ingénu amongst these experienced bon viveurs. The table rocked with laughter as the four reporters capped each other's anecdotes. Major Adams joined in, but Marcus felt out of it. The other men were all twenty years his senior. And his mind, anyway, was elsewhere.

Over the coffee and brandies the bragging turned to sex, with lurid descriptions of whores encountered during decades of foreign travel. Then Terry Franks sprang his Christmas surprise, announcing to the assembled company that the reporters had arranged for a couple of girls to be waiting for them back at their house.

'I suggest we settle our bill, piss off back there and let the delightful creatures entertain us.' He beamed like Santa Claus. 'They'll have their work cut out, but we're paying them enough!' He laughed uproariously. Marcus noticed the major looking a little uncomfortable. 'Oh, don't worry, old boy, it's on the house and we bought a gross of Durex this afternoon.' Cackling, Franks clapped Adams on the shoulder.

'Well, in that case . . .'

Then they all turned to the youngster in their midst.

'Marcus . . .?' Major Adams chuckled, a little embarrassed.

'If it's all the same with you, sir, I'll head back to the . . .'

'Of course. Take the jeep. I'll see you tomorrow morning sometime. Don't wait up.'

A ripple of laughter ran round the table. Marcus sensed relief that the young 'un wouldn't be there to witness the older men's antics. When the waiter came with the bill Marcus decided the moment had arrived.

'Well, goodnight, all of you. And thanks for a most amazing dinner and a thoroughly enjoyable evening.'

Terry Franks gripped Marcus's arm and pulled his face close to his own. 'Remember what I told you yesterday. Trust your Uncle Terry. He knows what he's talking about.'

'Thanks.' Marcus forced a grin and backed away from the table. 'Goodnight, all.'

Outside, the icy wind took his breath away. Snow was driving sideways. He pulled up the fur-lined hood of his parka and turned his back to the gale, trying to remember where he'd parked the jeep. Corporal Ivory was on a night out with some other NCOs and had given him the key.

But more urgent than finding the vehicle was his need to relieve himself. Marcus saw a couple of servicemen urinating against the wall of the hotel. When they'd finished he followed suit. The wind froze the urine as it left his body, adding a new layer to the cake of yellow-brown ice on the ground. In the cold, the alcohol was doing dreadful things to his vision.

There were at least a dozen jeeps parked in front of the Chosan, each with a guard organised by the hotel. After several false starts, Marcus finally found the right vehicle. He offered the guard a banknote but was badgered for more. Marcus had no idea how much he gave him in the end, but the man took it and left. He lifted the bonnet and replaced the rotor arm in the distributor, then got into the driving seat and pressed the starter button. The frozen engine laboured as if at death's door, but eventually it coughed into life.

Marcus sat there for several minutes, letting the machine warm up, while trying to decide what to do. A part of him regretted not going with the others, but he knew he couldn't rest until he discovered what had happened to Cho-Mi. And without Lee Ho Shin's help, he didn't know where to begin. When they'd visited the restaurant two days ago he'd blindly followed instructions. Nevertheless, he decided, come what may, to try to find his way there.

Seoul was a blacked-out city with no electric power, except in places like the Chosan where they had generators. The jeep's headlights picked out what looked like bundles of rags huddling in the ruins – refugees holding on in the hope that the war would turn. Sometimes Marcus saw faces lit by the yellow glow of bonfires, round blotches of despair.

Soon he was on the wide dual carriageway that led to the Capitol building, a point they'd passed when Lee had directed him to his uncle's premises two afternoons ago. He stopped the car to orientate himself. In the dark it was almost impossible to tell what was what. He was pretty sure they'd headed south-east before, but with no sun or stars to guide him he had no clue where that was. Then he remembered the compass he'd left in the car the day before and scrabbled under the seat to find it.

With alcohol-fuelled confidence, Marcus set off, his hopes rocketing as he recognised the tilted spire of a church half demolished by the war. Then the streets got narrower. He selected turnings by instinct rather than certainty, praying that some supernatural force would guide him.

Suddenly his way was blocked by rubble. A large building had collapsed into the road. Unless it had just happened, it meant he'd gone the wrong way. As he swung the car round and tried another route, the lights picked out hunched figures laden with possessions, moving in a slow stream. Towards the river, he realised. The migration was continuing around the clock.

After several more dead ends, he finally acknowledged that he was lost. There was no sign of the commercial area with its cafés and empty shops that Lee had led him to. Instead he emerged on to the banks of the Han. The snow had become a blizzard. Suddenly a ghoulish face pressed against the window of the jeep. It was just recognisable as female, the mouth an oval of lipstick.

'*Go for the refugee girls. Grateful for anything you give them . . .*'

For a millisecond Marcus considered opening the door, then he shuddered and drove on. There were people everywhere, tramping towards the bridges or sheltering beneath carts and awnings. He reached a broad avenue and turned along it, back towards the city centre. Then, with a heavy heart, he decided to give up his search.

It took twenty minutes to find his way through the ruined city to the suburb where he lived. He stopped outside the PR house and turned off the engine and lights, feeling very sorry for himself.

The snow had stopped falling by the time Marcus pulled himself together, but when he got out it crunched thickly beneath his boots. The house would be cold. The fire had gone out that afternoon and with no boy to fetch fuel they'd not been able to relight it. But they'd left an oil lamp burning inside and Marcus longed for its meagre comfort.

As he climbed the steps to the front door, he faltered, suddenly afraid. There was a figure huddled in the porch.

'Lee?' he croaked, heart racing.

No response. Then slowly the figure rose from the ground. It wavered as if lacking the strength to stand.

He drew closer and a mittened hand pulled back the cloth obscuring the face.

It was Cho-Mi.

16

HANDS TREMBLING, MARCUS unlocked the door. He didn't trust himself to speak, and there was nothing he could say that Cho-Mi would understand. She was shivering uncontrollably. Suddenly, confronted with her like this, he didn't know what to do. Could he hug her, or would it offend? The cultural divide felt like a chasm.

It was warmer inside the house, but not warm enough.

'Cho-Mi . . .' he whispered, helplessly.

'Mah-coos . . .' she replied, teeth chattering.

He tugged open the front of his parka and pulled her to him, letting the warmth of his body get to her. He held her tighter and tighter until the trembling abated. The snow on her hood melted from the warmth of his body and he pushed the cloth back. Her hair felt like silk against his cheek. She'd perfumed it.

'Cho-Mi . . . I love you. Do you understand?'

Marcus had never spoken these words to anyone before, and as he said them he wondered if he meant it. Love. Such a *big* word. She said something back, which sounded soft and endearing.

'*I* know . . .' he said, common sense returning at last. 'I'll light the cooking stove. We'll have a brew-up. Hot drink.' He made a movement with his hand, denoting the tipping of a mug into his mouth, but it did nothing to help her comprehension. 'I'll show you.'

Marcus led Cho-Mi to the room used as a kitchen and sat her on a chair. The stove was an American contraption which burned any fuel.

For the last few weeks they'd been using petrol from the jeeps. It not only cooked but provided warmth.

'This'll help,' said Marcus. He sensed that it was important to keep talking, even if she didn't understand. It established a normality. He struck a match and the burner lit with a *whoosh*. When he filled a kettle from the jerrycan of water in the corner, Cho-Mi seemed to come to life, taking it from him and placing it on the cooker. A tentative smile flickered on her lips. Marcus noticed her eyelids fluttering as she held her hands close to the stove for warmth.

'Do you like chocolate?' he asked.

She frowned.

'Perhaps you don't have it in Korea. Look. I'll show you.'

He went to the corner again and picked up one of the brown cardboard ration boxes stacked against the wall.

'The C-4 individual ration,' he said, showing her the box. Her incomprehension grew. 'It's inside. *Army food.*' He articulated the words slowly and carefully in some insane hope that by doing so she would understand.

A green tin contained the main-course rations and Marcus put it aside. Then he opened one of the smaller tins and pulled out the solid block of drinking chocolate wrapped in cellophane.

'We put this in hot water and Bob's your uncle.'

Cho-Mi turned it over in her hands.

'Here. Try one of these.' Marcus opened a pack of custard creams and handed her one. She bit into it and smiled. 'Good, eh?'

She was avoiding his gaze. Probably afraid of him, he decided. Not surprisingly. For a girl from a good home to have made her way through the blacked-out city to see a man of another race was extraordinarily daring. It didn't occur to him to wonder why she'd come, but he felt acutely responsible for her. And not a little anxious.

'I want to look at you.'

Very gently Marcus touched Cho-Mi's chin and lifted her face. She pressed his hand to her skin. Her palm was warm from the stove.

'I've been thinking about you all the time, do you know that? Ever since that first moment in the restaurant.'

Easy to admit such things, to expose his feelings when she didn't understand what he was saying. He could give voice to anything that came into his head, without fear of the consequences.

'Oh . . . if only we could *talk*. I'd give anything to know what goes on in that pretty head.'

She said something to him. Her words flowed like a gurgling stream, but she was eyeing the other tins, not him.

'You're hungry? Of course . . . Your family – what's happened to them? All gone? You're not the only one left in Seoul, are you? And did you stay here because of me?'

The last question tumbled out, more a reflection of Marcus's fear of having responsibility for the girl than excitement at the thought that she might love him.

He opened the green main ration tin. The three smaller tins inside it had their contents stencilled on the sides.

'Meat and noodles,' he muttered. 'That's disgusting. You'd hate it. But this one's all right.' He held it out. 'Frankfurters and beans. Like to try it?'

Marcus took Cho-Mi's eager but incomprehensible reply as a yes. The water was hot enough to melt the drinking chocolate, so he made that first, then emptied the beans and sausages into a billycan. She seemed uncomfortable with him doing all this for her, constantly trying to interfere.

Soon there was almost a feeling of warmth in the room and they each took off their outer layer of clothing and dropped it on the floor. Beneath her thick coat Cho-Mi was wearing the same high-waisted dress and soft jacket she'd had on when she sat for him.

'Ah . . .' Marcus said, understanding at last why she'd come. 'Same clothes as last time. You're a perfect model.'

She ate the beans and frankfurters straight from the billycan, using a spoon. From the speed with which she consumed them, Marcus guessed it was her first meal of the day. He cursed Lee Ho Shin for being so reticent that morning. *Had* her family abandoned her? And was it because of *him*?

When she'd finished the food, he fished more packets from the box.

'Salted crackers? They're pretty boring but apparently they contain some nourishment. Or there's some candy.'

Cho-Mi ate the crackers, then shook her head at the offer of more. Her gaze was cast down. Waiting.

For what? Marcus wondered. For him to make a move on her? He dismissed the notion, because he didn't want to think of her like that.

This wasn't one of Terry Franks's whores. No. If this was the true love he thought it might be, he wanted it to be right. To be decent.

Then, all of a sudden, it dawned on him how stupid he was being. The rules of behaviour he'd been brought up with didn't apply in a ruined city where morality had lost its meaning. He was wasting time. Corporal Ivory might be back sooner than expected.

'Would you like me to kiss you?' Marcus asked, her incomprehension stripping him of his inhibitions. But despite the freedom he'd just granted himself, he felt strangely paralysed. There was something he needed to do first. To give her what he guessed she'd come for.

Cho-Mi tensed as he rose from his chair and left the room. When he returned with his sketch pad, a smile flickered.

'Light's not exactly ideal,' Marcus said, turning up the wick of the lamp to a point just short of where it would smoke. 'But beggars can't be choosers, can they?' He reached out and lifted her chin again, then touched a forefinger between her eyes and drew it in his direction to indicate that she should look at him. She understood and slipped into the pose she'd adopted the day before.

She was pathetically beautiful. More so than ever in the soft oil-light. The shadows it cast gave Marcus the third dimension he'd wanted. Stroke by stroke, the face on the page began to radiate the likeness he'd been struggling to achieve. His pencil flew back and forth, embellishing and changing, bringing life to the flatness of the paper until perfection stared at him.

He looked up and beamed adoringly at her. It was an incredible feeling. A lightness in the head. The way romantic novels talked of love. And now it was happening to him.

Suddenly, without a word, Cho-Mi leaned forward and snatched the pad from his lap.

'Careful,' Marcus said. 'That's a work of art, that is.'

She turned it round, then got up and held the drawing to the light, her back to him. For a long time she stood there without moving, entranced by the image of herself. Marcus stood up and put his hands on her waist. She tensed at his touch.

'What d'you think?' His mouth was by her ear.

Cho-Mi didn't move, still gazing at the picture.

'If only you could speak English. If only you could tell me whether you're feeling what I'm feeling.' Marcus slipped his hands round to her front and pressed her against his stomach. She remained rigid, not breathing. He was hard now and he wanted her to feel it. To *know* of his desire, since she would never understand him telling her about it. He kissed her neck. Salty skin that was incredibly soft. He breathed in her smell, a mix of perfume and something indefinably womanly.

'I want you to understand that I love you,' he whispered, almost believing at that moment it was true. 'How can I make you understand that?'

Slowly she softened against him, going limp in his arms. Fired up by her powerlessness, Marcus reached forward and took the sketch pad from her, laying it on his chair. Then he turned Cho-Mi to face him. Her eyes were downcast and remained so when he raised her chin to kiss her. She kept her mouth shut as his lips brushed hers. Then, slowly, they parted.

As his tongue probed hers, salty from the crackers she'd eaten, Marcus knew he was on an unstoppable slide towards an act that he'd never before experienced. He would fill her with his love, so she could never be in doubt of it. Her hands moved across his back, tentatively, fearfully. She was holding her breath, as if to let it go would be to lose control of everything. He tried to part her clothing, searching for the shape of her flesh, the curve of her hips.

Then he was kissing her neck again, pulling frantically at the jacket. Peeling away the layers of fabric until her small white breasts were there for him to see and to touch.

She kept saying things to him, a stream of words that he took for passion.

The skirt was a sheath of cloth which he struggled with. She was crying now – tears, he told himself, of joy.

Then Cho-Mi was naked. A bony body with ribs showing and a dark smudge of hair below her belly. Marcus unbuttoned his trousers and let them fall, pressing her to him, feeling her flesh directly against his instead of through cloth. He manoeuvred her to the floor, laying her down on the coats they'd dropped earlier. Desperate not to come too soon, he tried to push her legs apart, but she clamped them together.

'Mah-coos. Mah-coos!'

There was fear in her voice. He knew she was wanting him to stop, but it was too late. He covered her mouth to silence her. Dark images filled his head. A terrible déjà vu. About to explode, he forced her legs

155

apart with his knees. She stopped struggling, her arm crooked round his neck. Biting his lip to hold himself back, he reached the threshold he'd never passed before, feeling it against the end of his shaft.

'I love you,' Marcus choked. 'Love you, love you.'

He pushed and the barrier broke. Cho-Mi jerked with the pain and he was through, shooting his love into her insides.

17

CHO-MI CRIED, HER whole body shaking. Marcus lay still, drained of all strength, feeling her trembling beneath him. There was no more need for words. He visualised his seed permeating her body and suffusing her with his love. He was still hard and held himself in like a plug, fearing that her feelings for him would drain away if he withdrew.

'Oh, my little darling,' he breathed. He badly wanted her to stop crying. 'I'm sorry if it hurt. But . . . but . . . love always hurts, so they say.'

Futile, silly words. She began to push against him and he realised that she was probably still in pain. So he withdrew. There was blood on the coat beneath her. He stood up and poured warm water into a billycan for them to clean themselves up.

'I'm sorry I hurt you,' he repeated, unsettled by her obvious distress. Yet any guilt he felt was counterbalanced by a glow of triumph. He'd become a man. Got one step further along the chain of life than Richard Carter had.

Cho-Mi sniffed back her sobs as she dressed. Marcus bent and kissed her mouth. She responded and then smiled at him, blinking away the last of her tears. They sat on the chairs again and looked at one another. Then she averted her gaze, waiting expectantly.

There was a crackle of gunfire outside, some distance away, but it made them both look towards the door. Then Marcus's brain began to work again. He couldn't keep her here. Didn't want her here when the major or Corporal Ivory got back. What he'd done – *they*'d done – was a secret between them and must remain so.

'I'll take you home,' he said.

She pulled herself up straight, her face contorting in a supreme effort to communicate what it was she wanted.

'It's going to be all right, Cho-Mi. We *will* be together. Somehow. After this is over, I'll find you. Wherever you are. And . . . and I tell you what – you can find *me*. Through the army. Between us, with you trying and me trying, we'll find each other. I promise.'

Cho-Mi concentrated hard, as if the sounds might suddenly convey a meaning. Then, with a crinkling of her brow, she put her hands together and pressed them against the side of her head.

'You're tired,' Marcus murmured.

She stood up and opened the door into the room where he slept.

'No . . .' he protested feebly.

She saw the two beds inside and laid herself down on one of them. Marcus followed her in.

'No, Cho-Mi. You can't. That's Major Adams's bed, anyway . . .'

He crouched and she tried to pull him down beside her. But instead he grabbed her shoulders and shook her.

'No. You can't stay here. *You-Can-Not-Stay-Here* . . .'

His tone of voice conveyed his meaning. She must have known it all along, but had decided to try it on. With her gaze cast down, she followed Marcus back into the room where he'd made love to her.

'I'm going to drive you back to your family,' Marcus told her solemnly. 'You must guide me. *Tell-Me-Which-Way-To-Go* . . .' He gestured with his hands.

Cho-Mi's distress at being turned out was obvious and it affected him. 'We won't be apart for long,' he whispered, hugging her tightly, with his chin resting on the top of her head. 'We must put our coats on now.' He picked hers up and held it for her, but she twisted away from him and snatched up his sketch pad.

Marcus was aghast. He'd promised her that she could have the portrait when it was finished and now it was. But that picture might be all he would ever have to remember her by.

'I'll make a copy of it and bring it to you, Cho-Mi. I won't go to bed. Work on it tonight and bring it to the restaurant in the morning.'

But the tears spilling down her cheeks told him it was hopeless. Gently he tore the page from his sketch book and rolled it into a tube.

The journey through the dark streets of Seoul passed in silence, except when Cho-Mi came to life to direct him into yet another side turning. Marcus drove with a heavy heart. His euphoria had evaporated.

When they reached the restaurant, it was in darkness. For a moment Marcus thought of trying to get Lee Ho Shin out of bed, if he was there, to interrogate him about the family's plans to flee. But looking at the shuttered house, he was struck by how alien it was. There was a culture here that he knew nothing about. The culture to which Cho-Mi belonged.

He realised then that it could never work between them. Never in a million years.

Cho-Mi's tears were flowing again. Marcus wiped them with his gloved hand, then kissed her moistened cheeks.

'I love you, Cho-Mi,' he said, through clenched teeth. 'Always will. Whatever happens.'

He watched her crunch through the frozen snow, with the rolled-up portrait clutched to her chest. The door, it turned out, wasn't locked and she disappeared inside.

He was never to see her again.

18

Christmas Day 1950

ON CHRISTMAS MORNING Tom awoke to the sound of someone singing 'Silent Night'. He got a lump in his throat thinking about Sara tugging presents from her stocking when they were young. He hoped his mother had gone to stay with friends, so as to be away from the house at this difficult time.

Then he began to wonder where Marcus was that morning, imagining some cosy billet in a warm house, attended by Korean servants. Officers had standards and, whenever they could, they stuck to them. Maybe the girl he'd fallen for would be there. Maybe she'd spent the night in his bed. He didn't like the thought of Marcus succeeding with such intimacies after his own embarrassing failure in Japan.

The men of 29 Brigade to which Tom was now attached had been told to have a lie-in. After reveille the headquarters sergeants came round with tea. Then everybody opened their parcels from home. One of Tom's was from his mother. Chocolate biscuits, tea and socks. Binnie had sent a card with a snapshot of the wedding. She looked so grown-up standing there in her long dress with a morning-suited Sebastian on her arm. It made Tom feel achingly homesick.

The morning passed quietly, with prayers and a talk from the brigadier, who then toured the camp saying hello to as many of the men as he could. The officers were doing their best to make the day special.

A huge marquee had been brought in from somewhere and they ate their Christmas lunch in shifts. Turkey, Christmas pudding and mince pies. Nothing was missed. And all served by the officers.

Afterwards Tom joined several of the men taking a stroll along the banks of the Han River. The pontoon bridge they were guarding was only for the military, but a short distance away one of the few iron-girder structures still standing was thick with a slow-moving mass of humanity. It looked as if the entire population of Seoul was on that bridge, pushing handcarts or wilting under those ubiquitous wooden shoulder frames, laden with all they owned.

At the church parade earlier, the padre had reminded them that Christmas was to celebrate the birth of Jesus Christ, 'who came on earth to save the world'.

Which world? Tom asked himself. Because it wasn't the one he was looking at.

The following week passed agonisingly slowly for Marcus. Lee Ho Shin never returned to the press house in the suburbs and the city was emptying fast. Cho-Mi was constantly in Marcus's thoughts. One day he found his way through the maze of streets to the restaurant where she'd lived, to discover that it had become a charred shell. Heart in mouth, he looked around for someone to ask what had happened here. Eventually an American patrol came by.

'We heard two different stories,' the GI told him. 'One was that it was an accident. The fire under the floor they use for heating?'

'Yes?'

'Got out of control. Then the other thing we heard was some rival set fire to it. Or criminals demanding money. Either way, they all fried.'

'The whole family?'

The soldier drew a finger across his throat and drove off.

Marcus told himself it wasn't true. The soldier had got it wrong and the family had simply destroyed the place when they fled, to prevent the communists having it. Any other explanation was too appalling to contemplate.

Soon anarchy broke out in the town. Police were amongst the worst of the looters, fleeing the city with packs bursting with silver. Seoul burned as it emptied. Thousands of refugees lit fires by the river as they waited to be allowed to cross, the flimsy wooden houses of nearby ghettos being broken up for fuel so that the people could survive another day.

As New Year approached, the journalists began to leave. Terry Franks dropped in to say they were heading south with the remains of the vodka liberated from the Russian Embassy in Pyongyang.

On New Year's Day itself, the Chinese finally launched their attack. The 'great bug-out' became a grey-green stream of tanks and trucks, jeeps and half-tracks, passing through the centre of Seoul.

Orders finally came for the press office to close. They packed their equipment into two jeeps, bribed an American quartermaster to give them extra cans of fuel and headed for the river, where they found the military retreat blocked by refugees. Prevented from using the bridges, thousands of Seoul's citizens had taken to the ice, walking their way to safety, before clogging the roads on the other side.

Marcus watched a loudspeaker plane circle the river, ordering people not to cross. But the hordes ignored it. Then mortars opened up, shattering the ice.

'This is awful,' said Major Adams. 'How can we call ourselves human beings?'

With a sick feeling in the pit of his stomach, Marcus imagined Cho-Mi in there – if she hadn't been burned alive – floundering in the icy water. He felt that the least he could do was to record everything he saw, but there was no time and his fingers were too cold to hold a pencil. He let his gaze roam over the scene, hoping it would sear itself into his memory so he could paint it later. Because he badly wanted the world to know about this. All those smug people sitting in their cosy homes in Wood Park – he wanted *them* to share the shame that he and all the UN soldiers must have felt.

From the south side of the river Tom watched the city burn. Thick swathes of smoke blotted out the mountains behind. The communists would inherit a ruin.

The human suffering he was witnessing was on a scale he'd never thought possible. He imagined Sara watching it with him, through his eyes. Sharing his horror. She'd been in his thoughts more and more in recent weeks. He suspected that she would always be lurking there, in some corner of his mind. An unseen companion determined not to let him forget her. The unanswered questions about her death were becoming an obsession. Marcus was wrong. It was not all in the past and never could be for Tom.

29 Brigade was preparing to leave. Tom helped pack up the

equipment and secure it for the next leg of the retreat. Eventually, he surmised, the tide would turn in Korea and the UN would drive the Chinese back. It had to happen that way, because the Western world couldn't afford to let it be otherwise. It would take time, but they had plenty of it.

And so did he.

The rest of his life, if necessary – to find out what had really happened on that day his sister died.

1982

19

Sunday, 2 May 1982

THE NEWSPAPERS WERE ecstatic about the RAF's bombing of the runway at Stanley Airfield. 'A remarkable feat of long-range aviation.' 'One in the eye for the Argies.' Fleet Street had gone Falklands mad since Galtieri's invasion, with the tabloids even sponsoring missiles to shoot down Argentine aircraft.

Tom Sedley put on his reading glasses and cast a despairing eye over the headlines. He opposed this war like he had most others. Men's lives blown away so that politicians could claim glory. Arguments about 'points of principle' tended to be lost on him after Korea.

After a few minutes he folded the paper and put it with his suitcase in the hall of the small terraced house, to read later. This was a day he'd not been looking forward to. The start of a week that was bound to be upsetting. He checked his appearance in the mirror, turning his head from side to side. Not for the first time he wondered whether he should touch up his greying temples.

For the past twenty years Tom Sedley had lived in a bubble of seclusion in the Regency elegance of Cheltenham, his life conveniently shrouded by the veil of secrecy that he was obliged to adopt because of his work at GCHQ, the government's electronic espionage centre. It had shielded him from the questions of friends and family, his mother amongst them. Did he have girlfriends? Men friends? Why wasn't he married? When he'd seen his mother it had always been at Wood Park. Never in the twenty years he'd been in Cheltenham had he let her come to visit him.

Tom checked that he'd not left any taps running, or the gas on, then closed the front door and carried his bag to the car. It was a bright day. The first good one after a week of rain. He sniffed the air, hoping for a trace of summer, but there was still a chill in it.

His mother had died the previous week and the small private funeral had taken place last Monday. A memorial service was planned at the actors' church, St Paul's in Covent Garden, in a few months' time, at which there'd be a collection for the Alzheimer's Society. The profession remembered Maureen Stuart fondly, even though her mental decline meant that she hadn't performed on stage or screen for many years.

Her death had been longed for – by herself, by him and by her companion of twenty-two years, her dresser Emily Harris. Senile dementia was a cruel illness that turned love into despair, but the whole awful business was over now. Tom had dreaded the aftermath of the death, expecting Emily to ask to remain in the house that had been her home as much as his mother's in recent years. In the event she'd left Heathside Close without a murmur, moving to Eastbourne to share a flat with a sister. She'd been planning it for a long time, she'd said.

Tom slung his bag on to the back seat of the Renault and climbed behind the wheel. He reckoned that it should take less than two hours to reach the North London suburb where he'd been brought up. Time had been frozen in Heathside Close, with his mother turning the house into a shrine to Sara, photographs in every room. He was not looking forward to being sucked back into that unhappy period of his life, but the administration of the estate was his responsibility. There was no one else.

The house was to be sold. May was a good month, the estate agents claimed. Half the proceeds would come to Tom, the rest being ear-marked for various actors' charities, with a handsome bequest to Emily. But before 16 Heathside Close could be put on the market it had to be cleared. Fifty years of clutter removed. Possessions and memories from his parents' lives, from his own childhood and from his sister's.

There were a few small pieces of antique furniture that he wanted for Cheltenham. Emily had already taken a chair and a table. The rest of the stuff was to be auctioned, or given to a charity shop. The furniture wasn't a problem for him, but the drawers full of junk were. Letters, newspaper clippings dating back to 1948 – Tom was determined to destroy them all. He had no wish to be swallowed up again by the tragic events that had blighted his teens and early twenties. Yet he knew it would all have to be gone through. Just in case. The next few days would be distressing, but he had taken a week's leave to cope with it.

Tom left the outskirts of Cheltenham and headed down the A40 towards London. Tom loved the Cotswolds. Felt cosseted by the damp, green countryside and the yellow stone of the villages. A landscape that had absorbed him easily and helped him eventually shake off his mentally damaging obsession about finding the truth behind Sara's murder.

He turned on the radio, pressing buttons until organ music boomed from the speakers. A church service. He'd never been religious, but he liked the music God inspired. Tom occasionally filled in at the local church when the regular organist was away.

There'd been no more than a dozen mourners at his mother's funeral. His father had died several years earlier and the schism between Tom's parents was so deep that Michael Sedley probably wouldn't have attended anyway, even if he'd still been alive. A few of Tom's mother's closest friends had been there, and a couple of the neighbours, people whom he hadn't met before. The families he used to know well, Binnie's and Marcus's, had all moved away.

Since his mother's decline into senility, his infrequent visits to Heathside Close had increased to once a month – Sunday lunch, mostly – more out of support for her companion-turned-carer than because it did anything for her. Recently, she hadn't even recognised him, claiming that her son Tom was a child, not a middle-aged man.

Emily Harris had moved in with his mother a few months after the divorce. Tom had returned from National Service to find his father living alone in a one-room flat in Manchester, muttering salaciously about the nature of Maureen's relationship with her dresser. Tom had sided with his mother, preferring her company to that of his father. And the suggestion that there was anything between Emily and his mother other than friendship, he'd put down to spite.

At Oxford, he stopped to buy food. The traffic was bad on the ring road there, so the journey to Heathside Close took a little longer than planned. When he finally arrived, he parked the car in the garage, then stood in the front garden, weighed down by shopping bags. The flower beds would need tidying before prospective purchasers came round, Tom realised.

He turned, gazing beyond the overgrown privet hedge at the house opposite. Once he'd known it almost as well as his own. He half expected

Marcus to wave at him from a window. Their bedrooms had faced one another across the street and they'd signalled in secret code when they were boys. It was nearly thirty years since they'd seen one another, two years after their return from Korea, when Marcus staged his exhibition.

Tom remembered the orderliness of the Warwick house. Such a feeling of certainty when he went in there. The house was like a well-oiled machine. Always food for an unplanned lunch in the fridge, biscuits in the tin, orange squash in the larder – unlike his own home where domestic planning was erratic at best. Marcus's father was tall, with neat crinkly hair that was never out of place. He always *knew* about things. Nothing surprised him. Marcus's mother had well brushed honey-blonde hair, Tom remembered, and was invariably perched at one end of the sofa with a book in her hand.

He turned towards his own porch, but let his gaze linger on the house next door where Binnie had lived. Her father had always been whistling. Tunefully and enthusiastically. Always making things, too. Carpentry was both a hobby and an obsession. The garage had become a workshop filled with lathes and power saws. And Binnie's mother? He tried to remember her, but a face didn't come. She was permanently in her husband's shadow, he seemed to recall. An ashen figure, wreathed in cigarette smoke, who'd never got over the death of her ten-year-old younger child from complications following flu.

Tom approached the oak-panelled front door and put the key in the lock. Everything about his own house carried a memory, too. The doorbell was mechanical, operated by a pull-down lever, its jangling a permanent reminder of the handbell that the teachers had rung in his prep-school playground.

He turned the key and pushed. The hall floor was of dark parquet in a diamond pattern, and gleamed with polish. Emily had been a good housekeeper. An umbrella stand made from a well-buffed shell case stood next to a mahogany side table. The carpeted staircase was to the left, and beyond it the doors to the living and dining rooms. He heard the steady tick of the long-case clock, which had been passed down from his grandfather.

As the emptiness of the place hit Tom, his eyes began to moisten. This was going to be *awful*.

He quickly took the shopping bags into the kitchen, telling himself to get on with things. Not allow himself to brood. Emily had defrosted the fridge and left the door open to ventilate. He put the perishables inside, switched it back on, then plugged in the kettle. Time for a brew. Old habits died hard.

He took his mug of tea into the living room, which was spacious, with two plump sofas and matching armchairs in pale green. The wood-block floor was partially hidden by a large Persian carpet. Framed prints hung on the walls, several of them theatre posters. At the far end of the room, French windows opened on to the garden. Tom unlocked them. It was cool outside, but he was desperate to blow away the mustiness of the place. In the flower bed beyond the patio, late tulips bloomed, their petals beginning to drop.

At the end of the lawn stood a little summer house. It had been a good garden for children, this. A good house too, with its loft large enough for a model railway on a huge trestle table. The loft . . . He'd forgotten the loft. Most of it was floorboarded but under the eaves there were spaces between the rafters, stuffed with heaven knew what. He had a nasty feeling that he might uncover boxes of old cowboy outfits.

Turning away from the window, Tom approached the walnut-veneered bureau, deciding it was as good a place as any to start. He'd gone through it superficially a week ago, searching for financial papers that the lawyers needed for probate. In the top drawer was a folder of press cuttings from the time of Sara's death, which he'd glanced at only briefly. It was his father who'd collected them, forlornly poring over the articles in the hope they would help him understand why the tragedy had befallen the family.

The lower drawers were full, the bottom one stuffed with photographs. They would be the worst problem to sort out. Pictures were so hard to destroy, each with the power to stir memories, some happy, many unwelcome. The drawer above contained letters. Some were copies of those sent to charities, explaining why his mother couldn't open flower shows any more. All of them would have to be gone through. Every letter glanced at, in case it was important. Tom peeled off a rubbish bag from the roll he'd bought in the supermarket and set to work.

Time passed more easily than Tom had expected. After dealing with most of the contents of the bureau he set to work upstairs in his old bedroom, which had become a box room in recent years. Soon several sacks of rubbish were lined up on the patio.

A pork pie and a supermarket salad served as a late lunch, which he washed down with a beer, sitting on the steps of the summer house. Electric mowing machines whined in the neighbouring gardens, people leading their lives as they had when he was young, half out in the open, half behind closed doors. He wondered morosely how many more betrayals were under way nearby? How many of this generation of families would be split by divorce or tragedy?

Two doors away, children played, their squeaky voices bubbling with glee. Tom smiled. It would have been nice to be a father. At times he wished he'd tried harder with his sexuality. There'd been a few unconsummated relationships with women, but at the age of thirty he'd finally admitted what he was and bonded with a man called Gerry. They'd met in a garden centre – 'next to the honeysuckles' as Gerry never ceased telling people within the small circle who knew about the relationship. Gerry ran a bookshop in Cheltenham and was involved in the Literary Festival. They were an odd pairing, Gerry a heart-on-sleeve extrovert and Tom the reserved Civil Servant for whom privacy was paramount. Keeping their shared life a secret from the people Tom worked with had been essential if he was to keep his job. And keeping it from his mother had been vital to his peace of mind.

The partnership had not been perfect. Gerry had needed to 'flap his wings' from time to time. Tom had put up with it because he had no choice, but it had remained a matter of contention. Eventually Gerry's involvement with festivals had taken him to America and the inevitable had happened. The letter saying he wasn't coming back had hurt Tom deeply. They'd been together for ten years. Then, a month ago, Tom had heard that Gerry had died, victim to some mystery illness plaguing the homosexual community of California.

He gathered up his lunch tray and returned to the house. The musty kitchen was in bad need of a make-over. The worn vinyl flooring curled at the edges and the kitchen drawers jumped their runners. Whoever bought this place would need to spend money on it. He washed up his plate and cutlery and left it to drain in the rack.

In the hall, Tom stopped to listen to the clock ticking in the dining room. It was a sound that he'd always found comforting. Entering the room, he paused by the piano he'd learned on, all those years ago. The keys felt strangely familiar as he played a little trill. The instrument needed tuning, inevitably. He stood there for the best part of a minute, leafing through the music contained in the piano stool, well aware that it was a delaying tactic. Because next on his list of tasks was to go into the bedroom where his mother had died.

On the morning it happened, Emily had rung in a state of great distress and Tom had come immediately. She'd tidied his mother up by the time he arrived. As if by magic, the dementia had gone from her face, leaving a half-smile. She was beautiful again, recognisable as the actress who'd broken many a heart.

Also up there was Sara's bedroom. Her memorial. Two ghosts, lurking on the floor above. Except, of course, he didn't believe in them.

He pulled himself together and climbed the stairs, entering his mother's room first. To his relief he felt nothing whatsoever of her presence. Emily had done a good job. All the clothes were gone, and the make-up. A jewel box on the dressing table was all that remained of how it had been. Tom made a mental note to get the gems valued. He looked out of the window. In the front garden opposite, a young woman was weeding. Marcus's old garden. And not far from her a pram. A new generation in place. The whole process starting all over again.

Sara's room was on the opposite side of the landing from his mother's. He couldn't remember when he'd last entered it. Never on his monthly visits. With trepidation he turned the handle and pushed the door open.

It was like a museum. Excessively tidy. Quite unlike when Sara had inhabited it. A little red rope across the front to keep visitors at bay wouldn't have looked out of place. The narrow bed had dolls and a teddy bear propped against the pillow. The quilted Beatrix Potter bedspread matched the curtains. It was the domain of a child, a little angel, not the almost-woman Sara had become. And yet, despite the room not being *her*, he felt a flicker of unease, an irrational dread that she or a part of her had been locked in here all these years.

Tom stepped on to the linoleum floor and opened the wardrobe. Sara's clothes still hung there. School uniform. A couple of dresses. Trousers. He pushed them apart until he could see the panel at the back, just to be sure that nothing untoward was lurking behind them. Then he closed the door again. In the chest of drawers next to the wardrobe he found socks, pullovers and blouses. But no underwear: the room had been cleaned of anything that might remind his mother of the nastiest aspects of Sara's death.

The innocence of the place extended to the shelf of Enid Blyton books on the right-hand wall, and to the undersized desk with its child's chair that she'd long grown out of. On the table was a Mickey Mouse pencil case their mother had brought back from Hollywood one year. It was the fictionalisation of a life that had been preserved here, not the life itself.

Tom took in a deep breath and let it out again. It was all right. Nothing to worry about. He'd been fearing that seeing Sara's things would trigger a relapse, returning him to the years following her death when he'd thought her spirit had attached itself to him. Using him as a counter-weight to the pull from the next world. He'd sought help about the obsession eventually and been referred to a therapist. It had been a huge relief when the treatment had worked.

He began to think of practical matters. The clothes to a charity shop, together with the child's desk and chair. Letting them be used again would be a far better memorial to his sister than this sealed-up shrine.

He moved along the landing. The spare bedroom had been Emily's domain, and like his mother's bore no trace of its former occupant. Tom felt very much better having seen these rooms. He was in control. It was manageable.

Then he looked up at the ceiling. The hatch into the loft was pulled down with a stick, which hung on the back of the bathroom door. A folding ladder extended from it. The smell as he climbed the steps transported him back. Pine and something strangely electrical that he'd always associated with the Hornby train set. Halfway up he reached for the light switch, his fingers finding it as if they'd done it yesterday.

The lamp came on, a large conical shade hanging over the long trestle table that occupied most of the floor space. The air smelled dusty and was warm from the sun on the slates. A grey water mark ran down the roofing felt at one point, ending in a stained circle on the floor. A tile missing, which he ought to get seen to.

Tom smiled as he looked at the model railway he and his father had put together when he was ten. It seemed quite unchanged, although it was caked with dust. A rectangle of tracks and a section that ran through tunnels, the whole surface landscaped and textured. They'd made the hills out of papier mâché, he remembered, sprinkling them with sawdust and painting them green. Tom picked up one of the engines and turned it over in his hands. His fascination for the train set had never been quite as strong as his father's, but he felt a rekindling of interest. This he wouldn't sell. This he would take home, even though he had nowhere to set it up.

As he'd feared, the eaves beyond the floorboards were stuffed with old suitcases and black plastic bags. Dust flew when he pulled the first one out. Soot coated his fingers as he undid the wire tie. Curtains. He closed it again and put the sack by the ladder. Several more bags proved to contain soft furnishings. He recognised his old bedroom hangings amongst them and a bedspread.

It was a quarter of an hour before Tom finished with the sacks, taking them one by one down to the garden for disposal. Then he leaned in to retrieve the first of the battered suitcases. It proved to contain letters to his mother, hundreds of them, mostly from fans. He remembered her superstition about throwing such things away. He picked through them, hoping to chance across something interesting or important, a famous name, perhaps. But he soon gave up. Closing the case again, he put it aside.

More letters were stuffed away in cardboard boxes, together with theatre programmes and flyers. It seemed as if every little detail of his mother's career was documented here. Tom sighed. All this was history. He couldn't simply destroy it. Somebody, somewhere would value it. Perhaps *he* should. Perhaps he owed it to his mother to make something of this memorabilia. To turn it into a book.

The next box contained some of his own childhood possessions. The crystal set and headphones he'd listened to while his parents thought he was sleeping. A couple of his early attempts at valve radios. Some battered Dinky toys, a cricket bat – and yes, a cowboy outfit. He put the Roy Rogers stuff with the other rubbish next to the ladder but set aside the rest of his things to be taken to Cheltenham with the train set. They were historic, Tom told himself. A part of his past worth preserving.

Behind that box he found a small blue suitcase, just large enough for an overnight. He had no recollection of ever having seen it before. The shell was of thick cardboard and the metal clasp had rusted shut. There was a screwdriver on the trestle table and he dug around the catch until the card tore. Inside was a thick exercise book with Peter Pan fairies on the cover. In the middle was a single word in red ink.

PRIVATE.

Sara's writing. Italic capitals. For some odd reason he could remember the square-nibbed Osmiroid pen she used to use. The clip on its cap had been broken.

Suddenly Tom shivered. It was as if someone had just trailed their fingers down his spine.

'Shit!'

He whipped round, staring at the ladder. The old, weird feeling had returned. Swearing again, he tried to remember the mental exercises the psychologist had given him to defeat the delusions.

He stood up, determined not to slip back into the madness that had tormented him for so many years. Ghosts weren't real, merely a figment of the human mind.

He flipped open the book. It was a diary. He recalled the police suggesting that Sara might have kept one and they'd gone through every nook and cranny of her room but found nothing. So had it been up here all the time? In this little blue case? Had she crept up to the loft whenever she wanted to add to it? If so its contents must have been very private indeed.

In which case it would be better not to read it. To burn the book so the past would stay where he wanted it, firmly buried.

But the hairs on Tom's arms were bristling. He was hearing his sister's whispers again. Being sucked into the vortex of thirty years ago and there seemed no way of stopping it. That nagging doubt was back. The suspicion the wrong man had been convicted. He stared down at the diary. Might this little book finally give him his answer?

The first page was dated July 1948. Two months before Sara's death.

No. He didn't want this. Couldn't bear the thought of plunging back into that tortured period of his life.

Tom snapped the book shut and returned it to the little suitcase. Then he marched to the far end of the loft to check out a tea chest that he suspected of containing old china. The bare boards creaked beneath his feet. He glanced back at the stairs one more time, then told himself to grow up. He was alone in the house. Just him and a load of dusty inanimate objects. Lifting the sheets of faded newspaper that covered the porcelain, he began removing pieces to examine them. He fantasised about finding a lost Ming vase, but soon discovered it was junk. A dinner set his mother had replaced when he was still in short trousers. He put the pieces back.

Then he flinched. He'd felt a hand brush against his arm.

'Damn . . .'

His mind still playing tricks.

Nevertheless he couldn't resist turning round and peering at that little blue suitcase under the eaves. Was it in any way possible that somebody – some *thing* – was trying to guide him towards it? He was just superstitious enough to believe it.

'All right, all right . . .'

He reopened the blue case and retrieved the diary. Then, feeling distinctly uneasy, he perched on a half-broken chair to read it.

The words came off the page and into Tom's head in the same way Sara would have spoken them – breathlessly, as if everything she experienced was unique. Her voice came through so clearly that it brought tears to his eyes. He wiped them with a shirt sleeve and turned the page.

There seemed to be little of relevance in the first entries. Tittle-tattle, mostly.

Saw J after school. She thinks she's so special, it's nausiating . . .

The spelling, never Sara's strongest suit, made him smile.

July's entries were few and irregular. Then came August and the school holidays. The family didn't go anywhere that year, Tom remembered. Their mother was in rehearsal for a West End play. Marcus was also stuck at home and the two of them had gone cycling for a few days, staying in youth hostels.

Horror of horrors! The sitting-room ceiling came down.

Ah yes. They'd had the builders in. Rewiring.

Dust everywhere and dreadful scratches on the piano when a lump of plaster hit it. The builder man swore like a navvy. I learnt some knew words and Mama had hysterix!!!

He remembered Sara hanging around the men, flirting naively and making them endless cups of tea.

Today they started replacing the wiring in the bedrooms. There are holes in the ceillings which you can see through from the attic, because they've taken up the floor boards there. I feel like a spy!

Two days later another reference to the workmen.

Very hot. The electrician took his shirt off today. He had fur all over his chest and was very musscular. I kept walking past him in my shorts and tennis shirt, but he seemed more intersted in Mama who was in the garden in her swimsuit. She'd put the reclina where he could see her. The man finished this afternoon and it's the last we'll see of him. I'm quite sad about it. I think Mama is too.

It was coming back to him. After the murder, all the builders had been treated as potential suspects. Interviewed by the police. Only eliminated when John Hagger was arrested. He turned another page.

The plasterer still hasn't been and there are holes everywhere. This afternoon the boys came back from their bike trip. They refused to tell me about it and went to T's room. So I decided to listen to what they were saying through the hole in the ceilling.

Tom's stomach clenched. He was remembering. He knew with excruciating certainty what was coming.

I couldn't hear anything, so I took a peep to see if they were there. The hole wasn't very big but it looked straight down on to T's bed. I nearly gave myself away by screaming when I saw what they were doing!!! Could only see T. His xxxx was standing up and very big. He rubbed it, then took hold of M's hand and tried to make him rub it for him. M didn't want to. He told T to do it himself. Then something squirted out. I suppose it was sperms. At supper M looked angry and didn't speak to T at all. I felt quite sick and couldn't look them in the eye. Boys are rather disgusting at times, even if as a woman one does find the male of the species rather fascinating.

Her precociousness made him cringe. Tom looked up from the page. Even after the passing of so much time he was embarrassed and not a little alarmed to think that she'd observed him masturbating. Sara had known the basics of sex – their mother had schooled them in it well before their teens – but to have seen that happening, then a few weeks later go into the woods with a stranger and be sexually assaulted . . . a coincidence, or could there have been some dreadful connection?

Something else dawned on him. *That* was the incident which had triggered Marcus's alienation. They'd tossed off in each other's company before, but never touching one another. That was the first and only time Tom had tried to get Marcus to pleasure him. His first overtly homosexual act, and Marcus had baulked at it. Turned against him from that moment on. *Before* Sara's death, not after.

His thoughts drifted back to Korea. Marcus hinting at this, but too embarrassed to spell it out.

He looked down at the diary again. That entry, dated 10 August, was followed by a gap of nearly three weeks. The next was on the thirtieth of the same month and written, to his surprise, in code.

ITXHI NKVIM INULO VEEWE MEIET SEPCR ETOLY INMTH EEGVE NIKNG SAGFT ERLSU PPKER FOWUR TIDME . . .

Tom wrinkled his brow. He quickly saw what the cipher was, one he'd learned long before joining GCHQ. He'd found it in an edition of the *Boy's Own Paper* during a wet summer holiday in Wales. To keep Sara quiet, he'd taught her the codes, and invisible writing too. In this example, the sentences had been broken into blocks of four letters with a fifth random letter added in the middle. He wanted a pen and paper to jot down his decipherings, so took the diary downstairs to the living room.

The decrypted result shook him rigid.

I think I'm in love. We meet secretly in the evenings after supper. Four times so far. A different place each time. He's told me that if I tell anyone he'll cut my tongue out. Dear diary, I'm so frightened. My tummy's gurgling the whole time. His kisses make my knees shake. What shall I do?

Tom sat there dumbfounded. A Pandora's box was opening. There'd been no hint of a boyfriend at the time of her death, secret or otherwise.

The next entry was for 7 September – a week before Sara died. The same cipher used.

TOXDA YIDLE TLYTO UCWHM YBLRE ASHTW HEFNH EKLIS SERDM EIZTM ADKEM EFGEE LAJLL FUUNN YINNS IDMEH . . .

He transcribed it quickly, his horror growing as he formed the words.

Today I let L touch my breasts when he kissed me.

L. Who on earth was L?

It made me feel all funny inside. He said that for us not to have secrets I must show him the most private parts of me next time we meet. What shall I do? If M and D knew about us they would send me away to boarding school. But he is my master. I am his slave and I must do what he wants.

Tom's heart thudded against his ribs. His head buzzed with a frenetic chatter. Sara's voice, his own, Marcus's, Binnie's, his mother's – the cacophony of 14 September 1948 howling back out of the darkness.

. . . I let L touch my breasts . . .

God! She was only a child! An angel, yet with a darker side to her than he'd ever known. Who on earth was L? He checked his deciphering to make sure he hadn't got it wrong.

L. There'd been a Lionel in the neighbourhood, but the youth was fat, had spots and flappy ears and they'd all made fun of him. No. Could it have been the electrician who'd rewired the house, maybe – the one she'd taken a shine to? He wrung out his brain trying to recall the man's name.

Tom turned the page, desperate for more clues, but found nothing. That was the last entry, written a week before she died.

Putting the exercise book down, he stared at the mantelpiece with its silver-framed photo of Sara. The old revulsion was back. The sick feeling in his stomach at the thought of his little sister's body being pawed and abused. He felt her presence in the room. Strongly. Not touching him any more – perhaps she didn't dare, now he knew what she'd been involved in – but close by. Very close.

He pulled himself together. For the sake of his own sanity it was vital to keep his head clear and not allow his imagination to run riot again. What Sara had written in the diary was incredibly important. It suggested that it could have been this L person who'd taken her into the woods, not John Hagger. It would explain the unanswered question that had dogged him in Korea, about what could have induced her to go there with a tramp.

He's told me that if I tell anyone he'll cut my tongue out.

An indication of L's inherently violent nature, or simply a threat to impress a gullible teenager?

The initial 'L' might be meaningless, Tom realised. She'd written that whole entry in code, so the abbreviation for her boyfriend might also have been a cipher. He rubbed his forehead. The list of candidates was a long one. It *could* have been one of the builders, or almost any of the young males in the neighbourhood. A close friend, even, which would explain why the man/boy had insisted their meetings be so secret.

How close a friend? Someone who took her into the woods because he knew them so well? Knew all the best hiding places?

Suddenly the room seemed deafeningly silent. Tom couldn't even hear the clock ticking. He was back where he'd been immediately after the killing, where even those closest to him were suspects.

20

Monday, 3 May 1982
6.30 a.m. London

THE BAGGAGE HALL of Heathrow's Terminal 3 was snarled with the early-morning arrivals from distant continents. Pan Am's flight from Boston had arrived thirty minutes early thanks to a stronger than usual jet stream.

Mary-Anne Hayden was not used to long-distance travel. It was her first trip to Europe, the first time her paper had sent her anywhere outside the United States. The *Boston Star* had a staff correspondent in London, who'd found herself overwhelmed with work since the Falklands crisis started. Mary-Anne was the answer to her plea for help.

She felt anxious about being here. Although the South Atlantic was a long way off, she had a fear the Argentines would bring the war to London. Terrorist attacks. A bomb on a ship brought into the centre of the city. She was also concerned about her cat back in Boston. A neighbour had agreed to feed her every day and remove the litter, but the divine creature would be lonely, living in the apartment by herself.

Mary-Anne pushed a hand through her thick black hair, then removed her spectacles and polished them on the sleeve of her cardigan. Sliding them back on to her nose, she looked around at the other passengers from her flight waiting for their suitcases. There was the man who'd sat across the aisle from her, whom she would have liked to talk to but who'd steadfastly ignored her. She'd felt sure that if only she could have struck up a conversation he would have found her interesting enough not to be put off by her appearance. Her face, she knew, was too broad and flat to be conventionally attractive. And her nose a little too prominent. But she'd been complimented on her eyes in the past.

The belt started moving. Her two bags were amongst the first to appear. She heaved them on to the trolley and made for the exit. Barbara Daley, the correspondent she was to assist, had told her to take a taxi to the correspondent's home in Hammersmith, where there was a spare bedroom that Mary-Anne could use until she found a place of her own. Neither of them had any idea how long she would be staying in London, but the editor who'd assigned her had suggested that it would be two months at least.

The taxi ride gave her a thrill. She'd seen the London black cabs in the movies, but to be in one for real was something else. As they reached the outskirts of the city, she soaked up everything she saw. There was a different feel to the place. A foreignness she couldn't quite put her finger on.

Barbara Daley had been London writer for the *Boston Star* for fifteen years. Mary-Anne knew little about her, except that she was around fifty and had a reputation for being abrasive. That was fine by Mary-Anne. She had no problems fighting her own corner. And this trip was the chance of a lifetime, both professionally and personally.

The word *cute* came to mind, when the taxi stopped outside Barbara Daley's address. A narrow town house on two floors, with pretty window boxes filled with pansies. The driver helped her with her suitcases, then she paid and he drove off at speed. As she watched him go, she wondered if she'd tipped him enough. Her watch, which she'd set to London time, said a quarter to eight.

'Hope she's up,' Mary-Anne whispered as she pressed the doorbell.

The door was opened after the second ring. Barbara Daley had a strong, lined face and untidy hair and looked questioningly at her visitor, while holding a phone to her ear with one hand and a half-smoked cigarette with the other.

'I'm Mary-Anne.'

The older woman beckoned her in, then began shouting into the phone about deadlines.

'We're five hours behind in Boston, which means I can just catch the last edition, if you'll only tell me . . . What d'you mean, you can't confirm it? All I want is a yes or no.'

Mary-Anne humped her suitcases into the small hall, which was cluttered with books and cardboard boxes, all occupying floor space. A painting of a rather beautiful nude girl almost filled one wall.

Barbara slammed the phone down.

'Assholes,' she hissed. 'That was the British Ministry of Defence I was talking to, Mary-Anne. Their press office is staffed by bored old men and ignorant young girls, all trained to give out as little information as possible.' She let out an exasperated sigh, then reached out her hand. 'Welcome to the UK, my dear. How was your flight?'

'Okay, I guess. Caught a couple of hours' sleep.'

'That's more'n I ever get on the red-eye. Boy, am I glad to see you. The Royal Navy has just sunk an Argentine cruiser called the *Belgrano*, with over a thousand men on board.'

'Oh my . . .'

'This morning the war got serious, believe me. There'll be a press conference at the Defence Ministry at eleven and I'll need you in the office to stop my desk jumping around while I attend it.'

'I suppose this is what they mean by hitting the ground running . . .'

'Sure is. Did you eat any breakfast?'

'I'm fine with that.'

'Well, let me get a couple of slices of toast inside me while you freshen up, then we'll make tracks for the office.'

'Is it far from here?'

'About twenty minutes on the subway.'

'The *Tube* . . .'

'Done your homework. Good.'

Mary-Anne decided the smile she was being given was patronising and realised she'd sounded like a greenhorn.

'Thanks for putting me up here.'

'No problem. Up the stairs and it's the room on the right. The blue room, as I call it. Make yourself at home. The bathroom's right next door. Just one for the two of us, so don't hog it. We need to leave in about ten minutes.'

With that the older woman started punching numbers on the phone as she headed for the kitchen. From the tone of the conversation that followed, Mary-Anne guessed that Barbara was talking to the night editor in Boston. She felt homesick suddenly.

The whole house smelled of cigarette smoke, which she hated, because very soon her clothes would start smelling of it too. Carrying the bags upstairs nearly pulled her arms from her sockets, but she made it. The room she'd been directed to was clearly used for junk as well as guests. Space had been cleared in a wardrobe and there was one empty drawer in the chest. The bed was a small queen-size with a little cabinet next to it. She sat on the edge and found it firm, which suited her well. A white towel had been laid out for her.

Ten minutes, Barbara had said. Eight by now. Mary-Anne opened the suitcase, placed her Bible next to the bed, then pulled out a trouser suit, blouse and underwear before taking her washbag to the bathroom. No time for a shower, although the sparkling fittings at one end of the tub were tempting. She stripped off and washed all over, before dressing in the clean clothes. She didn't spend long looking in the mirror, having been brought up to believe vanity a sin. Anyway, her eyes were rather bloodshot. She felt okay, but reckoned that sometime soon the time difference would hit her like a hammer.

Back in the bedroom she could hear Barbara on the phone still, so she began unpacking. Tucked down the side of one of the suitcases was a long cardboard tube. She held it for a moment, tempted to check that the rolled-up sheet of cartridge paper inside had survived the journey unharmed. This, after all, was the other reason she was glad to be in London.

Then she heard a shout from below.

'Mary-Anne, we've got to go.'

She put the tube back in the bag.

Wood Park

Tom hauled himself out of bed, his head throbbing. He'd downed the greater part of a bottle of wine the night before and had slept badly.

The thought that had kept him awake most of the night was that Sara's secret boyfriend might have been Marcus. No one knew those woods better. Sara had always liked him well enough and he'd certainly behaved oddly towards Tom after the event, behaviour that couldn't entirely be attributed to Marcus's nascent homophobia. But by the time daylight filtered through the curtains, Tom had persuaded himself that it couldn't be true. Marcus's shock at discovering Sara's dead body had been genuine, he felt sure of that. Not the crocodile tears of a murderer, revisiting the scene of his crime.

Tom stumbled down to the kitchen and put the kettle on. He'd decided on a plan of action – to trace Sara's intimates at school, girls she might have confided in. There could still be a teacher there after thirty-four years who would remember who his sister had hung around with. Or an old girls' organisation. Knocking on doors locally would also be worth a try, to see if anyone was still here from the old days.

He made himself a mug of tea, then set about boiling an egg and toasting some bread, laying a place for himself at the kitchen table. Doing things properly had always been important to him, even when alone.

The thought of taking Sara's diary to the police had of course been his first reaction, but his confidence in them was low. Inspector Wilkie, the investigating officer on Sara's killing, had been jailed ten years later for planting evidence in another murder case. After his trial, appeals had been lodged by several men sent down by him, but with John Hagger dead and no relatives campaigning on his behalf, that particular conviction had stood.

Tom had been sifting through his memory of the trial evidence, to ensure he wasn't deluding himself about the conviction being precarious.

There was the confession – Hagger had retracted it in court, saying it had been beaten out of him. The jury hadn't believed him, but Wilkie's record of corruption made it more likely in Tom's eyes.

The forensics – fibres from the tramp's jacket found on Sara's clothing and semen that matched his blood group. The first might have been planted by Wilkie as in the other cases, and the second wasn't conclusive, because the fluids could have matched many other men, as the defence had pointed out.

And there was a third, rather less scientific reason why Tom had always suspected that Hagger wasn't the killer. Sara had not actually been penetrated. The murderer's ejaculation had been premature – more likely with a young man than a 52-year-old, he reckoned.

It was news time. Tom switched on the radio and learned with horror about the *Belgrano* sinking. He shook his head in dismay. Whenever people died in war, he thought of Korea. Young men full of hope, shredded by metal. Good-looking boys like Pete Hewitt, who'd died within weeks of his return to the front line. Tom had visited

Hewitt's parents when he got back to England, their faces imprinted on his mind for ever. Ordinary, decent folk, destroyed by grief and incomprehension.

Tom transferred the egg from the pan to its cup and leaned the two slices of toast together so they would stay crisp. The tea had revived him and he brewed himself a small pot of the fresh ground coffee he'd brought from home, knowing there was only instant in the cupboard here. The smell did wonders for the musty atmosphere of the place. He cracked the egg and saw to his satisfaction that it was perfectly cooked.

The radio was still on. The Defence Secretary was to make a statement about the *Belgrano*. It wouldn't reveal much, Tom told himself. Submarine ops were always cloaked in secrecy.

When he'd finished his breakfast, he cleared away. Gerry had mocked his tidiness when they lived together, but Tom believed that if you kept control of the little things, the bigger ones usually fell into line.

He took a shower and dressed. Estate agents were coming to measure up in the afternoon, so he only had the morning for his inquiries. It was still early to knock on neighbours' doors or ring the school, so he decided to check out the newspaper clippings his father had collected, in case something jolted his memory.

As Tom sifted through the yellowing cuttings, it came back to him why he'd so hated what the papers had written. There'd been far more about the 'agony of a film star' than the details of the police investigation. He read quotes from friends saying how much the family was suffering, and marvelled again at the photo of his mother at a window, distraught and clutching a handkerchief to her eyes. He remembered wondering if she'd posed for it. It pained him to read it all again.

Even the builders who'd worked at their house a few weeks before the murder had been interviewed by the press, after the police excluded them from their investigation. Sycophantic quotes about what a nice ordinary family the Sedleys seemed to be, despite Maureen Stuart being so famous.

Tom shuddered and was about to stuff the cuttings back into their folder when he spotted a name. Robert Lester.

Lester. Beginning with the letter L. One half of the building firm Lester and Barnett. The name rang a bell. His mother had always been asking him to take a mug of tea for 'Mr Lester'. Because she didn't want Sara to.

Tom strode into the hall where the phone was and grabbed a directory.

Lester and Barnett, Temple Green Lane. Still in business. From his memory of the neighbourhood, their yard was five minutes' drive away.

He thought about it for a short while, wondering whether it was madness to go and confront the man after all this time. Then he swallowed his reservations and went straight out to the car.

The builders' premises were in a turning off Wood Park's main shopping street. A couple of vans stood in the yard, which had a rack for tall ladders on one side. Tom parked beside the vehicles and walked into the office. An elderly woman was typing out invoices.

'Yes?'

'I wanted to speak to Mr Robert Lester, please. Is he here?'

'*Robert?*' She looked at him as if he were mad. 'You mean Nigel.'

'No. It's Robert I want to speak to.'

'You'll have to shout, then. He's been dead more than thirty years.'

'Oh.'

She laughed at his confusion. 'Why d'you want to speak to him, anyway?'

He wasn't sure where to begin. 'It's about something that happened in nineteen forty-eight.'

She shook her head. 'We don't guarantee our work that long. No builder does.'

'It's not about work. It's to do with the house he worked at. A girl was murdered there.'

'Lordie, you must mean that actress's daughter. What was her name?'

'Sara.'

'No, the actress.'

'Maureen Stuart.'

'That's the one. Blimey, that's a long time ago. What are you looking for, then?'

'The girl was my sister. I . . . I'm writing a book about the case and saw Robert Lester's name in a newspaper cutting. Wanted to see what he remembered of it. Perhaps Nigel Lester was there too.'

'Forty-eight? Nigel wasn't born then.' She squinted, trying to see if Tom looked anything like his mother. 'You could always try Davy, I suppose. Bobbie's brother. He worked for the firm in those days, then set up as a builders' merchant. Retired now.'

'D'you know where he lives?'

'Yes. Did well for himself. Lives in Hadley Drive.'

'That's just round the corner from Heathfield Close, isn't it?'

'Exactly. Your mother still alive, is she? We see her old films on the telly sometimes.'

'She died a week ago.'

'Oh dear. Sad when they go, isn't it?'

'Very. What number Hadley Drive?'

'I don't know, love, but it'll be in the phone book.' She placed her hands back on the typewriter keys. 'Hope he can help. And if they make your book into a film, I'll be sure to watch it.'

'Thanks.'

Tom returned to the car.

Back at the house, he found the address in the telephone directory and walked round the corner to Hadley Drive.

The homes here were larger than the one he'd been brought up in, with gravelled entrances and built-in double garages. A man of about seventy was hosing down a Jaguar on the concrete apron.

'Looking for someone?' he asked, pointing the water jet away as Tom approached.

'Davy Lester?'

'That's me.'

Tom introduced himself and explained about the book he was supposedly writing. The older man looked a little disgruntled, but turned off the tap and invited him into the pine-cabineted kitchen.

'So you're Maureen Stuart's son.'

'Yes.'

''Orrible business that. 'Elluva long time ago, but I'll never forget it.'

'Were you one of the men who worked at our house a few weeks before Sara was killed?'

'No. Not me. My brother did the electrics, though.'

The man who'd taken his shirt off. Tom sensed he was on the right track.

'Robert. He died, I understand.'

'Yeah.' Lester took off his horn-rimmed glasses and polished them on a tea towel. Without them, his eyes looked washed out and curiously small.

'Long time ago?'

'Nineteen fifty.'

'What happened?'

'A work accident. He fell off the scaffolding and landed on his head. Killed outright. Nice way to go, except he was far too young. Survived his time in the war, then five years later, bang.'

'Do you remember him talking about my sister's death? Or about Sara herself? She took a bit of a shine to him, I think.'

Davy Lester sucked his teeth. 'It's a long, long time ago.'

'I know.'

'The only thing I do recall – well, it's not exactly complimentary, I'm afraid.'

'No matter. Speak freely.'

'Well, I seem to remember him saying he wasn't surprised at what had happened to the girl – your sister. Said she was a tarty little thing. Quite developed for a fourteen-year-old, and used to walk around the house without much in the way of clothing on.'

Tom bristled at the description. 'You think he was attracted to her, though?'

'What, fancied her, you mean? Dunno. She was only a child. He never said as much.'

'But he might have been?'

The older man looked at him out of the corner of his eyes. 'What are you driving at? What's this book of yours about?'

'It's a re-examination of the case,' Tom said quickly. 'A fresh look. You'll remember the man who was convicted claimed he didn't do it, and the police officer in charge . . .'

'Got done for stitching people up. I know. So you're trying to pin it on Bob?'

'Well, no. I'm just looking at who else it might possibly have been.' Tom realised he was being far from subtle. 'Sara wrote a diary, you see. And I've only just found it. It shows she was seeing someone in secret. Someone she called L.'

Lester frowned. 'But my brother was Robert.'

'Robert *Lester*.'

Tom could see that he was putting the other man's back up. He was an amateur at this, no trained investigator.

'It wasn't Bobby.'

'How can you be so certain?'

'Because I knew Bobby and you didn't.' Lester pointed an accusing finger at him. 'You're up a blind alley with this one, old son.'

'All I'm doing is looking at possibilities,' Tom insisted, determined not to be fobbed off by family loyalty.

'Yeah, but that's just the point. It *isn't* possible.'

'What d'you mean?'

'Well, because of what happened to Bob.'

'I'm not with you.'

'In the war. He got shrapnel in the guts. On the Rhine in forty-five. Right here.' Lester clamped a hand over his genitals. 'Lost his wedding tackle, poor sod. There's no way he did anything to your sister.'

Tom felt the ground sink beneath him. 'I'm so sorry. I had no idea.'

'Not many people did. Wasn't something he talked about. Imagine what it does to you when you fancy some bird and can't do anything about it. It's why some of us thought it wasn't no accident when he fell from the scaffolding.'

'I'm so sorry. Please forgive me.'

Lester waved his apology away.

'Doesn't matter.' He stood up. 'Anyway, if you'll excuse me, I must get back to cleaning my car.'

Tom shook his hand, apologised one more time and returned to Heathside Close, feeling thoroughly chastened.

Obsessed as he was by Sara's murder, it was easy to forget that other families had suffered tragedies too.

21

Holborn

MARY-ANNE WATCHED the Defence Secretary speaking live on the BBC. He said the *Belgrano* had been a threat to the British fleet, despite being outside the naval exclusion zone that the British government had declared around the Falklands. She didn't understand the implications of this but took a detailed shorthand note so she could mull it over with Barbara later.

The *Boston Star*'s London office consisted of one middle-sized room in a block near Holborn Circus, which accommodated several representatives of the foreign press. Like the house in Hammersmith, it smelled strongly of cigarette smoke. Barbara Daley had rapidly shown her how to replace the paper in the wire machines – Reuters and the Press Association – then told her to hold the fort while she went to the Defence Ministry.

'There's a navy guy who talks to me. I want to see if I can get an inside track on all this.'

Apart from monitoring the TV and the wires, the office had been remarkably quiet that morning, giving Mary-Anne time to browse phone directories for art galleries. The fact that there were so many made her realise just how large London was and how difficult her task was going to be.

At lunchtime, when Barbara returned, Mary-Anne was flagging. The time difference had caught up.

'C'mon. You need to eat something. And today the sandwiches are on me.'

They went into the street, buffeted by winds deflected by tall buildings, and headed down a narrow lane to an Italian café. Then, over a large cappuccino and a ciabatta with roasted vegetables and mozzarella, Barbara described the scene at the Ministry that morning.

'They have this guy who's the spokesman, you just wouldn't believe. Talks like a robot and reads his statements as if we're all beginners at a Pitman class. So goddam slow.'

'I saw him on the TV.'

'They showed it live?'

'Sure.'

'Shoot. Then you got as much out of it as I did. Don't know why I bothered going down there.'

'No chance to talk to your navy friend?'

'He was there but I didn't even get a smile. Nobody did. They're as uptight as hell. Outside military circles, people are saying the sinking of the *Belgrano* wasn't quite cricket.'

'Meaning?'

'Not the right thing to do, old boy.' Barbara put on a hoity-toity voice.

'And they're scared about what this sinking might lead to?'

'Maybe, and scared to show how pleased with themselves they are. Anything on the wires from Argentina?'

'Not a lot. Still searching for survivors. They're talking of several hundred dead.'

'To tell the truth, I'm stuck for an angle on this one, Mary-Anne. The paper will pick it all up from the wires, international reaction and all. I was hoping they'd give me the name of the submariner who fired the torpedoes, so I could go talk to his family . . .' Barbara winked theatrically.

'In your dreams . . .'

'Sure.'

Barbara put down her coffee cup. Mary-Anne realised her boss had been studying her face. The look of curiosity she detected was familiar. Here comes the interrogation, she thought.

'Tell me about yourself, Mary-Anne. How long you been with the paper?'

'About four years. Before that I did a master's in journalism in Florida, then worked for a couple of years freelance for the *Philadelphia Inquirer*.'

'Hard going, huh?'

'It sure was. Getting a staff job at the *Star* was one of the best days of my life.'

Barbara was frowning, as if seeing Mary-Anne's features properly for the first time.

'Forgive me, but your name doesn't quite go with your looks. Hayden – I mean that's so waspish, yet you look kind of oriental.'

'I was born in Korea. During the war there. My mother gave me to an orphanage. I was adopted by an American family and brought up in Pennsylvania.'

'I see. You don't mind my mentioning . . .'

'Of course not. You're not the first person to ask.'

'So how old were you when . . .?'

'My mother gave me away when I was a baby. I don't remember her at all.'

'That's tough. And your father?'

Mary-Anne shrugged. 'That's the big mystery. A UN soldier, I imagine. I got a hint the other day that he could have been British.'

'Oh yes? So you're going to try and find him?' Her eyes widened with excitement.

'Well . . . he could easily be dead.'

'Sure. But he may not be. So what are you, about thirty?'

'Thirty-one.'

'Sounds like you had a tough start in life.'

'Not really. The family who brought me up meant well.'

'That sounds ominous.'

'Well . . . they just didn't have any idea how I felt.'

'They treated you badly?'

'Depends on what you mean. They had two kids of their own. Later on. So they were several years younger than me. And they kind of used me as a nurse. The way they saw it, they'd saved me from a bad time in Korea – mixed-race kids didn't have much of a future there in the nineteen-fifties. So I owed them. They weren't unkind, but they treated me more like a servant than a daughter. And they hated me showing interest in where I came from. That was real taboo. *Ingratitude* was what they called it. They thought I was saying America wasn't good enough for me.'

'And you *wanted* to know about your past, of course . . .'

'At school the other kids called me 'gookie', which kind of made me determined to find out what they meant.'

'And to know who your real mom was. They stopped you, your adoptive parents?'

'They forbade me to make any attempt to find out where I came from. They said God loved me, which was all that mattered. And *they* were my past so why did I need to know any more than that?'

'So . . .'

'So it wasn't until college that I could start looking.'

'And?'

'I spent five years tracing nearly every orphanage in South Korea before I finally got my mother's name. Then another few years before I found someone who knew what had happened to her.' Mary-Anne's voice cracked. This was the hardest part to talk about.

'I'm sorry . . .' Barbara Daley squeezed Mary-Anne's hand. 'I'm prying and I have no right to. It's being a reporter – I don't know when to stop.'

'That's okay.'

'So . . . so what *did* happen to your mom?'

'She was beaten to death. By her brothers.'

Barbara's hand went up to her mouth. 'Oh my . . .'

'I only found out a few weeks ago.' Mary-Anne bit her lip. 'You see, Korean families are real proud of their lineage. Many can trace their ancestors back for centuries. So when the bloodline is polluted by someone from another race they don't take it too well.'

'So when did this happen? Soon after you were born . . .?'

'I think my mother must have gone into hiding with me. I was about four weeks old when her brothers caught up with her. She'd disgraced them, so they killed her.'

'That's so awful. But they didn't harm *you*.'

'That's what I don't understand. I'm sure they would have killed me if they could. I think she must have had an idea of what was in store for her and maybe asked a friend to take her baby. Anyway, I ended up at an orphanage for children of foreign soldiers. There was a church in Pennsylvania that found homes for them. Most of the babies were half American, of course.'

'But you're half British, you said. How did you find that out?'

'That's the darnedest thing. It was only a couple of weeks ago, as I said. I'd hired an investigator in Seoul to try to trace my mother's family.'

'So you could press murder charges, or what?'

'Oh no. Nothing like that. Anyway, I didn't know she was dead at the time. I just wanted to find out who they were. What sort of lives they led. Because *they* were my real family. Aunts, uncles, grandparents and cousins. I don't know . . . There's a whole part of me out there.'

'So what happened?'

'Like I said, a couple of weeks ago I got a call. The agency had traced a cousin of my mother who was prepared to talk to me.'

'You went out to Korea?'

'No. I'm no way ready for that. But we spoke on the phone. It was he who told me that she was killed by her own brothers. And the amazing thing was, he remembered my mother seeing a British soldier at Christmas time in 1950. So the dates would match for that man to be my father.'

'But he didn't know the soldier's name.'

'A lot was happening at that time. Seoul was overrun by the Chinese and he had to flee along with everyone else. They were all in fear of their lives. He didn't remember much about it at all.'

'So you've still no idea who your father is?'

'None at all. I have this fantasy image of a dashing young army officer who swept my poor mother off her feet.'

'How frustrating, you being here in England now and not knowing . . . Gee! Look at the time. We better hit the road to the office.'

They scraped the chairs back and made for the door. A light rain had started to fall. Without umbrellas they walked briskly, to avoid getting soaked.

'So you've come to the end of the road, kind of?' Barbara persisted, wanting to make sure there was no more to the story.

'Well . . .'

'There's something else?'

'I guess it's nothing really. Can't think it'll actually lead anywhere . . .'

'What is it?'

'Well, apparently, when I arrived at the orphanage I had a pretty unusual piece of baggage with me.'

'Really?'

'A picture. A drawing of a young Korean woman.'

'The plot thickens.'

'Yes.'

'Who was the picture of? I don't suppose you know.'

'I think it was my mother.'

'She looks like you?'

'A little. The eyes mostly. And the only explanation I can think of is that she knew she was going to die and wanted me to have something to remember her by.'

They reached the press building and hurried inside, out of the rain.

'That's quite a story, Mary-Anne.'

'Sure, but maybe it's just in my head.'

The lift had other people in it so they didn't speak again until they reached their floor.

'But how's that picture going to help you find your father, dear?' Barbara unlocked the door to the office.

'I think he was the one who drew it.'

'Why do you think that?'

Mary-Anne sighed. 'This is going to sound silly.'

'Go on.'

'Well, the way the picture was drawn, I think the artist had to have been in love with her.'

Mary-Anne was expecting scepticism on Barbara's world-weary face, but the older woman nodded appreciatively. 'I wish I could see it.'

'You can. I brought it with me. It's at your house.'

Barbara smiled. 'Good. This is *really* getting interesting. So, let me get this straight. You think your dad was a soldier and an artist too?'

'Yes.'

'And you've brought the picture over here, in case somebody recognises the style.'

'Well, yes. I know that sounds pretty far-fetched . . .'

'Not entirely. I know some people in the art world. And hey . . . maybe your guy had an exhibition when he got back from Korea.' She suddenly put a hand to her mouth. 'I've just thought of something which would make it all impossible, of course.'

'I know. He might have died out there.'

'Thousands did.'

'Yes.'

'Well. We can only try. I'll make some calls later. Meanwhile we'd better see what's happened to *today*'s war.'

22

Tuesday, 4 May
Putney, South London

IT HAD BEEN a struggle for Binnie to conceal her nervousness from Sebastian that morning, but since she seldom merited more than a casual glance from her husband these days, she thought she'd got away with it. As he went out of the door, he hadn't even asked what her plans were for the day, which was convenient, because she hadn't needed to lie.

She listened to the *Today* programme while running a bath. In the review of the papers, they made play with the headline in the *Sun* about the *Belgrano* sinking – *Gotcha!* Binnie found the jingoism sickening. And her husband chuckling over it, before he set off to the Ministry, was no more than she expected of him.

The rights and wrongs of sending a task force to the South Atlantic had divided their family. Amanda had phoned from Australia last night. 'Killing hundreds of Argentines for the sake of a pile of rocks – are you mad?' Their other two children lived in London. Stephen, working in the City, took after his father, saying that the aggressors needed to be taught a lesson. Their youngest child, Jane, was too preoccupied with her own life to care.

Binnie climbed into the bath, distressed as ever by the breadth of her hips and the lack of firmness in her breasts. She washed her hair, which she'd had cut and highlighted the day before. Then, after drying herself, she smothered her body with lotion.

The five-bedroomed semi-detached in Putney had been their home for twenty years. A mere two minutes' walk from the river, the children had loved it. But they'd all flown the nest now and the house was too big for her and Sebastian. He talked about selling up to buy a small flat in London and a larger place in the country, but Binnie loathed the idea. Putting up with Sebastian was bad enough here where she had lots of friends and plenty to occupy her, but to be alone with him in the wilds of Wiltshire – it didn't bear thinking about.

She dressed in a pullover and a light-coloured tweed skirt. Simple but feminine. Nothing that could be easily categorised or mocked. Then she spent some time on her make-up, carefully creating the appearance of not being made-up at all.

The past two months had involved a frenzy of activity, all of which she'd concealed from family and friends. What she'd been doing was entirely personal and utterly secret.

She breakfasted on muesli, swallowing her daily hormone pill with a mouthful of orange juice. By the time she was ready it was half-past nine. The sun was shining and a dry day was forecast. She had a two-hour drive ahead, with a midday rendezvous.

Binnie navigated the Volvo up the A1 to Peterborough, then branched off across country. It was a journey she'd made several times during the past eighteen months. Grove Marsh Prison was miles from anywhere, in the middle of the Cambridgeshire fens.

At a quarter to twelve she arrived and found a space in the visitors' car park from where she could keep an eye on the gate. This was a 'D' category open establishment, for prisoners unlikely to want to escape because their sentences were almost over. The wall surrounding the place was not much taller than a man and without any of the razor wire of the establishment Marcus had been in before.

At precisely twelve o'clock she saw him emerge from the gatehouse, carrying the small bag which she'd brought in to him last week. She flashed the lights and he began to walk towards her. There was a stiffness about the way he moved. He'd lost the pallor of the earlier stages of his sentence, but his face looked thin and drawn and his haircut was austere. He didn't smile as he neared the car, which worried her.

Binnie got out and gave him a kiss on the cheek. 'Welcome back to the world,' she breathed, her mouth by his ear.

Marcus grunted and slung his bag on to the back seat.

'You don't happen to have any fags, do you?'

'No, but we can stop in a village.'

'That'd be great.'

They got in and she began to drive, unsettled by the fact that he was making no attempt at conversation.

'Hello?' she tried after a while.

'Hello.'

'Say something nice to me, Marcus. You must be glad to be out at least.'

'Of course. Sorry. I should have thanked you for collecting me.'

'That's quite all right.'

'Four and a half years.' He shook his head in disbelief.

'But it's over.'

'Yes.'

The road south ran along the top of a dyke between cabbage fields, the flat horizon marked by the occasional tree and a line of telegraph poles.

'They tell me some people actually live in this godforsaken landscape by choice,' Marcus muttered, 'hard though it is to believe.'

'All right if you're Worzel Gummidge, I suppose.'

Marcus shuddered.

'Soon be back in London. Don't worry.'

They both fell silent again, as if needing to be clear of this wilderness before they could communicate further. It was another ten minutes before they found a village post office selling cigarettes.

'I'll have to ask you to keep the window open when you smoke,' Binnie said.

'Don't want me making a pong in your nice clean car.'

'It's Sebastian . . .'

Marcus turned towards her, wedging his shoulder against the side window. He was looking at her properly for the first time since getting into the vehicle. Her hair had been brushed until it shone and she smelled as if she'd rolled in flower petals. He studied her face. Plain English features that had worn moderately well. If anything, she'd improved with age. The lines around her eyes gave character, as did the few wrinkles in her skin. He still remembered the liberties he'd had to take with her portrait as a young girl to give her face personality.

'When did you stop wearing glasses?'

'Years ago. Have you only just noticed?'

'I thought you wore them sometimes when you came to see me.'

'Maybe once, when I'd lost one of my contacts.'

He went on looking at her. She'd visited him half a dozen times during his final eighteen months inside, the first real communication they'd had for years, apart from the occasional family do at Christmas. Turned up out of the blue one day, saying that she'd been worrying about him and felt bad that his own brother had never been to see him.

'You're not worried, sitting in a car with a convicted killer?' he asked, mockingly.

'If I were, I wouldn't be here, Marcus.'

'Well, anyway . . . this is very good of you, what you're doing. What you've *been* doing for me. I don't deserve it.'

'No. You probably don't.'

'And basically I'm an ungrateful son of a bitch.'

'I'm used to it. It runs in the family.'

She was a lot tougher than she used to be. He'd learned that during her visits. No longer the suburban mouse, but a woman with a mind of her own.

'Can I ask . . .' Marcus hesitated, looking for the right words. 'As I said, it's extremely good of you to take such an interest in my well-being, but can I enquire *why* exactly you're doing all this?'

Binnie hadn't expected him to ask outright. The answer was not one she wanted to put into words. 'I don't know, really. Because we've known each other since we were kids and I sort of care for you, I suppose.'

'Makes you feel good, eh, Bins? Is that it? A little act of charity to help you on your way to heaven.'

Binnie stamped on the brake. There was a loud hooting from behind and a small white van swerved past, a rustic face in the passenger window glaring at her.

'You supercilious bastard! Bloody well get out and walk if that's your attitude.'

For a moment Marcus considered doing just that. There was nothing he hated more than the conscience-troubled middle classes getting off on helping the downtrodden. He put his hand on the door handle, but the bleakness of what he saw beyond the glass deterred him.

'Sorry, Bins. That was a mean thing to say. I withdraw that remark.'

'I should damn well think so.'

She let in the clutch and they drove on again.

Peterborough came and went and they settled down on the motorway section of the A1, heading south towards London.

'Now tell me again about this place you've found for me,' Marcus said, reopening the conversation. Binnie had described it on her last but one visit, but he'd paid little attention. Her constant jolly positiveness whenever she came to see him had got on his nerves. And he suspected she was trying to get some sort of control over his life, which he was determined to resist. It was his own fault that he'd landed in prison. *He*'d wrecked his life, without any outside interference. If he was ever going to rebuild it he would manage it on his own.

'I told you. It's in Brentford.'

'Yes, but where the hell *is* Brentford?'

'On the wrong side of Kew Bridge from the gardens. The flat's quite small. A studio room, but it actually has a huge north-facing Velux window, so you'll have light to paint by.'

'And how am I supposed to pay for it?'

'That's for you to work out. The rent's quite modest. I've paid the first quarter. You can reimburse me when you've started earning again.'

He had a tight feeling in his chest. She'd already started controlling him.

'It'll get you started, Marcus.'

'Mmmm.' Started at *what*? That was the question.

He didn't want to discuss his future with her, so he turned on the car radio and pushed the tuner buttons until he found a pop channel.

'You don't mind?'

Binnie shrugged. She'd always known that today would be difficult. If it was to end the way she wanted it to, there was still a long way to go.

Marcus let the music pound his brain, hoping it would stop it churning. Binnie, because he and she went back so far, was a painful reminder of the ambition he'd once had. The trail he'd blazed through art school and the thrill of that first exhibition. A reminder too of the disappointments that had followed.

In some ways he'd preferred it in prison amongst men who were unaware of his past, or of the offence that had put him there. But he would have to get used to people knowing outside. His trial, after all, had filled the tabloids. 'War artist turned killer.' The art world he was returning to was a small one and he was far from sure he'd be welcomed by it. Yet painting was the only skill he had, and somehow he would have to make his living at it again.

Marcus cleared his throat. 'What does Sebastian think of you acting as Lady Bountiful to his disgraced younger brother?'

Binnie stiffened, then told herself not to react to his needling. His attitude was understandable after what he'd been through. It would be a long haul taming him.

'He doesn't know.'

'What d'you mean?' Marcus was astonished.

'Just what I said. He doesn't know.'

'What, not about any of it? Even the prison visits?'

She shook her head, keeping her eyes on the road.

'But whenever you came to see me you always said "Sebastian sends his best wishes".'

'Well, if you believed that, you're mad. Let's face it, sending you best wishes is not something Sebastian is ever likely to do.'

Binnie had developed a very hard shell in recent years, Marcus realised. In truth he didn't really know what sort of creature she was any more. During the prison visits their conversations had been trivial or circuitous. She'd asked if there were things he needed and had talked about her children. Very little had been said that was personal to him or to her. A plastic table in a room full of others didn't seem the place for an intimate conversation, even if they'd wanted one. And before that, in twenty-five years, they'd only met at family gatherings – Christmases, christenings, and the funeral of his mother. Awkward events where he'd usually been accompanied by a different woman from the last time they'd met, a woman never quite of the right class.

So, why her interest in him now? He had to know.

'I've never asked you this before, Binnie, but . . .'

'What?'

'You can tell me to mind my own business, if you like.'

'Oh, I will. Never fear.'

'Well then . . . what *exactly* is the state of your marriage?'

Binnie bit her lip. Then she shrugged. Frankness was going to be inevitable at some point, so why not now?

'Sebastian earns a good salary.'

'Ah, yes.'

'And may end up with a knighthood one day.'

'Lady Columbine Warwick. Is that what it's about?'

'No. It's many things. I have a nice house, nice clothes and the freedom to do what I want. And what does he get? Well . . . I never pretend to have a headache when he wants you know what.' She arched her eyebrows. 'And I'm a presentable consort at official functions. *And* . . . I never ask him why, when he's late home from the office.'

'God . . . It's all so prosaic.'

'Life *is* prosaic, for most of us.'

'You realise you'd have to live with the hated name Columbine if he got his "K"? They'd never let you be Lady Binnie.'

'I could live with that if it ever happened.'

'Your ladyship . . .'

'God, you can be a pain, Marcus. You know, all those things I've just listed, many people would think of as the ingredients of a pretty normal marriage.'

'Some people would call it no grounds for a marriage at all. What about love?'

Binnie sighed exasperatedly. 'You know why I married Sebastian. And every time I think of Amanda I know I made the right decision. She's a wonderful person. Your trouble, Marcus, is that you're too much of a perfectionist. Perhaps it's why you've never made any of your own relationships stick.'

Marcus squirmed. The failure of his love life was a great disappointment to him. 'I merely thought the *love* word might have crept into your marriage spec somewhere along the line,' he said edgily.

'I have never loved Sebastian.' She stated it simply and without feeling. '*You* know that.' She shot a glance sideways to try to see if he had any idea of the significance of what she was saying to him.

From his bemused expression she concluded that he didn't.

The traffic on the North Circular was light for a weekday lunchtime. It was a little after half-past one when they reached the Chiswick roundabout and turned off for Brentford.

This was a part of London that Marcus barely knew. As they passed stark towers of council flats his heart sank.

'It's a mixed area,' Binnie explained, sensing his reservations. 'Local authority and private. The road you're in has a bit of character.'

They turned up past a supermarket and a church and entered a street of terraced houses.

'What do they call this lot?' Marcus sniped. 'Edwardian artisans' cottages, no doubt.'

'Aren't you an artisan? Anyway, when you've earned some money you'll be able to afford something better.'

The house where they stopped had a 'To Let' sign outside.

'I'll get the agents to take that down,' Binnie murmured, nervously watching for his reaction.

Marcus got out and retrieved his small case from the rear seat. Binnie opened the front door to the house. Inside was a second door to the ground-floor flat, and a staircase.

'Upstairs?' Marcus asked, walking past her. His breath reeked of cigarette smoke.

'Yes.' She felt absurdly nervous as she followed him.

Marcus waited at the top of the stairs. She had to squeeze past to get at the lock. He sniffed her hungrily and rather obviously, all womanly smells having been missing from his life for the past four and a half years.

Binnie opened the door.

'This is the living room,' she explained, turning to catch his reaction.

'So I see.'

'Kitchenette in the alcove. Then, through there is a bedroom with a small bathroom.' She pointed to a narrow passageway. 'Well . . . shower room, actually.'

'I see what you mean about the light.' He looked up at the Velux. 'Positively dazzling. Glad there's a blind on it.'

'What d'you think?'

Marcus walked through into the bedroom. The double bed had been made up with the bedspread turned down as if ready to be used. Was she expecting him to make a pass at her? Sex-starved ex-con needing his oats? He had half a mind to do just that.

'Quite cosy, don't you think?' she called from the living room.

'Very.' He poked his nose into the bathroom. The basin tap was dripping. He tried to turn it off but it made no difference. There was a lime stain down the porcelain. 'It'll do for now, anyway.'

Back in the living room he found her bending over to take plates covered in cling film from the fridge. The hips had broadened over the years, but he didn't mind that. He smiled at her as she walked past him and set their food down on the small table.

'In fact, to be absolutely fair, you've done me proud, Binnie. Thank you.'

She beamed at him. 'I've prepared a salad lunch. Thought you'd be hungry. And . . . here. Open this, would you?' She handed him a bottle of champagne.

'Well, well.' Marcus couldn't help smirking as he took it, deciding that it was really quite nice to have a woman making a fuss over him again. 'Glasses?'

'In the cupboard over the sink.'

He found an assortment there, with no two matching.

'How long ago did I move in here?'

Binnie didn't understand what he meant for a moment, partly because an acute nervousness was setting in. 'Oh, I see. The lease started on the first of the month. Last Saturday.' She heard a slight tremor in her voice and prayed that he hadn't noticed it.

'You've been pretty busy, then.'

'Well, I was here most of Saturday, yes. There wasn't that much to do, really,' she lied.

'And Sebastian?'

'He was at Lords. With some university chums. They drink a lot of gin and watch a little cricket. It takes up most of the day.'

'Convenient.'

'Well . . . yes.'

Marcus popped the cork and filled two tumblers. 'Old lags' glasses,' he said, handing her one. The rims clinked dully as they touched them together.

'Mmm.' She swallowed a generous mouthful.

Binnie, Marcus realised, was not at ease. There was a slight colouring of her cheeks which convinced him that she really was expecting something sexual to take place between them.

'Well.' He smiled. 'Makes a nice change from prison tea.' He narrowed his eyes. 'Do I . . . do I get the impression there's quite a lot of your life that you keep secret from Sebastian?'

'I really don't want to talk about Sebastian . . .'

There was a pleading look in her eyes, which he responded to by moving closer to her, until they were almost touching.

'What *do* you want to talk about, then?'

Binnie looked down at his chest. She appeared close to panic and the colour in her cheeks had spread to her whole face. Then she lifted her face so that her mouth was level with his.

'I'm not entirely sure I want to *talk* at all,' she whispered.

Marcus hesitated, overcome with bewilderment. Life was difficult enough, without the complication of bedding his brother's wife. Yet the pressure in his loins was growing strongly and the thought of getting one over on Sebastian appealed enormously.

Then Binnie kissed *him*. On the mouth. Lightly at first, then full on, with her tongue searching for his like a terrier down a foxhole.

23

THEY LAY ON the bed with just a sheet covering them.

'That was all a bit rushed, I'm afraid,' said Marcus, as if apologising for a poorly executed portrait. 'Not one of my best efforts.'

He still had his shirt on, though unbuttoned. Binnie sat up and removed her bra, which had been hurriedly undone but was still looped over her shoulders. Then she turned towards him and placed her hand on his stomach.

'I don't mind.' She knew from experience that first encounters were seldom satisfactory. She fingered his spent cock, hoping for a return of its strength.

'Takes me a while to recharge my batteries,' Marcus mumbled. 'All that bromide in the prison tea.' He cleared his throat, feeling a strong need to reassert his dominance of the proceedings. 'Do this sort of thing often, do you?'

Binnie took her hand away and covered one of her breasts.

'I mean,' Marcus added awkwardly, 'I'm not suggesting . . .'

'Good.'

'But I take it this isn't the first time you've cheated on your husband.'

Binnie held the sheet to her chest. Marcus ran his hand down the ridge of her spine. There were small moles on her almost white back.

'No. It's not the first time, Marcus.' She swung her legs over the side of the bed. 'I think we should have some lunch, don't you? I went to a lot of trouble preparing it and I'll scratch your eyes out if you don't eat anything.'

She dried between her legs with a tissue, then put her clothes back on. Marcus paid a brief visit to the bathroom. When he returned to the bedroom he opened the wardrobe and found some of the clothes that had been kept in store for him while he'd been in prison. Binnie had asked him for the key to the place a few weeks ago. He dressed in old corduroy trousers and a denim shirt, and suddenly felt human again.

'I'm a lot better for that,' he said, walking back into the living room.

'Good. Glad to have been of service.' Binnie kept her eyes on what she was doing. 'I bought a chicken and ham pie and a quiche. Any preferences, or a bit of both?' She was busying herself at the table, laying out place settings.

'Since this is my first day out, I'll take whatever you're offering . . .'

His words prompted a disbelieving look and she returned to the fridge to pull out lettuce and tomatoes. Marcus came up and put his arms round her. She straightened up and leaned against him.

'Sorry,' he whispered. 'I'm extraordinarily clumsy, aren't I? Being inside has made me forget how to behave.' She put her hands on his and clamped them to her chest, letting her spine shape itself to his body. 'This has all come as a bit of a surprise, to be honest.'

Binnie turned to face him. 'Has it?' She lifted one eyebrow. 'Then it's probably best not to talk about it. Or even to think about it. Let's just *be*.'

'Sounds reasonable.'

'God! You sound like your brother. So damned phlegmatic.' She pushed him away. 'Now, I for one am *extremely* hungry.'

They sat at the small table, which had gatelegs and looked as if it had seen a few jumble sales.

'I'm not going to serve you, so help yourself.'

'Fine.' Marcus sliced some bread, then refilled their glasses with the bubbly.

While they ate, he tried to understand what was going on here. Was it possible that Binnie had been carrying a candle for him all these years? That her teenage crush on him had never really gone away? Then he reminded himself that she'd been unfaithful to Sebastian with other men. So, was sex just something she did when the opportunity arose? He needed to know. Because if the answer was the first alternative, it would be harder to deal with than the second.

'When did you first er, you know, cheat on Sebastian?' he asked, unable to think of a way to phrase the question more delicately.

Binnie looked across the table at him. Her instinct was to tell him to mind his own business, then realised her answer could be a way to finding out things about *him*.

'I take it you're not planning a tête-à-tête with your brother in the near future,' she said, checking.

'Sebastian and I have never confided in one another, you know that.'

She nodded. 'Then, if you really want to know what a bad woman I am, I'll tell you. It was about ten years ago.' She pressed her lips together, suddenly afraid. She'd never admitted this to anyone.

'And? Who was he?'

She took a deep breath. 'Well, actually he was a friend of the family. Called Henry.' She sighed, knowing it would be hard to make any of this sound good. 'In fact, he was the husband of my best friend.'

'Ouch.'

'We'd all been on holiday together, the two families sharing a house in Provence. The others went off to the beach and Henry and I found ourselves alone. And it just sort of happened.'

'Like you and me just now.'

'Well . . .'

'And when the holiday was over?'

'We went on meeting. In hotel rooms. But only for a few weeks. It was too dangerous. And in a way, the circumstances made it all rather sordid. The looks we got from the receptionists – it took the gloss off it. But the main point was, neither of us wanted to wreck our marriages. So we stopped it.'

'How very down to earth of you. I'd have thought that having started in Provence some of that reckless *amour* might have rubbed off on you.'

'It was sexual, not to do with love.'

'Ah. Yes, of course.' Marcus wasn't used to women separating the two sets of feelings. It could have been a man talking. And it made him feel even more inadequate about his own performance a short while ago.

'What about you?' Binnie asked, determined to get something in return. 'Did any of your *amours* ever come close to being legitimised?'

'Oh, it crossed my mind from time to time,' he declared airily. 'But for one reason or another it never happened.'

'Were you in love with any of them?'

'Oh yes! All of them, at one time or another. Falling in love was easy. Keeping it going was the part I found hard.'

'There wasn't any one woman you've always thought of as your soul mate, but for some reason or other . . .?'

From the distant look in Marcus's eyes she knew she'd touched a nerve.

'In my imagination, perhaps.'

'Who was that?'

He shook his head. He'd never told anyone. And never would.

'I remember one woman you lived with for several years. We met her one Christmas, I think.'

'Kaitlin. Irish, and with a temperament to match. It was friends of hers who got me into trouble. She was a very good sculptor. I met her in Paris when I was twenty-eight. I was living there then, you remember. Doing rather well. She stayed with me for five years.'

'What happened?'

'She got bored with me.'

The dismissive way he said it made Binnie think there was another reason. 'Fed up with waiting for you to commit yourself, more likely.'

Marcus smiled ruefully. 'Probably. We stayed friends, but she found another bed to share. What about my dear brother? He's had affairs too?'

'Sebastian has *women*. I don't know the details but I suspect he pays for them. It's a clubby thing. Lots of men in charcoal suits swapping phone numbers at the Reform. But I always know when he's been with one of them. There's a stupid, smug look on his face. And he comes home smelling of soap instead of sweat.'

'And does he know about your affairs?'

'No. I'm certain he doesn't. If he did I'd probably have a broken neck by now. At any rate, our marriage would be over. He would chuck me out.'

'Then you're playing with fire.'

'I've been very careful.'

'Until now.'

Binnie shivered. It was true that she was raising the stakes. True that she might trip herself up. Yet she couldn't stop. The prize was in her sights.

She caught his corduroyed leg between her knees, then slid her hand along it until she could feel his bulge.

'I think,' she said, 'we've *talked* about sex for quite long enough. Don't you?'

Wood Park

Tom's attempt at being a detective the previous day had yielded no fruit. Despite phone calls and knocking on several doors, he'd failed to discover the name of any school friend Sara might have confided in. In the afternoon the estate agents had taken more of his time than expected and he'd realised that if he allowed himself to be sidetracked by the past the week would slip by without him finishing what he had to do in the house.

Yet he was still determined to identify Sara's 'L' if he possibly could, and the only way was to tap other people's memories. If *her* friends were proving untraceable, he would have to resort to his own. It was an uncomfortable decision, because these were the very people he'd spent the last thirty years avoiding.

He decided to wit with Binnie. She'd never been close to Sara or even liked her particularly, but she was female. If there'd been a predatory male in the neighbourhood with a name beginning with L, she might well remember him.

Tom started with the premise that Binnie was more than likely still married to Sebastian. She was the type who stuck at things. The London phone book listed six Warwicks with the initial 'S'. He rang four without success, then got a recorded voice that was unmistakably hers.

Hearing its warm and gentle tones after all these years was an unsettling experience for him, so much so that he put the phone down without leaving a message. The pathetic teenage awe he'd once felt for her came flooding back.

Then he got a grip of himself. It would be madness to let the unfulfilled expectations of his youth stand in the way of getting to the truth. He stared out into the garden, trying to decide how best to handle it. Time was short. In a few more days he had to return to Cheltenham. If he left a message for Binnie and she didn't respond for a while, he would've lost his chance. So he decided to try his luck and turn up unannounced.

At ten past five Tom parked the Renault in a tree-lined street in Putney, a discreet distance from the house listed in the phone book. The windows of the Edwardian semi were closed, with the downstairs curtains drawn. He rang the bell. No response, so he returned to the car to wait.

The last time he'd met Binnie and Sebastian had been soon after returning from the Far East. There'd been a welcome-home party for him and Marcus, hosted by Marcus's parents. It was the first time he'd seen his fellow ex-National Serviceman since the fall of Seoul. Tom hadn't felt like celebrating. The broken home he'd returned to had felt like a morgue and he was still grieving for Pete Hewitt. He'd got maudlin and drunk, he remembered. In contrast, Marcus had been odiously cocky, telling anyone who would listen how he'd saved Tom from being bayoneted by a Chinaman. Binnie and Sebastian had listened avidly, then left the party early because of their baby.

An hour passed. Children returned from school, mothers walked by with buggies and, as six o'clock approached, people began coming home from work. They all ignored this middle-aged man in a car reading a paper.

Then at six-fifteen a taxi drew up and Sebastian got out. There was no mistaking him. The same straight, dark hair and confident jaw. Fuller round the waist maybe, but Sebastian had looked middle-aged from the moment his voice broke.

Earlier that afternoon, Tom had got a colleague at GCHQ to look up the MoD directory for him. Sebastian, it turned out, had risen to the rank of Assistant Under Secretary, head of a department dealing with advanced weapons projects. Tom watched him pay the driver, then walk up the short garden path to the house. Shortly after the front door closed, the living-room curtains were drawn back.

Talking to Sebastian was not what he'd come here for, so Tom decided to wait. He watched for another forty minutes, wondering what Binnie did for a living that kept her out so late. Then a Volvo swept past and he recognised her from the jutting chin and round face behind the wheel. No spectacles and the hair was lighter, but as she got out and locked the car door, her tall, slender figure in plain skirt and pullover reminded him forcefully of the young girl he'd once thought of as a future wife.

Tom overcame his nerves and propelled himself from the Renault. At the sound of the car door shutting, Binnie turned her head to see who it was. From her frown he judged that she hadn't recognised him.

'Binnie! It's Tom. Tom Sedley.'

She gaped. 'Tom . . .' Her voice cracked. 'What on earth . . .?'

'I was in London, so . . .'

'Yes. How amazing to see you. It must be—'

'Thirty years. I worked it out.'

'Good Lord.'

She looked quite shaken. Frightened, rather than glad to see him.

'Sorry to drop in on you like this . . .'

'It's – it's wonderful to see you. Come on in. Sebastian's back already by the look of it.'

Binnie looked acutely uncomfortable. Tom feared that he'd badly misjudged things by coming here unannounced.

'Look, if it's not convenient . . .'

'Don't be silly. Come in.'

'You're sure it's no trouble?' He could see she was annoyed that he hadn't phoned.

'Course not.'

Binnie opened the front door. The stairs rose up in front of her like a safety ladder. She knew if she didn't reach them soon she could be in an embarrassing situation. Her departure from Marcus's bed had been too hurried. She hadn't put any pants on and could feel his juices running down the inside of her leg.

'Seb?' TV noises emanated from the living room. 'He has it on all the time at the moment.' She touched Tom lightly on the arm. 'Incredible to see you again, but you'll have to excuse me. I need the loo rather urgently.'

'Of course.'

'Seb! We have a visitor.'

Tom heard the clink of bottle on glass in the living room. He wondered whether to go in, but decided to wait in the hall.

The door swung back. Sebastian lumbered towards him, clutching a whisky tumbler.

'Good Lord! It's Tom, isn't it? You old rascal. What on *earth* are you doing here?' He seized Tom's hovering hand, but his grip was curiously limp.

'Sebastian, how *very* nice to see you. You don't look a day older.'

'God! I should bloody well hope I do! You look about fifty!' He laughed explosively. 'Well, you *are* fifty.'

'Fifty-two.'

'Exactly. Have a drink, for God's sake.'

'Thanks. I'd love one.'

'Whisky? Sherry?'

'Sherry would be lovely.'

The room was all damask and reproduction French furniture which made Tom's toes curl. Sebastian crossed to a sideboard and filled a glass for him. On his way back he glanced at the TV.

'Have it on for the newsflashes,' he explained. 'Now, tell me everything. Where've you sprung from?'

'Well, I live in Cheltenham.'

'*Do* you, indeed . . .'

'I work at GCHQ.' Tom would never normally volunteer such information, but Sebastian was in the business.

'Good heavens. That's not why you're here, though.'

'Not at all. This is just a social call. There's something I wanted to discuss with Binnie. To do with my mother's estate. Something she might remember which I can't.'

'Your mother's dead? I'm so sorry.'

'Week before last. I'm in London sorting the house out.'

'That house in the Close?'

'Yes. My father died years ago so there's only me to finish things off.'

'Well, I never. Now where's that damn wife of mine?' He stepped past Tom and called her name up the stairs. 'Lives in a world of her own half the time.' He turned back into the living room. 'Yes, it's awful when they go, isn't it? My own mother died five years ago. Cancer.'

'And your father?'

'Got married again six months later. Went off to live in Spain. Happy as a sandboy.'

Binnie reappeared. She'd changed into jeans and a roll-neck sweater, brushed her hair and sprayed herself with perfume.

'Sorry about that. Sebastian's given you a drink, I see. You'll stay to supper, I hope?'

'Well . . .'

'Of course you will. I'll go and sort something out.' She turned away, but stopped when Sebastian said it was her Tom had come to see.

'Oh? How nice.' She looked a little bemused.

'Thinks you've got a better memory than me, or something.'

'Later,' said Tom. 'It can wait.'

Binnie arched her eyebrows, trying to divine what he wanted.

'My mother died a short while ago,' Tom explained, as if that was sufficient.

'I'm so sorry.'

'She had Alzheimer's.'

'Ah. That must have been hard.'

He could see that she was still waiting for an explanation for his unexpected arrival.

'Well, the reason I'm here, it's to do with Sara, actually.'

'*Jesus!*' Sebastian jabbed a finger towards the TV. 'Oh, good Lord . . .' The blood drained from his face.

Tom read the newsflash at the bottom of the screen. *RN destroyer hit by Argentine missile. Many casualties.*

Sebastian strode into the hall and picked up the phone.

'Oh dear,' Binnie whispered. 'Revenge for the *Belgrano*, I suppose.'

'There'll be some worried families in Portsmouth tonight,' Tom murmured.

Binnie hovered by the door, watching her husband press the receiver to his ear. Tom overheard the word *Exocet* and disparaging remarks about the French.

Very soon the phone was replaced.

'I have to go in.' Sebastian retrieved his jacket from the sofa. 'It's HMS *Sheffield*.'

'You're involved in the Falklands operation?' Tom was a little surprised.

'Only inasmuch as my department deals with advanced missile technology.' Sebastian tightened his tie. 'Car keys, Binnie?' He held out his hand. She left the room to find them. 'The ridiculous thing is we're supposed to know all about bloody Exocets. Use them ourselves. So the *Sheffield* should have been able to decoy the damned things. Need to find out what happened, before the Argies get lucky again.'

'Sounds very serious.'

'Very much so. If they get one of the aircraft carriers we're done for. Have to turn the whole fleet round and bring it home.'

Binnie reappeared and handed him the keys.

''Bye, Tom,' Sebastian grunted. 'Don't let my wife bore you.'

'Bastard,' Binnie murmured, after her husband had gone.

'I'm sorry. Hope my arrival hasn't caused . . .'

'Good Lord, no. He's always like that. Takes great pleasure in putting me down in front of other people. I'm quite used to it. Come into the kitchen. Do you eat pasta?'

'Absolutely.'

'Then I'll knock us up some supper while you tell me all about yourself.'

While Binnie worked at a chopping board with her back to him, Tom sat at the small gingham-covered kitchen table and told her a little about his life.

'It's government work. High-tech communications. Very boring.'

He described his social life with a small circle of friends, interested in art and literature.

'Not the theatre?' Binnie asked, remembering his aversion to his mother's world.

'Even the theatre, these days.' He smiled.

'Are you married?' She turned to look at him.

The inevitable question for which he was never quite prepared. 'No. I suppose the right woman and the right moment never quite coincided.'

She looked at him fondly. 'Such a pity. I often thought what a good husband you'd be. Even at one time imagined . . .' She didn't finish the sentence. '*Dear* Tom . . . Funny, isn't it? You and Marcus. Both unmarried.'

'Marcus too? I didn't know. We're not in touch.'

'Nor am I, of course,' Binnie added rapidly. 'But that's what I understand.' She chopped garlic noisily. 'I wonder if he's still in prison.'

'*Prison?*'

'You didn't know?' She turned round again.

'No.'

'Oh yes. He got eight years for manslaughter.'

'*What?*'

'It was awful. Didn't you read about it? It was in the papers.'

'I had no idea. What happened?'

Binnie took a deep breath. 'He'd fallen on hard times, poor lamb. Got in with a bad crowd. Irish no-goods. Tinkers. They all went off to a stately home in Norfolk in the dead of night to steal some paintings. They'd got inside undetected when the owner – some minor peer – heard a noise and discovered them. There was a struggle and Marcus hit him.'

'What with?'

'A heavy glass ashtray.' She grimaced. 'It smashed his skull.'

'That's appalling.'

'Yes. Awful.' She kept her eyes averted, avoiding his gaze. 'His defence was that he panicked. Lost control in the heat of the moment.'

'But smashing someone's skull . . .'

'I know.' She turned away.

Tom found the news acutely disquieting. If Marcus could lose control and kill someone just like that, what might he have done in the past?

'When did all this happen?'

'About five years ago.'

Tom thought back. He'd been distracted at that time and hadn't taken in what was going on outside his own small world. A new partner in his life, a man twenty years his junior, but it hadn't lasted.

'Well, well, well. And you think he's still inside?'

'Dunno. With remission I suppose he might be out.'

Binnie said it with the false innocence of a child. Tom began to wonder if she knew more than she was saying.

'But tell me about your mother,' she went on, changing the subject quickly. 'Alzheimer's. Was it terrible, the end?'

Tom described the awfulness of dealing with senile dementia. Binnie seemed quite shocked. Her own parents were infuriatingly healthy despite her mother being a lifelong smoker. They lived in Devon.

She laid the table and gave him a bottle of red wine to open. Then they began to eat. Tom thought obsessively about the man called 'L', racking his brains for any recollection that might make Marcus a candidate. Shortly he would raise the subject with Binnie, but for now he found, rather to his surprise, that he was enjoying the cosiness of just being with her.

'How's that daughter of yours?' he asked, remembering the squalling baby he'd seen when they last met.

'Which one?'

'Ah. I'm out of date. I meant your first-born.'

'Amanda. She moved to Australia with her husband and two children a couple of years ago. I've been out there twice. Amanda is a wonderful person. So utterly straightforward and normal. I can't imagine how she turned out so well, having me as a mother.'

'And you have other children?'

'Stephen was next. A beautiful baby, but the poor little chap caught polio when he was four.'

'How dreadful.'

'We thought he was going to die. But he made a remarkable recovery. He still walks oddly and his legs are pretty wasted, but he managed to get a degree and now works in the City. And then there's Jane.' Binnie let out a long sigh.

'Problems?'

'Of the hormonal sort. She was an appallingly difficult teenager. Totally out of control. Pregnant at sixteen. Beating *me* at that game,' she joked bitterly. 'I persuaded her to have an abortion. The boyfriend was *black*.' Binnie pulled a long face. 'I know that's not supposed to matter these days, but it did to me.'

'Aren't you a Catholic?'

'Yes.' She shook her head in dismay. 'Let's just say it was a very trying time, but I had to do what was best for Jane. Oh, Sebastian never knew about her pregnancy by the way, and still doesn't, so don't . . .'

'Of course not.'

'But that wasn't all. Jane then got into drugs. Left school without any A levels and lived in a squat for a couple of years. But –' Binnie said forcefully, holding a triumphant finger in the air '– she eventually found a job! In a hostel for the homeless. It pays her peanuts but she's now doing an Open University degree.'

'Fantastic.'

'Yes.' She crossed her fingers firmly. 'And she has a steady boyfriend. He's rather grim, but he seems to love her.'

'Well, that's . . . that's great.' Tom wanted to turn the conversation to the subject that had brought him here, but Binnie was in full flow.

'Yes. Yes, it *is* great. You know, in a funny sort of way I admire Jane even more than the other two. I mean she's tasted so much more of life than I ever did. And survived it.'

'Sounds like you've had a pretty fulfilling marriage . . .' he said, trying to bring the topic to an end.

Binnie gulped. 'Not quite how I'd describe it . . .'

'I meant the children . . .'

'Oh, I love *them* all right, yes.'

'Ah.'

'But I've never loved Sebastian, Tom. I'm sure you realised that.'

'I'm sorry, I didn't know.'

'Things are only all right between us so long as I do what he tells me.

Love, honour and obey – it's the last of those three words that counts for him.'

'Still, you've stuck it for over thirty years.'

'With difficulty. With difficulty, Tom.'

Binnie reached over and squeezed his hand. 'I can't tell you how nice this is to have you here. I always felt you were a person I could talk to. If you hadn't been out in Korea all those years ago . . .' She gave him a forlorn little smile.

This tale of a wasted marriage diminished her somehow in Tom's eyes. It irritated him that she hadn't fought back. Done something to make it good.

'I was full of innocence back then,' she continued. 'I suppose I thought Sebastian quite glamorous at the time. Oxford graduate. And he had a job.' She narrowed her eyes. 'You know how I got pregnant?'

'No.' And he wasn't sure he wanted to.

'He asked me to go to Brighton with him for the day. It was a Saturday. We'd gone to the pictures a few times up till then, but nothing very serious. I had the feeling there'd been someone at university he'd been in love with. Anyway, I thought it'd be fun and said yes. Well, he took me to a restaurant for a boozy lunch, then announced he'd reserved a room in a hotel.' Binnie shook her head. 'I was so naive. Said I didn't want to go with him, but he told me he'd already paid for the room so we had to. He'd worked it all out, you see. Planned it all, except for the little matter of contraception.'

'So that was it?'

'Lost my virginity and got pregnant,' she said ruefully. 'All over in about three seconds flat. And, although I didn't realise it at the time, I suppose that was my first experience of what he was really like.'

'How d'you mean?'

'He made it absolutely clear that nothing would stand in his way.'

'You're not saying it was rape?' A new little suspicion was germinating in Tom's head.

Binnie wrinkled her nose. 'No. Not real rape. I wasn't cowering in a corner screaming *don't do it*. It was more like facing a tidal wave, knowing there was no escape.'

'I remember Marcus saying the same sort of thing,' Tom mumbled. 'He couldn't argue with Seb. Used to get thumped if he did.'

'Quite.' She smiled nervously, thin lips in a flat, straight line. 'You know, I was really quite scared of Seb when I married him, Tom,' she admitted, in a small voice, 'and I've been scared on and off ever since.'

'What happens if you stand up to him?'

Binnie toyed with the remnants of her food, then pushed the plate away. 'He gets very angry.'

'Angry?'

'Well, violent at times.' She half-covered her mouth, as if trying to hold back the words. 'He strangled me once.'

'Seriously?'

She nodded, her eyes wide open. 'Seriously. I blacked out. When I came to, he had the phone in his hand to dial 999.'

A shiver ran up Tom's spine as he remembered the bruises on Sara's neck.

Binnie grabbed his hand. 'I shouldn't have told you all that. Don't ever repeat it to anyone, please.'

'Of course not.' But it had set his mind racing.

Binnie stood up and cleared away the plates. 'I'm serious. If Sebastian knew I'd told you, he'd kill me.'

Her words chilled him further. A threat of violence if she talked. The same threat that L had made to Sara thirty-four years ago. 'Don't worry. I won't breathe a word.'

Tom wrung out his memory again. He couldn't recall Sebastian ever showing an interest in his sister, but he'd certainly been there at the time. Aged nineteen, on vacation from Oxford. And having a liaison with a girl five years younger than him was certainly something he'd have been keen to keep hushed up.

'Cheese or fruit?' Binnie held the fridge door open.

The question he'd come to ask could wait no longer. Sebastian might be home any minute.

'Neither. Look, Binnie, there is a reason I've come crashing in on your privacy this evening . . .'

'Don't put it like that,' she said, her eyelids half closing. 'But I *was* wondering when you'd get round to it. You said something about Sara . . .'

'I've found her diary, Binnie.'

'Oh?' She turned away and busied herself at the sink, not looking at him.

'Would you mind sitting down again?'

She dried her hands on a tea towel. 'What does the diary say?' Her face had lost all expression.

'It reveals that she had a secret boyfriend in the weeks before she died.'

'Oh. Who was he?'

'That's the point. I don't know. She only referred to him as "L".'

'L?' Binnie blinked rapidly. She fingered her wedding ring.

'Ring any bells for you?'

'L . . . Just that? Nothing else?'

'Nothing else.'

'No description? What did she say about him?'

'That he was her master and she was his slave.'

'Bit melodramatic.'

'Yes. It also said he'd threatened to cut her tongue out if she ever revealed who he was.'

Tom watched for a reaction. For a brief moment there was disquiet in the eyes, then the mask descended again.

'Nice chap,' Binnie said.

'Mean anything to you?'

She shook her head. 'Of course, L may have stood for a pet name rather than his real one.'

'Quite. But you've no idea who it might have been?'

'No idea at all. And of course you're wondering if this mystery man was the real murderer instead of poor old John Hagger.'

'Exactly.'

'Well, I suppose we'll never know,' she said, turning her face away.

'Unless I can find out who L was.'

'Who do you suspect, Tom?'

He hesitated. Should he suggest it could have been Sebastian? Might the same thought have ever gone through her head?

'I'm thinking it could've been someone close. Someone right in the middle of our little community.'

'Like Marcus or Sebastian, you mean?'

'Well, yes.' Binnie's directness surprised him.

She shook her head. 'I'm sure you're wrong.'

He could see her mind racing. 'What are you thinking, Binnie?'

She shook her head again, then plunged her face into her cupped hands.

'What is it?'

She looked up at him and sighed. 'I've not been entirely honest with you, Tom.'

'What d'you mean?'

'I *have* seen Marcus. I saw him today, in fact.'

'Oh?'

'He was released from prison at noon. He got parole. I collected him and took him to the place I'd found for him. Just until he gets back on his feet. Sebastian doesn't know. You must promise me . . .'

'Of course.' Tom stared at her, trying to guess what this was all about.

'I started going to see him in prison about eighteen months ago,' she explained. 'Sebastian wouldn't have anything to do with him and I thought it was only right. And . . .' She seemed at a loss as to how to continue.

'And you ended up getting more involved than you planned?'

Binnie didn't reply for several seconds, keeping her eyes focused on the floor.

'I've always been fond of Marcus. You know that, Tom. Much fonder than I ever was of Seb. I know what you're saying about Sara. That this boyfriend could have been someone close. But Marcus?' She shook her head firmly. 'No. I'm certain it wasn't him.'

Tom leaned back in his chair and folded his arms. There was something touchingly vulnerable about her at this moment. Whatever she was involved in, she was out of her depth. And he feared for her.

'You will be careful, won't you, Binnie?'

'Careful?'

'With Marcus.'

'I don't need to—'

'He's killed someone, Binnie. Several people, if you include what happened in Korea. There's a side to his character that you may not be aware of. I saw it once and it nearly cost me my life.'

'Tell me . . .'

'No. It's too complicated. I can't explain it to you. Just trust me. And be careful.'

Binnie nodded solemnly. 'Of course I will. But you don't have to worry.' She reached across the table. 'It's sweet of you to care. Now . . . let me at least give you some coffee. And then we can talk about *you*. I'm dying to hear about the loves in your life.'

Tom had no intention of telling her about Gerry and the others.

Discussing his own sexuality with people outside his intimate circle of friends was out of the question.

'No coffee for me, thank you,' he murmured. 'And I ought to be going. There's no end of things still to do back at Wood Park.'

'Oh, don't go. We've so much to catch up on. How long are you in London for?'

'Until Sunday.'

'Then we must meet again. Give me your phone number and I'll ring you tomorrow.'

He wrote it down for her.

Binnie gave him a lingering hug on the doorstep. 'Oh, Tom . . .' she whispered. 'If only, eh? If only . . .'

Tom walked back to his car with his mind in turmoil. The Warwick brothers. A fine pair. One of whom he was almost certain was 'L'.

But which?

24

Wednesday, 5 May

MARY-ANNE HAYDEN awoke with a start. The bedside clock said nine o'clock. She listened, expecting Barbara to be bustling about, but the house was silent, apart from the whine of a passing jet. They'd planned to be late starting that morning. The HMS *Sheffield* attack had kept them in the office until two a.m., filing updates for the last edition.

She got up and tiptoed to the bathroom. Barbara's door was shut. If circumstances allowed, they'd planned taking the morning off so they could show the sketch of Mary-Anne's mother to one of Barbara's arty friends. It was four a.m. in Boston and the office wouldn't make demands on them for several hours yet.

Mary-Anne took a shower and dried herself in front of the full-length mirror. There were mirrors everywhere in the bathroom, which lent the tiny room a sense of space but made her self-conscious. Her body was heavy on the hips and slightly deficient in the chest area. It was hard to know where to look to avoid seeing herself.

She was giving her hair a final rub when the door burst open.

'Sorry,' Barbara croaked, bleary-eyed. Then she took another look. 'On the other hand, to be greeted by such a pretty sight first thing in the morning . . .' Her mouth twisted into a lopsided smile. As she backed out, closing the door again, she said, 'Don't be long, please.'

Mary-Anne reddened with embarrassment. She finished quickly and returned to her room to dress.

★

After breakfast, Mary-Anne spent a few moments in her bedroom with the Bible on her lap, praying for a successful outcome to the day. Then she grabbed the cardboard tube and went out to Barbara's elderly Peugeot for the trip to the Fulham Road.

'Jennifer Manley's a real sweetheart,' Barbara declared as she wove the car through the traffic. 'We met at a do at the US Embassy. She was seeing a diplomat at the time. Jen has a genius for picking talent. Always has a couple of new young painters on the go. Mostly figurative. Oils and acrylics. Unfortunately for her, by the time they're commanding big prices they've moved on to smarter galleries. As I say, she has an eye for talent, but a poor head for business. You'll love her.'

'You think she'll be able to identify the painter of this picture?' Mary-Anne gripped the tube tightly.

'Maybe not. But she might have ideas on how to set about it.' Barbara saw the disappointment on her passenger's face. 'It's a start, my dear. The best I can come up with.'

Mary-Anne touched Barbara on the forearm. 'I know. And I'm grateful.'

'So you should be,' Barbara growled, giving another of her twisted smiles.

The Jennifer Manley gallery was in a turning opposite St Stephen's Hospital. Barbara found a parking meter in the next street and they walked back to the shop.

The gallery smelled of linseed oil. The paintings, not too many, were spaced out on the walls, except for one small seascape on an easel by the window, where it could be seen from the street. Jennifer turned out to be English and closer to Mary-Anne's age than Barbara's. She had an elongated face, long, dark hair and her body shape was disguised by a voluminous purple caftan. She and Barbara greeted one another with a warm embrace.

'And this is Mary-Anne,' Barbara explained, as they disentangled themselves. 'Hotfoot from Boston with a mystery picture for you to look at.'

'How exciting,' said Jennifer, beaming at the newcomer. 'I love mysteries!'

'It's not that special,' Mary-Anne said, removing the cap from the tube. 'As a work of art, I mean. Though it's special to me.'

'Most paintings are like that,' said Jennifer. 'They mean lots to some people and nothing to others. Anyway, show me.'

As Mary-Anne flattened the sheet of cartridge paper on a display table she saw the eagerness fade from Jennifer's face.

'Oh yes,' she said. 'Very nice.'

The word 'nice', Mary-Anne realised, was not a compliment.

'As I told you, it's of Mary-Anne's mother,' Barbara reminded her.

'At least, I think it is,' Mary-Anne added cautiously.

'He can certainly draw. It is a he? Yes, of course. You think the man may have been your father, Barbara said.'

'Yes. Does the style . . .?'

'Well, to be honest there isn't any particular style. I don't mean it's not a well-executed sketch, but there's nothing in it that would point me, or anyone else for that matter, towards a particular artist.'

'Oh.' Mary-Anne was disappointed but not entirely surprised. 'So you wouldn't know how to trace him.'

Jennifer shook her head. Then she frowned. 'When did you say this was done?'

'1950.'

'And the artist was a British soldier?'

'I think so. We were wondering if there might be a record of him. Maybe he was an official war artist.'

'There weren't any in Korea. I don't know how I know that, but I do. However, there's nothing to say this fellow didn't show his pictures when he got home.'

'If he survived,' Barbara added.

'Well, quite. I tell you what. How much time have you got?'

Mary-Anne looked at Barbara for guidance.

'Should be okay for a couple of hours.'

'Then come with me, Mary-Anne.'

Jennifer led her into a small office at the back of the gallery. She pointed to a corner stacked with slim cardboard boxes, each of which had probably once contained a ream of A4 stationery. There were dozens of them.

'My predecessor left them when I took over the gallery. I've meant to sort them out for years, but never got round to it. He was a watercolour man and seems to have kept the flyers for all the exhibitions he ever went to. I've no idea how far back they go, but if you can spare the time, help yourself. There might just be something of interest there. Come back another day if you can't finish them.'

'That's very kind of you.' Mary-Anne dreaded how long this was likely to take.

'Okay?' Barbara's back was half turned. 'If you're happy doing that, Jen and I will sit and gas for a while.'

'Sure,' said Mary-Anne sharply. She'd been hoping for some help with the task. 'I'll be just fine.'

The other two women strolled around the gallery, looking at the paintings on display, then sat at Jennifer's desk and talked. Ever curious, Mary-Anne half listened for a while, then gave up.

Opening the first two boxes, she discovered her task mightn't be that hard, thanks to the meticulousness of the previous gallery owner. Inside each was a sheet of paper showing the years covered by the contents. The first ones she looked at were from the 1960s and 1970s and she began to fear they wouldn't go back far enough. Then she found 1955 to 1958 and, by the time she'd finished, had boxes covering the years 1954 to 1960.

She heard the doorbell go and twisted round to glance into the gallery. A tallish woman in jeans had come in and was talking with Jennifer, holding out a small sheet of paper. Selling something, Mary-Anne concluded. The woman seemed in a hurry to leave again, as if not wanting to make any sort of impression. Perversely, Mary-Anne took steps to remember how she looked and for a brief moment their gazes met.

Then she returned to her task. The main problem was the gap between the date of her painting and the first of the boxes. The Korean War had finished in 1953, but the soldier-artist who might be her father would probably have left before that, his unit being replaced on the battlefront by another. He might have returned home as early as 1951 and had an exhibition the same year. In which case this was all a waste of time. She was assuming a hell of a lot, she realised. Firstly that he had survived the war. Secondly that he'd done more than paint the odd picture of Korean girls, and thirdly that he was a good enough painter to merit an exhibition.

Still, she had a real chance here. She started with 1954. It wasn't just flyers in the box, she discovered, but reviews and magazine articles too. It would take an age to check line by line for references to Korea. But she set to with a will.

Twenty minutes later Mary-Anne had finished the box and progressed to 1955. There were many fewer bits of paper for that year and she was soon on to 1956, her heart sinking as she moved further away from the Korean War.

By the time Barbara came in to announce they had to go, she'd finished 1959.

'No luck?'

Mary-Anne shook her head. 'Always a long shot, I guess.'

Barbara saw the depth of her disappointment and touched her on the cheek. 'We'll think of something else. But right now we have to move our butts.'

Mary-Anne looked at her watch. Nearly midday. Seven a.m. in Boston. The desk would soon be clamouring for news.

She replaced the boxes in their corner, picked up the cardboard tube and joined the other two women at the front of the gallery. They were bidding each other a fond farewell, standing beside the easel with its vivid seascape. The physicality of their embrace made Mary-Anne uncomfortable. She stared at the floor while they hugged. Stared down at the legs of the easel. Then she noticed that the string preventing the back leg from sliding away had broken and a cardboard box had been placed behind it as a chock.

'Jennifer . . .' She pointed at the floor.

'Oh. You missed one!' Jennifer laughed, as if the whole business was really rather ludicrous.

'Could I . . .?'

'Of course. Fetch another box from the back room, so the easel doesn't collapse.'

Mary-Anne did and replaced the one on the floor. She lifted its lid. 1952–53.

'We really don't have time for this, Mary-Anne,' Barbara scolded.

'Two seconds.' Mary-Anne placed the box on the table and started picking out the flyers. Half a minute later she'd found it.

'Look,' she said, triumphantly. 'The Dugdale Gallery. An exhibition of watercolours depicting scenes from the Korean War, by Marcus Warwick. Served as a lieutenant with the Middlesex Regiment.'

'*What* name did you say?' Jennifer gaped.

'Marcus Warwick.'

'But that's ridiculous.'

'What d'you mean?'

Jennifer strode over to the table and picked up a small square of paper, holding it out for them to see.

'But . . . that's the same name,' gasped Mary-Anne. 'How come . . .?'

'Extraordinary,' Barbara wheezed.

'It was given to me an hour ago,' Jennifer exclaimed. 'A woman came in.'

'I saw her.' Mary-Anne grabbed the sheet of paper.

> Portraits and other commissions sought.
> Oil, acrylic and watercolour.
> Marcus Warwick.

'There's a phone number,' said Barbara, still in a hurry to leave. 'You could call from the office.'

'But . . . do you know him?' Mary-Anne asked, wanting confirmation that this wasn't a dream. She had visions of a David Niven character, a gentleman artist of impeccable taste and style.

'No, I don't. But I have an uncomfortable feeling I know *about* him.'

Mary-Anne frowned. 'What d'you mean?'

'It may be a different Marcus Warwick, of course, but a painter of that name hit the headlines somewhat, a few years back.'

'Really? How?'

Jennifer screwed up her face, trying to remember. 'You're not going to like this. As far as I can recall it was an art theft that went wrong. He'd got involved with some gang stealing paintings from a stately home. And he ended up killing the owner.'

'Oh, my God . . .' Barbara covered her mouth with a hand.

Mary-Anne stared at Jennifer in disbelief.

'I'm sorry . . . But I don't think I'm mistaken.'

Mary-Anne's daydream evaporated. If this was her father, then she was descended from a criminal.

'How many years ago?' she asked, unable to disguise the tremor in her voice.

'I couldn't say. Could be five. Could be more.'

'But wouldn't he still be in jail if he killed someone?'

The two other women looked at each other and shrugged.

'Sure,' said Jennifer. 'I could be wrong about this.'

'But if she's *not* wrong, Mary-Anne . . .' Barbara's face creased with anxiety. 'Are you sure you still want to meet him?'

Mary-Anne pulled herself up straight.

'Too damn right I do. I don't have any choice in the matter after waiting so many years to find him.'

Holborn

The first photos of the burnt-out HMS *Sheffield* were appearing on the agency wires by the time the two journalists arrived back at the *Boston Star* office. They'd picked up sandwiches on the way back from Fulham and began to eat them at their desks. Initially, the warship being still afloat and most of her crew safe reduced the impact of the story on Mary-Anne. But the shock of the deaths came home to her when she saw the tear-stained faces of relatives on the lunchtime bulletins.

'You want me to go to Portsmouth and talk to the families?' she offered, hoping to demonstrate that her personal mission in London wouldn't interfere with her professional one.

'No, thanks. The desk can pick that up from the wires. No, I've heard there's a confidential briefing on the *Sheffield* attack for UK defence correspondents this afternoon. I know one of the guys. Think I'll try and get a steer from him when it's over. It's the big question we need to work on today – do the Brits have the ability to do this Falklands War, or will they come crawling to the USA for help?' Barbara noticed that Mary-Anne was only half listening. 'Have you rung this guy Marcus Warwick yet?'

'No. I was going to but . . .'

The phone rang and Mary-Anne picked it up.

'Yes. This is Mary-Anne speaking.'

Barbara looked up, saw the young woman's eyes narrow, then widen with astonishment.

'You're here in London? But that's amazing.' Mary-Anne thrust her fingers through her hair. 'Yes, of course. Of course we must meet.' She listened, mouth agape. 'Yes, yes, give me the number. Well, evenings are not so good. We work late. Breakfast would be fine. Tomorrow?

I'll ring you tonight to confirm that. Thank you. Thank you. Goodbye.'

'Sounds like you have a sugar daddy,' Barbara purred.

'You'll never believe who that was.'

'No, I'm sure I won't.'

'You remember me saying I employed an agency to find my relatives in Korea?'

'They came up with a cousin, you said.'

'Kind of. Well, that was *him*! He rang me in Boston just before I came over here, which is how he knew I was going to be in London.'

'And now he's here?'

'At the Inn On The Park hotel. On business. Here for a week.'

Barbara stared at her with a faraway look. 'You know, my dear, I think someone up there's looking out for you. Maybe you'd better ring Mr Warwick right away.'

Fear had stopped Mary-Anne doing it up to now. The fear that if this man *was* her father, she wasn't going to like what she got. But Barbara was right. She couldn't put it off any longer.

She dialled the number. The voice that answered sounded gruff and half asleep.

'Is that Marcus Warwick?' she asked timidly.

'Who wants to know?'

'I . . . I was ringing about a portrait.'

'What are you talking about? What portrait?'

'I wanted one done. Of myself. I got your number from Jennifer Manley's art gallery. Somebody left one of your leaflets there this morning.'

There was silence from the other end, then a snort of confusion. 'Leaflets? I don't know what you're talking about.'

Unsettled by his tone of voice, Mary-Anne read it to him.

'Oh God . . .' There was a long pause. 'So you want me to paint your portrait? Any particular reason?'

The question threw her. 'Well, no, I just . . . Could I come round and see you?'

'When?'

'Tomorrow morning? About ten o'clock?' She looked at Barbara, seeking her approval. The older woman shrugged and nodded. 'Can you give me the address?'

There was a kerfuffle at the other end, then a muffled expletive. 'Look, you've caught me on the hop. I've been away. Haven't quite got myself sorted yet. Perhaps you could ring again.'

'When?'

'Well, tomorrow morning, perhaps. Then I'll be able to tell you if it's okay to come for a sitting.'

'Just for a talk would be fine, if you're not ready to paint yet. So we could discuss prices and all.'

'You're American?'

'Yes.'

'Mmmm. Ring me tomorrow around nine.'

'I'll do that. Goodbye Mister Warwick.'

Mary-Anne put the phone down and covered her eyes with her hands.

'Not easy,' Barbara mumbled.

Mary-Anne shook her head. 'It's the not knowing that's the worst part. Was that my father I just spoke to? Or someone who has no connection with me whatsoever?'

'With a bit of luck, you'll find out tomorrow.'

Mary-Anne nodded and wiped her eyes with a tissue.

'You know,' she said, sniffing, 'I have an awful feeling he was drunk.'

Brentford

Binnie had finished her mail run round London's minor art galleries by two in the afternoon. She'd planned on having a couple of hours with Marcus, then getting home in time to be clean and tidy for Sebastian's return from the office, assuming some other military disaster didn't delay him.

There were no spaces outside the Brentford flat, so she left the Volvo in the nearby supermarket car park and walked, letting herself in with the spare key.

'Christ . . .' she gasped when she saw the state of the place. The little home she'd made so neat and tidy for him had been turned into a pigsty. 'What happened?'

Marcus lay on the sofa, dressed only in underpants and an unbuttoned shirt. His thick hair stuck out in all directions and his bleary, green-brown eyes had a vicious look in them.

Binnie pushed the door shut and leaned against it. A whisky bottle and a glass stood on the floor next to the sofa. On the table was the remains of an attempt at breakfast, egg-stained plate and toast crumbs. A folder of unfinished work, which she'd brought from the store the other day, along with his clothes, was spread out on the floor. Some of the sheets from it had been torn up in disgust and scattered round the room. She took in a deep breath.

'What on earth happened, Marcus?'

He glared at her like a simmering volcano.

Binnie thought fast. He'd had a crisis of confidence and drowned his sorrows. Only to be expected after what he'd been through. Sympathy was needed.

'I'll help you tidy up . . .'

'Don't you fucking dare!' He levered himself upright and stood unsteadily.

'Marcus . . .' She reached out an arm to support him, but he smacked it away, with a swing of his wrist. 'Ouch!' She backed away, trembling, remembering suddenly that in a previous moment of lost control he'd killed someone.

'What the bloody hell have you been up to?' he bellowed, his breath sour with drink. His eyes were an unhealthy colour and watery.

'I don't know what you mean.' Her stomach twitched with nerves. What she'd done that morning had been on her own initiative. She hadn't told him of her plans.

'You been telling people I'm back on the street.'

'Oh, that. Trying to drum up work for you, that's all,' she answered, trying to stay calm. 'You should be grateful.' She bit her tongue, realising she'd chosen her words badly.

'*Gratefu—*' Marcus swayed menacingly towards her.

Binnie backed away, hands groping towards the door. 'How did you find out, anyway?'

'Bloody phone call. Some bloody Yank woman wants her picture painted. No fucking idea why. Posterity, proberly. Wants to live for ever. 'S what they all want. And *you* . . .' He jabbed a finger towards her. 'You bloody . . .'

'There's nothing wrong with posterity, Marcus.' She'd reached the door and pressed herself against it. 'We'd all like some of that. And remember. It's talented people like you who create posterity. The rest of us can only buy it. Anyway, it's work! Money coming in. Aren't you glad?'

'How fucking dare you? Telling me what to do. Organising my life. Going behind my back. You're an interfering bitch. Know that? An interfering bitch.' He tottered perilously and made a grab for the back of a chair to steady himself.

'You're drunk, Marcus. Hideously drunk.'

'I'm not bloody drunk . . . Anyway, so what? My business. You can't tell me what to do. What d'you think you are, a bloody social worker? Taking pity on the poor misguided ex-con. Think you can set me back on the straight and narrow, do you? Any minute now you'll be dragging me to confession. Oh, and by the way, how does *that* go down with your priest?' He jabbed a finger towards the bedroom. 'Shagging your husband's brother mus' be some kind of mortal sin, isn' it?'

Mortified, Binnie put her hand on the door handle, ready for a quick exit. Everything she'd done for Marcus had been for one reason and one reason only. Because she loved him. Always had, ever since he'd painted her picture when she was a girl. And she'd had sex with him because she'd never done it with anyone she really loved before and needed to know how it felt. But he was as impossible now as he'd always been. As mean and selfish as his brother, and at this particular moment physically repulsive to boot.

Marcus regained control of his legs and drew himself up to his full height.

'And talking of shagging, I've got news for you.'

Binnie imagined he was about to reveal some vile venereal disease he'd contracted in prison.

'What?' she croaked.

'You're a lousy fuck.'

Tears coursed down her face. She seldom cried, but he'd cut her to the quick. She fumbled with the door lock, then groped her way to the ground floor. Outside in the street an overweight young woman ambled past, pushing a buggy and trailing an older child by the hand. They stared at her like gawpers at a motorway crash. She began to run, scrabbling in her bag for a handkerchief.

When she reached the car, she slid into the seat and locked the door. Her face was burning.

'Bastard! Evil, shitty bastard.'

Nothing had changed. She'd spent her whole life deluding herself. Binnie felt incredibly foolish. And feverishly angry. Furious at the lifetime of misery and humiliation that the Warwick family had subjected her to.

25

Wood Park

OF THE TWO brothers on his suspect list, Tom had decided to confront Sebastian first. But it took him two hours to get through on the phone. The Ministry of Defence was in meetings mode.

'I have a gap in my schedule at about one-thirty,' Sebastian told him tensely. 'If it's really important, we could have a sandwich together in my office.'

'It *is* important, Seb.'

'Then get here by one-fifteen at the latest so they can process you through security. Come to the north entrance and ring my outer office from reception. Someone'll come down and get you.'

Tom felt as though he was on a roller coaster, racing without brakes towards an uncertain outcome. During another night of not enough sleep, the thought that Sebastian was more likely to be 'L' than Marcus had become deeply entrenched. The way he'd forced himself on Binnie all those years ago, the violent nature she'd described, the loss of self-control resulting in the near-strangulation of her – it fitted. Yet he had no idea how he was going to handle the conversation with him.

He took the Tube to Charing Cross and walked through the wallflower-scented Embankment Gardens to the Ministry. Nerves were setting in, a fear that he had nowhere near enough hard evidence to justify an outright accusation. He was beginning to wish that he'd turned everything over to the police and let them do the dirty work.

Tom was fifteen minutes early. Big Ben struck one o'clock as he crossed the road to the river bank. He leaned on the stone balustrade, watching a tug towing a chain of lighters upstream against the tide. Sometimes he missed London. The buzz, the pulse of the place felt like a challenge, one he'd spent his life avoiding. He looked across at the Royal Festival Hall, which filled much of the bank opposite. Despite his love of music, to his shame he'd never been to a concert there.

He walked down as far as Westminster Bridge, then returned to the stately Portland stone north entrance of the Ministry, his anxiety intensifying.

Passes were filled in, and when a brisk young woman came down to get him he was scanned by a metal detector and passed through an airlock that sniffed him for explosives.

'The place is a madhouse at the moment,' the woman confided, as they waited for the lift.

'I can imagine.'

'You're an old friend of Mr Warwick, I understand.'

'On an all too brief visit to London. So, very glad he can squeeze me in today.'

'He's got another meeting at two, so when the moment comes . . .'

'I'll go quietly. Never fear.'

When they arrived at Sebastian's outer office, Tom was told that the 'Assistant Under Secretary' was on the phone. Three people were working there, bent over their desks in attitudes of intense concentration.

Suddenly the door opened and Sebastian welcomed him into the inner sanctum. A plate of sandwiches and a bottle of mineral water followed, carried in by the woman who'd brought him upstairs.

'Sorry about last night, Tom,' Sebastian said, pointing to a chair. 'Bad business. And we've still not got to the bottom of it.'

'Technical failure?'

'Or human error. We don't know yet. It seems the anti-missile warning systems interfere with the ship's satellite communications, so that might have been a factor. Anyway, sit down and tell me what I can do for you.'

Tom took a seat in a leather armchair. It was lower than Sebastian's and he felt at an immediate disadvantage.

'Tuck in,' said Sebastian, helping himself from the plate of sandwiches.

'Thanks.' Tom took one filled with chopped egg. 'As you know, Seb, I'm clearing out my mother's house.'

'Can't be much fun.'

'No.' He studied Sebastian's face. Not a flicker of concern over what this meeting might be about. 'I found something of Sara's.'

Still no reaction.

'Not surprised. The house was full of her stuff. My own parents told me that when they left the neighbourhood.'

'Yes. But this was a diary.'

'Aha.'

'We had no idea it existed.'

'I see. And by the look on your face it revealed something significant.'

'It certainly did.' Tom's belief in Sebastian's guilt was beginning to evaporate. 'Sara was having a secret love affair in the weeks before she died.'

'Love affair? Bit young for that, wasn't she?'

There was a look of mild curiosity in Sebastian's eyes, but no more than that. Either he was very good at bluffing, or he couldn't have been the one Sara was seeing, Tom concluded.

'Yes. She referred to this man as L.'

'L.' Sebastian shrugged. 'Is that supposed to mean something to me?'

'That's what I wanted to ask you.'

'Ah. So that's what this is all about. Well, the answer's no. I haven't a clue who L was. Have you?'

'It's what I'm trying to find out, Seb.'

'Well, my mind's a total blank, I'm afraid. It *was* thirty-four years ago.'

'What *do* you remember of that time, may I ask?' Tom inquired, beginning to feel a little foolish at having come here.

'When Sara was murdered? Not much. I'd spent the previous week up at Oxford and only returned to Wood Park on the day they found her. I remember helping with the search.'

Tom's heart sank. He'd got it all wrong.

'I thought you spent the holidays at home that year.'

'A few days here and there, I seem to remember. But, um . . .' For the first time Sebastian began to look uncomfortable. 'Well, to be frank, I had interests elsewhere at the time. There was a girl up at Oxford I was madly in love with. A brilliant student. History, I think. Well out of my league, far too clever for me. But it didn't stop me doing everything I could to get her. Actually, between you and me, she was the first woman I bedded. Or rather, she bedded me. Can't think why I'm telling you all this . . .'

'Go on.'

'Well, not much more to be said. Except that I didn't match up to her requirements. She was far more experienced than me. Told me she'd had fifteen lovers. Can you believe that? In those days. Anyway, she was much more sophisticated than I was. I sort of hung around her like a poodle, begging for scraps.' He shuddered at the memory of it. 'Never again. Taught me a lot.'

'Such as?'

'How easy it is for a man to lose his dignity, Tom.' Sebastian straightened his back. 'I'm still not sure why she kept me on the end of her string. I think she was flattered by the way I kept coming back for more, despite her belittling me the whole time.' He tried to laugh it off, but the memory of it was paining him. 'Looking back, it was a thoroughly humiliating experience. Which was why Binnie was so refreshing when we eventually got together.'

'I can imagine. When was that, exactly?'

'Let me think. After I graduated. Summer of nineteen fifty. Oh, did she behave herself last night? Didn't say too many bad things about me?'

'Not at all.'

'Because, you know, I absolutely adore Binnie. I know I say dreadful things to her at times, but the truth is I'd be lost without her. It's funny, though. There's still a whole part of her that I simply don't know. There's a . . .' He held out his hands as if measuring a fish he'd caught. 'I don't know, a section of her mind that's completely closed off from me. A private world inside her head that she never allows me to enter. And when she retreats into it, with the shutters down, nobody else seems to count. Even the children when they're around. Strange.'

A world where she dreamed of how things might have been, Tom guessed.

'Did *she* have any ideas on this chap Sara was seeing? Last night, I mean.'

'No. None at all.'

'You know, it was probably bloody Marcus.'

Tom put down his half-eaten sandwich. 'Why d'you say that?'

'Because he always was a totally untrustworthy little sod.'

'But you don't remember any special looks between him and Sara? Anything that might . . .'

'Oh no, no. Nothing at all. I'm just being my usual odious self.'

Suddenly Sebastian frowned and snapped his fingers. 'I've just realised what this is about. You think this L person killed your sister.'

Tom spread his arms. 'I don't know what to think.'

'Mmm.' Sebastian's frown deepened. 'And actually, to be brutally frank, you thought for a moment it might have been me.'

'All I'm doing is asking people if they remember anything,' Tom said defensively. 'Asking anybody who was around at the time.'

'Okay. Okay. I won't take offence, then.'

'Please don't.'

There was a tap on the door. The PA came in to announce that the Secretary of State was on the phone.

'Tom . . . I'm sorry.'

Tom got up to go. 'Sure. No problem. Good to have had this chat.'

'Take some of the sarnies with you.'

'Thanks, but I'm fine.'

They shook hands and Tom was ushered out.

'I'll escort you downstairs again,' the woman told him. 'I'm sure you'd find your way all right, but it's the rules.'

'Of course.'

Outside in the street again, Tom felt extremely foolish. Why the hell was he wasting his time pretending to be a private eye? He had no idea how to conduct an investigation. All he was doing was embarrassing himself.

That damned whispering was in his ears again.

'Oh, for God's sake, Sara . . .'

A passer-by stared at him as if the remark had been addressed at her. 'Sorry . . .

He'd be locked up as a lunatic before long if he didn't watch himself.

And if his wretched sister *was* haunting him, why the hell couldn't she just tell him L's real name?

Wood Park

Back at Heathside Close Tom finished clearing the attic, packed the train set away for Cheltenham, and lined up Sara's things that were to be taken to a charity shop. The other stuff from under the eaves was already at the local council's tip.

At a quarter to five he went to the kitchen to brew some tea. Tomorrow would be another busy day. The auctioneers were coming to value the furniture in the morning, then he had a meeting with the solicitor which could go on for hours.

The whole process of winding up his mother's life was making him feel old suddenly. While she was alive there'd been a generation above him. Now he was all there was left of his family. And with no descendants to follow him, he dreaded reaching retirement age. Particularly if he had to spend it alone.

He poured boiling water into a mug, then switched on Radio 4 to make sure there were no new disasters in the South Atlantic.

He was removing the tea bag when the phone rang.

'Tom? It's Binnie.'

His heart sank, suspecting she was wanting another get-together to delve into his private life.

'Hello, Binnie.'

'I've had a thought.' Her voice sounded peculiarly strained.

'About . . .?'

'What you said last night. Sara and this chap she called L.'

Startled, Tom reached for a notepad and pen. 'Have you, indeed . . .?'

'I mean, I have to stress it's only a thought. I never heard Sara say anything and I never saw anything suspicious between them . . .'

'Them . . .?'

'She was much younger than me, so we didn't exactly connect.'

'I understand that.'

'So don't take this as gospel or anything. It's simply an idea.'

'Tell me, Binnie.'

'Well, I'm sure you won't remember, but Marcus painted a portrait of me once. When we were in our teens.'

Marcus.

'Yes. Yes, I do remember.'

'Well, just for fun, he signed it Leonardo.'

Tom shivered.

'Leonardo . . .'

'You know, as in Da Vinci. It was his smug little joke.' There was a certain bite to her voice.

'L for Leonardo . . .'

'Exactly. I mean it could be nothing at all. And I can't *really* believe Marcus could have . . . But . . . but in the light of what you were saying last night and what Marcus has just been in prison for . . . I thought you ought to know.'

'Yes. Thank you.'

Tom tried to rein himself in, knowing that he'd already been down a blind alley with the other Warwick brother. He reminded himself how genuinely shocked Marcus had seemed when they'd found Sara's body. He didn't know what to say.

'Tom, are you there?'

'Yes. I'm here. Binnie . . .'

'It's probably nothing. I can't *really* think Marcus and Sara were seeing each other, can you? I mean she was only fourteen and he thought her a real flibbertigibbet.'

'Is that what he said?'

'Well, yes. As far as I can recall.'

Tom was remembering Korea. If Marcus *had* killed Sara it would explain things. Both his refusal to question Hagger's guilt and the near-fatal hesitation in the copse. If Marcus thought he was under suspicion from Tom, what better solution than to let him be killed in action?

Binnie was still talking.

'I don't want you to think I'm accusing him or anything. You know what I've always felt about Marcus. But I just thought you ought to know. So you can eliminate him, if nothing else.'

'You did the right thing, Binnie. Thank you. I must talk to him. You know where he is, you said. This flat you fixed him up with.'

'Ye-es . . .' She sounded reluctant and unnerved. 'I promised I wouldn't tell a soul, though.'

'I need to talk to him, Binnie.'

'Yes. Yes, of course you do. Let me . . . let me see what I can arrange. I'll try and speak with him. Get him to ring you, perhaps.'

'That'd be fine.'

'So . . . I'll call you later, then.'

'Thanks, Binnie.'

Tom put the phone down and shook his head in bewilderment. Marcus *could* have been putting it on when they found Sara's corpse. And he *had* kept well out of the way after the killing, but there'd been an alternative reason for that. Tom told himself not to jump the gun. This was the third time he'd thought he'd got a lead. The third time he might be wrong.

26

Thursday, 6 May
Hyde Park Corner

THE LOBBY OF the Inn On The Park seemed full of Asian faces. Late for her breakfast date, Mary-Anne realised that the man she was to meet could be any one of them. But she followed his instructions and hurried to the house phones to ring the room.

'I'm in the lobby,' she announced breathlessly.

'What are you wearing?'

'Oh, um, I guess it's a suit. In a kind of beige. And dark-rimmed glasses.'

'Wait for me by the elevators.'

Mary-Anne had no idea what to expect of Lee Ho Shin. His description of himself as a 'cousin' of her mother was, as she understood it, a loose term. His exact relationship wasn't clear, but it didn't greatly matter so long as he could cast some light on whether Marcus Warwick was indeed her father.

Recently she'd been mugging up on the ways of the traditional Korean family. Records of the male bloodline would go back hundreds of years, she'd learned, but the women's lineage didn't count, because they were only there to breed. It was a primitive concept that she feared might affect the way Lee Ho Shin behaved towards her.

About ten people emerged from the lift. One of them whom she judged to be in his early fifties made a beeline for her. His dark hair was slicked across a bald crown and he wore spectacles with heavy frames. There was a smile playing on his lips.

Mary-Anne bowed. She'd learned the basics of Korean culture and knew this would be expected. He bowed back, murmuring his name. Then his hand thrust out a business card.

'Oh, thank you. I'm sorry. I don't have one. I should have thought . . .'

'It does not matter.' His voice was low and steady. 'We are not in Korea now.' The twinkle in his eyes came as a relief to her.

He guided her to the coffee shop and they settled at a table near the window, overlooking Piccadilly.

'It is so fortunate that my work bring me to London at same time as you, Miss Hayden,' he said, in an accent with a slight American tang.

'I still can't believe it,' said Mary-Anne. 'Can I ask what kind of work you do?'

'My company make electronic components. For computer, TV and car. We are second biggest in Korea. I am sales director. It says so on my card.'

Mary-Anne still had it in her hand. 'I'm sorry, I didn't read it yet.' She did so. 'Sure. There it is.'

'And you are reporter for *Boston Star*, Miss Hayden. If they send you to London you must be very important person.' The twinkle in the eye again.

'Of course I am, Mr Lee Ho Shin.'

'You can say Lee. It is easier for foreigner.'

'Oh. Well, thank you. And please call me Mary-Anne.'

The formalities over, they studied the menu card and ordered.

'I guess bacon and eggs is not what you have for breakfast at home,' Mary-Anne commented, suspecting small talk was required before they could get down to business.

'Rice. Always rice.' He laughed self-deprecatingly. Then he scrutinised her intently. 'So tell me. I like to know. Have you found your father yet?'

'I'm not sure. I'm hoping to meet someone this morning who might be him. I believe he was a soldier in Korea and sketched some pictures there.' She shrugged to show she wasn't setting much store by it.

'What his name?'

'Marcus Warwick.'

Lee Ho Shin's eyes narrowed, and there was a hint of a smile. 'Wowick . . .'

'Is that name familiar?' she asked, realising that trying to read his face was like watching for Vatican smoke signals.

'Wowick,' he repeated, staring into the middle distance. 'Mister Wowick. I think maybe, yes, that is the name. Captain Wowick they called him.' He nodded as if appreciating a good wine.

Mary-Anne liked the sound of *Captain*. She clamped a hand to her mouth.

'But I not absolutely sure,' he added quickly. 'Maybe if I can meet him . . .'

'How did you come to know him?'

'You see, in year 1950 I was refugee. Many, many Korean were refugee. I come to Seoul from Pyongyang. My parents dead. I was student. I just want to become engineer, that all I want. But I need money, so I must find work. Because I speak English, the British soldier take me as translator. I go with . . . with people like you . . .'

'I don't understand.'

'Reporter. I go with reporter.'

'You worked with press liaison? For British army public affairs?'

'Yes. And this captain, maybe called Wowick, he came to join us. He very much like to draw pictures. I take him round Seoul to show him the city, then he ask to eat some Korean food. So I take him to my uncle restaurant. And Cho-Mi, your mother, she working there. She serve the captain his food, and I think he like her very much.'

Mary-Anne was speechless. This was the first she'd heard that her mother was a waitress and it was a relief. In her darkest moments she'd feared she worked the streets.

'And they fell in love?' she whispered, tears welling up.

Lee tilted his head to one side. 'Maybe so. I don't know.'

Mary-Anne couldn't hold back. She dabbed her eyes with her napkin. 'I'm sorry.'

'I didn't mean to upset you.'

'No, no. It's not your fault.' She wiped her eyes, conscious of people looking at her. 'I'm so sorry for this. You don't want some strange woman emoting all over you at breakfast.' She blew her nose.

'Please. Don't worry.'

'It's so unfair. *That's* what upsets me. Cho-Mi's life sacrificed because mine began. Where's the justice in that? Why couldn't her brothers let her be happy?'

Lee Ho Shin cast down his gaze. For a while he didn't speak. 'You don't understand,' he murmured eventually. 'In Korea . . .'

'Oh, I understand she disgraced the family by giving birth to a half-caste child. But to *kill* her for it . . . It's so unchristian. I mean I've no idea if they were Christian or not . . . The point is, if they'd let her be, maybe she could have found her lover again after the war.'

Lee Ho Shin avoided her look. 'Maybe your father not want to see Cho-Mi again,' he said sombrely. 'Maybe just want her that one time because she a woman.'

Mary-Anne swallowed. 'Of course. I'm romanticising. Love may not have come into it at all. I realise that.'

The waiter arrived with their coffee and eggs. As he placed the plates in front of them she sipped at her juice.

'Forgive me,' she said when the waiter was gone. 'I'm so American. Always inventing Hollywood endings.'

Lee looked at her quizzically. 'But you are half Korean and half UK.'

'True. But I *feel* American. I don't know what it means yet, being half Korean and half English.'

'Perhaps you will find out here in London. And of course if you come to Korea.'

'Yes. I'd like to do that some time.'

'You can stay at my house. My wife will make you very welcome.'

'Thank you. That's kind.'

As they ate, Mary-Anne told him a little about her upbringing in America. How she'd always felt an oddity there because of her looks. He asked if she'd travelled much and she admitted this was her first trip outside the United States.

'You've been to London before?' she inquired.

'Three times.' Lee glanced anxiously at his watch. 'You will see Mister Wowick today?'

'Oops. I should've called him. What's the time?'

'A quarter past nine.'

'Will you excuse me if I go to the lobby and ring? How much time have you got?'

'My first meeting is at ten.'

'I won't be long.'

Mary-Anne hurried to find a phone. Five minutes later she was back with a grin on her face.

'He'll see me as soon as I can get there. I'd better be on my way. Thank you so much for breakfast and it was such a pleasure meeting you at last.'

Lee took hold of her hand. 'Perhaps I can ask you something.'

'Of course.'

'Mention my name to Marcus Wowick. If he is your father, if he is the Captain Wowick I knew in 1950, I would like to meet him again.'

'Of course. I'll arrange a get-together. Wouldn't that be fantastic! The father, the daughter and the man who made the introduction that led to my life being created. What a reunion.'

'That would indeed be something.' Lee Ho Shin beamed.

Lee watched Mary-Anne walk away. He'd found it hard, sitting opposite a woman whose eyes so reminded him of Cho-Mi. It had taken him many long years to put those dreadful times behind him.

The name Warwick had been engraved on his heart for thirty-two years. It had been a pretence to have claimed to remember it only when she mentioned the word. Captain Warwick was someone he'd dreamed of finding one day – the man he held responsible for the grotesque and untimely death of the cousin he'd loved.

He hardly remembered what Captain Warwick looked like any more. Just the eyes. The cold look in them as he'd turned away the last time Lee had seen him.

It had been in May 1951, quite by chance. Having fled south with his uncle's family after the evacuation of Seoul at the beginning of the year, he'd at last found work with the British Army again, with a unit newly arrived in the country. He'd travelled north with them to the Han River where they were to relieve another regiment. It had turned out to be Marcus Warwick's.

He'd caught sight of Warwick clambering aboard one of the trucks that had brought the reinforcements. Called out to him. There was no doubt that the Englishman had recognised him, but he'd turned his back. Just stood there, waiting for the truck to drive him to Inchon and the sea journey back to Hong Kong. Closing his ears and his mind to what he might have to say. Lee had been unable to give him the news that Cho-Mi was expecting his baby and had had to flee her own family as a result. Unable to explain that she'd become a beggar, living off scraps, and was badly in need of help from the man who'd been the cause of her distress.

Lee Ho Shin caught the eye of a passing waiter and asked for the bill. The confrontation he'd so long wished for was coming closer.

Wood Park

Tom spent a frustrating morning dealing with a garrulous and rather unknowledgeable valuer from the auctioneer's office. The tasks involved in winding up his mother's life seemed to grow daily. Every postal delivery increased the number of people to be notified about her death. She was on the list of dozens of charities and seemed to have regular correspondents amongst her fans, contacts maintained by Emily, he assumed.

The estate agents had shown half a dozen clients round since they'd measured up on Monday. Two had come back for a second look. All of which served to increase the pressure on Tom to have the loose ends sorted by the time he returned to Cheltenham on Sunday. He would need to prioritise. In effect, the unmasking of L was going to have to take second place.

Brentford

Marcus had awoken at four a.m. with a throbbing head. He'd staggered out of bed and washed down some paracetamol with a large glass of water. It had been several years since he'd got so drunk and he was badly out of practice.

By the time the American woman phoned he'd consumed several mugs of tea and forced down some breakfast. It hadn't cured his hangover but he was functioning again.

He'd decided to let Miss Hayden come and talk to him about her portrait, because, as Binnie had said, it was a chance to earn some money. Impossible to start work today, because his hands wouldn't stop shaking. But they could discuss what she wanted, the number of sittings he would need and the cost.

The flat looked as if a gang of teenagers had held a party in it. As Marcus started to clean up, he felt worse and worse about what he'd said to Binnie. He'd been a bastard. Selfish, outrageously rude, wallowing in hurt pride. An abject apology was called for. On his knees. The truth was that he'd quite liked her fussing over him. He was bad at managing on his own.

But to apologise he would have to contact her. She'd said in no circumstances to ring her at home – fears about MoD security monitoring their calls, because of Sebastian's work being top secret. It sounded odd, but that's what she'd said. So he had no option but to wait for her to contact *him*. And, however appalling he'd been to her yesterday, he felt certain she would. Women always gave him a second chance.

Marcus kept thinking about his first afternoon of freedom and the way she'd given herself so wholeheartedly to him. After the hurried and unsatisfactory start, he'd turned in a good performance in the end, judging by the noises she'd made. That was the unkindest of all the things he'd accused her of yesterday. In the 'bed' department Binnie hadn't been 'lousy' at all.

Mary-Anne had never been so scared in her life. Everything pointed to the man she was about to meet being her father. Yet the picture of him that had formed in her head in the last twenty-four hours was not of a man she could love, or respect. A criminal. A thief and a killer. And maybe a drunk, too. A man to whom her mother might have meant nothing. Yet she knew that she had to meet him. To find out for sure. Her search for her roots had been the primary quest of her adult life. She couldn't curtail it because of fears of what she might discover.

The house in Brentford, when she saw it, was not what she was expecting. A shabby piece of suburbia rather than somewhere an artist might live. She got the taxi to go past and drop her at the end of the road, so she could have a moment to adjust. She'd imagined Marcus Warwick's home being like the brownstone terraces in Boston. Faded, but still with a sense of grandeur.

She took a deep breath and walked back to the house, ringing the top bell like he'd said. Something buzzed and the door clicked open. The stale air inside the hall smelled of unseen tenants. She climbed the stairs, the vital cardboard tube clutched in her left hand.

When the door to the flat opened, Mary-Anne half expected some instant recognition – blood smelling blood – but there wasn't any. She'd imagined an artist's beard and he was clean-shaven. Good looking once? Hard to tell. But the eyes were compelling, seeming to see right into her head.

'How d'you do?'

Marcus Warwick shook her hand. There was a strong smell of drink on his breath but he didn't appear intoxicated. He was frowning at her and she guessed she wasn't quite what he'd expected either. As he moved towards the centre of the room, he half turned his head.

'You're younger than I'd imagined.'

'Oh. I'm sorry.'

'All I meant was that people who want their pictures painted are often older. Or else wanting their children done.'

Mary-Anne glanced about the room. Quite small and smelling of cigarette smoke despite the windows being open and a breeze passing through. An easel stood beneath the skylight – more for effect, she guessed, judging by the lack of evidence of use.

'Cup of tea?' Marcus asked. 'Although being American I expect you'd prefer coffee, which I can also do.'

'Coffee would be great.' She was struggling to control her heartbeat.

As he moved towards the kitchen area, Mary-Anne noticed that his legs didn't seem to move as though they were directly connected to his body. *Very* hung-over, she concluded. She felt like a spy, knowing so much more about him than he did of her.

'You *are* Marcus Warwick?' she asked, checking.

'For my sins.'

'And . . . do you live here alone?'

Marcus glanced back, as if surprised by the personal nature of the question.

'As it happens, yes. At the moment.' His gaze lingered on her. She felt disturbed by it, suspecting that she was being assessed sexually. 'What about you? You live here in London?'

'For a month or so. I'm a journalist with the *Boston Star*. Over here for the Falklands . . .'

'Ah, yes.'

'You think Britain will win?' she asked, fearful of plunging straight into the only question she really wanted to ask.

'God knows. Be disastrous for the country if it all goes wrong, but at least we'd be rid of that woman.'

Mary-Anne watched him switch the kettle on. It started singing immediately, so it must have just boiled. Hands shaking visibly, he put Nescafé into two mugs. Then, to calm her own nerves, she took a peek at his bookshelves to see what he read. Thrillers, mostly. She picked one off the shelf and found it had someone else's name in it.

'The flat's rented and the books came with it,' Marcus explained, emerging from the kitchen alcove with the two mugs. He caught sight of the cardboard tube she was holding and grimaced. She guessed what he was thinking. That she would show him the contents and say 'I want one like this'.

'Here we are.' He placed the mugs on the table. 'Now, let's get to business. What did you have in mind?'

Heart pounding faster than ever, Mary-Anne held out the tube. 'I wanted to show you this.'

'What is it?'

'A picture of my mother, I think.'

'You *think*?' Marcus's brow furrowed.

'I'm pretty sure.'

'Was she by any chance the oriental half of your parentage?' he asked matter-of-factly.

'Yes. She was Korean.'

'*Korean* . . .' He looked startled suddenly, then frowned at her.

'Yes. I was born in Korea.'

Mary-Anne watched for some sign that he'd guessed why she'd come, but couldn't see any. He continued to frown, as if digging deep into the past. When he still made no move to open the tube, she decided to take the initiative, pushing off the plastic cap and extracting the roll of cartridge paper for him.

Behind the frown, Marcus was reeling with shock. Through the lenses of this young woman's spectacles he'd seen Cho-Mi's eyes. He shivered. It was as if Korea's bitter north wind had found its way in through the open roof light. With fumbling fingers he held tightly to the tube of paper, not daring to unroll it.

'Where did you get this?' His voice cracked as he asked the question. He told himself it was coincidence. That millions of Korean women had those eyes. And yet hers were now brimming with tears.

He steeled himself and unrolled the cartridge paper to reveal the face he'd drawn more than thirty years ago.

'How did you get this?' he gulped.

Mary-Anne dabbed the corners of her eyes with a tissue. 'It was handed in to the orphanage in Korea. With me, when I was a baby.'

'W-when? When was this?'

'30 October 1951. I was about four weeks old.'

'I see.'

Marcus had no need to do the calculation. Cho-Mi had been a virgin when he'd pumped his love into her and, unless others had got to her soon after, this woman was probably his child.

His *child*. This not particularly attractive mongrel woman with an American accent. It wasn't sinking in.

He spread the picture out, to give himself time to think. It was a good portrait. One of his best, even after all these years. And it brought hammering back to him the overwhelming power of his infatuation for the skinny little waitress during that bitter cold Christmas in Seoul.

'You *did* draw this?' she asked, seeming to need it spelled out.

'Oh yes,' he croaked. 'Yes, I did this.'

'And you and my mother . . . you made love together?'

Marcus held up a finger.

'Just once,' he whispered. 'Then the war tore us apart. She disappeared. I . . . I thought she was dead.'

'Well, she *survived*.' The stress that Mary-Anne put on the word made it sound like an accusation. She removed her glasses and dabbed her eyes more thoroughly.

'I . . . I don't know what to say.' Marcus didn't feel in any way equipped for this sort of situation. Physically, mentally, he seemed to lack the proper responses. 'From what you're telling me, it sounds like you could be my daughter,' he said lamely.

Mary-Anne was speechless. It was the moment she'd dreamed of, yet the joy she'd hoped for was totally absent.

'And – and you, I think, are my father,' she stuttered.

Then they both stood up and moved round the table to embrace. But not for long, pulling apart awkwardly without looking at one another.

'This is a terrible shock,' Marcus bumbled. 'I mean, not *terrible* . . . wrong word. A *great* shock. A fantastic one. I simply had no idea.'

Marcus never dreamt that a child could have come from that brief surge of passion on an ice-cold floor. And he still couldn't grasp that this woman had his blood in her veins, his genes. A female whom a few minutes ago he'd been assessing in a totally inappropriate way. He stared at the picture again, then up at her.

'The eyes,' he said, slowly getting himself under control. 'Same as your mother's. And the shape of the face.'

'But I think I have your nose,' she told him, laughing nervously.

'Sorry about that.'

'Oh, it's nice. Something we have in common.' She forced a smile.

Marcus couldn't say it to her, but the face in the picture was so much more beautiful than hers. He'd soon forgotten how lovely Cho-Mi had looked, but he'd always remembered the strength of his longing for her. She'd become his 'if only' girl, as the years rolled by with his life skidding from one failed relationship to another.

'I think I'd better sit down again,' he said, flopping on to the chair.

Mary-Anne blew her nose to clear her eyes. 'You've no idea how often I've wondered about you.'

'Of course. You must have done.'

'What you looked like, or even whether you were alive.'

'How . . . how did you know I was English?'

'I managed to trace a relative in Korea. A cousin of my mother. A man called Lee Ho Shin.'

'*Lee* . . . Good heavens.'

'You remember him? He told me my mother met a British soldier who liked to draw. And it turned out to be you.'

'But how on earth did you track me down?'

'Luck. Hard work. And a little help from God, I think. I found an old leaflet advertising your Korean paintings exhibition.'

'But that's extraordinary.'

His shoulders had slumped and he'd taken on something of a hunted look. Mary-Anne knew that she should go easy on him but time was running out.

'Can I ask you some things?'

'Of course. Anything.' Marcus propped his chin on his fist, as if his neck no longer had the strength to support his head.

'Did you love my mother?'

He blinked and she could see him calculating how to satisfy her with his answer.

'I can honestly say I've never felt the same passion for any other woman.'

'Then why did you let her go?'

'Oh . . . you don't understand.'

She watched him pick up a small round tin from the table and tease strands of tobacco from it, laying them out in a rectangle of white paper.

'It wasn't that I let her go, Mary-Anne. It was the war. We were all fleeing the Chinese.'

'But if you loved her, you'd have tried to save her . . .'

His eyes closed for a moment. Then he licked the gum of the paper and rolled the cigarette between his fingers.

'Or am I being naive?'

Marcus lit up and drew in a lungful of smoke. 'Well . . . I'm afraid you probably are, Mary-Anne.' He said it as gently as he could. 'The truth is, your mother and I were like two leaves floating on a stream, pushed briefly together by the current. There was a short lull in the war, during which we met and fell in love. Then the fighting started again and we all had to leave Seoul. Civilians in one line, soldiers in another. There was no way for us to be together.'

'But you did love her?'

'At the moment of your conception – totally.'

Mary-Anne realised that it was the most she would get from him. Then his eyes began to flicker with guilty curiosity.

'What . . . what happened to her? Why did you end up in an orphanage?'

'That's a sad story. She fled with her family to a place called Taejon.'

Her father nodded, his eyes misting over. 'I remember it. Swamped by refugees, all fighting for a square inch of space.'

'Then, when it became obvious she was pregnant, her family turned against her.'

Marcus winced.

'Well, she managed to survive somehow and gave birth to me. But she must've known her brothers would come looking for her, because she gave me away so I'd be safe.'

'And what happened to her?'

'Her brothers found her and killed her.'

'Oh Lord . . .'

Mary-Anne watched her father's face crumple. It relieved her to see his grief. Perhaps he really *had* loved her mother.

'She'd disgraced the family by bearing a foreigner's child, you see.'

He turned his face away.

'It must have happened to many women who went with foreign soldiers.'

'I suppose so.' Marcus shook his head at the awfulness of it.

Suddenly Mary-Anne looked at her watch. She imagined Barbara tapping her foot at her assistant's extended absence from the office.

'I have to go back to work in a minute,' she said, knowing there was one more vital question she needed an answer to. 'Can I ask you something?'

'Of course.'

'I heard that you'd been in prison. Is that right, or was it a different Marcus Warwick?'

Marcus's face fell. 'It's right, I'm afraid.'

'They say you killed someone.'

'It was a dreadful accident. The whole business was a terrible mistake.'

'I'm sure it must've been,' she said kindly.

'I'm not really a bad man, Mary-Anne. A foolish one, maybe. A bit wild at times. I've made mistakes. Plenty of them. But please don't think of me as bad.'

'I won't.' She smiled warmly at him. She believed what he said. 'I have to go now.'

'But there's so much I want to ask about *you*,' Marcus pleaded. 'You'll come again soon?'

'Yes, please. If I may.' She began rolling up the portrait of her mother.

'And you don't want your own picture painted . . .'

'Oh no, thank you.' She laughed, hoping she hadn't offended him. 'I'm not so picturesque. I tell you what – maybe I could take you out to lunch one day, so we can talk some more.'

'That would be very special. Being taken out to lunch by my daughter.' He chuckled to himself.

'When it looks a quiet news day, I'll ring and see how you're fixed.'

'I shall look forward to it.' Marcus shook his head. 'You know, I can still hardly believe any of this. I shall wake up in a moment and it'll all have been a dream.'

'A nice one, I hope.' Mary-Anne slid the rolled picture into its tube and replaced the cap. Then she wrote down her phone numbers for him and stood up.

'Well, goodbye, *dad*.'

They laughed awkwardly at her use of the word, then hugged one more time.

'You know, you've made me so happy,' he said, holding her by the shoulders. 'If circumstances had been different, who knows, your mother and I might have given you some brothers and sisters.'

Mary-Anne kissed him on the cheek. Then she remembered the message that she was meant to pass to him.

'Oh, I almost forgot. Lee Ho Shin is in London.'

'What?'

'On business. Said he'd love to meet, if it turned out you were the Captain *Wowick* he remembered.'

'Well, I'll be blowed!'

'Think about it. Maybe when we do lunch, he could come too.'

The suggestion seemed to unsettle Marcus, but he nodded his agreement as he opened the door for her.

'Don't come down,' she said. 'I can find my own way.'

'I'll see you very soon, my dear. Thank you so much . . . for finding me.'

Mary-Anne hurried down the stairs and stepped into the street in a daze. She wanted to cry and to laugh all at the same time.

But she couldn't do either until she'd found herself a taxi.

Marcus went to the bedroom window, which overlooked the street. With tears in his eyes, he watched Mary-Anne hurry down the road, her heels clicking on the pavement.

'My daughter . . .' He shook his head again and pinched himself.

Then someone else caught his eye. Binnie, emerging from her Volvo on the other side of the road.

'Oh, God . . .'

She'd come to give him what for. And he was far from ready for it.

Binnie glanced only briefly at the oriental woman who'd just come out of the house, assuming that she was something to do with the ground-floor flat.

It had been hard plucking up the courage to come here this morning, but she was driven in part by desperation.

Once her anger of yesterday had subsided, she'd thought long and hard about her position. She'd taken enormous risks already. Giving up so easily on her plan to start a new life with Marcus was madness. And all because of some stupid things he'd said when drunk.

She locked the car and crossed the road. There was an added reason why she needed to throw herself back into the fray. She felt bad that she'd told Tom Marcus had called himself Leonardo all those years ago. He was under suspicion now and might need her protection.

Marcus thought of not answering the door. Of pretending to be out. Or dead. But he knew the apology he owed would lose its value the longer he delayed it.

When the bell rang he buzzed Binnie in and stood at the top of the stairs, bracing himself.

'I brought you some aspirins,' she announced halfway up, holding out the pills like a peace offering. He could see that she was frightened as to how he would react.

'A veritable saint . . .' He put his hands up in mock surrender. 'What can I say?'

'About?'

'Yesterday.'

'Oh, that!' She was pretending not to care. Overdoing it. 'I never pay attention to men when they're drunk.'

'So you haven't come to plunge a dagger into my heart.'

'Not if you've sobered up. Can I come in?'

'Of course. Sorry.' He stepped aside to let her through.

Binnie stood in the middle of the room, looking around and smiling with relief.

'Well, well. This is an improvement.'

'I behaved like a pig, Binnie. I'm terribly sorry. And whatever I said, forget it. I was talking nonsense yesterday.'

She kissed him on the cheek. 'God, you reek of booze.'

Marcus covered his mouth, watching her inspect the room, her confidence growing visibly. He wondered what price she would extract from him for her forgiveness.

'You'll never believe what's just happened,' he said bouncily.

'What?' She looked worried again, as if whatever he was about to reveal would be her fault too.

'I've become a father.'

She gaped at him. 'What on earth are you talking about?'

'You saw her. She left just as you arrived.'

'A Japanese woman? I assumed she was the tenant of the ground-floor flat.'

'Korean. *Half* Korean.'

'Oh . . .' He could see her mind ticking. Calculating when and how.

'The other half's Warwick, you see. I met her mother in Seoul. Christmas nineteen fifty. A beautiful girl called Cho-Mi.'

'Met? You mean she was a prostitute,' Binnie said, assuming the obvious.

'No. She worked in her father's restaurant, actually. And we fell in love. I mean really. Truly. It was love at first sight.'

Binnie didn't want to hear this.

'And I did a drawing of her,' Marcus added.

'Ah, yes.' Binnie turned her face away. 'Of course you did.'

'What does *that* mean? It was a good one.'

'I'm sure it was, Marcus.' She gave him a condescending smile. 'You certainly know how to flatter girls with your pencil, even when you're being cruel to them with your tongue.'

He was about to apologise again when she added something.

'You realise it was that sketch of me which made me fall in love with you all those years ago?'

'Binnie . . .' He felt unnerved by her admission. Cornered.

'You signed the picture Leonardo, as far as I remember.'

He blinked at her, puzzled as to why she should remember that.

'Did I? God, I'd forgotten. Picasso, Rembrandt – I used to stick any old name down, depending on whose style I thought I was copying. Pretentious twit . . .'

Binnie was looking at him oddly, as if wanting to tell him something important but not quite daring to. Marcus decided to get back to what he'd been talking about, before she came up with any other declarations of how she felt about him.

'Anyway, this girl Cho-Mi – well, we . . . you know . . . she and I had it off. The first time for both of us. Just the once,' he added quickly, not wanting to wrong-foot Binnie by playing up the importance of the relationship. 'Then the war went crazy and I never saw her again. I was certain she must've died. Thousands did in that cold. But I found out today that she survived and, nine months later, gave birth. To *my* child.' He spread his arms in amazement.

'How on earth did she find you, this . . .?'

'Mary-Anne. The girl got adopted by an American family. Grew up there. She's a journalist now, over here for the Falklands War. But it was that portrait of her mother, Binnie. That's what did it. That's how she found me. Through the picture. Isn't that incredible?'

Binnie smiled knowingly, as if to her it wasn't incredible at all. 'And the mother? Now she's found you, she'll want her arrears of child support, I suppose.'

'Binnie . . . she's dead.'

'Sorry. I was being catty. Quite uncalled for.' To compensate, she gave him a radiant smile and kissed him on the cheek. 'Congratulations, then. This girl, your daughter, was she the one who rang yesterday, wanting her portrait painted?'

'Yes. Except what she really wanted was to find out if I was her father.'

'Married?'

'I didn't ask. I know hardly anything about her yet. She had to go back to work.'

Binnie nodded thoughtfully. Then she put her arms round his neck. 'You know, there's so much about *your* life that *I* don't know, Marcus. And I really want to.' She braved the alcohol fumes and kissed his mouth.

Marcus felt desperately frail today, and far from sure where things were heading. Bedding Binnie to spite his brother and relieve his sexual frustration was one thing, but the deeper relationship she seemed bent on pursuing was another matter altogether.

'It'd bore the pants off you,' he murmured sheepishly.

She smiled at his choice of metaphor. 'You can bore my pants off any time you like.' She kissed him again. 'And I'd love to meet your daughter.'

'Mmmm.' He wasn't at all sure he wanted that to happen. The less Mary-Anne knew about his private life the better. 'It's extraordinary, you know – there's somebody else from Korea who's turned up in London. A chap called Lee Ho Shin. We employed him as a translator when I was there. In fact, it was through him that I met Cho-Mi.'

'Lee Ho Shin . . .' She seemed to be toying with the foreignness of the name. Then suddenly her face lit up with an idea.

'This girl's come here to track down her English connections, right?'

'Well, *me* primarily, yes.'

'Of course, but she should also meet her uncle.'

'I can't think of anything worse.'

'No, but listen. You've got two people turning up out of the blue from Korea. Well, I've got a surprise for *you*. Someone else from our past has just reappeared on the scene.'

'Who?'

'Tom Sedley.'

'*Tom* . . .' Marcus felt a twitch of uneasiness.

'Yes. His mother's died and he's in London sorting out the house in Heathside Close.'

'God! Was she still living there?'

'Yes. Tell you what. Why don't I throw a small supper party? Sebastian and me. You and your daughter. Tom and your Korean translator, Lee whatsit.'

'Are you mad? Suppose Sebastian . . .' He waggled his finger backwards and forwards to indicate the two of them.

'Look, the best way to make sure he never suspects anything is for him to see us together in normal social circumstances.'

'There *are* no normal social circs when it comes to my brother and me.'

'That's why having all the others there makes it so good. There'll be so much distraction, so much to talk about. And everyone'll be on their best behaviour. No chance for awkward questions or nasty scenes. It'll be a chance to bury ghosts and explore new pastures.'

Marcus wondered what particular ghosts Binnie had in mind. He was racking his brain for reasons why this party shouldn't happen.

'What about Mary-Anne? Maybe she saw you when she left here. She might recognise you and give us away.'

'No, no. I was watching her. Not even a glance in my direction. Far too preoccupied with having found her father.' Binnie clapped her hands. 'The more I think about it, the more I think we have the makings of a fascinating evening.'

'Or a total fucking disaster.'

'Nonsense. It'll be great. How about tonight?'

Marcus groaned.

The woman was out of control and there seemed to be nothing he could do about it.

27

Wood Park

THE PHONE CALL inviting Tom to the party came as he opened the door to the estate agent bringing yet another potential purchaser to view 13 Heathside Close.

'What's prompted this idea, Binnie?'

'Well, apart from it being an obvious chance to reunite old friends, it's to celebrate Marcus's return to the world and the fact that he's just become a father.'

'I *beg* your pardon . . .'

Binnie explained what had happened and how she'd caught an accidental brief glimpse of the daughter. 'Smart and businesslike from what I saw.' She told him too about the visit to London of the Korean whom Marcus had used as an interpreter in 1950.

'Did you know the man, Tom?'

'This is all quite extraordinary! I certainly didn't know him, but I may have seen him once. What's he doing here?'

'On business of some sort. I don't know what. It's going to be fascinating, getting you all together. You can come?'

'Well, of course. Tell me, you haven't mentioned Sara's diary to Marcus, have you?'

'No. Thought I should leave that to you. Perhaps not tonight, though, Tom – might spoil things. Let this just be the reunion to end all reunions. A time for all of us to put our differences behind us. Shall we say seven-thirty?'

'Fine.'

'Oh, and Tom . . . What I told you yesterday. I got it completely wrong.'

'What – about Marcus signing himself Leonardo?'

'Yes. It was Picasso. I'm so stupid.'

Tom replaced the receiver and swore to himself. It had happened again. Every time he thought he was getting somewhere, the basis for his suspicions crumbled.

He stared out of the window. A blackbird was wrenching a worm from the front lawn. Digging up the truth about Sara's death was going to be every bit as hard.

Holborn

Mary-Anne was astonished to receive a call from someone claiming to be her aunt by marriage. Even more so to be told that her uncle was a senior official at the Ministry of Defence who might be called away from the party at short notice if something dramatic were to happen in the South Atlantic. She accepted the invitation immediately and with gratitude, knowing full well that Barbara would give her the evening off if there was even the remotest possibility of getting an inside track on the Falklands War. She took down the address.

'And would you mind contacting Lee Ho Shin and bringing him along?'

'Sure I will. I can tell you he'll leap at the chance of seeing my father again. Thank you so very much for this.'

As she replaced the receiver, she noticed Barbara giving her a proprietorial look, as if wanting some of the credit for tracking down her lost parent. Mary-Anne had an uncomfortable feeling that she was expecting something in return.

Putney

It was an unusually warm day for early May and the lawn would be dry enough for people to walk on if they wanted to. Trying not to think about all the things that could go wrong later, Binnie prepared a buffet supper. She'd bought champagne from the off-licence and quiches, salads and ham from the supermarket. She also made a large bowl of coronation chicken to ensure that no one went hungry. She'd considered attempting a rice dish for the Korean but had decided against, knowing that it couldn't compete with what he was used to. The work was therapeutic, taking her mind off the perils that her life had unexpectedly become surrounded by.

It had been a spur-of-the-moment decision to propose a party. A desperate attempt to disperse the gathering storm clouds. A way of dealing with an increasingly intractable situation by tossing the components into a pot and letting them sort themselves out. Binnie had done it often enough when the children were small, believing that if she left them to their own devices and with a minimum of interference, things would turn out the way she wanted in the end.

At ten to seven she heard the front door opening. Sebastian marched into the kitchen, scowling.

'Now what the hell's this all about, Binnie? It's simply not on to leave a message with my secretary saying I'm going to have a houseful of strangers when I get home.'

'*We*, not I,' said Binnie. 'It's *our* house. And only two of them are strangers.'

'My bloody brother's a stranger and a good thing too. How come you're in touch with him, anyway?'

'He rang. Out of the blue. He's just been released from prison and was so excited at discovering he had a daughter, he wanted everyone to know. Particularly his family. And that's *you*, Sebastian, whether you like it or not.'

'Well, it's all highly inconvenient. Life's far too serious at the moment to have to bother with such trivia. It's most inconsiderate of you to invite them here without my say-so.'

With that he stormed from the room and marched upstairs to change.

'Too bad,' murmured Binnie, trying not to tremble.

Brentford

Although he'd been expecting it, Marcus jumped when the buzzer went.

'It's Mary-Anne. Running late, I'm afraid. Sorry.'

'I'll be right down.'

'And there's a chill in the air. You might want a coat.'

He took a final mouthful of the whisky he'd poured five minutes ago and dug out his old camel duffel coat that was hanging in the bedroom cupboard. It was rather nice to have a daughter thinking about his welfare, he decided.

Mary-Anne had phoned earlier, to say she was going to the party with Lee Ho Shin in a taxi and they could pick him up on the way. He'd told her it would be a long detour for them, but when she'd said her newspaper was paying, he'd accepted.

Marcus was not looking forward to this evening. It was only to appease Binnie that he'd agreed to go to the party. Neither his brother nor Tom Sedley were top of his list of people he wanted to be reunited with. And as for Lee Ho Shin, he felt far from sure that the memories they shared would be happy ones.

Lee Ho Shin was on tenterhooks as he watched the doorway of the small house for his first sighting of the man he'd come to England to find. For many years during and after the Korean War he'd imagined what he would do if they were to meet again. He used to be very clear about what he wanted Marcus Warwick's fate to be. But with the passage of the years and the entry on to the stage of Mary-Anne, his desire for retribution had moderated. If the man showed remorse and a love towards his daughter, it might be enough. Marcus Warwick's future, therefore, lay entirely in his own hands.

On the taxi journey from Hyde Park Corner, Mary-Anne had told Lee about the prison sentence her father had served. The fact that Marcus Warwick had caused the death of yet another innocent soul only served to reinforce Lee's prejudices about the man.

When Marcus emerged from the house, he saw an oriental figure climb out of the cab to greet him. Mary-Anne watched like a ringmaster as the two men approached one another. Like wrestlers, she thought, summing each other up. Lee Ho Shin bowed. Marcus had forgotten the small amount of Korean etiquette he'd once known and held out his hand.

'I would never have recognised you, Lee.'

The Korean smiled enigmatically. 'I must say the same.' In truth he'd always had difficulty telling one European from another.

'We need to get into the cab,' said Mary-Anne. 'We'll be awfully late.'

'Don't worry about that,' growled Marcus, patting her affectionately on the arm. 'Keeping my brother waiting is always a good thing to do.'

The two men occupied the back seat, with Mary-Anne on the fold-down opposite. Marcus could see that she was extremely nervous about this evening. Join the clan, he thought.

'So when did you two guys last meet?' she twittered.

'December nineteen fifty,' said Marcus, wanting her to hear his version first. 'We all had to leave Seoul in a hurry, because the Chinese were coming.' He turned to the man beside him. Lee had wedged himself in the other corner as if to ensure there should be no physical contact between them. He sensed the man's hostility. 'Mary-Anne tells me you're a businessman these days, Lee. And successful too, by the look of you.'

'Yes. I think so.'

'You were studying engineering, I seem to remember.'

'Electronic. And you are painter? Also successful?'

'On and off.' Marcus looked up at Mary-Anne, wondering if she'd briefed Lee on his past.

'I told Lee a little about your recent troubles,' she confirmed nervously. 'I hope you don't mind.'

Marcus shrugged. His past was something that he and others would have to learn to accept.

'And your brother?' asked Lee. 'Mary-Anne tell me he work for Ministry of Defence. He was also in Korea?'

'No. Sebastian was born too early for National Service. Never served *in* a war, though with his job he may have sent a few men to their deaths in one.'

'That sounds a little extreme,' Mary-Anne soothed.

'What he do at Ministry?' Lee asked. 'Important man? In charge of Falklands task force, maybe?'

'Good Lord, no. To be honest I've no idea what he does, but I'm sure it isn't *that*. Is this your first time in London, Lee?'

'No. I been many times. Good for business, because we make electronic component very cheap and sell here. Maybe I can get military contract from your brother.' He laughed nervously, showing a mouthful of bad teeth.

'Worth a try,' said Marcus drily.

The taxi crossed the Thames at Kew Bridge, the water gleaming in the evening light. Willow trees on an upstream island cast wide black shadows on the river's surface. A flight of geese rose to negotiate the bridge, then dipped down again.

'Funny,' said Mary-Anne. 'The light's kind of different from in Boston. Silver instead of gold.'

'Not feeling homesick, I hope,' Marcus purred, hungry for any scrap about how she felt, or what her life amounted to.

'Oh no. Not at all.' She looked thoughtful for a moment. 'How could I, now I know I'm half English . . .'

Fifteen minutes later, after a tense journey in which neither man felt ready to broach the subject of the Korean War, the taxi purred into the heart of Putney. As Marcus recognised the suburban street that he hadn't visited for a decade at least, he felt his gut was about to void itself into his trousers.

Mary-Anne paid the driver. Marcus thrust his hands into his coat pockets and stood beside Lee, staring at the house in silent anticipation. It was Mary-Anne who eventually rang the bell. Binnie opened the door to them, her smile looking as if it had been embroidered into place. Behind her stood Marcus's brother, dressed in striped shirt and dark trousers, making a valiant effort not to scowl.

'This is so exciting,' Binnie gushed. 'Marcus — wonderful to see you again, looking so well. And you must be Mary-Anne.'

'That's right.'

'Let me look at you. Your father's nose, perhaps?' She laughed politely.

Alarm bells rang in Marcus's head. His daughter was staring at Binnie in amazement. As if she'd seen her before.

'But aren't you . . .'

'. . . Marcus's sister-in-law and therefore your aunt, I suppose,' Binnie interrupted speedily, desperate to stifle whatever the girl was about to reveal. 'I can't tell you how thrilled I am by all this.' She turned to the third of their guests. 'By a process of elimination you must be Mr Lee. You're all most welcome.'

'Don't keep them standing in the doorway, woman.' Sebastian reached past her, grabbing Mary-Anne's hand. 'Delighted to meet you.'

'Oh, the pleasure's mine, I assure you.'

Marcus wondered whether *he* would merit a greeting from his brother. He hadn't even looked him in the eye yet.

'God! Still got that old coat, Marcus?' Sebastian took it from him, with a look of disgust. 'Do try and get him to buy a new one, Mary-Anne. The only person who wears a duffel these days is Michael Foot.'

'Who's Michael Foot?' asked Mary-Anne.

'Leads the Labour Party, but don't worry about it,' Marcus muttered, guiding her forward into the living room. 'No one else does.' Then he saw Tom standing there, a grey-haired version of the youth he remembered, wreathed in a self-conscious smile. The two of them reached out to one another and clasped hands.

'Extraordinary,' said Marcus.

'Amazing,' Tom replied, eyeing him warily.

'Have a drink,' said Sebastian, thrusting a tray of champagne glasses amongst them. He offered it to the ladies first. 'Hope you're not allergic to this stuff.'

'I hope *not*,' Mary-Anne giggled. 'Thank you.' She rested her free hand on Binnie's arm. 'You know, it's extraordinary, Mrs Warwick, but I'm sure I saw you two days ago.'

Binnie looked startled, then quickly composed herself. 'I don't think so. And please call me Binnie.'

'That's interesting,' said Sebastian, hovering. 'Where d'you think you saw her?'

'In Jennifer Manley's art gallery in Fulham.' She pronounced it 'Ful-Ham'.

Marcus flinched. The very disaster he'd anticipated was beginning to unravel.

'Surely it was you that handed in the slip of paper with my father's name on it?'

Binnie blanched.

Marcus quickly took Tom to one side, mumbling how sorry he was to hear about his mother. But the diversion didn't help.

'What slip of paper?' Sebastian's question to Mary-Anne was deceptively casual.

'A handbill offering his services as a portrait painter. That's how I knew where to contact him.'

'Well, it certainly wasn't me who handed it in,' Binnie declared, her face a mask. She turned to Lee Ho Shin. 'Come and talk to me, Mr Lee. You're here on business?' She took his arm and led him away.

Marcus risked a glance over his shoulder. His brother's suspicious glare made him feel weak at the knees. He scooped up his daughter to prevent her digging herself in any deeper and introduced her to Tom.

'We live in extraordinary times, Tom. Extraordinary times.' He hooked an arm round Mary-Anne's shoulders. 'Did I ever tell you about the girl I met out there in Korea?'

'I have a vague memory of you saying you'd fallen in love, yes.'

Marcus beamed a 'What-did-I-tell-you?' smile at his daughter. But Mary-Anne wasn't paying attention.

'I'm sure it was her in that gallery,' she whispered.

'Look, you're wrong,' Marcus snapped. 'And for God's sake drop the subject.'

Mary-Anne's cheeks turned bright scarlet. 'Sorry.'

'Not your fault,' he said, rapidly moderating his voice. 'Didn't mean to snarl, but families are like minefields. Need to know the territory before you venture into them.' He felt desperately maudlin all of a sudden and gave her a paternal squeeze. 'You know, I so wish I'd learned about her years ago, Tom. Having a family might have kept me on the straight and narrow.'

Tom looked quizzically at Mary-Anne. 'You know about his troubles, do you?'

'Yes, I heard about that.'

'All in the past,' muttered Marcus. 'All in the past.' He quickly took his daughter's arm, feeling he'd better do some explaining. 'Come with me a minute. Excuse us for a moment, Tom. Family matters . . .' He led Mary-Anne over to the far wall, where a large nineteenth-century landscape painting hung above a bookcase.

'There's one thing you need to know, my dear, if we're all going to survive this evening. My brother and I don't get on. Not at all. Never have. And one reason he dislikes me is that Binnie has always preferred me to him.' He gave a nod and a wink, hoping she would understand. But she didn't appear to. 'So that's why it's important he doesn't know Binnie's been helping me get on my feet again.'

'I see.' She'd begun to work that out, but something in what he'd said didn't quite add up. 'If Binnie preferred you, why did she marry your brother?'

Marcus squirmed at her insensitivity. 'Well . . . to be honest it's because when I was away in Korea my big, grown-up brother got her pregnant.' He smiled uncomfortably. 'Something of an occupational hazard with the Warwick family . . .'

Mary-Anne appeared rather shocked at the flip way he'd said it and tried to conceal her feelings by looking away.

Sebastian was making a beeline for them. Marcus braced himself.

'A top-up, brother?' Sebastian offered, clutching a bottle. 'I see you're not on the wagon.'

'Making up for lost time, I'm afraid. Not much of this stuff in prison.' Marcus held out his glass.

'Yours is still full, I see, Mary-Anne.'

'I like to take it slow. Tell me, Mister Warwick . . .'

'It's *Sebastian*, please.'

'Are you involved in the Falklands War?'

Sebastian arched his eyebrows and pursed his lips.

'Peripherally, yes.'

'I'd be so glad to talk to you about it.' She wrinkled her nose at him. 'I suppose I should really call you *Uncle* Sebastian!'

Sebastian emitted a high-pitched laugh. 'What an extraordinary situation this is! I come home from work this evening to be told I've suddenly acquired a niece. And now she wants to talk about the Falklands, of all things. What *is* this?'

'I'll come clean. I'm a journalist, I'm afraid.'

'Oh dear.'

'But a very tame one.' Mary-Anne hooked a hand through Sebastian's arm and led him away, telling him about the high editorial standards of the *Boston Star* and why she was in London.

Marcus glowed with pride as he watched Mary-Anne cross the room, still not quite believing this was his daughter. What *was* she? What sort of creature? One thing was clear. Although her physical features were mostly Korean, her self-assurance was entirely American.

Glad of the brief breather, he took in what was happening elsewhere in the room, trying to calculate his chances of surviving the evening. Tom and Lee Ho Shin were in conversation with Binnie over by the doorway to the hall. Binnie's neck was red with stress. As if aware he was looking at her, she turned and beckoned him over.

'Marcus . . . Lee's been telling us about how you met Mary-Anne's mother. And how he made you eat . . . what was it called again?'

'Kimch'i,' Lee reminded her, his lips fixed in a tense smile.

'Cabbage and chillies. Is that right?'

'A bit strong, as far as I remember,' Marcus commented. 'But not bad.'

'I can't tell you how nice it is to have the three of you here,' Binnie gushed. 'All the time when these two were out in Korea, Mr Lee, I was dying to know what it was like.'

Marcus pursed his lips at her gaucheness.

'They were my best friends in those days, but I hardly saw them when they got back.'

'And *I* have not seen Captain Wowick for very long time,' Lee reminded her. 'So there is something I like to discuss with him. You excuse us?'

'Of course.' Binnie took Tom's arm and led him away so that the other two could talk in private.

'*Captain* Warwick,' Marcus exclaimed, arching his eyebrows. 'Long time since anyone's called me that.'

Lee was staring at him with the same cold intensity that Marcus remembered from Seoul.

'In the taxi you tell Mary-Anne the last time we meet was December nineteen fifty,' he accused. 'You wrong.'

'Oh?' Marcus was taken aback.

'We meet again five month later. On the day you leave Korea, I think.'

It came back to him suddenly. 'I'd forgotten that.' At the time in question he'd been more than ready to escape from the country and everybody who lived in it. 'We were boarding the trucks, I think.'

'And I try to tell you Cho-Mi expecting your child, but you don't listen.'

'No. That can't be right.' Marcus was struggling to recall the details. 'Don't remember anything about Cho-Mi. Just a vague memory you were after money.'

'Money, yes. For Cho-Mi. Because she have to leave her family.'

'I don't recall that . . .'

'You refuse to listen.'

Marcus felt his neck begin to glow. He'd shut his mind to the past by then. And ever since. He wished fervently that others would do the same.

'Lee . . . this is all a very long time ago. I'd been fighting a war for the previous nine months. I can't remember what I said or did or thought at that time. Apart from the joy of knowing I was getting out of that God-awful country of yours.'

Lee's stare became stony-hard. Marcus had just confirmed the opinion of him that he'd held for the past thirty years.

'Then I tell you now, so maybe don't forget again. Cho-Mi live like a beggar when she pregnant because her family no want her any more. I go to work for British Army again to get money for her. But when I go to give to her I don't find her so often because she keep moving. Because she afraid. Afraid what her brothers will do to her. And when I find her again she tell me she have to go with American soldiers to get food, so her baby don't die inside her. Cho-Mi become prostitute, Captain Wowick. Because of you.'

Marcus turned away in despair. 'It was the war, Lee. It happened to many girls. You can't blame me for that.'

'But only happen to Cho-Mi because she pregnant with your child.'

Marcus spread his arms. 'What do you want me to say? I knew nothing about it. But even if I had known, there was nothing I could have done. You can understand that, surely? I was just a soldier. I couldn't choose where I went or what I did.'

'You know what happen to her in the end?'

Marcus screwed up his face. He'd had enough. 'Yes. Awful. Her brothers . . . Mary-Anne told me.'

Lee pressed closer to him, his voice dropping to a whisper. 'I was only one from family who knew where Cho-Mi was when she have her baby. I tell her if she give up her child, then maybe her family take her back.'

Marcus braced himself. Lee was not going to stop.

'So I take baby to orphanage for her. Then, soon after, her brothers find me. They beat me near to death until I tell them where Cho-Mi is. They make me take them to her.' Lee paused, licking his lips as if trying to remove the bitterness he'd tasted for more than thirty years. 'Then, Mister Marcus Wowick, they make me help them kill her.'

'God almighty . . .'

Horrified, Marcus stared at the Korean open-mouthed.

This was the woman whose life had brushed against his for the briefest of periods. And Lee was blaming him for what had happened to her. And to him. Saying Marcus was responsible.

He knew in his heart that there was nothing he could have done. War was war. Dreadful things occurred. He'd seen his fill of them. He stiffened his back, determined to set the record straight. 'You Koreans have a very cruel and brutal culture, Lee.'

A clicking sound came from Lee's throat.

'I repeat, Lee. None of this is my fault.'

Lee was dumbfounded. The blame he'd wanted Marcus to shoulder was being dumped back on him and his countrymen. He felt the blood drain from his face. There could be only one ending now, the one he'd hoped to avoid.

'Ah so . . .'

He turned his back on Marcus and walked away. He would dearly have loved to leave that house there and then, but circumstances didn't permit it. Instead he fixed his gaze on his hostess and the other Englishman who'd been in Korea. What he needed now was a breathing space. To have conversations of no consequence in the hope that it would give him time to think.

As Binnie and Tom absorbed him back into their chatter, he looked beyond them to where Sebastian was talking with Mary-Anne. There was something in the way Marcus Warwick's brother was eyeing her that Lee recognised. He'd seen it in 1950 when the captain first met his cousin. It was the look of a conqueror, of a man whose own desires were all that mattered.

He watched Mary-Anne. She was no fool. No innocent like her mother. But these Warwicks were of no use to the girl. Having a father like Marcus was worse than no father at all.

Slowly an idea began to form in Lee's head. A remarkable scheme. One that might draw both of these brothers into his sights.

Mary-Anne had been softening Sebastian up by telling him what a lovely house they had.

'It's so interesting to meet you, Sebastian. You seem so different from my father.'

'Oh, we are. Chalk and cheese.' He chuckled. 'You know, I can't get used to you calling Marcus *father*.'

'It's really odd for me too.' Mary-Anne put on what she hoped was a winning smile. 'Tell me, if it's not a secret, what exactly do you do for the MoD?'

'You know, if you want to ask something about the Falklands, the press office are the people you should go to.'

'Oh sure, but I—'

'No. I want to hear about *you*. Tell me about yourself. And your mother. How did this all come about?'

Mary-Anne told him. In some detail, in the hope that it would distract him from her indiscretion about seeing Binnie in the gallery. She watched Sebastian's eyes as he listened, their black hardness slowly softening as curiosity took over. Finally she detected the look that many men had when conversing with women. The look that said, 'There's only one part of your body I'm really interested in and it's not the one I'm staring at.'

'Well, well,' he said when she'd finished. 'What a fascinating and rather appalling story.'

'It's dreadful that people could do such a thing to a young woman whose only crime was to have fallen in love.'

'Indeed. But tell me, what do you make of *us* all?' Sebastian made a sweeping movement with his arm.

'Too early to say, I guess.'

'That's being honest.'

'Well, I've only just met—'

'Of course. I wouldn't expect . . .'

'I mean, I don't really know any of you yet. For example, I seem to have some cousins.' Mary-Anne pointed to the framed photographs on the bookcases.

'Indeed you do. I'm surprised my wife didn't round them up for this little event. Mind you, one *is* in Australia.'

Mary-Anne got Sebastian to tell her about them. She noted his pride in his son's achievements and his less effusive comments about his daughters. The man was a chauvinist pig, she decided, and she well understood her father's dislike of him. If this was chalk, then she preferred cheese, despite its numerous imperfections.

'Of course, it's a fascinating time to be in London,' she declared, desperate to nudge the conversation where she needed it to go. 'In the States, we're so impressed at the way Mrs Thatcher has stood up to General Galtieri.'

'She had absolutely no other choice.'

'But it's brave. The Falkland Islands are such a long, long way away.'

'That's why we have a navy, my dear.'

'But the loss of HMS *Sheffield* must worry you.'

'Of course. But we'll manage.'

'You don't think you'll have to ask the US to help, if it all goes wrong for you?'

She saw him bristle. 'That's utterly inconceivable. Washington would never agree and we would never ask. Anyway, they're helping us already, as you know.'

'Communications and intelligence.'

'And the uprated Sidewinders for our Harriers. Essential if we're to see off the Argentine Skyhawks.'

'Uprated?' she asked innocently.

'The ones the Royal Navy had for its Harriers are an old version, which happen to be identical to the missiles on the Argentine aircraft. In an air battle the odds would be in the enemy's favour because they have more planes.'

'In what way are the new missiles uprated?'

Sebastian's eyes now had the look of a man who gets a kick out of impressing young women.

'The old ones have to be fired from behind the enemy plane,' he explained. 'They need a full-on view of the engine exhaust to get enough heat to home in on. The new ones are much more sensitive. They're called all-aspect – in other words, they can be fired from in front of the target as well as behind it. It gives us a huge advantage.'

'I see. How interesting.' Mary-Anne pretended that the significance of what he'd said had escaped her, but deep down she was excited. The information was new, she believed, and signified a deeper American involvement in the conflict than had hitherto been realised. She would only know for sure when she checked with Barbara, but maybe she had her scoop. At that moment Lee Ho Shin joined them.

'Your wife tell me you are specialist in electronic system, Mister Wowick.'

'It's Sebastian,' said Sebastian, getting to his feet. 'And yes. My department hands out development contracts for new weaponry.'

'Very interesting,' said Lee. 'I too am electronic specialist. Maybe we can talk . . .'

'But first you need some food,' Binnie announced, leading Tom and Marcus towards the kitchen. 'It's help yourself, I'm afraid.'

'The servants having a night off?' Marcus joked, desperate to lighten the uncomfortably intense atmosphere that had settled on the gathering.

'Absolutely,' Binnie laughed, rather too loudly, as if it was the funniest thing she'd ever heard. 'Everybody into the kitchen and grab a plate.'

Tom watched as the others started helping themselves. He'd been quietly observing Marcus, wondering what the Korean had told him that had caused him to look so ashen. Wondering too why the conversation had ended so abruptly.

There were other chemistries at play. He'd seen intimate glances pass between Binnie and Marcus, suggesting a rather closer relationship than Binnie had admitted to. He'd begun to wonder if the reason she'd changed her mind about Marcus signing himself Leonardo was because they'd just started an affair.

Mary-Anne interrupted his musings when she came up to him with a plate piled with salad.

'So, you're kind of my father's oldest friend.'

'Friends when we were young,' said Tom carefully. 'Lost touch some time ago.'

'Then this must be the most amazing reunion for you guys. Did you share the same trench in Korea?'

'Not quite. Neither of us knew the other was there, actually. We met up by chance.'

'And I saved his goddam neck once,' Marcus growled, listening in from the other side of the kitchen table.

Tom scowled, then began helping himself to the food.

'Really? How?'

'By spiking some poor Chinese boy in the chest,' Marcus proclaimed.

'Oh.' Mary-Anne was taken aback. 'You killed the guy?'

'Oh yes. If I hadn't, Tom wouldn't be standing here now.'

Tom gave her a sideways look, as if to say 'Don't listen to him'. He noted how nonplussed she looked at the idea that the killing for which Marcus had been imprisoned wasn't the first time he'd ended someone's life.

'Of course,' she said, covering her surprise. 'I guess that's what happens in war.'

'It's a simple matter of choice,' Marcus assured her. 'Either he dies, or you do.'

'But is that choice only valid in wars?' Binnie chipped in, gliding round the serving table to see that people were getting enough to eat. 'Or could it apply in non-war circumstances?'

'Well, I . . . I can't quite imagine . . .' Marcus stuttered.

'Oh, you know, if a mugger came up with a knife. Would you kill him? If you had a suitable weapon? Assuming you thought he was going to kill *you*.'

'Well, yes, I probably would. Self-defence.'

'And if it wasn't your actual life at stake, but the life you were going to lead?' she pressed.

'I don't get you.' Marcus looked acutely uncomfortable.

Tom noticed the flush on Binnie's face and wondered if she was drunk or on an adrenalin high.

'Suppose somebody had the power to destroy your life. To make it seem pointless carrying on. And by killing that person you could change everything and be happy and successful.'

'Then it would be murder, you silly woman,' Sebastian chipped in.

Binnie glared at him. 'But in war you'd happily kill someone who got in your way.'

'Different rules,' Marcus said, nodding.

'Of course they are,' said Sebastian. 'They have to be.'

'But *should* they be different? That's my point,' Binnie persisted.

A tense silence descended, then Mary-Anne let out a loud laugh.

'Oh boy! Did *I* start this one?'

It pricked the bubble and the tension dissolved into chuckles and the clink of forks on plates. They drifted back into the living room, where Binnie opened the French windows and switched on the patio lights.

Tom watched her, wondering what had prompted that discourse. He saw her go on to the terrace to check everything was tidy, then come back in, looking around the room until her gaze settled on Mary-Anne. She went up to the young woman and began asking about her work.

Playing the professional hostess, Tom realised. And she did it well. For a brief moment he envied Sebastian for having Binnie as his consort.

He glanced around the room. Lee Ho Shin had cornered Sebastian by the kitchen door and was bending his ear. Marcus was standing by himself on the far side of the living room, examining a painting.

The moment had finally come for them to talk.

'One of yours?' he asked, joining Marcus.

'I'm flattered. But as it happens, no.'

'I knew nothing about your brush with the law,' Tom ventured, 'until Binnie told me.'

'Then you obviously don't read tabloid newspapers.'

'Must have missed it.'

'I was a bloody fool, Tom. Things hadn't been going well. My work had gone out of fashion and I couldn't seem to keep a woman for any length of time. You know how it is.' He eyed Tom meaningfully. 'Or perhaps you don't, women not being of much interest to you, I suspect.'

Tom ignored the jibe. 'So how did you get involved with these thieves?'

'One of them was a bloke I drank with. They wanted expert advice. Someone to go along with them on a robbery and point out which pictures were most valuable. I was at a low ebb. Thought it'd be harmless enough. They didn't want to sell the paintings abroad or do damage to them. Just claim the reward money from the insurers. A victimless crime. But . . . oh God . . .' He shook his head at the stupidity of it. 'You see, I'd never done anything like that before. I was scared out of my wits. And when this old man came into the room clasping a cricket bat and saying he'd called the police, I just lost it. Picked up the nearest heavy object I could find and took a swing at him.'

'And that was that.'

'Yes. Cracked his skull and he died of a brain haemorrhage. They picked us up half a mile away.'

'How was prison?'

Marcus shot him a sideways glance. 'Not something I ever want to repeat.'

Tom noted the feeling with which he said it. He glanced around to check that the others were out of earshot. It was time to start his interrogation.

'Last time we met you were full of plans for an exhibition,' he began.

'God, that was a long time ago.' Marcus shrugged, indicating he didn't really think it was worth going into. 'Had a few shows over the years. But you know, half the time what people want to buy in a painting is not the picture itself, but the name scrawled in the bottom-right corner. I'll let you into a secret, Tom. I nearly went into the faking business when times were hard. And I could have done it, you know. I had the skills.'

'And signing somebody else's name on your work wouldn't have been new to you, would it?'

'What do you mean?'

'Didn't you sign yourself Leonardo when we were kids? And Picasso. On Binnie's portrait, for example?'

'Oh, that . . .' Marcus sounded relieved. 'Juvenile delusions of grandeur. Yes, I seem to remember scribbling various painters' monikers from time to time.' Then he frowned. 'But now you mention it, on Binnie's picture I don't believe I did. Her father bought it from me. My first earnings. Wanted me to sign my own name, in case I became famous one day.' He frowned again. 'Extraordinary of you to remember that.'

'I didn't remember it. Binnie mentioned it. After I told her about Sara's diary.'

Tom watched the blood drain from Marcus's face. Suddenly he knew he was on to something.

'Diary?'

'Yes. I found it in the loft at Heathside Close.'

'What . . . what does it say?'

'She refers to you a couple of times.' Tom decided on bluff.

'Oh?'

'As L. Which I assume means L for Leonardo.'

Marcus gripped Tom's arm and propelled him towards the French windows.

'Let's get some air . . .'

Tom abandoned his plate on a side table, startled at the dramatic effect his ploy had had. Outside, his pulse quickened rapidly as they crossed the patio with its tubs of tulips. They stopped beneath a cherry tree, heavy with blossom.

Marcus shot a glance over his shoulder to check they were far enough from the doors.

'What *exactly* did she write?' he croaked.

Guilt was etched so deeply on Marcus's face, Tom felt himself trembling.

'She seemed to think she was in love with you.'

Marcus clamped his hands to his head. 'Love? Come on. What did that kiddo know about love? It was a silly infatuation, Tom. That's all. She was fourteen, with a vivid imagination.'

Tom couldn't believe what he was hearing. Was this a confession?

'Why didn't you tell the police you were seeing her?'

'Seeing?' Marcus gulped. 'She said I was seeing her?'

'Secret assignations. Why the hell didn't you tell *me* about it, Marcus?'

Marcus squeezed his eyes closed. 'Because . . . because it wasn't relevant, that's why. What happened between me and Sara had nothing to do with her murder, Tom. You've got to believe that.'

Tom stared at him, incredulous that he should suddenly be proclaiming his innocence. 'She wrote that your kisses made her knees shake . . .'

'Oh, Christ . . .' Marcus covered his mouth and turned away.

'She said you touched her breasts. And that next time you saw her, you wanted her naked.'

Marcus shook his head furiously. 'It's rubbish, Tom, rubbish. Fantasy.'

'You met in the evenings after supper, she said. It's all there in the diary, Marcus. If the police had found it, you'd still be in prison. Or hanged.'

'No, no! You're getting it wrong, Tom. You don't understand.'

'You saw her that last evening.'

'Yes, but . . .'

'Got out of control, did it? Scared, was she? Screamed, perhaps? And you killed her because you were frightened of being found out.'

Marcus gripped Tom by the shoulders, his thumbs pressing into the bone. Tom imagined these same hands crushing Sara's throat. He had an overwhelming desire to beat Marcus to a pulp.

'No . . .' Marcus hissed. 'I did *not* kill her.'

'How on earth do you expect me to believe you?'

'Tom, we've known each other a long time . . .'

'During which period you've never said anything about this.'

'I'm telling you the truth.'

'The police can judge that.'

'Jesus . . .' Marcus clasped his hands to his face again. 'You can't do that to me. Listen. I'll tell you everything, Tom. Every bloody thing. Because you've got to believe me. You've simply got to.'

Tom backed away from him, shaking his head. Emotions suppressed for decades were breaking free. 'You pretended, you bastard. In the woods, when you showed the police where she was. Pretended you knew nothing about it.'

'Tom. Tom, listen. When I saw Sara lying there dead, I . . .' He shook his head. 'God, this is hopeless.'

'Look. We'll go to the police together. Get it over with tonight. Eh?'

'Police? No way. Tom, there must be no police. I've got a record now. They'll go after me. Stitch up a case and it'll be the slammer again.'

'Yes, and for the rest of your bloody life, I hope.'

'Listen, listen.' Marcus led Tom deeper into the garden, beyond the spill of the patio lights.

'I'm listening.'

'Yes, okay. I'd been seeing Sara. Yes, I touched her like she said. Yes, I knew she was besotted with me. But the point is . . . she knew more about . . . you know, *sex* than I did. Or seemed to. You know how ignorant you and I were at that age. Always talking about it. Speculating on what one did to women and what it felt like. But never *knowing* anything. But *she* . . . Christ, how can I put this so you'll believe me?'

'Try telling the truth.'

'This *is* the truth. Look. She was sexually precocious. That's the only way I can put it. *You* know that, Tom. She flaunted herself. You saw it.'

'Go on.'

'Well, one day in the Close, I was doing something to my bike, and she started chatting to me. All sort of flirty and teasing, you know. And . . . she said she'd seen us once. You and me. In your bedroom.' He raised an eyebrow. 'You know what we got up to sometimes. There was a hole in the ceiling or something.'

'I know. She wrote about it in her diary.'

'Christ, well, there you are! Doesn't that tell you what she was like?'

'Go on with your story.'

Marcus paused to take a breath. 'Putting it crudely, she said she'd seen what us boys did with our dicks and wanted to . . .' His face creased with embarrassment. 'Well, she wanted to do it for me.'

Tom struggled to keep calm. 'So?'

'Well, I . . . I mean, come on. We were teenagers. Spotty bags of hormones.'

'So you said yes.'

Marcus nodded. 'She said it would have to be a secret. No one must know. And I said too bloody right.' He grimaced at the awfulness of what he was having to reveal. 'There was a shed on my father's allotment. We went there one night after supper and we . . . started kissing and fumbling. And yes, she did what she'd said she wanted to do. Sorry, but you wanted to hear all of it. Well, then things got . . .' Marcus struggled for the words.

'Okay . . . I suppose I wanted more. It was all new, you know, getting sexed up. With a girl, I mean. And I was scared somebody would see us at the shed. So, stupidly, I arranged to meet her the next time in the woods.'

'This was . . .?'

'The night she died,' Marcus gulped.

Tom was tempted to grip Marcus by the throat, but controlled himself.

'Hear me out before you jump to conclusions. Okay. I took her to *our* hiding place in the woods. And, yes, some of our clothes came off. We started feeling each other up – I'd never done that before. With a girl. I mean *fully*. But she was leading *me* on, Tom. That's the truth of it.'

'What happened?'

'Well, I lost it. I tried . . . you know . . . to stick it in her. Yes, I admit that. Crazy. She was fourteen, so it would have been a crime. But anyway – I couldn't get it in and, you know, came anyway. All over her legs. And then she started crying.' Marcus shook his head at the memory of it. 'And . . . and I panicked.' He looked as if he couldn't go on.

'Tell me.'

His voice dropped to little more than a whisper. 'I put my hand over her mouth to try to quieten her . . . Mouth, that's all. Not her neck.'

'Then you strangled her.'

'No, Tom,' Marcus moaned. 'That's the whole point. I didn't. I did the thing I've been most ashamed of all these years.'

'What?'

'I left her. I got up off the ground and ran, terrified that someone would find us there. She was under age. That's what I was most scared of. Being caught trying to have sex with an under-age girl. But if I'd been man enough to stay with her, comfort her, calm her down, she would probably be alive today.'

Tom stared into Marcus's eyes, searching for some twitch that would confirm this was a lie.

'I don't believe you.'

'It's the truth. The God-awful truth. And I've lived with it, and with my shame, for thirty-four years.'

Tom folded his arms. 'It's bollocks. I mean if *you* didn't kill her, who did?'

'John Hagger, I suppose.'

Tom stared incredulously at him. 'Hagger was innocent, Marcus. The police stitched him up.'

'Are you sure?'

Tom shook his head. Of course he wasn't. Not sure of anything. 'What're you saying? That Hagger was hanging around in the woods, saw what was going on and moved in as soon as you ran away?'

'Well, who else? They found fibres from his clothes on her. Maybe he even tried to have sex with her, too. Or perhaps it was just coincidence that his . . . stuff and mine were of the same blood group. It's technically possible.'

Tom kept looking at Marcus, coldly, analytically. Sifting and resifting what he'd just been told.

'Why on earth should I believe you, Marcus?'

'You've got to. For God's sake, man, I did not kill her!'

The vehemence of Marcus's denial was so strong that Tom began to wonder if the right man *had* been convicted after all.

He glanced towards the house. Binnie and Mary-Anne were still chatting to one another in the living room, but Binnie kept peering into the garden.

Looking anxiously in their direction.

28

For a couple of minutes Tom and Marcus didn't speak again, then Binnie called to them from the house.

'Come back in, you two. Aren't you cold out there?'

Anxiously her eyes searched their faces as they re-entered the living room. 'You all right?' Her question was addressed to Marcus.

'I need your loo,' he mumbled.

'Up the stairs, first on the left. You may meet your daughter on the way down. If she's still in there, there's a bathroom on the landing above.'

Tom watched him go, shoulders slumped.

'You talked about Sara's diary,' Binnie accused him. 'I did ask you not to this evening, Tom.'

'He admitted he was the one seeing Sara, Binnie.'

'Oh.'

'But he denied killing her.'

Her mouth twisted into a knot of anxiety. 'And do you believe . . .?'

'I'm not sure.'

'Well, you should. I simply can't imagine . . .'

'He still thinks it was Hagger.'

'Yes.' Binnie seemed relieved. 'Why not? Ah, here's Mary-Anne again. You've hardly talked to her yet. She's an extremely interesting woman.' She led Tom over to her and paused for long enough to see that the two of them really were engaged in conversation, then drifted towards the stairs.

Tom asked Mary-Anne to tell him her story, but listened with only half an ear. Her physical appearance made him feel uncomfortable, her mongrel face a reminder of what Korea had done to him and of what the armies of foreigners had done to Korea.

As he half listened, his mind churned through Marcus's story, searching for clues as to whether it was truth or lie. What Marcus had said was just plausible. There was no secret about Sara's precocity. It had even been spelled out in court. And although Marcus's description of what he'd done had stirred powerful feelings of hatred inside him, Tom had to accept that his sister might have borne some responsibility for what had happened between the two of them.

But not for her death. For that someone else was culpable. And he still didn't know who. As he watched Mary-Anne's mouth move, he itched to leave this house and give himself space to think.

'But that's enough about me,' Mary-Anne declared suddenly. 'Now I want to hear what you and my father got up to as kids.'

Tom looked wordlessly at her. Then, hesitantly, he began to talk. Telling her about the good times. About his mother the film star. Anything he could think of that was happy and exciting and that pre-dated the summer of 1948.

Marcus had reached the toilet just in time to be sick in the bowl. Afterwards he sat on the lavatory lid with his head in his hands. A few minutes later there was a knock on the door.

'Marcus?' Binnie's voice. Little more than a whisper.

'Go away.'

'Can I help?'

'No.'

She tried the door, but he'd locked it. A few moments later she whispered again.

'Marcus . . . Come on out. We can talk in the bedroom.'

He knew he couldn't stay in there for ever, so he flushed the toilet again, washed his face with cold water and opened the door.

'You look dreadful.'

'Stomach's a bit off. A hangover from this morning's hangover, I expect.'

'You poor thing.'

They were standing on the landing. She took his arm and turned towards a bedroom, but he resisted.

'I'm going home, Binnie.'

'Must you? I'll call you a taxi. Happy to pay for it.'

'No. I'll walk.'

'Don't be daft. It'll take you all night.'

'Fine by me.'

Binnie studied him with concern.

'What happened out there in the garden? With Tom?'

Marcus stared coldly at her. He'd always said this party was going to be a disaster. She should never have arranged it. At the back of his mind he began blaming her for the state he was in.

'We talked about old times.'

'And?'

'And that's it. Now I'm going home.' He made for the stairs.

'We'll see each other tomorrow?'

He stopped with his hand on the banister.

'I don't know. Ring me, perhaps.'

Then he descended to the ground floor, with Binnie following closely.

'I'll ring first thing,' she whispered, 'and maybe bring lunch again. Or we could go to a pub.'

'We'll see. Maybe I'd be better left on my own for a bit.'

'I don't think you should brood . . .'

'I'll be the judge of that.'

They looked towards the kitchen. Through the open door they saw Sebastian and Lee Ho Shin huddled at the table, studying what appeared to be photographs.

'What on earth are they looking at?' said Binnie.

'Pictures of electronic gizmos, probably,' Marcus suggested. 'Lee seems to sell the things. Better say goodbye to them, I suppose.'

Sebastian looked up and saw them. Lee slipped the pictures back into his wallet.

'Do you think he knows?' Marcus croaked.

'Knows what?'

'That you and I have been fucking, dear.'

Binnie bit her lip. 'If he asks about Mary-Anne seeing me hand out those leaflets, I might have to admit I've been helping you get settled again.'

'That should alleviate his suspicions,' Marcus replied, his voice heavy with sarcasm.

Binnie picked up a couple of plates from the living room and took them with her to the kitchen.

'You two seem to have found something in common,' she commented, depositing the crockery on the draining board.

Lee Ho Shin stood up. 'I so sorry, Mrs Wowick, for keeping your husband talking. He has such interesting job.'

He turned to Marcus with an icy look of triumph in his eyes. Like someone who'd stumbled on buried treasure and planned to use it to fulfil a lifelong ambition.

'Marcus is going, Seb,' Binnie announced.

'Is he? Lee was also making departing noises.' Sebastian remained seated and his face was a little flushed. 'Will you arrange cabs for them?'

'Certainly.' She went into the hall to make the call.

Marcus looked down at his brother, loathing the offhand way in which he'd always treated Binnie. 'We don't seem to have talked, Seb.'

'No.'

'Still . . . why change the habit of a lifetime?'

'Quite.'

Marcus reached out a hand to the Korean. 'Cheerio, Lee. Nice to see you again after all these years.'

Lee didn't take the hand but bowed stiffly instead. Then he walked straight past Marcus, saying, 'I better ask if I can go with Mary-Anne.'

After he left the room, Marcus and Sebastian stared wordlessly at one another. From the anger smouldering behind his brother's eyes, Marcus suspected that Sebastian had guessed about him and Binnie. Time to cut his losses. Without another word he turned on his heels and followed Lee into the hall.

Tom's conversation with Mary-Anne was coming to an end. He hadn't intended to tell her about Sara's untimely death and his doubts about the conviction of John Hagger, but the words had tumbled out. The young woman was too good a listener. The journalism training, he guessed. What he *had* kept to himself was the discovery of the diary and what Marcus had just revealed to him. Coming to terms with her father's most recent act of criminality would have been hard enough for the girl. Learning what he'd done as a teenager could well have been too much for her to handle.

'I'm so sorry about your sister,' she said when he finished. 'Heck . . . *Sorry* is so inadequate after what you went through.'

'It was a long time ago.'

'And you've no idea who really—?'

She was cut off in mid-sentence by Lee Ho Shin appearing beside them.

'I have to be going,' he announced. 'Mrs Wowick has ordered a taxi. D'you want to share it, Mary-Anne?'

'Oh, sure. That'd be great.' She turned back to Tom. 'You know I'd love to talk some more with you. Could I take your phone number?'

'Of course.'

She wrote it down. When she looked up again, she saw her ashen-faced father hovering in the hallway, pulling on his old duffel coat.

'You don't look well,' she said, going up to him and touching him caringly on the arm.

'I'll be okay.'

'You're coming in the taxi too?'

Marcus shook his head. 'The walk will do me good.'

'I've told him it's ridiculous,' said Binnie. 'It's miles. Actually, there's a train he could take.'

'We could drop you at the station,' Mary-Anne suggested, glad not to have to make that long detour to Brentford again. She envisioned Barbara Daley waiting impatiently at the house in Hammersmith to see what story she'd come up with.

A couple of minutes later the cab arrived. Although he wasn't travelling in it, Tom was the first to leave.

'Dear Tom.' Binnie smiled anxiously at him as he stepped into the porch. 'We really mustn't lose contact again.'

'No. We won't.'

'I feel we haven't talked nearly enough. Drive carefully, now.'

'I will.'

Lee Ho Shin and Mary-Anne made their farewells too. Marcus bade them a hasty goodbye with a promise to call his daughter in the morning, then began walking unsteadily down the road. The party was over.

Before climbing into the taxi, Lee took a last look at Marcus. There was something very pathetic about the figure shuffling away along the pavement. But not pathetic enough to make him rethink what he'd decided. An opportunity had presented itself to him this evening, which would give him more than he'd expected from his sudden visit to London.

After closing the front door, Binnie turned to face Sebastian, expecting an interrogation. But he was smiling to himself. Preoccupied. Ignoring her. Which suited her fine. So she went to the kitchen to start clearing up.

A couple of minutes later, as she stood at the sink washing glasses, Sebastian entered the kitchen behind her. She braced herself for his questions.

Instead she felt his hands close round her breasts and his stubbly mouth suck the soft skin at the base of her neck.

'What are you doing?'

She tried to twist away from him, but he held her tight. She could feel his hardness against her rear.

'Seb . . .'

'I'm going to fuck you.'

'Do I get any say in this?'

'Not on this occasion, no.' He took one of her rubber-gloved hands and wrenched it up behind her back.

Binnie cried out in pain as her shoulder joint cracked. She leaned forward in an effort to ease the pressure.

'There's a good girl. Just how I want you. Face down, arse up.'

With his free hand he undid the fastening at the side of her skirt and let it drop to the floor.

'Seb, please . . .'

'You are my *wife*,' he hissed, giving an extra twist to her arm.

He slipped his fingers under the waistbands of her tights and pants and eased them down, then slid his hand between her thighs. Binnie knew from experience that passive submission was the best way to survive Sebastian's carnal flare-ups. She eased her haunches away from the sink and let herself go limp. Her husband spat on his free hand, then wiped his saliva into her.

He entered her without further preamble, thrusting deep, his rhythmic motion pushing her forward until her head was jammed against the taps. Then, as he climaxed, he pushed her face into the washing-up water.

Suddenly Binnie panicked. Sebastian was going to kill her. Her lungs were almost empty. Desperate to breathe in, she began to struggle, but he held her face firmly in the water, one hand on her neck, the other on her twisted wrist. She tried to kick out at him, but her ankles were ensnared by her skirt and tights. Then, as suddenly as he'd dunked her, he released his grip.

She stood upright, gasping for air. As the shock set in she began to sob.

Sebastian did up his trousers, poured himself another glass of wine and sat at the kitchen table, smiling to himself as Binnie pulled up her clothing. She fought to control the tremors engulfing her. She hated giving him the satisfaction of seeing how much he could hurt her.

Sebastian cleared his throat.

'So, how long has it been going on?'

'What?' she choked.

'You and Marcus.'

'I don't know what you mean.'

'Binnie,' he said, his voice low and threatening. 'I *will* have the truth. There are two ways to do this. The easy one or the—'

'All right.'

She turned to face him, wanting to see his expression when she told him.

'I went to see him in prison a few times,' she said, savouring every word. 'Several times, in fact. He needed support from his family – that's you, in case you'd forgotten – and he wasn't getting it.'

Sebastian's contemptuous demeanour didn't change.

'I found somewhere for him to live when he came out. Where he could work. And on the day of his release, I picked him up and took him there.' She stopped, suddenly afraid of what her husband would do when she told him the rest.

'Go on.'

'And we made love. With considerably more feeling than I've ever experienced with *you*.'

Pain flickered in Sebastian's eyes, then it was gone. Her satisfaction at hurting him was short-lived. His powers of self-control were far, far greater than hers.

Sebastian went on staring at her, until in the end she had to look away.

'You had sex with my brother.' His voice was low and menacing. 'Do you know what that makes me feel?'

'I can't imagine.'

'Sick. *Sick.* To think that you would sink to *that.*'

'I happen to love him.'

'*Love?* You're mad. I mean, *Henry* . . . I could understand why you fancied *him.*'

Binnie gaped. How long had he known?

'But Marcus is vile,' Sebastian went on, his lip curling. 'Disreputable, criminal, booze-soaked . . .'

'In fact, the man you'd least like me to have an affair with. Is that what you're saying?' She felt a grain of satisfaction at last.

'You must never see him again.'

'Impossible.'

'Do you intend to destroy our marriage? You'd be penniless, you know.'

Binnie didn't reply. Its destruction seemed well under way now, but she needed him to make the decision, not her.

'Well?'

'If that's what you want,' she whispered.

She noted a trace of perplexity on Sebastian's face. The bastard was calculating the benefits and disbenefits of divorce.

'Promise me that this thing with Marcus is over,' he demanded, almost plaintively.

'I can't do that.'

'Then you leave me little choice.' Sebastian stood up and headed for the door. At the threshold he paused. 'I'm going to sleep on it. I'd be obliged if you'd use the spare room tonight.'

Binnie watched him go. Yes, she would move her things. Willingly. But she couldn't do anything until the trembling stopped.

29

Wood Park

WHEN TOM GOT back to Heathside Close, he snatched up Sara's photo from the living-room mantelpiece, glanced briefly at the deceptively childish face, then laid it face down. Sara, he'd now finally realised, had lost her innocence thirty-four years ago. This evening he'd lost his.

On the journey home he'd seethed at Marcus's callousness for concealing his involvement in Sara's death. A part of him wanted Marcus punished for it. The obvious thing was to go to the police, but Tom knew that, because of his fear of prison, Marcus would deny what he'd said in Binnie's garden, making it his word against Tom's. And with no additional evidence, there'd be no prosecution. And what could they charge him with, anyway? Obstructing the course of justice? Certainly not murder or rape.

As the dreadful story went round and round in his head, Tom reached the depressing conclusion that his pursuit of the truth had hit a brick wall yet again.

Friday, 7 May
Holborn

Mary-Anne's story on the latest-version Sidewinder missiles supplied by the US to the Royal Navy had been filed to the paper shortly before midnight, backed by Barbara's belief that it was indeed a scoop. But when the two of them arrived in the office this morning and checked the usage report, they discovered that the piece had been spiked.

Mary-Anne was bewildered. 'Perhaps it wasn't news after all,' she suggested.

'Sure it was. Nobody knew of it. I checked with the paper's Pentagon guy.'

'Then, *why* . . .?'

'I don't know, honey, but I'm sure going to find out. In the meantime make us some coffee, would you?'

Mary-Anne filled the filter machine and switched it on, then sat down to read the London papers. There seemed to be a lull in the Falklands story after the initial naval actions. The loss of the *Belgrano* had struck such fear into the Argentine navy that their ships were staying close to home. Some newspaper columnists were expressing impatience for the British forces to land on the islands, predicting that an invasion could be days away. Others suggested it would be weeks yet.

'Here you go.' Mary-Anne handed her boss her coffee.

'Thanks.' Barbara gave her a warm smile. 'So tell me what you found out about your new family.' She stirred sweetener into her cup. 'We didn't get around to it last night.'

Mary-Anne wrinkled her brow, not at all sure she wanted to.

'I guess it's all so new,' she parried. 'Do *you* have a lot of family?'

'Hundreds of 'em. In Washington State.'

'See them from time to time?'

'Almost never. They're farmers, most of 'em. Don't like me and I don't like them.'

'What is it with families? Why can't they just be normal, ordinary folks?'

'How many normal, ordinary folks do you know?'

Mary-Anne thought about it and realised there were very few.

'The truth is most people are awkward cusses, full of shit they'd rather not talk about,' Barbara pronounced.

'I guess that applies to my father. You know, there was a guy there last night who was supposed to be his oldest friend, yet they hadn't seen each other for thirty years. Can you believe that?'

'You know why?'

'No. But something awful happened when they were kids. This guy's sister got murdered.'

'And he suspected your pa did it? That's why they haven't spoken?'

Mary-Anne was astonished. That obvious connection simply hadn't occurred to her. 'He said some old hobo was sent to prison for it, but he wasn't convinced he was guilty.'

'So maybe that was the reason why he and your father stopped talking to one another?'

'I don't know. I didn't ask.'

'And you call yourself a journalist?'

Mary-Anne blushed at the rebuke. She *should* have asked. It had all gone too quickly last night. But Barbara's suggestion that her father might have been involved gave new meaning to what she'd seen in the garden last night. Her father and Tom Sedley talking extremely heatedly. At one point she'd thought they would come to blows.

'Look, if you want to go talk to this friend of your pa's again, midday onwards may be a good time,' Barbara offered. 'It looks quiet, and once I'm back from the press conference at the MoD, I can handle things here on my own.'

'Well, thank you. I just might take you up on that.'

Mary-Anne flicked through her notebook for the number she'd written down last night.

Brentford

Marcus stood in one corner of the studio flat with his back to the wall, his hands thrust deep into his pockets. The place felt like a condemned cell this morning.

He knew what to do. The same as he'd always done when things went wrong. Deny them to himself. Pretend they hadn't happened. Escape.

Not from the police. He didn't think Tom would turn him in. What he had to get away from was the whole Wood Park connection – his supercilious brother, queer Tom . . . and the long tentacles of Binnie. It had worked for the past three decades. He'd kept his sanity by keeping his distance from all of them. And his present suffering had only come about because that distance had been bridged.

One person above all was responsible for it.

She'd rung at half-past eight that morning, which Marcus guessed was when Sebastian left the house for the MoD. He'd told her not to come over, but she'd insisted, speaking in the thin, high voice of someone suffering from shock.

'Seb knows about us,' he'd deduced.

'He forced it out of me.'

'Shit.'

She would be here by midday. He dreaded the shrilling of the bell.

His sexual liaison with Binnie had all been a hideous mistake. She was clearly very serious about him. She wanted him, *really* wanted, in the way she had when she'd been seventeen. But the point was he still didn't want *her*.

He'd kicked himself for being so naive. For thinking it was just a bit of fun. But this morning it would be over. He would be firm but fair. Thank her for all she'd done, but say that it couldn't continue.

And where would he run to this time? The answer had come to Marcus in the sleepless small hours. An angel had entered his life. A sweet one, not the dark creature who'd tempted him into madness thirty-four years ago. Her arrival so timely it could almost have been preordained. Mary-Anne had come to save him. From himself. He would become the father she should have had, all those years ago. Involve himself in her life in whatever way she would allow. And he would start painting again. Not here in England, where his name sparked jokes and hostility in the trade, but in America – if Mary-Anne would make it possible for him.

Wood Park

First thing that morning, Tom wrote a list of things that had to be done in the house before he returned to Cheltenham. There were certain matters that could be dealt with by phone at a later date, but he would still have his work cut out. With time pressing, the unanswered questions about Sara's death would have to go on hold once more.

Then came the phone call from the American girl. He didn't really have the time to see her, but she'd been insistent and something in her voice made him suspect she'd guessed that his estrangement from Marcus had been linked to Sara's murder. She was coming at lunchtime. Wanting to see where her father had been brought up. He couldn't really spare the time, but couldn't refuse her either.

Here at about half-past twelve, she'd said. Would she have lunched? No, but not to worry. Tom did worry, though, and went to the supermarket to buy a pizza.

At twenty to one there was the rattle of the taxi outside. Tom opened the front door. There'd been a sharp rain shower earlier and the garden path was still wet when his visitor walked up to the house.

'What a beautiful place!' Mary-Anne declared. She was carrying a small package, which she presented to him. 'I didn't know what to bring, so I got you some French cheese.'

'You shouldn't have bothered, but thank you. Come on in. You'll find boxes everywhere, I'm afraid.'

'You really want to move from here? It's such a great house. So much character.'

'I haven't lived here since I was a child,' he reminded her. 'And my work's in Cheltenham.'

'I forgot. This was your mother's place. You told me last night.'

'I'm not surprised you don't remember. There was a lot to take in. All those strangers. All those undercurrents. You must find us a pretty weird lot.'

'Not at all.'

Tom could tell by her voice she was being polite. He led her to the kitchen and offered her a glass of wine.

'Oh, no, thank you. I had two glasses last night which will last me all week. Some iced water would be fine.'

The way she said it, combined with the heavy-framed spectacles and rather austere cut of her thick, dark hair, made Tom suspect a puritan streak in her, a characteristic that certainly hadn't come from her father. He told her the pizza would be out of the oven in a few minutes and he set the table with some salad things and opened the Camembert she'd brought.

'You're so organised, Tom. Can I ask if you're married?'

'You can, and I'm not.'

'Me neither, though I'd like to be one day. If anyone'll have me. So you live alone in Cheltenham?'

'At the moment, yes.'

'From that I conclude it hasn't always been so.'

'No.'

The brevity of his answer unsettled her. 'I'm sorry. I had no right to ask.'

He spread his hands to show that it didn't really matter.

'How come my father never married? Do you have any idea? I didn't get round to asking him yet.' She kept folding and unfolding her arms.

Tom felt a strong urge to give her a few likely reasons, but restrained himself.

'My knowledge of Marcus's life ended in the nineteen fifties,' he reminded her, 'and only restarted a few days ago.'

Mary-Anne caught sight of the garden through the kitchen window.

'That yard must've been great for playing in, when you were kids,' she suggested, crossing the room to get a better look.

'It was. And we had the park and the woods too. For Londoners we were pretty spoilt.'

'Just you and your sister? No other siblings?'

'That's right.'

'And did Sara have her own separate group of friends? She was three years younger than you, you said.'

'She did. School chums, mostly. But the Close was like a club. All the kids in the street mucked around together.'

'You have any pictures of her?'

Tom hesitated, then decided there was no reason not to show her. He went to the living room and came back with the photograph.

'This was taken a couple of years before she died. She'd grown up somewhat by the time . . .'

'She's real cute. Was my father keen on her?'

It was no casual question, Tom realised. Mary-Anne had come here because she wanted to know everything.

'Keener than I knew at the time,' he said.

'Is that what you two were talking about last night? In the garden?'

Tom opened the oven door and used gloves to slide the pizza on to a bread board which he placed on the table. Mary-Anne hovered, concerned that she should be doing something to help.

'I didn't want you to go to all this trouble.'

'It's only a bought pizza.' He sliced it and put a piece on her plate. 'Do sit down.'

'Well, it's very good of you.' She smiled thinly. 'Thanks. But you didn't answer my question yet.'

'No. I didn't.' He was undecided about how much detail to go into. The most graphic elements were too embarrassing for him to discuss with a young woman.

'Look,' Mary-Anne said, cutting her pizza slice into small pieces, 'let me tell you where I'm coming from. Finding out who my dad is didn't exactly start well. I spent a long time tracking him down, only to discover he'd just been released from jail after killing someone. It was a shock.'

'It must've been.'

'There are so many things I don't know about him. And then last night you told me about your sister being murdered and sexually assaulted, and that shortly afterwards there was a breakdown in your friendship with my father. And, seeing you two in the garden having a not entirely friendly conversation, I began to wonder . . .'

'. . . Whether I suspected Marcus of killing her? No. At the time I didn't. But this week, I have to say, things changed.'

'Oh? Why was that?'

Tom told Mary-Anne about the diary and the reference in it to L. As he spoke she watched him attentively, while taking small mouthfuls of pizza.

'So that *was* what you were talking about last night,' she said when he'd finished. She was beginning to look upset.

'Well, yes . . .'

'And? I need to know everything, Tom.'

He summarised what Marcus had said to him, omitting the most intimate elements.

When he'd finished, Mary-Anne put her head in her hands. 'Oh boy.'

'He assured me he didn't kill her, though.'

'And you believed him?' she asked, looking up again.

Tom hesitated. 'Rightly or wrongly, yes, I did. You could say I gave him the benefit of the doubt. But what I can never forgive him for is keeping quiet about it all these years.'

'Of course not.'

'I'm sorry to be telling you all this, Mary-Anne, but maybe it's best you know precisely what sort of man you've just become related to.'

Mary-Anne put her knife and fork together. She'd hardly eaten anything.

'This is awful. I can't take it in. To be so closely involved in Sara's death, then not tell anyone – that's more than cowardly. It's evil. Wicked.' She shook her head. 'So many lives affected by what happened back then. Like ripples in a pond.'

'And we all thought it was old history until this week.'

She grimaced. 'It must be terrible for you. Tell me, do Binnie and Sebastian know all this?'

'No. At least I assume not.'

Mary-Anne stood up, paced up and down the kitchen, then stared out of the window again.

'I don't know what to do, Tom. Should I have it out with him, get him to be honest with me, or just go back to the States and forget I ever found him?'

'That's up to you.'

She came and stood by the table again. 'I feel awful.' She bit her lip. 'But then I always knew it was risky, starting this search for him. But when you don't know what sort of people made you, there's a terrible yearning to find out.'

'I can understand that.'

She stared wistfully out of the window.

'Would you mind showing me which house my father was brought up in?'

Tom took her into the front garden. The sky had cleared and in the bright sunshine the damp path was steaming.

'There.' He pointed to the pebble-dashed home on the opposite side of the road. 'At one stage Marcus and I rigged a phone line between our bedrooms. Worked fine until a removal van drove through it one day.'

'You were real buddies.'

'You could say that.'

'And who lived next door to you? More kids?'

'Binnie.'

'Wow. You were all here together. She's the same age as you two?'

'Yes.'

'Did you compete for her?' Mary-Anne asked, turning round to study his reaction. 'I mean, was she a girlfriend or just a friend?'

Tom frowned. 'At one point I was keen on her, I have to admit. But Binnie was always sweet on Marcus.'

'Even then?'

Her reaction surprised him. She seemed to be confirming his suspicions.

'Ah. You think . . .'

'Well, don't *you*? There were some pretty strong signals passing between them last night. Now, will you tell me the real truth?' Mary-Anne put her hand on his arm. 'I'm entitled to know.'

'What else can I tell you?'

'Forget the benefit of the doubt. At the bottom of your heart do you still believe that my father killed Sara?'

Tom hesitated, uncertain what he believed any more.

'One thing I *am* convinced of – if it wasn't Marcus who killed Sara, it wasn't John Hagger either.'

'Why do you say that?'

He let out a deep sigh. 'It's a long story.' But he explained briefly about the court case, the man's protestations of innocence and the crooked policeman.

'Wow. This story gets worse and worse. So . . . if it wasn't Hagger and it wasn't Marcus, then who?'

'I don't know. And I'm not sure I've got the energy left to try to find out.'

'Maybe somebody who was jealous,' Mary-Anne suggested. 'Some young man secretly in love with Sara, who went off the rails when he saw what she was doing with Marcus.'

Tom shook his head. It didn't fit with his memory of Wood Park at the time.

'Or a girl.'

Tom did a double take. 'Some girl jealous of Sara, you mean? Wanting Marcus for herself?'

'Why not?'

They looked at one another without speaking. Then he frowned, not wanting to believe what she was suggesting.

'I wouldn't have thought a female would have the strength,' he protested.

'Not true. Strangling someone's quite easy, if you're really determined.'

Tom turned and looked at the house next door. The obviousness of what Mary-Anne was implying shocked him. It had simply never occurred to him.

The home that had belonged to the Rowbotham family was a dark house now, surrounded by tall junipers. He remembered them being planted. Small bushes that had been stuck into the ground by her home-building father, when Binnie was still a young child.

Brentford

Marcus, quaking with disquiet over what he was about to do, opened the door to the flat and watched Binnie climb the stairs. In one of her hands was a plastic bag from a supermarket and in the other a more substantial piece of luggage.

'Good heavens,' she exclaimed when she saw him. 'Get you!'

A barber had done a reasonable job on his hair that morning and he was wearing a clean shirt and a tie.

'Hoping to see Mary-Anne later,' he explained awkwardly. 'I've rung her office a couple of times, but the bossy woman who answers won't tell me where she is.'

'I see. How are you feeling?'

'Okay. What's in that suitcase?'

'Some things, that's all. I thought I'd stay for a few days, if you don't mind.'

'What's happened?' Marcus asked, his alarm growing. 'What's going on?'

'I've told Seb that I love you,' Binnie replied, reaching the top of the stairs. She put the bags down and kissed him.

'Binnie, for heaven's sake . . .'

'Now, don't give me any trouble. I've had enough from your brother.' She walked past him into the flat and towards the kitchen. 'Can you bring those bags in?'

This was hopeless. Not at all what he'd planned. But he couldn't just chuck her out. Apart from anything else, she'd paid the rent for the place.

'Hungry?' she called.

'Well, now you mention it . . .'

'I've brought some smoked salmon. Thought I might as well spend Seb's money, while I still have access to the joint bank account.'

Marcus dumped the suitcase on the floor, then handed the supermarket bag into the kitchen alcove. Totally uncertain how to handle this rapidly worsening situation, he backed into the main room and began rolling a cigarette.

'My God – you've even washed up your breakfast things,' she exclaimed.

'That's right. I'm a reformed character.'

She poked her worried face round the kitchen door. 'How reformed?'

'Binnie, what's happened? With Sebastian?'

'We had things out last night. Both of us realised we can't go on living together.' She tried a reassuring smile, but it didn't work. 'I think he's considering whether to divorce me.'

'He can't. He's an R.C.'

'He joined the church to marry me, so I suppose he can leave it to get a divorce.'

'But this is disastrous.'

'Why?'

'Because . . . because it's impossible, that's why.'

'Nonsense.' Binnie slipped back into the kitchen. He heard her sorting out plates and cutlery. 'There's a cold bottle of Muscadet here. Could you open it?'

Marcus's resolve crumbled. Meekly he went to the kitchenette and drew the cork while she laid the table. When he brought the bottle back into the room, he saw that she'd brought wine glasses.

'Where did those come from?'

'I bought them. We only have tumblers in the cupboard. They were quite cheap.'

'Look, there's no point in buying things for this place.'

'We can take them with us when we move.'

Marcus took a deep breath. 'Binnie, there won't be any moving. Not you and me. I'm planning to go away somewhere, but on my own.'

'Going away?' Binnie sank on to a chair. 'What d'you mean?'

'I need to get away from everything. Everybody. To start again.'

She forced another smile. 'I think that's a great idea. Where shall we go?'

'Not *we*, Binnie. Not we.'

'Marcus, don't do this to me.'

'Look, you've been wonderful, Bins. Couldn't have managed without you, coming out of prison and all that. And . . . well, you know. Everything. It's been terrific. You made me feel like a man again.'

'What are you saying?' she squeaked.

'I'm saying, it can't happen any more. Us going to bed and things. All this.' His arm swung in a wide sweep, ending on her suitcase in the middle of the floor. 'You can't move in here. Look, Seb'll get over it. He'll forgive you. You can blame it all on me. He'll understand.'

'Marcus darling, you're talking rubbish. You and me, we *can* make a go of it. There's room for me here. I won't get in your way.'

He held up a hand. 'Stop it, Binnie. I've told you there's nothing between us. Understand?'

'That's not what you said in bed yesterday.'

'Fuck . . .' He turned away in exasperation and lit his roll-up.

'Don't turn your back on me, Marcus! I love you. That's for real. Don't you understand, after all these *fucking* years? Ever since I was sixteen. Mad about you. Ready to kill for you.'

He spun round. 'What did you say?'

'Nothing.' Binnie defied him to read anything into her words. 'I love you, Marcus.'

'But I don't love *you*,' he yelled.

'But in bed . . .'

'It was a fuck, Binnie. A shag. Not a bad one, but it wasn't love. Okay, I said things. But those words come with the orgasm. They're meant at that moment, but *only* at that moment.'

'Then let's go to bed again now,' Binnie howled, desperate for a reprieve.

Marcus jabbed a finger towards her. 'I don't want you in my life, okay? Just get that simple fact into your blinkered, self-deluding little head. I've managed the past thirty years without you and I'll manage the rest, thank you very much.'

Binnie's expression switched suddenly. From acute anguish to smouldering anger. Marcus could see what he'd done, turned her love into hate, but there'd been no other way. She loathed him now, because as far as she was concerned he'd deceived her. Led her on. Led her into wrecking her marriage.

There was a sharp knife on the table. Binnie's hand made a grab for it, but he got there first and snatched it up.

'You'd better go,' he said icily. 'Before one or other of us does something we'll regret.'

30

Holborn

IN THE AFTERNOON, Mary-Anne got a phone call from her father. Her voice trembled when she realised it was him. She wasn't ready for this. Learning what sort of man he was had turned her inside out.

He asked to see her, expressing his fond eagerness to get to know her properly and hear about her life in America. She prevaricated for a while, trying to make her disapproval apparent in her tone of voice. But in the end she agreed to meet for lunch tomorrow. With no paper on the Sunday, Saturday was their day off.

Now it was evening. The two women were sitting in the *Boston Star* office, watching the TV news bulletins. When they were over Barbara announced that she was taking Mary-Anne out to dinner.

'That sounds nice. Any special reason?'

'Because you're a doll and you deserve it.'

'Well, thank you, even if it's not true. Where are we going?' Mary-Anne's knowledge of London was still very limited.

'Covent Garden.'

'The Opera House?'

'Little Italian place round the corner from it. I rang while you were out and booked a table.'

There was no story for them to file that day and since the last one hadn't made it into print, they were disinclined to try too hard. As they were leaving the office, the phone rang. It was Tom, asking Mary-Anne for Marcus's phone number.

Mary-Anne gave it to him.

'You've had some new thoughts?' she probed.

'No. New questions, perhaps. I'll let you know if anything comes of it.'

'Thanks. I'm seeing him for lunch tomorrow, by the way. If he says anything about Sara or Binnie I'll ring you.'

Outside, it was a pleasant evening, so they decided to walk along Holborn and through Lincoln's Inn, which reminded Mary-Anne of older parts of Boston.

'You can smell the history,' she commented, as they made their way westwards.

'Over there's the Old Curiosity Shop. You know, Dickens?'

'Wow.' She took a quick closer look, then they crossed Kingsway and Drury Lane, entering theatreland.

The restaurant was opposite the Theatre Royal, a narrow cubbyhole of a place which had all the right smells. The table reserved for them was away from the others, in a corner by itself.

'I always ask for this one. At the other tables you're always clashing elbows with someone you don't know.'

This evening, Mary-Anne detected a nervousness in Barbara which she hadn't seen before. Absurd though it seemed, it felt like they were on a date.

Barbara ordered Frascati and sparkling water, while Mary-Anne perused the menu. Italian food was a cuisine she knew well and she quickly chose.

'Shall I tell you why your Sidewinder story got spiked?' Barbara asked, once they'd ordered.

'You found out already?'

'Sure.'

'Go on, then. Don't keep it to yourself.'

'Well . . . what your host told you last night, my dear, it was classified information. Top secret.'

'What . . . like he could go to jail for telling me? That sort of secret?'

'Not quite. But when the paper's Pentagon guy checked it out, alarm bells rang in the State Department and the White House.'

'Oh my gosh!'

'The editor got sat on from a great height. And I mean great. They told him if the *Star* published the story, it would do untold damage to US diplomatic efforts to get a settlement in the South Atlantic.'

'Because they don't want to be seen siding with the Brits so much?'

'Precisely. State's still hoping to perform some miracle that'll prevent all-out conflict on the islands themselves.'

'Oka-ay. That makes me feel a little better. I kind of felt it must've been because of the way I wrote the piece.'

'Don't worry. Your stock's riding high, hon. Both with them and with me. Now, tell me what you found out about your pa today.'

The starters came while Mary-Anne was describing the suburb of Wood Park.

'The kind of place young kids and grown-ups love, but where teenagers go out of their minds with boredom.'

'No bars or movie houses where the horny can make out?'

'Exactly. Except in the woods. Which is where fourteen-year-old Sara Sedley went with my father and ended up dead.'

Barbara put a hand to her mouth. 'Tell me the worst.'

Mary-Anne did. And as she talked about the dark secrets she'd learned about her father's character, she became embarrassingly emotional.

'I'm sorry,' she sniffed. 'But I don't know what to believe. He said he loved my mother, but maybe it's a lie. He said he didn't kill this girl, but how do I know that?'

'Most men are liars, Mary-Anne. It's in the genes. But that doesn't mean he's a killer.'

'Except he did kill in Korea. And again five years ago.'

'The first of those was war and the second sounds as if it could have been more of an accident.'

'Sure, but what I fear most, Barbara, is that he faces eternal damnation. God will not forgive him for what he did to that young girl. Unless I can persuade him to repent.'

'Doesn't sound the sort of guy who'd respond well to having a Bible waved at him, honey.'

'Maybe not. But when I see him tomorrow I'm sure going to try. Couldn't live with myself if I didn't.'

Barbara squeezed her hand. 'Have a drink, sweetheart, and forget about him for now. You haven't touched that glass of wine I poured you.'

An icy calm had enveloped Binnie by the time Sebastian arrived home, shortly after nine.

'Binnie!' His voice reverberated around the ground floor.

'I'm in here,' she called from the sitting-room sofa.

When he entered the room, his face was flushed. With drink or anger, she couldn't tell, but she braced herself.

'Where's that bloody brother of mine?'

She pretended to look under the cushions. 'I don't know and I don't care.'

Sebastian stared at her in astonishment.

'He's bloody dumped you, hasn't he?'

Binnie turned her face away.

'Might have known.' He gave a loud, sneering laugh. 'What happened? Go on. Tell me.'

'There's nothing much to tell, Seb,' she replied huskily. 'He's an even bigger bastard than you are, and I've been rather foolish. That's all.'

'Foolish. That's putting it mildly.'

Binnie was expecting a stronger reaction than that, suspecting that he would still want to end the marriage. She didn't look at him, but could hear his heavy breathing, as if he were in the grip of powerful emotions.

'Binnie, I want you to tell me the truth.'

'I have.'

'I mean about Marcus and Tom. There are things going on, aren't there?'

'What d'you mean?'

'The party last night. I saw them in the garden. Arguing. Tom nearly hit him. It was Sara, wasn't it? Tom's still obsessed by her death. Doesn't believe it was Hagger.'

'Yes.'

'Thinks Marcus killed her.'

'Marcus and Sara were seeing each other.'

'I knew it! Damn well guessed it when Tom told me about the diary.'

'But Marcus denied killing her,' Binnie said carefully. 'That's what they were arguing about in the garden.'

'And what do *you* think?'

It was several seconds before she answered.

'I don't think, Sebastian. I *know*.' She looked him full in the face. 'Marcus has admitted it to me. He did strangle Sara Sedley.'

Wood Park

Tom's afternoon had been hijacked by the estate agent returning with a young couple eager to buy the house. It wasn't just the property they were after, but its recent history – the fact that a famous actress had lived there. They planned a commemorative plaque on the front wall and asked for some of her furniture and pictures to be sold with the bricks and mortar, so that they could preserve the atmosphere of the place. It was early evening before Tom managed to work out an acceptable plan and agree a deal.

Now it was three hours later. He sat at the kitchen table with a dirty plate and a half-finished bottle of wine. In front of him was the phone number that Mary-Anne had given him for Marcus. He'd tried it twice but there'd been no reply.

Whatever the time pressures on him, Tom knew he couldn't leave his latest suspicion unexplored. During the day he'd grown angrier, suspecting now that it wasn't only Marcus who'd duped him over the years. Deception and lies. Marcus and Binnie. What a pairing.

Tom tried the phone again.

This time he got through.

Brentford

Marcus put the phone down. He hadn't answered the earlier calls, fearing it was Binnie ringing. This time he'd worried that it might be Mary-Anne calling with some alteration to their arrangements for tomorrow.

Tom had wanted to drive over and talk to him right away, but Marcus had managed to put him off until the morning. Wouldn't say what it was about, but it wasn't hard to guess. The man was obsessed with a dreadful event of long ago that should've been left buried. Marcus, on the other hand, was concerned not about the past but the future. His own. With his daughter.

The doorbell jangled, making him jump.

'Bloody hell! Who the fuck's this?'

Was it Binnie back, wanting to cut his throat? Thank God for doorphones. He didn't need to let her in.

He picked up the handset.

'Hello?'

'Marcus?' A man's voice.

'Who's that?'

'Sebastian. We need to talk.'

Marcus shuddered. 'I don't think so.'

'It's not about Binnie. Something else has come up.'

Marcus hesitated, fearing he'd be putting himself in physical danger letting his brother in.

'Come on, for Christ's sake. It's raining out here.'

Marcus pressed the door release then hurried to the kitchen, taking a sharp knife from the block on the worktop and slipping it into his pocket.

Sebastian's jacket was spattered with raindrops when he came through the door. He glowered at Marcus, his face flushed with tension and anxiety.

'Look, it's all over. Finished,' said Marcus, backing round to the far side of the table to use it as a barrier. 'I hope she's told you. She had some fantasy about her and me . . .'

'I said it's not about Binnie,' Sebastian grunted.

'Oh.'

'Can I sit down?'

'Of course. Drink?'

'No.'

Marcus sat opposite him. He'd never seen his brother in such a state. His stare was darting all over the place and his breathing was rapid, like a man scared out of his wits.

'Well?'

'Your fucking Korean friend . . .'

'Lee Ho Shin?'

'Lee Ho *Shit*, more like it.'

'What's happened?'

'He's a North Korean spy, did you know that?'

'*What?*'

'He's trying to blackmail me into giving him details of a missile guidance system we're working on. It uses something very high-tech called a laser-gyro.'

'Good God. *How* blackmail you?'

Sebastian looked shamefaced. 'I made a complete and utter fool of myself.'

'Seems to run in the family.' His brother seemed disinclined to explain, so Marcus prompted him. 'In what way did you make a fool of yourself?'

Sebastian's mouth twisted as he plucked up the courage to reveal what had happened.

'At that bloody awful party which my wife organised last night . . .'

'Where you and Lee seemed to be enjoying yourselves.'

'Little bastard . . . Played me like a fish.'

'How?'

Sebastian let out a long sigh. 'We, er . . . we found we had something in common.'

'That much I gathered.'

'A liking for girls.'

'You and a billion other men.'

'I mean girls you pay. For doing the sort of sex your wife would object to.'

'You dirty sod . . .' Marcus was enjoying his brother's discomfort.

'Fuck off and listen. Don't know how I could've been so stupid, but Lee told me about a girl he'd used in London last time he was here.'

'The pictures he was showing you . . .'

'Yes.'

'. . . when Binnie and I came into the kitchen and you couldn't stand up because you had a hard-on.'

Sebastian's face reddened with anger and embarrassment.

'Look, I happen to be very easily tempted in that department. Okay? I admit it.'

'A bloody addict by the sound of it. Addicted to funny sex. What is it? Schoolgirls or black leather and whips?'

Sebastian glared at him. 'All you need to know is that Lee and I arranged to meet this evening. He took me to the address he'd mentioned and . . .' His eyes glazed over as if they were still seeing the girl.

'What, the two of you had her? At the same time?'

'Since you ask, yes. Then separately. It was while I was flying solo, as it were, that Lee took some pictures. I didn't see him do it. The girl had my full attention . . .'

'I can imagine.'

'Afterwards, when we were out in the street, heading for a bar, he showed me the prints. Polaroid stuff. Said copies of the pictures would go to all the daily newspapers and the head of security at the MoD unless he received full details of our laser-gyro system by tomorrow midday.'

Marcus gaped in astonishment. 'But that's the oldest trick in the book. And you fell for it.'

'There's nothing very subtle about your friend Lee, Marcus. But he *is* a master at understanding human weakness.'

'Not hard in your case, by the sound of it. And he's not my friend, by the way.' Marcus's unease was deepening rapidly. 'Why are you telling me this, Seb?'

'Because I want you to relieve me of the problem.'

'Relieve?'

'Kill him.'

Marcus's jaw dropped. 'You're mad.'

Sebastian solemnly shook his head.

'You want me to commit murder to save your ruddy neck?'

'It's not murder. It's war. The communists are still the biggest threat this country faces. You killed plenty in the 1950s. One more shouldn't make any difference.'

'You're mad. D'you know that? Totally fucking mad. Why on earth should I do your dirty work for you?'

'Because if you don't, you'll be back in jail for the rest of your life.'

Marcus felt his insides give way. 'What are you talking about?'

'Sara Sedley. There's a diary. Tom found it.'

'I know.'

'I understand it says you had sex with her. And Binnie tells me you admitted to her that you strangled the girl.'

'Bollocks! I never said any such thing.'

'She's prepared to stand up in court and swear you did.'

'Jesus!' Marcus reeled backwards. 'Hell hath no fury . . .' He felt the walls closing in. All his plans to escape were crashing about his ears.

'You'll do it, I take it?' Sebastian demanded.

Marcus's heart hammered out of control. Binnie would be brilliant in court. She would deny their affair. Deny that this was her revenge for his telling her to get lost. The fragrant wife of a top Civil Servant – he wouldn't stand a chance. The diary and Binnie's testimony would finish him.

She'd got him nailed to the wall.

But now, he suddenly realised, he could go a little way towards nailing her too.

'All right,' Marcus croaked. 'I'll do it.'

'Good man.'

'But on one condition.'

'What's that?'

'That you forgive Binnie for her little indiscretion with me. And that you take her back, keeping her on a leash so damned tight it nearly chokes her.'

31

Saturday, 8 May
Brentford
8.55 a.m.

Tom ARRIVED AT the house in Brentford five minutes ahead of the time agreed. He half expected Marcus to have run for it during the night, but the door buzzed open soon after he pressed the bell.

Marcus looked a shadow of his former self. If it meant he was suffering, Tom could only feel glad about it.

'Nice place,' Tom said as he was ushered inside. 'Live here before you went to prison, did you?'

'No. Binnie found it for me.'

'Ah, yes. She told me. Do I get the impression you two were having an affair?'

''Fraid so.' Marcus grimaced. 'How did you guess? Oh, never mind . . . Look, I was dead grateful for her help when I came out of clink, but she rather went beyond her brief.'

'Meaning?'

'Oh, it's all horribly complicated. I'm in deepest shit, Tom. Sit down and I'll tell you about it. Cup of coffee?'

'No, thanks.'

'Something stronger?'

Marcus looked like a man seeking an excuse to start drinking. Tom shook his head.

'How long has the affair been going on for? It started before you went to prison?'

'God, no. And I had no intention of starting one after I got out. She came on to me like a bloody siren. Had it all planned. Jumped me when I was vulnerable. Should be a law against people like her.'

Tom doubted it was as simple as that. 'And Sebastian?'

Marcus winced. 'That's the problem. He came round last night.'

'I'm surprised you don't have a broken nose.'

Marcus plunged his face into his hands and rubbed his temples. 'I don't know what to do, Tom. I've got no fucking idea.'

'About what? He's given you an ultimatum?'

'Oh yes. And what an ultimatum.' He looked up pleadingly. 'Can we wind the clock back, Tom? Return to the good old days when we could talk freely and openly to each other. About absolutely anything.'

'We can try.'

Marcus looked pathetically relieved as he began to describe his relationship with Binnie and how it had ended. He told Tom about the sudden arrival of Sebastian last night and the extraordinary story he'd come out with.

'Jesus . . .' Tom exhaled.

'He thinks I'm going to kill Lee Ho Shin for him. He's mad. Stark raving bonkers. But if I don't do it, he and Binnie will stitch me up in court and I'll be sent down for life for a murder I didn't commit.' He was staring down at his hands as he said it.

'You're quite sure you didn't kill Sara? *Look* at me, Marcus.'

Their stares met.

'I didn't kill her. You've got to believe me.'

Tom decided that he probably did.

'Who else knew about you and Sara?' he asked.

'Nobody.'

'You're sure?'

'Well, yes. If anybody had known they'd have told the police. Surely.'

'Unless the person who knew was the one who killed her.'

Marcus blinked.

'Somebody so upset at what you two were up to that they followed you into the woods.'

'No.' Marcus shook his head insistently. 'I don't believe that.'

'Somebody who was jealous. Another boy keen on Sara . . . or a *girl* keen on you.'

Their gazes met again. Tom saw that Marcus's thoughts were coming into line with his own. That he was thinking the unthinkable.

'I can't believe that.'

'Binnie was very keen on you, Marcus. Besotted, in a repressed sort of way.'

'I know, but . . . No. It's nonsense.' He looked totally bewildered. 'She . . . she couldn't have. No.' He shook his head again.

For a few moments Tom let it sink in.

'There's a ruthless streak in her, Marcus. You're seeing it now. She's ready to get you jailed for life in order to get what she wants.'

'*Wants?*'

'Her security back again. If she can't have you, she still needs Sebastian. And to get Seb back she has to help extract him from the mess he's in. She's a woman who looks after number one, Marcus.'

'You can say that again.'

'So what have you decided to do? About Lee Ho Shin.'

Marcus screwed up his face. 'I told Seb I'd kill Lee . . .' He laughed insanely. 'Crazy. I can't possibly, of course. But I have no idea what to do. Advise me, Tom. Advise me.'

'You have to go to the police.'

'You're mad. I'm not doing that. Seb and Binnie would get me banged up for ever.'

'But if you run away and Lee shows his photos, sending Seb's career down the pan, they'll still have you put away.'

'I know,' Marcus moaned. 'I'm stuffed whichever way I turn.'

Tom's mind struggled to find a solution. Suddenly he came up with it.

'What's the arrangement for contacting Lee?'

'I have to meet Sebastian in Whitehall at eleven o'clock. He gives me an envelope with papers in – material that might convince Lee at first glance, but which doesn't actually have anything secret in it. Then Lee rings him at eleven-fifteen at a call box, telling him where to meet. He's already told Seb he wants me to be the one bringing the stuff. Can't think why. So I meet him, hand over the envelope and get given the photographs of my brother with his dick stuck up some poor girl's arse.'

'And then you're supposed to kill him.'

'And take the papers back so there's no link to Sebastian. The bugger's got it all worked out in theory. But not in practice. Suppose Lee insists that the meeting happens in a pub, or some other crowded place. How on earth am I supposed to stick a knife in him and get away with it?'

'Quite.' Tom scratched his head. 'Okay. So here's what we do. You go ahead and meet Seb as planned. Then, when you know where the rendezvous with Lee is, you give me the bumph and I take it on from there.'

'You'll meet Lee?'

'Yes.'

'And?'

'So will the police. With luck you'll be kept out of it.'

'And Sebastian?'

'He'll have to fight his own corner. So long as there's nothing classified in that envelope he gives you, he should be all right.'

'Yes, but he and Binnie can still put me behind bars.'

'Not without the diary.'

Marcus started laughing as he realised what Tom was saying. 'I can't tell you how grateful—'

'Don't mention it. Now, if I can use your phone I'd better start alerting people.'

Marcus frowned at him. 'You know who to contact?'

'Certainly. I've spent the last thirty-odd years trying to stop spies getting our secrets. I'm not going to let this one get away with it.'

Marcus gaped in amazement. 'You work for MI5? I had no idea.'

'It's not MI5. The spying I deal with is electronic. But I have plenty of contacts. Now. Where's your phone?'

Binnie parked in the supermarket car park at Brentford. It was a chilly morning and rain was threatening. Her hair was pinned behind her head in a way that changed the shape of her face. She put on dark glasses and pulled on a beret. Then, dressed in a long fawn raincoat that she hadn't worn for years, she walked for five minutes to Marcus's street. She knew what she had to do today, but not how she was going to do it.

About fifty yards from the flat she saw a familiar figure emerge from the house and climb into a car. Tom. She turned quickly away and ducked down a side street until the car passed by. Then, trying not to look conspicuous, she strolled back round the corner as if nothing was amiss. To her consternation Marcus had now emerged and was heading straight for her, hunched up in that filthy old duffel coat. Binnie repeated her move into the side street, praying that her disguise had been good enough to deceive at that distance.

Once Marcus's footsteps had passed behind her, she turned and slipped back into the road. He was walking at a steady pace. She followed, keeping about fifty yards behind him, on the other side of the road. If he turned to look, she planned to crouch and attend to a shoe. At the main road, he turned right and overtook some women with prams. Binnie used them as a screen until Marcus was uncomfortably far in front, then she passed them too.

Ahead was the entrance to the railway station and Marcus was making straight for it. Things were about to get complicated.

Hammersmith

Mary-Anne had never been fondled in that way by a woman before and, in her unaccustomedly tipsy and emotional state last night, she hadn't immediately rebuffed Barbara. If it was sisterly comfort being offered she would have welcomed it. But when it became clear that Barbara had considerably more than a hug in mind, Mary-Anne had shaken herself free.

This morning at breakfast Barbara had apologised, but in a cursory way, giving Mary-Anne the impression that this wasn't the first·time the older woman had misjudged the object of her desires.

'Forget about it,' said Mary-Anne. 'I should be flattered. It's not often people of either sex find me attractive.'

'God, you say such stupid things at times.' Barbara lit her first cigarette of the day.

'Have you ever been to the Newspaper Library at Colindale?' Mary-Anne asked, eager to change the subject.

'No. I can't say I have.'

'Thought I'd go this morning. Want to see what was written when that girl got killed back in nineteen forty-eight.'

'I don't even know where Colindale is.'

'I looked it up. If I get my skates on I should get maybe a couple of hours there, before coming back into town to meet my father.'

'I wish you good hunting. As for myself, I'm going to play a little sedate tennis with Jennifer this morning. And I expect we'll do lunch. So I guess you and I will meet again sometime this evening.'

318

'Sure.' Mary-Anne got up from the table and took her breakfast plate to the kitchen.

'Just leave it in the sink. I'll do it.'

'Well, thanks. I'll be on my way then.'

Mary-Anne stepped out of the front door and headed for the Tube. What she hadn't told Barbara was that she intended to spend the afternoon finding a room to rent.

Embankment
10.55 a.m.

Binnie felt quite clear about what she was doing. Utterly certain that it was right. There was a power greater than herself involved in all this, just like last time, steering her towards her destiny. Her guiding light, she called it.

There was no indication that Marcus had seen her. His mind seemed to be elsewhere and he was paying little attention to anything. At Brentford station, she'd slipped into the next carriage as the doors closed and watched at each stop in case he got off. At Waterloo she'd followed him into the Underground, her heart hammering her ribs.

The Tube had been packed. There was a drivers' work-to-rule, with many trains cancelled. Crowded platforms. She'd almost lost sight of Marcus in the crush. One stop later he'd got off. As he emerged from Embankment Tube station, he was still alone. Somehow Binnie'd expected to see a woman appear from somewhere and attach herself to his arm, some moll whose previously unknown existence might explain why he'd rejected her.

She watched him shuffle past the flower sellers, gaze cast down, as if not wanting to see or be seen. Then he stopped suddenly in the shadows where the road passed beneath the railway bridge. He turned round. So did Binnie, walking quickly back towards the Tube station entrance. She bought a newspaper from the booth and pretended to read it while observing the street over the top of the page.

And there Marcus was, still standing beneath the bridge, staring out towards Whitehall, hands thrust into his coat pockets. Waiting for someone. Binnie's pulse quickened to the point where her head began to throb.

Marcus spotted Sebastian as he rounded the corner from the Defence Ministry. He was late, hurrying towards a phone box on the corner of Northumberland Avenue. It was nearly a quarter past already, the hour when Lee was due to ring. The phone booth was occupied, however. Sebastian hovered outside the door, hopping from foot to foot, but the woman inside turned her back on him.

It took an age before she finished. When Sebastian pushed past her to get inside, he snatched up the receiver but kept his hand on the rest, waiting for the call.

Marcus prayed it wouldn't come. That Lee Ho Shin would have had second thoughts. Or had fallen down a lift shaft. But a couple of minutes later he saw Sebastian talking. Then, shortly after that, his brother joined him, sweating profusely.

'Here. Take this.' He handed Marcus an envelope. 'It's what you give to your evil little friend. It's got rubbish in it, but he won't realise that immediately.'

'Sounds like you've done this before,' Marcus remarked bitterly.

'Don't be ridiculous.'

'You realise if I get caught you're going down with me.'

'Don't you bloody dare get caught.'

'This is insane.'

'It's war, Marcus. You're in the service of your country.'

'Bollocks. I'm being blackmailed by you and that mad wife of yours. Where and when am I supposed to meet him?'

'In the long-term car park at Heathrow Airport, at one o'clock. Row D, Bay 24.'

'Sounds like he's got a plane to catch.'

'You make bloody sure he doesn't. And I want those photos.'

'How many are there?'

'I don't know,' said Sebastian, shamefaced. 'Don't ring me when it's over, whatever you do. The phones—'

'Tapped. I know.'

'You'd better come round to the house. I'll keep Binnie out of the way. Now, you need to get a move on. The Tubes are hellish. Oh, and watch yourself. Lee wanted me to confirm that it was you coming to the rendezvous. Hope you didn't do anything to upset him all those years ago . . .'

Sebastian turned and began marching up Northumberland Avenue towards Trafalgar Square. Marcus stared at his brother's back, remembering Lee's anger when they'd met at Binnie's party, his conviction that Marcus was to blame for Cho-Mi's death. He shivered, clutching the envelope tightly.

'Tom,' he murmured to himself. 'You're a bloody hero. You'll never know it, but you may just be saving my life.'

Binnie had watched the assignation from a distance. She couldn't believe what she'd seen. It wasn't a woman Marcus had ditched her for, but money. An envelope full of the stuff, which her monstrous husband had just handed over as the pay-off for kissing her goodbye. Blood thicker than water. The Warwick brothers' mafia. A wad of cash to set Marcus up wherever he wanted to go.

A red tide threatened to engulf her, but she held it back. The moment would come soon enough. Marcus was on the move again, walking towards Whitehall, past the tall, grey ministries that employed toads like her husband. Binnie followed, determined not to let him out of her sight.

Tom was keeping an eye on the road behind him in the wing mirror of his car. He'd parked at a meter opposite the Ministry of Agriculture. He spotted Marcus approaching, a brown A4 envelope in his hand. As he drew near, Tom pushed open the passenger door.

'Am I glad to see you,' Marcus huffed, sliding on to the seat. He was sweating profusely.

Tom took the envelope from him. 'What's the deal? Where do I meet Lee?'

'Heathrow Airport.'

'I might have guessed.'

Marcus gave him the details. 'And I've brought you a present.' He opened his coat and drew out a kitchen knife, its blade wrapped in layers of paper to protect it.

Tom looked at it in alarm. 'I hope to God I shan't be needing that.'

'You never know. Take it.' Marcus frowned for a moment. 'Just thought of something. Lee's expecting it to be me.'

'So?'

'He might not make contact if he sees it's someone else.'

Tom felt rather relieved at the possibility. He'd launched himself into this business without thinking through how dangerous it might be.

'Tell you what,' said Marcus, struggling out of his duffel coat. 'Put this on. He saw me wearing it the other night. With the hood up he won't see your face until the last minute.'

Reluctantly Tom took the coat. It smelled of turpentine and tobacco. Then he turned to Marcus and looked squarely at him. There was one last piece of the jigsaw that needed slotting into place.

'There's one more thing I want from you, Marcus, if I'm to do this for you.'

'Oh God . . .'

'The answer to a simple question.'

'What?'

'That day in Korea when you saved my life . . .'

Marcus turned his face away.

'You hesitated.'

'Yes.'

'Why?'

Marcus sucked in air as though it was a narcotic.

'I don't know.'

'You were thinking it might have been better for you if I was dead.'

Marcus screwed his face up as if in pain. 'Perhaps. For a split second.'

Tom took a deep breath and let it out again. 'Because you killed Sara.'

'No. Because I thought you suspected I did, Tom.'

'I see.'

'I'm not a very good person. Can you forgive me?'

Tom didn't answer immediately. Forgiveness meant putting things behind him for ever and he wasn't quite ready for that.

'Perhaps. In time. Now . . . You'd better be off. I've got people to talk to.'

'Will you let me know how it went?'

'Of course. You're going home now?'

'No. Meeting my daughter for lunch in South Kensington. Got the best part of an hour to kill, so I thought I'd soothe my nerves in the National Gallery.'

They shook hands. For one disturbing moment Tom thought that Marcus was going to kiss him.

322

Binnie followed Marcus up Whitehall and round the edge of Trafalgar Square. She was baffled by what she'd seen. The envelope she'd assumed to be full of money was now in the hands of Tom Sedley. There was a male conspiracy afoot, but whatever it was, nothing would deflect her from what she intended to do.

Marcus made his way up the grand staircase of the National Gallery, letting the tranquillity of the place soothe his fevered mind. He didn't dare believe yet that his troubles were over. Looking for comfort, he turned into the rooms containing works from the eighteenth and nineteenth century. This was *his* art. These were the works he'd studied, the men whose styles he'd tried to copy. Not the Canalettos, whose architectural exactitude was beyond him, but the English painters. He stopped in front of a Gainsborough. He felt a kinship with this man. Like Marcus, he'd known how to flatter his sitters. But how many had fallen in love with him?

Marcus sat on a bench, but couldn't relax. Ever since leaving prison his life had spiralled downhill. Now it was hanging in the balance. He'd put too much store on Mary-Anne agreeing to help him. If she turned him down he had no other plan up his sleeve. Nowhere else to go. And why should she come to his aid?

What, after all, had he ever done for her?

Fingers trembling, Tom extracted a ticket from the machine at the long-term car park. The barrier lifted. A jumbo jet screamed a hundred feet above his head. The air was rancid with the smell of burnt kerosene.

He wished now that he'd never suggested doing this. Yes, the police would be here, but they'd wait for him to do the deal before they made their move. Him and Lee. Alone. Himself no hero, the other man an unknown quantity.

Looking round anxiously, Tom followed the signs saying SPACES. All the way to the end. Past D Section, where he was to meet Lee Ho Shin. It was packed tight with cars and blocked off with cones. A zone not in use today. Empty of people. The Korean had done his research.

Tom was fifteen minutes early and extremely nervous. This wasn't his scene. He was a back-room boy, not used to coming face to face with a spy.

He saw no sign of the police but told himself it was okay because if he saw them so would Lee.

He parked the car and looked across to the perimeter road. Two men in suits waiting with small suitcases at a bus stop. Not Lee Ho Shin. Heart thudding, Tom looked at his watch for the tenth time in as many minutes. Then, to soothe his nerves he switched on Radio 3, but quickly turned it off again and opened the window. Needed to be able to hear.

Suddenly Tom remembered Marcus's coat. He pulled it from the back seat and struggled into it. Then, from beneath the seat, he took out the knife and carefully unwrapped the blade.

Crossing the road from the National Gallery towards St Martin-in-the-Fields, Marcus began to sense that he was being followed. He looked round but saw no one he recognised. No evidence of a tail. Trying to convince himself he was imagining things, he walked on to the Strand and down Villiers Street to Embankment Underground station. He was in a hurry now, having remembered the Tube drivers' go-slow. He wanted to be there at South Kensington, even if it was far too early for his meeting with Mary-Anne. Because nothing must prevent him from seeing her.

Marcus had made up his mind to admit all his past sins and throw himself on his daughter's mercy. He'd sensed from her manner that she'd probably been brought up with a crucifix above her bed, and if she wanted him to embrace God at this late stage in his life then he would willingly do so.

He passed through the ticket barrier and took the stairs to the District Line. The dense crowds in the station increased his paranoia. He kept glancing behind but saw no one he knew.

The platform was solid with people.

'Shit . . .'

If it was like this everywhere, the trains when they came would be stuffed. Marcus pictured himself still stuck here in an hour, with Mary-Anne cursing his name for not showing up.

He eased along the platform, hoping for more space at the far end. Sullen faces to left and right, many resentful at his pushing through the crowd.

A loudspeaker babbled apologies. Next train in two minutes. Marcus spotted a gap. A punk clutching a can of lager was being avoided by other passengers. Marcus managed to ease his way past and to the front of the platform without being lynched. Then the space behind him began to fill.

A rumble in the tunnel. A sudden rush of air. Marcus's pulse quickened. He hated crowds. Hated the pressure building behind him.

He braced his legs as the train thundered in, motor noise dipping as it slowed. Two lights on the front like low eyes. Above, the flat screen of the cab and the dark outline of the driver. Fear rippled through him. Always the terror of falling on the tracks. Ever since a boy. The familiar onset of giddiness. He tried to step back, but the crowd held him.

Okay, Marcus told himself. Done it a million times. Take a deep breath.

Ten yards away now. Five.

Suddenly something hard in the small of his back. Like the end of a pole. His heart raced. Imagining it? No. The pressure grew. Harder and harder . . .

His arms went up. His mouth cranked open. He sucked in air to shout. Glass front of the cab zooming in. Balance going. Tipping forward. The driver's horrified eyes staring into his own.

There was a bang and a screech of brakes. The crowd drew back in horror. A woman screamed.

Binnie moved steadily along the platform, weaving through the crowd. Her mind was floating free. Like coming round from an anaesthetic. No pain. There would be no pain ever again. Because the cause of it had been removed.

She left the station by the river entrance. Climbed the stairs to the footbridge over the Thames. A pleasure boat passed below as she walked across the bridge's middle span. Faces craning up to look. She waved back, feeling extraordinarily peaceful.

As the ensign of the motor launch passed beneath her, Binnie let go of the tightly rolled newspaper she'd been clutching, its pages scattering on to the fast-flowing tide.

32

Heathrow Airport

Two minutes to one. Heart in mouth, Tom tucked the A4 envelope under his arm and walked towards Block D. Eyes scanning left and right. Where the hell was Lee? It had started to rain. He pulled up the hood of Marcus's duffel coat.

Vehicles entered the car park in a steady stream. He prayed that some were filled with lean, fit police.

Tom found Bay 24 where Marcus and Lee were supposed to meet. A red Toyota was parked in it. The car was empty. Tom stood back from it, irrationally thinking there could be a bomb in the boot.

The rain was getting heavier. He held the envelope so that it could be seen. Dark, wet splodges on the buff manila.

Minutes passed, each an eternity. Every few seconds another plane screamed overhead. He glanced towards the gate again. The terminal bus was beginning its circuit of the stops.

Tom looked at his watch. Five past. How long before he dared abort?

Ten yards away, in the opposite direction from the one in which Tom was looking, the door of a rented Mondeo opened silently. Lee Ho Shin climbed out and stood upright, his stare locked on to the back of that familiar coat. The bitterness he'd stored in his heart for thirty-one years had been honed razor-sharp in preparation for this moment. The only killing he'd done before had been when he'd been forced to. This time it would be of his own volition.

He flattened his right hand into a blade and raised it above his head, moving forward stealthily. He'd been taught unarmed combat when he volunteered his services to the North. Never used in anger before, but he was angry now.

Tom heard the faintest of sounds and spun round.

'Christ!'

The Korean's hand hacked downwards. Tom flinched and the blow caught him on his right collarbone. Pain shot through him like a knife and his arm went limp.

'Aagh . . .' His knees buckled and his vision went haywire. 'What the hell . . .?

Then Lee saw who it was. He gasped. 'Why you here? Where Marcus Wowick?'

'Shit . . .' hissed Tom. 'What did you do that for?'

'Where Marcus Wowick?'

'Couldn't come,' Tom gasped, holding out the envelope with his left hand as if to protect himself from further harm. Where were the goddam police? 'Bloody hell . . .' The pain was excruciating.

Lee snatched the envelope from him.

'Photos,' Tom muttered, still not understanding Lee's intentions. Some absurd sense of duty told him that he had to complete his mission. 'Gimme the pictures.'

Thrown by the discovery that he'd attacked the wrong man, Lee put a hand in his coat pocket and pulled out the Polaroids, holding them up for Tom to see.

Pink flesh bending over more pink flesh. Tom reached for them, but Lee shook his head.

Then Lee opened the manila envelope. A sheaf of papers inside. He flicked through them and swore. Worthless. Every last one of them. They were treating him like an idiot.

'You colonialist dog!' he screamed. 'You cheat me! You just like Wowick. You rape my country. You . . .'

Lee ran out of English words and a torrent of Korean ensued. Out of the corner of his eye Tom spotted a police vehicle speeding towards them through the ranks of parked cars.

Suddenly Lee saw it too. Blind with rage he hurled himself at Tom, hands chopping frenziedly, searching for the nerves and arteries that could bring about death.

It was Korea again. The copse, the terrible, terrible pain and the certainty of imminent extinction. And no Marcus to save him this time. Tom reached inside the coat as Lee's hand sliced at his face. He slithered sideways and the blow smacked against his temple, stunning him. As he fell to the ground, his hand closed on the knife handle.

Lee raised his arm to strike at Tom's throat. As the fingers speared downwards, Tom thrust with the knife, his arm jolting as the blade found flesh and bone.

Lee grunted. The eyes widened in surprise, the mouth agape. Tom saw a grey mass of rotten teeth as the man toppled across him. Pain worse than anything he'd ever experienced shot through his broken shoulder as the Korean's weight slammed down on him. He heard screeching brakes and hoarse shouts, then he blacked out.

33

Two weeks later
Friday, 21 May

THE FUNERAL OF Marcus Warwick at Mortlake Crematorium was supposed to be a simple affair for the family and one or two old friends, but the event attracted the attention of the press. A certain amount of the story had become public knowledge, but the media scented that there was more.

The death of the notorious painter/thief under the wheels of a District Line train was being described as a probable suicide by 'sources close to the police'. His sister-in-law had told the adjourned inquest that Marcus had been overcome with remorse in the days before his death, when a long-lost diary revealed his involvement with fourteen-year-old Sara Sedley, murdered back in 1948. Mrs Warwick told the coroner that Marcus had admitted to her that he had killed the girl.

The incident in the Heathrow car park had not reached the ears of the media. Lee Ho Shin's corpse had been flown secretly back to Seoul for disposal, the South Korean authorities belatedly discovering that he'd been in regular clandestine contact with his elder brother who'd become a senior official in the North's communist regime. Sebastian Warwick had been allowed to keep his position at the Ministry of Defence for now, but had been warned that a sideways move to Agriculture was imminent.

Tom stood in the second row of the little chapel, his right arm in a sling. Next to him, dressed in black, was Mary-Anne, her face half concealed by a veil. The extraordinary tale of how she'd tracked her father down through the painting of her mother had also intrigued the papers. In the row in front of them stood Sebastian and Binnie, straight-backed and still. Tom saw her hand lightly touch her husband's, a gesture confirming their dependence on each other if they were to survive these difficult times.

The service was brief, with a short eulogy given by the chaplain from the open prison where Marcus had spent most of the last year of his life. The priest revealed that Marcus, a firm atheist, had phoned him the day before the tragedy to tell him he'd begun to consider the possibility of God's existence. At this, Mary-Anne sobbed into a handkerchief.

At the end of the service, before the coffin slid through the curtains on its journey to the incinerator, they listened to a scratchy recording of Nat King Cole singing 'Mona Lisa', which had been one of Marcus's favourite songs.

Afterwards, the dead man's brother and sister-in-law led the mourners outside. Sebastian stepped straight into a black official car and was driven off at speed, hiding his face from photographers waiting by the crematorium gates.

While Binnie talked with the prison chaplain, Tom and Mary-Anne walked round to the side of the red-brick chapel where the wreaths were laid out.

'Funerals are such a terrible way to end a life,' Tom commented, lamely.

'Funerals like this one certainly are,' she replied. 'The unspoken things were so much louder than what *was* said. What happened to your shoulder, Tom?'

'I had a fall moving furniture. Broke my collarbone.'

'I'm sorry. That must've hurt.'

'It's getting better. And the house sale's going through, so I can't complain.'

'I'm happy for you.' Mary-Anne blew her nose as they looked down at the flowers. 'Pretty,' she commented, finding the wreath that she'd ordered. 'That's good. He'd have liked those. Now . . .' Her voice dropped to a whisper. 'Tell me what you think. I need to know. Did he fall or was he pushed?'

'I don't think we'll ever know that, Mary-Anne.'

'What's your gut feeling?'

'I saw him earlier that morning. There was no indication that he wanted to die.'

'My thoughts too. He was on his way to see me. Tell me, do you happen to know where Binnie was when it happened?'

Tom shot her a sideways glance.

'You told me on the phone that he broke up with her the day before he died,' she reminded him. 'Couldn't she have . . .?'

'Sebastian says Binnie was with him. Claims she drove him to Whitehall in the morning because he had something to do in the office, and home again later.'

'And do you believe that?'

Tom didn't respond for several moments. He took Mary-Anne's arm and they walked into the crematorium gardens, to be well out of earshot of the others.

'One thing I've learnt in the past couple of weeks,' he told her, 'is that as far as my oldest friends are concerned, nothing is ever what it seems.'

'Meaning?'

'That I always had the impression Sebastian didn't give a damn about Binnie. Yet when I talked to him the other week, he told me very sincerely that she meant the world to him.'

'So?'

'So it's not impossible that he's lied to the police about her whereabouts in order to save her neck, in the hope she'll settle down and be a good wife to him again.'

'Knowing she might have killed his own brother?'

Tom shrugged. 'He always despised Marcus. Anyway, people do extraordinary things for love.'

Mary-Anne contemplated what he'd said for a moment or two. 'Do you remember her talking to the papers back in forty-eight?'

'Who, Binnie?'

'Yes. I was at the newspaper library in Colindale on the morning my father died. Looking to see what got written when Sara was killed. There was an interview in the *News Chronicle*, where Binnie talked about all the kids in the neighbourhood being such close friends and how the heart had been plucked out of the community by what happened to Sara.'

'That last part was certainly true, but I had no idea Binnie had appointed herself spokesman for us all.'

'If she did kill your sister, it shows how manipulative she was, even then.'

'It certainly does.'

'And now she's got the husband she hates to cover up for her . . . That's some woman. One thing I'm certain of. The idea of my father committing suicide makes no sense to me whatsoever. He genuinely wanted to see me, I'm certain of that.'

'Did he tell you what he wanted to talk about?'

'To really get to know me, he said. To hear all about my life in the States.'

They walked on through a pergola smothered with roses in early bud, then turned and headed back towards the chapel.

'I'm going back to Boston tomorrow,' Mary-Anne announced suddenly.

'Oh? But the real Falklands War's only just started. I heard on the radio that our troops have landed at San Carlos.'

'I know. But for the first time in my working life I'm putting personal considerations above professional ones. The truth is that it hasn't been a happy experience for me here in England. All this disaster with my father, I have a feeling I caused it somehow. If he hadn't been coming to see me he might still be alive.'

'That's rubbish, my dear.'

'Even Lee Ho Shin disappeared off the face of the earth without saying goodbye. I feel like I'm some kind of pariah. Everything I touch goes bad.'

Tom looked away, remembering how frighteningly close he'd come to death at Lee's hands. Should he tell her what had really happened? No. She was a journalist, and it was a subject best kept buried, for all their sakes.

'That's nonsense. Of course you're not to blame for anything. But your paper can't be happy that you're abandoning the story at this crucial stage.'

'They don't have any say in it. I've submitted my resignation.'

'That's pretty drastic. What are you going to do?'

Mary-Anne lifted the veil from her face and looked Tom straight in the eye. 'I'm going to study for the priesthood.'

'Good heavens. Women can do that in the States?'

'In my church, yes. I just think that God must have had a job in mind for me when he let me survive back in nineteen fifty-one. And reporting wars from a desk in London isn't it.'

'Well, you have my admiration.'

She blushed a little. 'It's a little early for that. Let's see if I succeed first. Uh-oh . . .'

'What is it?'

She nodded in the direction of the chapel. Binnie was walking towards them.

'I don't think I can face her, Tom. Please excuse me.'

'Of course. But look, keep in touch. Let me know how you get on.'

'I will.' Mary-Anne shook his hand and was gone.

As Binnie came towards him, Tom wondered how much she knew about Lee Ho Shin. He suspected that to get her on side Sebastian would have had to reveal almost everything.

'Hello, Binnie.'

'Awful . . . awful.' She grimaced.

'Yes.'

'I spoke to him the day before it happened, you know.'

'Yes.'

'I'd gone round to see him, to say that Sebastian had accused me of having an affair with him.'

'You mean you *weren't*?'

'Of course not. As I told you, I'd been to see him in prison and helped him get set up when he came out, that's all. Marcus was lonely. He wanted more, of course.' Binnie arched her eyebrows to convey what she meant. 'So I told him it wasn't going to happen. That's when he broke down and told me he'd killed Sara.'

The outrageousness of her lying astonished Tom. Only two people knew what had really passed between Binnie and Marcus at their final meeting and one of them was dead. With such effrontery she could easily get away with murder. And almost certainly had. Twice.

Tom's powerlessness to do anything about it infuriated him. But the evidence to press charges against her simply wasn't there. No witnesses to her crimes, either time around. He shuddered at the thought of how he'd worshipped her all those years ago.

'I've decided to go away for a while,' Binnie announced, pulling herself up straight. 'Amanda's keen for me to visit them in Australia. Says I can stay as long as I like. Her youngest is only two, so she could do with a hand.'

'And Sebastian?'

Binnie rolled her eyes. 'It'll do us both good to have some time apart.'

She waved to someone about to climb into a car. 'I must go. That's Warwick *père* over there. Recognise him?'

Tom stared. 'No. He looks pretty frail. And who's the dark-haired woman helping him?'

'His Spanish wife. Little gold-digger. Sebastian's father had a stroke last year and she's clinging to him like butter to a blanket to make sure she gets his money if he has another one. They're staying with us for a few days.' She kissed him on both cheeks. 'Keep in touch, Tom. Be happy.'

'I'll try.'

Tom watched Binnie close the car door behind her father-in-law, then climb into the front seat. Her face had aged several years in the last few days. Whatever she claimed, he knew that Binnie had made a desperate bid for happiness with Marcus and had lost it. He doubted she would ever get a chance with anyone else.

There was no one left from Marcus's funeral. Outside the crematorium the next bunch of mourners was gathering. Tom walked back to his car. As he put the key in the lock he gave a last glance at the chapel. Smoke was coming from the chimney behind it.

'Happy now, Sara?'

He felt nothing. No sign at all that she'd been here.

2004

Epilogue

The Embankment, London
January 2004

'SO, WHAT DID you want to tell me, Binnie?'
After Binnie had approached Tom outside the National Film Theatre, they made their way along the South Bank, towards the new Hungerford footbridge. Two elderly people, whom a passer-by would mistake for a couple. It felt so strange having her walking at his side, a situation Tom had so often imagined when he'd been young. Ahead of them, the setting sun had turned the sky a livid purple. He took it as a warning.

'There's so much,' she answered, tensely.

'Is it a confession you're wanting to make?' In some ways he hoped it wasn't. That the tramp had indeed killed Sara, and Marcus's death had been an accident. For his own peace of mind, he'd tried to convince himself of that in the intervening years.

'What do you suspect me of, Tom?'

'Let's start with Sara.'

Binnie didn't reply.

'Should I take your silence to mean you know rather more about her death than you've ever admitted?'

'I . . . it's difficult for me. Not that straightforward.'

'On the contrary, I'd have said it was totally black and white. Either you do or you don't.'

She looked around her to make sure they weren't being overheard. Tom stopped walking and turned to face her. 'Well? Which is it?'

337

'Please, Tom.' She reached out a gloved hand and touched his arm. 'This isn't easy for me. What I want to do is make things better for both of us.'

'Did you or didn't you kill her, Binnie?' He was losing patience with her.

'Hear me out, Tom.' She chewed her lower lip, trying to decide what to say. 'I won't deny I was the cause of Sara's death.'

Although he'd waited so many years to hear them, Binnie's words shocked Tom to the core.

'You *murdered* her, Binnie.'

'Well, no. Not really. I never intended that she should die, you see.'

'What d'you mean, *never intended*? She was strangled. With great force.'

'Please. Hear me out. I want you to understand. It's very important to me that you do.' She took hold of his arm. 'Do you mind if we keep moving? I'm so cold.'

They started walking again. Tom suspected it was so that Binnie could avoid looking him in the eye.

'You see, I wasn't really in control of things at the time. I was in the grip of some overwhelming outside force. It's hard to describe.'

'It's an emotion known as jealousy, Binnie.'

'No. It was more than that. It was an absolute certainty that I had to prevent her taking something that was mine.'

'You mean Marcus.'

'Yes. I was so in love with him, my life wasn't going to be worth living if I didn't stop her.'

'And the only way of doing that was by *strangling* her?' It felt utterly unreal hearing this, with commuters marching past on the way to their trains.

'Don't be too hard on me, Tom. I was only seventeen at the time. A teenager. You're not in control of your emotions at that age.'

He felt like knocking her head against one of the lamp-posts they were passing.

'But you never told anyone. You let John Hagger get sent to jail for your crime. You were ready to see him hang.'

'I know, I know. It was wrong of me, but I was sort of trapped by what I'd done. I can't explain it. Please try to understand.'

'And Marcus? You pushed him in front of that train.'

Binnie didn't reply.

'Well?'

'Tom . . . It was an accident. Honestly. It's the truth. Yes, I'd followed him that morning. I was desperately upset. Just didn't know what I was going to do. I'd given myself to him, you see. Totally.' She made it sound as if that explanation justified everything. 'I was ready to scrap my marriage, lose my children – my whole former life. Just for him. Then he threw it in my face. Surely you can understand how I felt.'

'So you pushed him under a train.'

'No. Well . . . Yes, I was there in the station. Behind him on the platform. I'd finally decided I had to speak to him, you see. To make him see sense. So I reached through the crowd to touch him. To let him know I was there. Then I don't know what happened. He just seemed to fall forward.'

Tom stopped walking and stared disbelievingly at her. 'You'd better try your story on a jury, Binnie, because I don't believe a word of it.'

'Tom.' She seized hold of both his arms. 'I'm telling you these things because it's important that you know the truth. For both our sakes. So we can start with a clean slate. But if you ever tried to take it further, to talk to the police about it, I would have to deny this conversation ever took place.'

'God almighty! How do you sleep at nights, Binnie?'

She took a deep breath. 'With difficulty at times. Not because of what I've done, but because of what I've lost. I have nothing in my life now, Tom. Sebastian and I divorced years ago. I live alone, and it's hard.'

'You've got your children.'

'They have their own lives. And, to be honest, they don't want to see me.'

Binnie hooked her hand through Tom's arm and they continued walking, his uneasiness deepening by the minute.

'I'm so sorry, Tom. So terribly sorry for what I did to you.'

'To *me*?'

'Yes. Sara's death blighted your life. I've always suspected it's why you never married. Am I right?'

He ignored her question and looked away, out across the river to the multicoloured fascia of Charing Cross station.

'Is that why you came to find me, Binnie? To apologise to *me*?'

'Yes.' She breathed in deeply and stopped walking, keeping a firm hold on his arm. 'And to ask you something.'

No, Tom thought. No questions. He would not let her pry into his life.

'You see . . . I had the feeling, a long time ago, that you were quite keen on me.' Binnie put on the smile she'd used when she was little. The self-consciously mysterious one. 'Was I right?'

Tom felt off balance suddenly. She'd found his Achilles heel.

'Maybe. A long time ago.'

'I knew it.' She beamed with satisfaction, as if everything she'd just revealed to him was no longer of any significance. 'Oh, life's so strange,' she sighed. 'The silly thing is, I always liked you too. You were the one I could really talk to. Much more than Sebastian or Marcus.'

'Well, there you go . . .'

'If only I hadn't got pregnant. Maybe when you returned from Korea, we'd have married.'

It was entirely possible, Tom realised.

'We could have been so happy together.'

'I doubt that, Binnie. I doubt it very much.'

They continued on to the stairs up to the footbridge. Then they began to climb them.

'I'm certain we could have been happy. I'd have made sure of that.' She gave his arm a squeeze. 'I *know* it, Tom. Now listen. I have a proposition to make. You live alone still, don't you?'

He didn't answer, but she took his silence as a yes.

'Well, so do I. And it's silly, isn't it? Don't you think it's time we put the past behind us and joined forces, for the final straight, as it were? I *so* want to make it up to you, Tom, all the suffering I caused you. Please let me try.'

The unexpectedness of Binnie's proposal knocked the wind from Tom. Could it possibly end like this? His teenage fantasy coming to fruition in the most unexpected of ways? The chance to spend his final years sharing a kitchen table with her as he'd once imagined?

For one extraordinary moment he was tempted, a vista appearing of some little piece of good coming from all this evil. A slow healing of all the pain and misery.

They reached the top of the stairs and began to walk across the bridge. Then suddenly, Tom had the odd sensation that a third person had joined

340

them. A presence that he could feel but not see.

They reached the middle of the bridge and leaned on the railing, staring down at the thick brown water swirling through the middle span, the river running with the full force of the ebb tide.

Tom felt Binnie shiver beside him, and guessed that she was longing for him to put his arm round her shoulders.

'Please, Tom. Will you give us a chance?'

He still didn't answer, unable to think of exactly what to say.

'You see, without your forgiveness and without the hope of being happy again, I'll have nothing to live for. I might as well end it now. Throw myself in the river.'

Tom turned to look at her. She was both longing for and dreading his answer. Then her face became a blank. Devoid of all expression. She was withdrawing into her secret world, protecting herself in the way she'd always done when people didn't comply with her wishes.

'I'm sorry, Binnie, but it's absolutely out of the question. You see, I can never forgive you for what happened in nineteen forty-eight. Because Sara would never forgive *me* if I did.' He began to back away from her. 'And now, if you'll excuse me, I have a train to catch.'

Suddenly her expression hardened. 'Don't disappoint me, Tom.'

'Is that a threat, Binnie?'

She didn't respond, but her eyes were like stones. The switch from love to hate had been instantaneous, as it must have been with Marcus.

'Are you implying that if I don't agree to your plans, I might fall under the wheels of some sort of public conveyance?' He backed further away from her, fearing that she might lunge for his throat or try to push him over the rail.

'Because if you are, I should give you a warning. This conversation *will* be written down. Word for word. And it'll be lodged somewhere safe, with instructions to pass it to the police if I suffer a sudden and unexplained death. That would be evidence they *couldn't* ignore. Goodbye, Binnie. I think it'll be for the best if we don't meet again.'

Tom began walking towards the north side of the river, but stopped after a few paces and looked back. Binnie was gripping the rail, staring down at the water.

What if she jumped? Would her death be on his conscience?

Something tugged at his sleeve. A powerful force telling him that he'd done enough. As much as any mortal could.

He walked on, quickening his pace and without glancing back again.

London was lit up all around him. A sparkling, vibrant capital city. The crisp river air carried with it a tang of the sea. Tom filled his lungs with it.

Air that had never smelled so fresh.